The Hatch and Brood of Time

Books by Ellen Larson

The NJ Mysteries
The Hatch and Brood of Time
Unfold the Evil

The Hatch and Brood of Time

The First NJ Mystery

Ellen Larson

Poisoned Pen Press

First Revised Edition 2014

10 9 8 7 6 5 4 3 2 1

Library of Congress Catalog Card Number: 2013941233

ISBN: 9781464202230   Trade Paperback

Poisoned Pen Press
6962 E. First Ave., Ste. 103
Scottsdale, AZ 85251
www.poisonedpenpress.com
info@poisonedpenpress.com

Printed in the United States of America

To the memory of my mother,
Jane Alberta Baker Larson

Prologue

It had been an old-fashioned winter in that intensely suburban corner of northeastern New Jersey called Bergen County. A wet and heavy snow, laying siege on Christmas Eve, withstood the January buffet of freeze and thaw and was reinforced in early February by a blasty blizzard of snow and sleet. The neat backyards and shrub-encircled homes were sealed beneath slabs of snow with a razor-sharp glacé crust. Alpine peaks, raised by straining snowplows, overflowed the verges and encroached upon the streets, subduing the noise of suburban traffic to an unaccustomed and equally old-fashioned quiet.

At the heart of the county, bounded to the west by a frozen Oradell Reservoir, to the east by a well-sanded Knickerbocker Road, and to the north and south by lines born of the surveyor's pencil, was the Borough of Haworth. Near the center of town, half way up steep and slippery Tank Hill, just opposite the upper exit of Haworth Elementary School, lived Natalie Joday. On many a snow-silenced winter's eve, Natalie could be found in her tiny second-floor apartment, sitting cross-legged beneath an afghan on her sofa, diligently preparing for the next day's work, or indulgently catching up on her reading. Either way, when lurking memories of troublous times broke the tranquil surface of present occupation, she would throw an arm across the back of the sofa, bury her chin in the bend of her elbow, and gaze out the frosty picture window as others might gaze at a crystal ball.

Below her the lights of half the borough twinkled in a snowy nighttime world of unfamiliar shapes and shadows. A double row of oversized yellow streetlights blazed along Haworth Avenue, starting atop Tank Hill and running down, extending through the center of town and over the railroad tracks before curving left and ending in a darkness that was White Beeches Country Club. Bright house-lights clustered galaxy-like around an amorphous central downtown glow. In contrast to these steadfast tokens of order and safety, flashing blue and red lights shown forth now and then, reflected by ice and snow and window glass, presaging the swoosh of a sander lurching through the slush, or the scrape of a snowplow's metal blade on the pavement.

Whenever those skipping colored lights appeared, Natalie held her breath, and braced herself—just in case. Just in case the rotating flashes should be followed not by the muffled but homey sounds of plow, sander, and slush, but by the squeal of car brakes and the slamming of car doors and the ringing of the doorbell above the crackle and jargon of a police radio—insistent spinning lights invading her home and streaking across her walls in painful bursts of blue and red that did not go away.

Then, as sander or plow slid cautiously down Tank Hill, making its way to White Beeches and swiftly out of hearing, whisking those intrusive lights away to bedazzle other homes, Natalie would breathe again, tension would fade, and guarded winter silence would return.

Chapter One

Natalie sat down at her computer on the afternoon of February 11th, 1992, with a cup of French roast coffee and renewed purpose. Inspecting her kingdom, she found, under a thatch of papers, two fugitive pens and a highlighter, which she retrieved and jammed into a clay flowerpot abloom with variegated journalistic impedimenta. The papers she gathered together, patted into order, and placed in the filing cabinet beneath the window. Mind and desk thus cleared for action, she propped up her spiral notebook at a convenient angle, pulled the keyboard to her stomach, and looked at the monitor for the fifth time:

Animal Activists Against Abduction

Sandra Cappi, Harrington Park reference librarian and animal lover, has announced the formation of a nonprofit organization to combat a growing epidemic of dog and cat thefts from private residences throughout Bergen County. The newly formed Housepet Abduction Hotline will offer members a monthly newsletter, and maintain a twenty-four-hour toll-free number for the general public.

A study (available from HAH) compiled by Ms. Cappi and her colleagues, based on county-wide police reports and statistics gleaned from the files of the Westwood ASPCA, reveals that the incidence

> of missing housepets doubled in the second half of 1992. From July to December, 18 dogs, 9 cats, and an Angora rabbit were "missing, presumed stolen." The number of strayed pets reunited with their owners decreased dramatically over the same period. Such information has led this group of concerned Bergen County residents to conclude…

"To conclude…" Natalie said informatively. She rested her fingers on the keys, straightened her back, and tucked in her chin.

"…that," she continued decisively. Her eyebrows puckered in studious preoccupation.

"To conclude that…" she said ingeniously. Her fingers slipped from the keyboard and her gaze wandered.

The telephone rang, and Natalie launched herself from her chair, hovering over the keyboard just long enough to hit Command S, flew to the kitchen, and placed a hand on the phone. She took a calming breath, and, after the third ring, nestled the receiver against her ear.

"Natalie Joday." She leaned against the counter and crossed one foot in front of the other.

"Oh. I thought—I'm sorry…Is this the Joday residence?" The young woman's rich voice, hedged in smothered emotion, conveyed in those few words a history of conflict and incident that instantly captured Natalie's attention.

"Yes it is."

"Is Daniel Joday there?"

"Sorry, no." Natalie's interest faded as quickly as it had been aroused: It was going to be one of *those* phone calls. "Daniel doesn't live here anymore." She shoved a hip against the counter and went to retrieve her coffee. If this was going to be a question-and-answer session about her brother's character and activities, she would need material sustenance.

"Oh. Is Natalie Joday there?"

"Speaking."

"Natalie? Oh—you said that, didn't you? I'm sorry. I'm not…. This is Sarah Dow. I don't know if you remember me or my sister? Lydia? I…she was a friend of your brother's? A couple of years ago?"

"Of course I remember you." Natalie, coffee in hand, wandered into the living room, eased onto the sofa, and stretched out her legs. "I reviewed you as Millicent in *Hello, Dolly* at Northern Valley in, uh 1989…no, 1990. You live up on Closter Dock Road somewhere. Big house, Japanese garden, high stone wall with broken glass on the top. You sing."

"That's right."

"Yeah, sure." Natalie took a sip of coffee. "So, how're you doing?"

"Okay. No. Not okay. It's my sister. She's gone. She's missing. Three days. Yesterday they found her car. I really—"

"Jeez…" Natalie sat up, removing her feet from the coffee table.

"I don't know what to do." The words came slowly, squeezed out around the edges of her fear. "The police aren't doing anything! I mean, I suppose they are, but if they don't tell us what it is, how do we know it's enough? They say it's too soon. Too soon for what? I know my sister—she would never, never just disappear like this. I know! But I can't get them to listen to a word I say."

"Yeah," said Natalie. "The cops have a real hearing problem with people they don't consider professionals. Especially family."

"Really? I thought it was because I—everybody is treating me like I'm hysterical, and telling me I'm only making things worse. But I feel this terrible urge to do something!" A ripple of suppressed ferocity traveled along Sarah's words. "I may not know anything about finding missing persons—but so what? My father thinks I'm being selfish, trying to interfere. He doesn't… but I can't do any harm, can I? And I can't sit here and do nothing! I just can't."

"No, you can't. You have to do something."

"You really think so?"

"Of course." Natalie ran her fingers through her mop of brown hair, holding it off her forehead. "Can I do anything to help? Have you considered putting an ad in the paper?"

"No, I hadn't thought of that. You mean to find out if there's anybody who has any information about where she is? That's a good idea. Do you still write for the *Star*? Could you tell me who to get in touch with?"

Natalie did so.

"Thanks," said Sarah. "I didn't expect you—I mean I didn't intend to dump all this on you out of the blue. I'm sorry I'm such a wreck."

"You don't need to apologize," objected Natalie. "This is scary stuff."

"That's it." Sarah's voice fell to a whisper. "That's it exactly. I'm so afraid that something has happened to her, that someone might have hurt her. That's why I'm trying to get in touch with Daniel."

Natalie's tone stiffened. "Mmm hmm."

"Because he was her friend, I mean," added Sarah hastily. "Someone she might have confided in. And not only Daniel—I'm trying to get in touch with anybody who knew her well. I know it's not much, but I'm just trying to do…something."

Natalie's grip on the phone tightened. "I think it's a good idea."

Sarah sighed. "It's the only one I've had so far. Lydia and Daniel were very close once, and I thought—I'm sorry to be bothering you, but this is the only number I had for him."

"You're not bothering me. Daniel's not living here—hasn't for over a year. But I'll get in touch with him."

"Isn't there a number where I could reach him?"

"No." She reached for the pad of yellow paper and pencil she kept on the shelf beneath the coffee table. "But I'll get the message to him right away, I promise. What's your number?"

"555-4289."

"Okay. And, Sarah…" Natalie paused, wavering between conflicting emotions. "If things get rough, or if there's ever anything I can do…"

"Thanks, but, that's okay. I know you didn't know her very well."

"I meant if there's anything I can do for *you*."

"Me?" Again that super-charged delivery. "Thanks."

Natalie left the sofa and went to stand by the picture window. She waited for the disturbing feelings aroused by the conversation to dissolve, leached away by the passing of time. It was another cold, blustery day. The wind picked up the loose snow from the storm and sent it swirling; skittering whirlwinds danced along her driveway and crashed into the drifts. Lydia Dow. Although Natalie hadn't said as much to Sarah, her memories of Lydia were, though few in number, very clear. Rich, foolish, insulated Lydia Dow, unwittingly typifying a lifestyle that Natalie—raised in harsher surroundings—had learned to despise. Lydia Dow with her almond-shaped sky-blue eyes and expression of calculated dreaminess.

She recalled Daniel's voice challenging the logic of her instant disapproval. "How can dreaminess be calculated?" Daniel had asked. "You can be dreamy, or you can be calculated, but you can't be both. Your problem is you just don't like her."

"That's not the issue," she had argued. "It doesn't matter whether I like her or not." But in her heart she had known it was true; she had not liked her, not one bit. Lydia Dow. She had burst dramatically in and out of Daniel's delicately balanced life, oozing sympathy for his past hardships, but flaunting the promise of wealth and easy living before his wistful eyes. And always dancing tightrope-style along the verge of a tempestuous scene. Lydia Dow. Blind to the feelings of those closest to her, thoughtless enough to be capable of anything.

Natalie touched the cold window with a forefinger, breaking the spell of memory. "What's she pulling this time?" Whatever her sympathy for Sarah, she was damned if she would have anything to do with Lydia.

Her cat, chocolate-colored and silky-soft, leaped onto the sofa and rubbed his moist nose against the back of her hand. She reached out to scratch the white strip between his ears, realized she was still holding the phone, and bestirred herself to dial a number.

"Hello."

"Hi, it's Nat. How are things?"

"Descending rapidly through intolerable to vile."

"Oh, sorry to hear it. Is Daniel there?"

"Momentarily. I'll get him for you."

There was a pause, and then: "Yeah?"

"Hi. Me. Have I called at a bad time?"

"A classic—you know, like in the movies when the hero says, 'Sit down, Vanessa, there's something I have to tell you,' and then the phone rings."

"Oh, dear."

"Never mind. As you are so fond of saying, life goes on. What's up?"

"I've got a message for you from Sarah Dow."

"Who?"

"Sarah Dow—Lydia's sister?"

"Oh! More melodrama."

"Yeah, well, she would like to speak with you urgently."

"Who?"

"Sarah!"

"Oh, sorry."

"Do you have the number?"

"I doubt it. It's been ages since I had anything to do with those people. You'd better give it to me."

She did.

"Got it," he said. "See you Saturday?"

"Or die," she said. They hung up.

The cat sprang to the floor and trotted at her heel as Natalie, with furrowed brow and pursed lips, padded back to her little office on the far side of the kitchen. Her expression did not change as she read the words on the monitor, nor did it as she looked at the cat.

"To conclude," she said, placing her hands on her hips, "there is an organized effort at pet-napping going on—right in our own backyard."

The cat, unimpressed, took a few steps away from her, turned around, and meowed. Natalie, finally taking the hint, retraced her steps and opened the outer door. As the cat bounded down the stairs and into the wide world beyond her reach, she called, "So watch your tail, Trickster!" Then, likewise putting out the whispering warnings of human folly that murmured in her mind, she returned to her work.

Chapter Two

Toward the end of March the blackened, gritty snow finally yielded and began its retreat from Bergen County, unburdening the long-suffering shrubbery, and, incidentally, tragically flooding the perennially inadequate sewer system in downtown Closter. The sun, regaining the ascendancy, shone fiercely four days running.

On the late afternoon of March 31st, Natalie found herself in Hackensack at the offices of the *Bergen Evening Star*, lingering in the post-deadline lull to see how a piece she had done on antique barber poles would look juxtaposed against the weekly "Fashion Facts by Beverly." She had little use for the idea of dressing to impress, and none at all for the pretense of conforming to transient fashion trends. Which didn't mean she lacked the knowledge of how to dazzle when she wanted to, or the wardrobe and figure to carry it off.

She lounged wrong-way-about on a folding chair in the newsroom while she waited. The chin that rested on her crossed arms was pointed, the mouth curved and firmly set. Her long nose separated steady gray eyes beneath dark, arcing eyebrows that imbued every expression with one species or another of inquisitiveness. At the moment, Natalie's face was a picture of curiosity. She was watching Ginny Chau, recently hired and highly touted crime bureau reporter, update her database of professional contacts. Ginny's remarks, as she color-coded the denizens of Bergen County by highly subjective degree of journalistic usefulness, were both entertaining and enlightening.

"Theodore Linstrom," said Ginny briskly. "Zoning Committee vice-chair. A Person of Power. Blue group." Ginny, twenty-five, did not believe in deference to governmental authority. "Maryanne Roberts, state assembly. Yellow group."

"Not a Person of Power?"

"Yellow. Personal friend." Ginny tossed her head, making her silver earrings jingle. Natalie sighed in envy, and Ginny smothered a smile. "Fire Chief Andersson," she continued. "Political appointee. Pink."

"Isn't fire chief an elected office?"

"Sure, but Andersson was appointed two years ago when McKinney had to resign on incompetence charges."

Natalie bowed her head before this example of the attention to detail that distinguished those reporters of superior status.

Ginny's mouth moved sideways. "Something about ordering the removal of all the barber poles in the county because they were fire hazards. The Historical Society was not amused."

Natalie laughed, then yawned, pushing her unruly hair back from her forehead. Teresa, one of the print shop girls, came zigzagging through the office with a stack of freshly minted *Stars*, which she dumped one-by-one onto empty desks with an air of extreme boredom. As she approached Natalie, however, her expression brightened.

"Hi, Natalie!" She held out a copy of the paper. "How's your rully cute brother?"

"Rully fine," obliged Natalie. She peeled off the first section and tossed the remainder of the paper onto an empty chair. Teresa giggled, gave Ginny her copy, and loafed away.

Ginny and Natalie settled back to take a critical view of the front page layout before hunting up their respective material. Ginny's phone rang and she made a noise of impatience as she answered it.

Natalie stared at the front page. The lead story had been awarded a color photo and a four-column spread:

Semi-frozen Body Found Beneath Parkway: Police Suspect Foul Play

The partially frozen body of a woman was found this morning by members of the Bergen County Highway Beautification Crew. The body was stuffed in a recess in a tunnel beneath the northbound lane of the Palisades Interstate Parkway in Alpine, halfway between exits 1 and 2, the District Attorney's office announced. Initial reports suggest the body, that of a white female in her late twenties, had been in the tunnel for about two months. No positive identification has yet been made.

Natalie frowned at the shadowy but cleverly composed photo: an ambulance backed up to the dark mouth of an arching, head-high tunnel beneath a parkway crowded with bumper-to-bumper traffic, and in the front a foreshortened squad car parked on a muddy bank. Ginny's voice brought her back to the newsroom.

"L–Y–D–I–A? Like the tattooed lady? Never mind, I got it… Positive ID. Twenty-six years old…Missing since February 8th of this year…Forty-three Closter Dock Road, Alpine…555-4289…Okay…Homicide…Okay…I got it. Thank *you,* ma'am!"

Ginny cradled the phone and looked at Natalie, her eyes shining with the world-class enthusiasm that had gotten her so far so fast. "Perfect timing." She stood up, snatching reflexively at the hem of her skirt, and reached for her briefcase. She tore off the top half of the front page, folded it in quarters, and stuffed it into her jacket pocket. "This is my chance to show Tyler-chan he's not the only frog in the crime bureau pond anymore." She switched off her computer. "Wish me luck!"

"Good luck," said Natalie softly, without looking up. Ginny, awash with the purpose and excitement on which she thrived, fetched her faux-fox coat from the cloakroom, and clattered eagerly away.

◇◇◇

Natalie sat, head bowed, adrift in the disorientation that accompanies the abrupt reordering of the universe after sudden violence.

Never a pleasant experience, even for a reporter trained to cope with the unexpected, this time it was especially wrenching. Natalie was overwhelmed by the memory of Sarah Dow's anguished voice, and her desperate and misunderstood need to act. What torments Sarah must have endured since they had spoken she could not even guess. Her spirit flinched under the sharp prick of conscience.

"I should have called her back," she whispered. But she had been oh-so-confident that Lydia was up to her old tricks and would reappear when it suited her; so ready to let her sympathy for Sarah as an individual be washed away by a subtle undercurrent of resentment against the Dows and their kind.

Daniel would have been more compassionate. Natalie, absent a morbid desire to revive memories of a difficult time in their lives, had not mentioned Sarah's call or Lydia's disappearance to her brother in the intervening weeks. Nor, for what she presumed to be a similar healthy aversion, had he brought up the subject. But she had no doubt that he had tried to do what he could to help. It would be like him to feel genuine concern for an old friend—old lover, rather—and to lend support to the family, regardless of who they were or what had happened in the past.

Natalie raised her head. She got up, walked around the desk, and slipped into Ginny's padded chair. She picked up the phone, punched up an outside line, and dialed the number still echoing in her mind. After fourteen rings she heard Sarah's voice.

"Hello." It sounded flat; empty.

"Sarah? This is Natalie Joday. I just heard the news. I'm so terribly, terribly sorry. If there's anything I can do…" Her voice trailed away, as, with a surge of emotion, she remembered how meaningless such words had once, long ago, sounded to her.

There was a silence—not the silence of choice, where someone does not or will not speak, but the silence of one who cannot speak, broken only by the sound of hoarse breathing. When words came, they were forced one by one through an unwilling throat. "Could you come over?"

"Of course," said Natalie. "Now?"

"Could you?"

"Yes. I'll be there in twenty minutes." They hung up. "Damn," whispered Natalie. "Damn." Grabbing her shoulder bag, she retrieved her jacket from the cloakroom. She went into the hall and hurried down the steps to the parking lot, headed to a place she had never wanted to be, into the heart of a family she had never wanted to know.

›››

When driving through residential Bergen County, one is never aware of the borders that separate one town from the next; each street in each town seems much like the last. One sees row upon row of large, attractive houses, built in the Forties and Fifties, each house surrounded by ornamental shrubbery, dogwood, and a well-manicured lawn, and shaded by magnificent oaks and maples, a few of which are remnants of the hardwood forest from which the county was carved. Rigorously enforced zoning regulations restrict commercial development to confined locales; thus each community has its own "downtown" shopping area, which is generally its only distinguishing feature. Most towns have a duck pond set in a grassy park, a gazebo, and a war memorial; some boast a restored railroad station from the bygone days of the passenger train.

Hackensack Road was crowded with late traffic, and Natalie fidgeted in the bucket seat of her twelve-year-old Volvo. She made better time through Oradell, and when she hit Haworth Avenue she was racing, past her home without a glance, across Schralenburgh, over to Hardenburgh, and through downtown Demarest. When she reached rolling Closter Dock Road, she slowed to peer at the house numbers on the high brick walls that protected the most opulent homes in Bergen County from the interlopers driving by. Eventually she spotted No. 43.

She eased the Volvo through the open gate and onto a driveway of white crushed rock, then followed a sharp left-hand bend through heavy rhododendrons—a standard landscaping device that effectively masked the three-story mock-Tudor home beyond from the sights and sounds of the road. The driveway swung back to the right, and then looped around a sunken garden in the center of which sat an Italian-style fountain. To one side, a little white sign, decorated with a painted sprig of lilac, read: Company Parking. Natalie pulled into the rectangular area and switched off the engine while the wheels were still rolling. The car jolted to a stop.

A flagstone walkway led across the lawn to the front of the house. The grass was already green, and the circular flower beds were bright with crocuses and hyacinths. She passed between two ancient oaks and came to a broad front door beneath a peaked roof. She stepped onto a wide sandstone stoop and rang the bell, glancing discreetly through the diamond-shaped window in the center of the door. She took a deep breath.

A shadow moved across the bright light within, but the door did not open. Natalie pursed her lips, but then reminded herself that this was a house in mourning—they had every right to vet their visitors. She clasped her hands behind her back and gazed about the yard. To the left she noted a garage, tennis court, and swimming pool. To the right, almost hidden behind budding forsythia, was a little cottage. But as the minutes ticked by, a sense that she was not wanted—that she could do no good—crept out of the recesses of her mind and took shape as the thought *I don't belong here*. She pursed her lips again, and rang the bell, harder and longer.

The door opened inward with a jerk, and she beheld a man of about fifty, with a broad handsome face and a thick powerful body. He stood possessively in the breach and scowled at her, feet apart and burly shoulders squared to the fore. "What do you want?"

His inflection suggested that she was the most recent in a long series of unwelcome guests. It wasn't so much a question, Natalie felt, as a brief prelude to peremptory rebuff.

"I'm—" Giving her name up front was a professional reflex, but his attitude alarmed her, and she decided discretion was called for. "I'm here to see Sarah."

"I just bet you are." He emitted a barking laugh. "What are you—reporter or something? Ambulance chaser?"

Natalie started to shake her head, framing a denial, then changed tack. "Coincidentally, I am a journalist, but I'm not here—"

"You people are vultures, aren't you?" His eyes crinkled up at the corners and he thrust forward his square chin. "Haven't you ever heard of respect for the bereaved? Look lady, you better just scuttle back to whatever sleaze factory you came from." He made a move to close the door.

Anger—heedless of his loss or her own intentions—flamed within her, sparked by his unfairness and fueled by his raw belligerence. She placed a hand on the closing door.

Her eyes were as hard as his own, her voice as belligerent. "I think you'd better tell Sarah her friend has arrived."

"You don't seem to be able to take a hint!"

"You don't seem to be able to comprehend that I'm expected!"

He treated her to another in the series of already clichéd looks of condescension and scorn. Then he gave in—all at once and without admission of defeat. He turned, leaving her stranded in the open door, and walked through the foyer then across the living room to the foot of a staircase.

"Sarah?" he bellowed. "Sarah!" He spoke as if to a banished child. "You got company!" Then he disappeared through an archway to the right, leaving in his wake an atmosphere of angry disapproval and the echo of a slamming door.

"Jeez..." Natalie sidled into the foyer, closed the door, and looked around. The living room was decorated in a modern application of silver and white and glass. She unzipped her jacket and lowered herself onto the edge of a chair with a white petit point seat.

She heard a door open somewhere upstairs and the creak of hardwood floorboards. A young woman appeared on the landing at the top of the first flight, took half a step forward, and stopped.

Natalie raised her head. She had not seen Sarah since *Hello, Dolly* three years previously, when she had attracted considerable attention with her aureole of ruddy hair, natural flair for acting, and, above all, her mesmerizing singing. At the moment the aureole was a dull and matted tangle around her sad oval face, all eyes, and her too-thin frame was lost beneath a gray sweatshirt and faded jeans.

Sarah shoved her hands into her pockets. "Better if you come up."

Natalie moved, following her up two flights of stairs, down a long hall, and up another flight, in silence.

Sarah's room was spotlessly neat and distractingly bedecked with innumerable little china figurines lined up in tidy rows on every available horizontal surface. There was a glass case full of riding trophies and ribbons on one wall. A built-in cabinet housed a television, VCR, tape deck, CD player, and shelf after shelf of CDs. In the only empty corner, an acoustic guitar, minus one string, leaned up against one of two massive speakers.

Sarah motioned Natalie to a paisley armchair, and dropped herself into the depths of another. "After we hung up I realized I was out of line asking you to come." She put a thin hand to her head, rubbing her blue-veined temple. "I tried to call you back, only you weren't home. I just wanted to say—you didn't have to come, but I'm glad you're here."

Natalie, reflecting that this sentiment, in reverse, summed up her own attitude better than she herself had been able to, sat down without comment.

"I don't want to be alone," Sarah continued. "That must sound dumb. There are three other people in the house. But their emotions seem so overdone, so fake. And at the same time, not enough! Not nearly enough. Even Harry seems to be just pretending."

She twisted in the chair, and her voice became bitter. "Well, I can't pretend. I've been expecting it, almost since the beginning. But now that it's here, it's so unreal!" She brought her fists down on her thighs. "I knew it! I knew it! No matter how many times they said there had to be another explanation, I knew it!"

Natalie watched helplessly as Sarah's emotions rampaged through a maze of shock, anger, bitterness, and grief from which there was no exit. Her face flushed and her silvery voice grew strained and harsh. "God, these past weeks…Rose following me around all the time wanting to touch me—hugs and pats and squeezes every ten minutes—and saying insipid things: 'Sarah dear, try and be strong.' Dad just can't control his anger—can you believe that?—*his* anger, because she was so 'irresponsible' as to run off and leave her financial affairs in limbo. At least that shows he thought she'd be back." Sarah buried her face in her hands. "Even Harry—"

"Wait a second." Natalie was willing to lend support but wanted also to understand. "I'm getting lost. Who's Harry, who's Rose, what financial affairs?"

"Well, it was her money!" Sarah's angry eyes reappeared from behind her hands. Then she made a self-deprecating gesture. "Sorry. I forgot you don't know anything about us. It's just—I felt like you knew me when we talked on the phone." She looked down at her lap. "And you were so nice when you interviewed me during *Hello, Dolly*. I heard a lot about you from Daniel, too—not that I spent that much time with him, of course." She looked at Natalie shyly. "You look so much like him."

"My hair is darker."

"A little. Anyway, I always assume everybody knows everything about us—the unspeakable secrets of the unfortunate Dow family." She lowered her voice in mock horror. "'Insanity runs in that clan, you know.' That's what people must think."

"My experience is that people know a lot less about us than we think they do." Natalie arched an eyebrow. "So you'll have to fill me in if you want me to understand."

Sarah, her brown eyes searching for relief, looked at her straight on for the first time. "I want you to understand."

"Okay. Explain it to me. How come it was her money?"

"It was our mother's, originally, and she left it to Lydia. Dad has absolutely no right to be so possessive about it—or so obvious—but that's the way he is. He married our mother for her money—and, by the way, that's from him, not from her. Dad…" She paused, her eyes glittering as they moved back and forth.

"Wait. I don't have to call him that anymore. I don't care if he is my flesh and blood. With Lydia gone I can call him Eric, and she won't think I'm being disrespectful. It's awful to have to call total strangers Dad and Mother. Isn't it?" She laughed without humor. "Or is this a symptom of my selfish ingratitude and growing instability?"

"Frankly, after having just met your father, I can think of a lot worse names than Eric."

"Oh!" Sarah sat upright, hooking spidery fingers around the edge of the chair. "Was he—angry? It was when he heard your name, wasn't it?"

"Actually, I didn't give him my name."

"Oh. That was lucky. He didn't like your brother." She ducked her chin in embarrassment. "Thought he was after Lydia's money."

"Nice."

The chin came up. "And yet after Mother left us, my father was proud to tell us that he had only—that was his word—*only* married her for her money and had not loved her. Hey, I've taken Psych 101! I know a defense mechanism when I see one—but how could he talk like that before two girls, nine and fifteen, whose mother had just disappeared?"

Natalie stared in open amazement. "She disappeared too?"

"Yes." Sarah's voice grew harsh. "She ran away with the milkman, or maybe it was her stockbroker. I don't know the details. She was crazy too. But mostly she just hated Da…Eric, and to prove it, she gave everything she owned—everything—to Lydia. By God if anybody ever wondered why he kept Lydia under his thumb, I can tell you I never wondered!" Her anger burned bright for a moment. "He wanted control of the money! Well, he's got it now!" Then she remembered, and her defiance gave way. Tears welled in her eyes, and her delicate face softened and fell.

"I loved her so much—and she loved me. That was the one dependable thing in the whole universe. And now it's gone." The tears flowed, and she pulled a wad of shredded tissues from her pocket.

Natalie's throat tightened and her eyes misted over.

"Sorry," mumbled Sarah, when the spasm had passed.

Natalie thought it best to keep her talking. "How come Lydia got it all? What about you?"

"I don't know." Sarah shrugged. "I don't care about money."

Natalie's eyes flicked around the room.

"I guess it was because she was older," continued Sarah. "She's better than me at business stuff anyway. She was very responsible about the estate. Extremely conscientious. Don't you see? That's how I knew from the first day that something had happened. Disappearing was the one thing in the world she would never, *ever* have done. It would have been like putting the stamp of approval on the worst thing that had happened to us. She would rather have died than follow in our mother's footsteps—reenact her mistakes. And of course she knew what it would have done to me, to have that happen, to someone I loved…again." Sarah shook her head. "No way. I mean I may have my problems, but I knew my sister."

Sarah looked so positive about this that Natalie felt compelled to believe her.

"Of course," Sarah added, with a return to her self-disparaging tone, "nobody agreed with me. *Eric* was just sure she'd turn up safe and sound somewhere—probably attached to some good-looking loser—so of course Rose and Graham said they thought so too. If I disagreed with the party line I was being hysterical."

"Who's Graham?"

"Oh…he's this guy." She rolled her eyes and recited: "He's Rose's deceased first husband's second cousin."

"And Rose?"

"Dad met Rose about two years ago, and they dated some. Then she moved in, and they got married recently. She's not so bad. Frankly, she could have been a lot worse. I mean, she left us alone. Only…somehow she did it so pointedly that it felt—intrusive."

"I know the type," said Natalie.

"Well, anyway, last July, Rose asked if her 'cousin'—that's what she calls him—could stay in the guesthouse while he wrote his book. Dad...Eric...always does anything Rose wants—so Graham came. We couldn't stand him from the first—Lydia and I. I don't think Eric liked him either, though he'd never let on. Lately I've noticed Graham is even wearing out his welcome with Rose. I wish he'd finish his book and leave. How long can it take? It's exhausting being nice to Graham; he's so smooth about everything—no, not smooth...slippery."

She looked away for a moment. "But that's not the worst of it." Her tone became confidential as she turned back to Natalie. "I think there was some grand scheme to pair him off with Lydia. Last fall, in a letter, she gave me the idea that she was changing her mind about him, warming up to him—she denied it was anything romantic, but I sensed a big change in her mood. God. I suppose Graham's just a common mooch, the kind of guy who doesn't care who supports him as long as he doesn't have to do it himself. I mean I don't think he's a jailbird, or somebody out to rob us as we sleep, but—" She stopped mid-sentence, aghast.

Natalie leaned back slowly in her chair, dropping her eyes.

Sarah swallowed hard. "I'm sorry." She covered her mouth with shaking hands. "I can't believe I said that. I didn't mean it like that."

"Never mind." Natalie took a deep breath. "Really. It was a general statement and I shouldn't take it personally. It's okay. Go on."

Sarah shook her head. "It's not okay! Because I really like your brother." She emphasized every word. "I mean really a lot, not just saying so. I admire him—his gentleness, his loyalty. Whatever he did, he paid for it, and that's in the past."

"Yes, it is."

"Actually," confessed Sarah, "I had a terrible crush on him when he was going with Lydia. I don't know what he thought of me—I was still in high school—but I thought he was wonderful. I used to bug Lydia to take me with them when they went places. Of course I covered my real feelings—but it gave my supporting role as The Confidante in my sister's love story an added texture to be always talking about Daniel."

Her smile of remembrance faded. "Then, when everything got so awful for them, and they broke up, I felt as if I had betrayed her. As if somehow I had got what deep in my heart I had always wanted. Like I had been willing them to split up so that he might notice me. Like it was my fault."

Natalie squirmed in discomfort. "Stop it, Sarah, please," she pleaded. "You keep taking the blame for everything."

"I can't stop! I try, but I don't know how!" Tears ran down her face and she fumbled for a fresh tissue. "I thought maybe the reason he didn't call back in February was because he knew it was all my fault."

Natalie's eyes widened. "He didn't return your call?"

"It's okay. It doesn't matter. I shouldn't have tried to involve him. Anyway, Harry has been tremendous." Sarah made an effort to collect herself. She blew her nose, and spoke in a more conversational tone. "I've never told anyone this—I couldn't very well tell Lydia—but, when I met Harry, the first thing I noticed about him was how much he reminded me of Daniel. Now you're going to ask me who's Harry."

"Actually, I've worked that one out."

Sarah smiled. "I'd have gone crazy these past seven weeks if not for Harry. He's the only one who didn't try to tell me everything would be okay. I'm so lucky to have him. But he can't bring her back. No one can. Something happened and I wasn't there to help. When Lydia needed me most—I wasn't there! If only I could have done something!" She lapsed into tears.

Again Natalie's emotions welled in response to Sarah's plight. She could think of no comforting words with which to soothe, no innocuous questions with which to distract. She was wondering if, after all, she wasn't doing more harm than good. Then there was a tap on the door.

A voice said, "It's me."

Sarah looked up through her tears, blew her nose, wiped her eyes, and went to the door. She opened it, and tried to smile, fooling neither Natalie nor the man standing in the hallway. An anxious expression crossed his pale, handsome face.

"Hi," he said, as they embraced. His manner was one of wanting to help, but not to intrude. He touched her hair with a gentle hand, pushing at the tangles. "I just wanted to let you know I was here, and I'm okay. Do you want me to come back later?"

She shook her head. "No, it's okay. Come in."

"Rose asked me to tell you she's fixed some cold cuts and fruit salad."

"I'm not hungry." She turned to Natalie. "How 'bout you?"

Natalie shook her head. She became aware that the newcomer, having closed the door, was trying to catch her eye. She stood up to greet him.

"Harry Suter," he said, extending a hand.

"Natalie Joday," she said, grasping his palm.

The hand that shook hers came to a momentary halt, and then resumed motion with a slightly looser grip.

Natalie's glance fell, but then her chin came up and she looked him in the eye. "Perhaps you've heard of my brother."

"Yes." Harry lowered his eyes.

Natalie sat down, trying not to feel resentful. But she could not help being amazed that the slightest reference to Daniel could arouse such a reaction from a man who had never even met him.

"She called when she heard the news," Sarah explained, reseating herself in the armchair. "I asked her to come over. I'm really glad she did."

Harry looked up at Natalie and smiled. "You're a lifesaver," he said sincerely. "I knew she didn't want to be alone. I got here as quick as I could."

He was a tall man, about Natalie's age, well dressed in a conservative gray suit, with a white shirt and open collar. There was a hanky folded in his coat pocket. His curly brown hair was clipped short; his square chin was dimpled. He reminded her not at all of her brother.

He went to the bed and sat. His shoulders slumped and an expression of mingled exhaustion and sadness took possession of his face. "I could use a little moral support myself if you've got any left over. I'm beat." He plucked the hanky from his pocket and wiped his face. "I just got back from the police station. What an experience! Not that I hesitated when they called and asked me to come down as soon as I conveniently could. And believe me, with everything going wrong at the New Globe, it was not a convenient time." He looked at Sarah. "I'm worried Mr. Montgomery really thinks we're going under, not just being dramatic about it. This latest fund-raiser I'm supposed to be organizing is going to be a complete flop."

Sarah mustered a supportive smile. "Don't say that."

Natalie glanced at her watch.

"Anyway," continued Harry, "of course I went to the police station right away. But once I got there—the way they treat you! The questions they ask! And what kind of work hours do these people keep? I thought they were going to grill me all night. The worst was that they had the most god-awful way of making me think they suspected me. As if they knew I'd done it and it was just a matter of time before they worked out the details."

"Done what?" asked Sarah.

"Well, you know, the murder."

"Well, who would ever think you did?"

"That's what I'm saying, Sarah!" In his debilitated state, he could not hide his exasperation. "I mean, of course I didn't do anything, but the way they have of asking questions makes you think they think you did! They've still got Graham down there—I saw him in the hall. He made a point of saying, in that catty way of his, that he couldn't understand why they gave me such a hard time, when they were so nice to him. But I bet they're rounding up everybody who was at the dinner party the night before Lydia disappeared." He shot Natalie an uneasy glance, then looked back at Sarah. "Of course they wanted to know everything about the fight. I hope Graham doesn't make any trouble—"

"Wait a minute." Sarah put up a hand. "What are you talking about? What kind of questions were they asking you?"

"What you'd expect, I guess. 'What was your relationship with the deceased? Where were you on the afternoon of Monday, February 8th? When did you—'"

"I don't believe this!" Sarah's eyes were open wide, her voice an angry wail. "Why are they wasting their time? They refuse for weeks on end to believe something happened to her, and now when they're forced to admit something did happen, they still can't do anything useful? Why aren't they out there trying to find whoever murdered my sister?"

Harry faltered, lowered his eyes in silence.

Natalie roused herself. This, then, was why she had come. This was what she, despite their short acquaintance and disparate backgrounds, could do. She must help Sarah find her way amidst the invasion and upheaval to come. What she had delusively thought to be the end of one nightmare re-materialized as the beginning of another.

Natalie, speaking in a clear voice, took the first step. "Are you saying, Harry, that the police think the murderer was someone who knew her?"

Harry did not look willing to go down that road. "Maybe," he hedged. But it was enough.

Revelation broke across Sarah's face in waves. Endless as the recent weeks had been, filled with long hours picturing every imaginable horror, they had not been long enough for her to think these thoughts: Someone close to her might be suspected of murdering her sister. Worse yet, she herself might be suspected, and so be subject to unbearable mortification; most abominable of all, someone close to her—her father, Rose, or even Harry—might actually be the murderer. She was bowled over by the shock as it hit; she was drowning and unable to breathe.

"Sarah!" Harry bounded off the bed as Sarah, with a bloodless face and unfocused eyes, slumped sideways in her chair. "I'll get a doctor!" He started for the door.

"No!" gasped Sarah. "I don't want anybody!"

"Help me get her onto the bed," said Natalie, at Sarah's side. Harry stared at her. "She needs to lie flat. She's just fainted, that's all." She maneuvered Sarah's head forward and onto her knees. "Don't breathe so hard, Sarah, you'll hyperventilate. Come on, Harry," she said impatiently, "give me a hand!" He moved.

They got her onto the bed, and Natalie sent Harry to the bathroom for cold water and a washcloth. While he was gone, Sarah, breathing more slowly, stared at the ceiling, clenching and unclenching her fists.

"My God," she whispered, "can't somebody make this stop?"

Natalie felt her chest tighten in urgent sympathy with Sarah's appeal. How cruel a trick of life it often is to stumble without warning upon the truth. "I wish I could," she said, despite the years of struggle which had taught her, against her will, that she could not.

›››

Time dragged as Sarah, inconsolable but afraid to be alone, waited for grief to pass, or to become somehow bearable. At eleven o'clock Harry went to the all-night pharmacy in downtown Closter to procure the strongest nonprescription sleeping aid he could find. "Don't tell them where you're going," Sarah begged before he left. While he was gone, she found the energy to shower and change into her pajamas.

By midnight she was asleep. With a nod to Harry, Natalie picked up her jacket and declared her intention to leave. They crept stealthily out of Sarah's bedroom and closed the door, walking a few yards down the hall before speaking.

"Do you think she'll be all right?" Despite his whisper, Harry's anxiety was patent. "Don't you think she should see a doctor?"

"She said she didn't want to."

"Because she doesn't want her father to know she's so upset. He'd recommend she see a doctor, all right—he already thinks she's a nutcase." Harry's voice, propelled by his emotions, rose uncontrollably.

Natalie shushed him, and then whispered, "What's the matter with him, anyway?"

Harry shook his head and made a helpless gesture. "Eric Dow likes to put people in their place and keep them there.

One time—" There was a creak on the stairs below, and Harry froze, all eyes and chin.

"Harry?" A voice whispered in the darkness—a female whisper.

Harry relaxed, relieved if not pleased. "Rose."

They went to the head of the stairs, and Natalie beheld a slight ash-blond middle-aged woman in a salmon pink robe, poised apprehensively on the landing below. The woman sighed in relief when they appeared.

"I thought I heard voices. Is she all right? Is she asleep at last? Come down to the dinette—I'll fix you both a cup of decaf." As she turned, Natalie caught a whiff of coconut cologne. The trio descended the stairs and turned left. They tiptoed through a darkened kitchen and into a family breakfast room on the south side of the house. The knotty-pine walls were covered with framed theatrical posters, and, above a long picture window, there was a bookshelf stacked with crumpled play scripts and old programs. Natalie and Harry sat.

Rose poured coffee from an electric percolator into three cups already waiting on the table. "This is such a terrible thing. I just couldn't even think of going to bed until I was sure poor Sarah was all right. Thank the Lord she has friends to turn to. I wanted to go to her—but I knew she wouldn't like that." She smiled wistfully. "She and Lydia were so close. It's a double blow for Sarah—those poor girls never had a real mother, and Lydia practically raised Sarah. I never felt it right to try to fill that role."

Harry slumped forward in his chair, leaning his elbows heavily on the table and putting both hands around his cup. He looked as miserable—in a helpless, resigned way—as anyone Natalie had ever seen. She concluded that he was extremely familiar with Rose's verbal précis of Dow family relationships.

Rose stirred a half-teaspoon of powdered creamer into her coffee; despite the late hour and the trials of the long day, her posture was elegant and her makeup flawless. "Harry, didn't you tell Sarah I had prepared a tray for her?" She turned to Natalie. "Are you hungry? Everything's all fixed."

"No thanks, really." Natalie looked at the thin brew in her cup. What she really wanted was to go home.

"Of course Eric isn't the most sympathetic of parents, either," continued Rose. "I know that. But believe me it's not that he doesn't care. He's one of those men that have difficulty showing their emotions. His generation was brought up to believe that too much permissiveness and emotionalism are bad for one's children. He went up to bed hours ago, poor fellow. First the tragedy of the girls' mother, and now this. It's such a shame. He and Sarah should be able to share their grief—it's what they both really need. Don't you think so, Natalie?"

Natalie, asked to confirm something she disagreed with, was at a loss for words. Harry looked at her in mute sympathy. She searched for a noncombustible response. "Well, this is such a difficult time for everyone."

"That's exactly right!" Rose greeted Natalie's cliché as if it were PhD material. "This is such a tragedy. These past few weeks have been so awful—and now this. I hope they catch the hoodlum that did it and lock him up on bread and water and throw away the key. You know I read that the crime rate in Bergen County has quadrupled in the last fifteen years. Eric says the reason is they let *the* most dangerous criminals out on the streets after a slap on the wrist! What we need is a less lenient penal system. Don't you think so, Natalie?"

Caught between her battered sensibilities, and her appreciation that Rose—however annoying—had no idea how volatile her question was, Natalie snatched the quick way out.

"I'm afraid I really must go home." She stood up and started to put on her jacket. "Thanks for the coffee, Rose. We should all get some rest."

Rose shook her head and sighed. "I know I won't sleep tonight."

Harry stood up, staggering a little, and Rose reached out to steady him. "Poor Harry! You've felt the strain these past weeks too." She turned to Natalie, patting Harry's arm maternally. "I don't know what Sarah would have done without him. He's been a rock." Her expression was smiling and serene, while Harry's was hooded and haggard.

"I've got to get my coat." He slipped out from under Rose's arm and went unsteadily through the kitchen to the hall.

When he was out of earshot, Rose turned to Natalie and gripped her arm. "I'm so worried about him. Do you think we should let him drive when he's like this? Do you think he's been drinking?"

"No!" said Natalie. "No. I'm sure it's just stress."

"I'm sure you're right. He'll bear up. It's Sarah I'm worried about. You know she has a history of emotional problems. I don't know what this will do to her—come again soon, Natalie." Her voice grew louder as Harry reappeared. "Sarah needs her friends now."

She opened the dinette door for them, and they stepped into the night. Natalie took half a dozen steps, frowned, and stopped. She looked back over her shoulder, and saw Rose standing in the open doorway, watching them. How on earth had Rose known her name? Natalie shook her head and hurried across the yard after Harry. If she was lucky, she would never find out.

Lights shone from the windows of the cottage behind the forsythia. "I guess Sergeant Allan has given Graham the all clear," said Harry, nodding at the cottage. "I'm surprised he came home—he's usually on the prowl all night and asleep all day. Maybe the experience actually got through to him."

They reached the driveway. Her car had been joined by a white Subaru DX and an olive green Nissan. Harry moved to the driver's side of the Nissan while Natalie squeezed between cars to the door of the Volvo.

As she fumbled with her keys she heard a sharp intake of breath behind her. Turning, Natalie beheld Harry across the roof of the Nissan. Away from the Dow family, and protected by the darkness, he had given way, without struggle and without embarrassment. She saw the glint of tears on his cheeks.

"You okay?"

Harry shook his head. "I've been dreading this day for seven weeks. I've tried not to think of myself; tried to do what would make it easiest for Sarah. But it's—no use."

Natalie shook her head. "I'm sorry, but given the circumstances I don't think there's much you could have done. She has to—"

"I tried to get her out of there—away from those people. We could have gotten married—gone anywhere in the world. Anywhere but Alpine, New Jersey. But she wouldn't go. She didn't have the strength to leave when we had the chance."

"You're both in shock over this, Harry. Later on—"

"It's too late." He turned, got into his car, switched on the ignition, and drove away.

◇◇◇

At one a.m. the streets were empty, and Natalie raced home in record time. As she pulled into her driveway, and beheld her snug white house nestled amid the mountain laurel, and her cheerful yellow home light, she experienced a deep sense of relief. Having fulfilled what she saw as her obligation, she swore a silent oath never to cross the Dow portal again. She trotted up the cedar staircase to her apartment, the vision of a firm mattress and a supine position uppermost in her mind.

She had pulled off most of her clothes and flung them into a heap on the bedroom floor when the telephone rang. Was it Sarah, awake and awash again? She let it ring a long time before she went to the kitchenette and picked it up.

"Yes?"

There was a silence on the line, as though someone had been about to hang up. Then: "Natty?"

Only one person in the world called her that. "What?" she asked quickly.

"Hi. Me. Sorry to bother you at this hour. Have you been out?" There were harsh voices in the background, and other sounds she found hauntingly familiar.

She ignored his question. "Where are you?"

Daniel cleared his throat. His light tone was edged with distaste, as though attempting to disassociate himself from the words he must speak. "I'm at the Hackensack Courthouse. I called Matt, but he's out of town. I've been calling you for hours. Nobody at the *Star* knew where you were—"

"Has something happened? Have they—"

"No! They picked me up for questioning, that's all. But—they're worried I might try to skip town, and they want me around while they check out my movements on the afternoon of February 8th. They also need my version of what happened at a dinner party in Alpine on the night of February 7th. They want to know what my relationship with Lydia Dow is—was."

"You're kidding? You are kidding."

"I'm not kidding, Nat."

"But I just—that was three years ago. You told me you hadn't seen her—"

"Let's not discuss that now." His voice was sharpened by a warning edge. "We'll talk about that when you get here, okay?"

"Okay." *You fool,* she thought, *you blind fool.* "Okay. I'll be there in twenty minutes."

"Thanks. I'm on the second floor. Room 215. Down the main hall and up the stairs to the right."

"Yeah." She headed back to her bedroom to get her clothes. "I remember the way."

Chapter Three

"He's not going to leave the county," said Natalie to Sergeant Allan. She looked at Daniel. "Are you going to leave the county?"

"I'm not going to leave the county."

Brother and sister turned matched pairs of cool gray eyes, set in twin expressions of frankness, toward the sergeant.

Sergeant Allan's eyes flicked from brother to sister. It seemed to him that the sister's frankness was rooted in personal conviction, while the brother's grew from shop-worn expedience, the caesura of which allowed a glimpse of a more complex motivation. He pursed his lips and drew a thoughtful breath.

Natalie kept her eyes on the sergeant. He was young to be in charge of a murder investigation, and his loose-fitting suit and close haircut were proof that he shared his generation's preoccupation with style. But his presence was commanding enough to give assurance of experience and more than sufficient intellectual reserves. The three of them were alone in Room 215, a pale-green chamber with a desk, three chairs, a bench, barred windows, and not enough air.

The sergeant shook his head, exhaled, and stood up. "I'm going to try and reach his parole officer again."

Daniel shot a resigned glance at Natalie.

"Believe me, I wish you could," she said. "But he's in Trenton at a rehab conference. Can't you call Inspector Conklin? Please? He's known Daniel for years."

"We'll see." The sergeant, signaling neither commitment nor hostility, left the room.

As the door closed, Natalie looked sidelong at her brother. One would never guess from his outward appearance—neatly ironed pink shirt tucked into gray trousers; chestnut hair running back from his forehead in uniform waves; an air of patient relaxation as he sat, long legs crossed, fiddling with his watch—that he had spent the last eight hours answering the questions of inquisitorial homicide detectives who took it for granted that he was being less than straightforward. It was brought home to Natalie, not for the first time, that her brother was the only person she knew—man or woman—who could conjure the appearance of felicitousness under any circumstance.

Shaking her head, she looked more closely. His attention was given over to the task of resetting the date and time on his watch, his dark eyebrows sweeping high above his downcast eyes. Natalie frowned: he needed a shave, but she could see the unnatural flush of color and slight swelling along his jaw, making his trademark smile more lopsided than usual. She withdrew her gaze and focused on the cracked face of the wall clock. Four a.m.

They sat in austere silence for twenty-five minutes, their exchange limited to alternating looks of boredom and patience. They were both too experienced to choose that time and that place for a family conference. Their yawns alone broke the silence.

Finally, a uniformed officer poked his head into the room. "Sergeant Allan would like to speak with you, Miss Joday." Natalie sprang up, but at the door she hesitated, and looked back.

Daniel's smile had evaporated, and his eyes, raised to hers, betrayed his fear. She knew the memory that had made her stop and turn had come to him as well: She had once left him sitting in that very courthouse. Two years had passed before she had seen him outside of a jail cell or courtroom. She set her jaw and stepped into the hall.

The officer followed her out, locked the door, and headed to the stairs. It took him a dozen strides to realize he was alone. With a little jump, he swiveled around. Natalie, fists wedged into the pockets of her jeans, leaned against the dark-green tiles of the wall and studied her sneakers. The detective walked back and gazed at her questioningly.

She looked up with a smile. "Would you please tell Sergeant Allan I'd prefer to speak with him here?"

"Lady, we don't generally do business in the hall."

"I know," admitted Natalie. "Can you just ask him? I'm sure he'll understand." The detective looked skeptical, shrugged, and headed for the stairs again. Natalie touched the back of her head to the wall.

Sergeant Allan appeared by return, wearing an expression that said "this is not what I need at this hour." He addressed her with a sense of injury, his hand over his heart. "I work six years to rate an office, and you want to talk to me in the hall."

"Sorry."

"Don't you think you're being just a tad overprotective?"

She nodded. "I knew you'd understand."

There was a pause, during which the sergeant studied her. "Okay," he said, "I'll play. Here's my problem. On February 7th there is a dinner party at the Dow residence in Alpine. Eight people attend, one of whom is your brother, ex-boyfriend of Lydia Dow. There is food, alcohol, music, small talk. There is a fight that nobody can explain, and the guests leave shortly thereafter. Twenty-four hours later Lydia Dow is missing—almost certainly already dead. Yesterday morning, seven weeks later, her body is found. As part of my investigation I want to account for the movements and activities of the seven people who saw her the night before she disappeared. Are you with me?"

"So far."

"Right. Your brother has a history of trouble with the law. He has jumped bail."

"That was over five years ago, Sergeant."

"I know, Miss Joday. So let's talk about today. He has no fixed address, no real income."

"He's working!"

"He's stocking shelves three hours a night at the A&P."

"This is working!" Natalie pulled her hands out of her pockets and turned up her palms. "This is working steady. Not full time, but you know how tight the job market is. Besides, he attends classes two days a week at BCC." She shook her head in exasperation. "This is nothing! You can't arrest someone because he's only working part-time."

"I'm not going to arrest him, Miss Joday."

Natalie's eyes flashed, but she wanted more. "And you can't detain someone because his address doesn't appeal to you."

The sergeant tipped his head back and spoke with authority. "I can detain a material witness until my investigation is complete if I have grounds to believe I won't be able to find him when I want him."

Natalie conceded the point with a shrug.

The sergeant continued in a more matter-of-fact tone. "I'm not trying to be difficult. And I'm fully aware that you've been grappling with police procedure for more years than I have. Long enough to see it from my angle. Look. He's had three residences so far this year: he starts off sharing some crummy hotel room up in Rockland County with a guy he didn't seem to know too well and hasn't seen since; then he spends six weeks with his girlfriend in Cresskill until they have a blowup and she shows him the door; and for the past two months he's with one of the A&P boys in Bergenfield in an illegally parked trailer with no phone." He made a gesture, half in wonder, and half in exasperation. "Hey, it's only March!"

Natalie lowered her dancing eyes. "So housing is expensive around here. Is that the problem? He can stay with me."

The sergeant crossed his arms. "Now how did I know you were going to say that?"

"I suspected you as a student of human nature the moment I laid eyes on you."

He hesitated, smiled sidelong at her, and then returned to business. "Will he stay at your place?"

"Ask him."

"I will. It's believing him that's the problem."

Natalie's tone was earnest. "Look, Sergeant, the fact is Daniel is cooperating with you and he will continue to cooperate with you."

"You're sure of that."

"Yes, but I don't expect you to take my word for it." She made a gesture of supplication with her open hands. "If you would just call Inspector Conklin, he could give you an unbiased opinion. My brother has already gotten one tough deal, and he doesn't need another one."

"I called Conklin. He explained about—the circumstances."

"Oh. Thanks."

"Not necessary. It's part of my job."

Natalie frowned. Was it possible the sergeant had made up his mind before he had sent for her? Might even have meant to ask her to take Daniel in? She glanced up at him, trying to read him, but he was fumbling for something in his jacket pocket, and she could not read his expression.

Eventually he pulled out a notebook and flipped it open. "Okay, let's move on to specifics. You are Natalie Joday, you live at 128 Haworth Avenue, Haworth, New Jersey, and your phone number is 555-5999. You are unmarried, twenty-nine, drive a 1980 maroon Volvo, license number 2BO N2B. You grew up in Haworth and graduated from Northern Valley Regional High School in 1982. You moved to Englewood and attended the Farleigh Dickenson School of Journalism. You took a year off to work as a volunteer in Africa in 1986, and returned to graduate from college in 1987. You moved back to Haworth four years ago and got a job with the *Bergen Evening Star*, first as a stringer and then a staff reporter, where you are considered to be a valued and dependable employee. You are on a first-name basis with the mayor of Haworth, two top-level state officials, and a US senator."

"Wow," said Natalie. "I'm impressed."

Sergeant Allan shook his head in modest denial. "I'm on good terms with your night editor."

"I didn't realize Chip knew my license number."

"We get that kind of stuff ourselves."

"Oh, right. So my bona fides are established?"

"Yes. Everyone should have such a sister. If your brother will agree to stay at your place until further notice, I'll accept that."

"Thanks, I appreciate it."

"You appreciate it," snorted Sergeant Allan. "What about him?" He nodded toward the locked door.

Natalie, brushing the question aside, took his nod as an invitation to move, and did so. The sergeant unlocked the door and ushered her inside.

Daniel took in his sister's glowing face, inhaled deeply, and looked expectantly at the sergeant.

"You're out of here," said the sergeant, "on one condition. I need to know that I'm going to be able to find you again. Are you willing to stay at your sister's for a while—I mean, stay put?"

Daniel lifted his shoulders in bewilderment at the low degree of difficulty. "If she'll have me."

Natalie glanced from one man to the other with a broad smile. "Then it's settled."

Sergeant Allan gave a curt nod. "Okay, you can go, Joday." Daniel stood up and turned to retrieve his coat, but the sergeant wasn't finished. He placed a restraining hand on Daniel's arm, and when he had his attention, said, "Thanks for your cooperation."

Daniel nodded, and turned again as the sergeant released him, but not quickly enough to hide the flash of guilt that crossed his half-obscured face. Natalie caught it, and, watching Sergeant Allan out of the corner of her eye, she knew he had spotted it too. For an instant, reflected in the mirror of the sergeant's eyes, she saw her brother as he and many others must see him: unreliable, unhelpful, untrustworthy. She looked away, and concentrated on zipping her jacket.

Released, brother and sister walked down the hall together, picking up speed and energy as they went. They bounded down the stairs, and Daniel drew his sister's arm through his own, pulling her tightly to him. They burst through the doors and into the crisp outside world, where a baby-blue predawn sky promised a fine day.

Daniel threw back his head and eyed his sister. "You are a magician—you are my guardian angel. Anything I have or can obtain by honest means is yours, save only my faithful steed Skyrocket and my black high-top Reeboks, which are too big for you anyway. Name your desire!"

Natalie laughed, momentarily stymied. "Let's see, what I really want is..." She affected a puzzled expression, and then laughed again. But as she thought about it, her smile faded slowly away, as stars do at the coming of dawn.

⋙

They hunted up an all-night diner on Howland Avenue where they devoured a celebratory breakfast in the company of half a dozen discriminating truck drivers who had wandered over from Route 17. Huddling over tall frosty glasses of fresh orange juice and a starter plate of toast, they traded tales of the previous night.

"They were waiting for me at the A&P when I got there at 7:30." Daniel buttered his toast, taking his time with the corners. "Two plainclothes guys who didn't identify themselves for the damned longest time. Things got a little hairy at one point—I thought they were going to evacuate the A&P. Chuck was not amused, but it was great, the way he tried to protect me. Pass the marmalade? Eventually we figured out what was going on, and I left peacefully. No, really!" He shook his head in response to Natalie's skeptical glance at the swelling on his jaw. "There was just a little jostling at the beginning. Anyway, I got to the courthouse around eight. I started trying to call you around nine."

"While I was spending the evening at the Dows' with Sarah."

Daniel choked on his orange juice. "You're kidding!"

Natalie shook her head as the waitress appeared with their specials. "Ironic, isn't it? I'm sitting around listening to Sarah's boyfriend talking about the grilling he got at the courthouse, and you're being grilled at the courthouse and ringing up my empty apartment."

"I had no idea you were in contact with those people!"

"I wasn't." Natalie rattled the pepper shaker over her eggs with vim. "I heard the news at the office and called Sarah to offer condolences—I know, I know, I was never a buddy of anybody named Dow. But Sarah—got to me that day she called. Speaking of which, when I delivered her message, you gave me the distinct impression you hadn't been in touch with Lydia for ages." She raised her eyebrows.

Daniel poured maple syrup on his pancakes. "Well, I don't think I actually said that…."

"I said, 'distinct impression.'"

"Okay, okay." Daniel lifted his hands in a gesture of surrender. "Sorry…I did—intentionally—give that impression. It's true I may have been trying to hide, but not from *you*, okay?" He paused to collect his thoughts, and from the look on his face it was not a happy exercise. "You may not remember, but when you called, Rebecca and I were in the late rounds of our breakup, and in fact I left her place for good the next morning."

"Oh. Was that then?" Natalie took a sip of coffee.

"Yeah, that was then. Well, one of Rebecca's accusations was that I was seeing somebody else, and the dinner party at the Dows' the preceding weekend was introduced as supporting evidence. So when you called, it didn't seem to be the appropriate moment to say 'Oh yeah, Sarah! Lydia's kid sister! You know I was hoping she'd call—great ladies, those Dows.' So I stonewalled. I honestly didn't think it would make the slightest bit of difference." Daniel paused to take a sip of tea. "Sorry to expose these pathetic details of my life."

"Listen." Natalie leaned forward. "This is no time for delicacy. From what I saw last night we're dealing with folks who breed problems like some people breed hamsters. Nor are they likely to have the spare time or natural inclination to worry about anybody else." She waved her fork at him. "And we both know it's a mistake to trust the police to do an even-handed job. We need to damned-well keep on top of the situation; which means we both need to know exactly what's going on and never mind the niceties. Let's keep our priorities straight! Agreed?"

Daniel nodded, his gray eyes darkening as he looked at his sister's face. "Agreed." He took a deep breath. "I need you,

Natty. I can't handle what's coming—I know that—and you're the only one who's ever given two cents for me." Worry lines crossed his forehead, and his voice dropped. "Look, here's my idea of a priority: I don't want to go back to prison for something I didn't do. I just couldn't take it. No joke. I can't even take thinking about it."

"I know, Danny," whispered Natalie.

"Okay." He straightened up and his face cleared. "To it, then. What do you want to know?"

"The whole story, from when you first met Lydia—and don't skimp on the details."

"There was a time when you didn't want to hear her name."

"Very true, but times have changed." She signaled to the waitress for a second cup of coffee.

Daniel cast his thoughts backward. "I was aware of her in high school, but no more than that. We were the same age—but I was smoking dope in the boiler room while she was organizing bake sales for the French Club trip to Montreal. So our paths didn't cross until my last semester, junior year. We were in a drama workshop, and we had to do a scene together. We met after school to discuss it and ended up hitting it off. We spent half the night talking over every play we'd ever read. We chose something from *Moon for the Misbegotten*."

"How appropriate."

"I thought so. Anyway, we did the scene and—it was magic! Well…" Daniel flashed a grin, and took a bite of his hash browns. "Maybe it was and maybe it wasn't. But at the time—you know how it is. Lydia was very serious—very intense. Every moment was thrilling. Of course I knew from the first she was stinking rich."

"An added attraction."

Daniel reached for the ketchup. "I was going to say, it kept us from getting closer. I didn't want her to find out how different my life was from hers."

"Oh."

"After I dropped out of school I never saw her. And then there was Lara and blah, blah, blah. Cut to my release from prison three-plus years ago. Lydia was one of the first people I ran into after my trip to California."

"I remember."

"You were highly skeptical about our relationship."

"Why be diplomatic? I thought she was a pain vampire." Natalie took a sip of coffee and shrugged. "I may have overreacted."

"No. You were right." He put down his knife and fork. His eyes were full of pain, but his voice was calm. "I didn't get it at the time—I didn't get it when we broke up later that summer. But I got it this past February. The truth is she *liked* it that I'd been in prison, that I'd been 'led astray,' and had 'suffered the consequences,' but was at heart a 'good guy.' She was attracted to the idea of me as much as she was attracted to me. If I'd been smart enough to realize that at the time…well, nothing was easy in those days."

"I remember."

Daniel grasped his teacup in both hands and looked into its depths. "I was trying to make up for lost years in a big way, and Lydia seemed to understand. There wasn't any point in hiding my history anymore—since I was a local news headline—and it was an incredible relief! Because she cared for me anyway. She told me that with me she had 'discovered a moment of immortality.' She seemed so deeply, passionately happy—at first. But it all went nowhere fast. Oh, sometimes we talked about the future, about doing theater—forming our own company—or starting some kind of artsy-craftsy business. But that always brought up the money issue again, because of course I didn't have any, and I couldn't help but feel like shit that she'd have to finance everything—even if she didn't mind. Particularly if she didn't mind. And then there was her father."

"Yeah. Mr. Understanding."

Daniel put down the teacup. "You met him last night?"

"Oh, yes."

He nodded. "This was *the* issue between us. She didn't want her father to know she was 'seeing me.' She justified it by pointing out that I wasn't wild for her to meet my father either, and I took it, but it wasn't really the same thing. After a while, meeting always in secret got old. It was also a pain to have to call her at 'special times,' instead of when I wanted to. This led to a lot of misunderstandings. Lydia thought it was romantic to be dodging a disapproving father, but I thought it was... humiliating. Then, in the end, he somehow *did* find out about me—and, boy, did all hell break loose. The payoff came when he tracked us down at the Fourth of July fireworks extravaganza in downtown Demarest. He knocked me into a fifty-gallon ice chest full of Dr. Pepper, grabbed Lydia by the hair and, before a spellbound house, roared that if he ever caught me within a mile of his daughter again he'd break every bone in my body. Scored to 'The Battle Hymn of the Republic,' and featuring the community chorus waving sparklers."

"A taste for melodrama runs in the family."

"Well, that's what I thought." Daniel reached for another slice of toast. "When I got around to *thinking*. Talking it over with Matt one day, I had to wonder if parking in dark alleys and bathing in ice water were really good for my self-esteem. Lydia and I saw each other a couple more times, and I got the idea she would have gone on. But she wouldn't defy her father, and I wouldn't see her on the sly anymore, so nothing came of it. All in all, breaking up was about the only smart move we ever made."

"Hmm." Natalie made a little sandwich of egg and toast crust as she spoke. "Sarah said her father had a tight hold on Lydia, but I wasn't sure if she was reading the situation correctly—or speaking for herself."

"She got it right, from what I experienced."

"You were staying at my place then, right? I knew you broke up, but I had no idea it was so messy."

"Do you think I wanted you to know what a sap I was?" Daniel glared at her, struggling to keep his voice low. "Even now, when I remember what it felt like landing in a bath of cold water and soda cans...Well, if any good came of it, it was that I decided those were not the sort of people I should be hanging with."

Natalie tilted her head at him. "So what made you change your mind?"

"You're referring to this past February?" Daniel made a rueful face. "Good question. I've thought a lot about that. So much time had passed—hadn't I learned anything? Here's what I've concluded: I think I made a fundamental mistake. Sometime around the first of the year I decided I had finally made it, finally pulled my life together—and I relaxed."

"This is a crime?"

"You haven't heard the best part." Daniel took a deep breath. "Early in February, I ran into Lydia at the 7–Eleven in Closter. First time in two and a half years. I was glad to see her. I hoped she was doing well. I found myself thinking of her as an old friend—someone it had been fun to yack with about plays and books. Neither of us was embarrassed—it felt great. Then she asked me to dinner at the house the next evening. It would be casual, she said, just a few friends. Sarah would be there, and I would be surprised to see how she'd grown. She wasn't at all dramatic about it, Nat, and I thought, well, good—she's calmed down, I've calmed down, life is not half bad.

"And there was another thing. I had never been in her house. Castle Dow. The Big House…the forbidden palace surrounded by the hedge of thorns. And I hadn't been virtuous enough to find a way in. Even when her father was out of town on business, she'd been too scared to let me come over. That had made me feel lousy. So I wanted to be able to say to myself 'That was then, when you were immature, and your life was nowhere, and you got dumped into an ice chest, and this is now, when you are stable, and moving forward, and have old friends who ask you around to dinner parties, no matter who their fathers are—or yours.' So I went."

"How was it?"

"A nightmare." Daniel closed his eyes for a moment. "She wasn't there when I arrived—she had gone out to buy club soda and pick up Sarah's boyfriend. But when she walked through the door it took me about two minutes to see that nothing had changed, we were still in the land of make-believe. Lydia was just playing a different role, one I couldn't get a handle on at all. And my role—well, I had been typecast as the token felon, presence guaranteed to spice up the dullest party."

"Oh, Daniel!"

He ignored her sympathy. "I kept saying to myself, 'I thought I knew this person once…what was I seeing?'" He shook his head and mocked, "Now look who's being melodramatic."

"Well, let's enforce practicality. Who else was there?"

"Sarah. Sarah's boyfriend, what's his name?"

"That would be Harry."

"A couple in their early thirties, neighbors I think. Then there was this weird guy, Graham. And, oh yeah, their stepmother."

"Rose!?"

"Yeah, Rose."

"What was she doing there? I mean, wasn't she a little out of her element?"

"She didn't seem to think so." Daniel pulled in his lips at the corners.

"So what happened?" urged Natalie.

"First we had a little cocktail hour, and stood around chatting about how interest rates had plummeted and what it had done to the economy—Lydia was always a whiz at finance. I tried to hold my own by saying something intelligent about balance-of-trade deficits, and failed. Remind me to study more for my final in macroeconomics. Then we admired the furniture and the paintings. Then Graham played the piano and Sarah sang a couple of songs. We had dinner. It sounds exactly like what I always thought normal was supposed to be. Only I still felt so out of place! But it wasn't the money—or my record, either. I don't know what it was. But after spending years wanting to get in, I found myself itching to get out." He frowned, then let it go with a shrug. "Well, anyway, then came the blowup."

"I heard there was a fight."

"Yeah. I never worked out what caused it. I guess a lot went over my head that night. Well, here's what I know:

"After dinner people broke into smaller groups. Rose latched onto this other couple, cornering them in the living room, and they talked about holiday plans and golf handicaps and import regulations. Lydia insisted that Sarah and I have coffee with her to talk over old times. Just exactly what I really didn't want to do. Graham and Harry went downstairs for a game of pool."

Daniel held a table knife in both hands, flipping it over and over. "The phone rang, and Lydia jumped up to get it, which left Sarah and me alone. Suddenly, from the basement, we heard this huge crash—it was a mahogany rack full of pool cues falling off the wall, I later learned. Then we heard a scuffle. Sarah and I shot up out of our chairs and ran to the hall. Rose, coming from the living room, was there ahead of us. We streaked past Lydia, who was on the phone, oblivious to what was going on. We clattered down the stairs thinking somebody's being murdered, and Lydia, raising her voice above the din, was saying, 'No, thank you, I'm not interested in hearing anything more about it, you can send something in the mail if you want.' Surreal.

"We got to the rec room just in time to see Harry taking a swing at Graham. Not bad for an MBA, either. Graham went over sideways, but came up again—real quick—with a pool cue in his hands. He took a full-power swing at Harry, who ducked behind the pool table—but Rose nearly got the follow-through right in the face. I jerked her back. She shook me off and threw herself at Graham—screaming bloody murder. I dove in behind her and made a grab for the cue. Graham let go, barked 'Shut up!' at Rose and slapped her—not gently. But it didn't even slow her down—she went right for his face. I got my arms around him and pinned him against the wall, at the same time trying to keep Rose from gouging his eyes out. Meanwhile, Sarah was making sure Harry kept out of it. Then came a lull, while everyone breathed hard and wondered what the hell to do.

"At that moment Lydia made her entrance, took in the whole scene, put her hands to her mouth, and went into hysterics. Bad theater—anticlimactic. But it defused the situation. One by one everybody snapped back to 'normal.' Rose took charge, insisting everybody apologize to everybody else and pretend nothing had happened. Nobody objected. It was sickening. Apparently we were all supposed to brush it off and carry on like civilized adults. Well, if that's the way civilized adults behave, I'll stop trying to be one, thank you.

"Graham was the first to leave, full of smooth apologies and lame jokes. Then the other couple—I can't remember their names—made their excuses and left, and I knew I had to split. I explained I had an eight o'clock class the next morning and wanted to get a good night's sleep, and took off. God it was awful. All I could think as I left was, thank God no one knows where I'm living or where I work or even my phone number—I'll never have to see any of these people ever again." Daniel closed his mouth and fell silent, looking at his empty teacup.

Natalie, while fully appreciating this concluding sentiment, found plenty to wonder about in the rest of the tale. She wrapped a paper napkin around her forefinger. "Where was Eric?"

Daniel stirred. "Ah yes…the irony of it all. He wasn't there. Lydia said he was on a buying trip and wouldn't be back till the next day, so she had had the courage—*the courage*, she said—to invite me. I was so angry with her for saying that. So angry. And now I can't…"

He closed his eyes for a moment, and when he opened them again to gaze at his sister, his look was haunted and bereft. "We'll never get a chance to heal the damage we did to each other. My last memories of her…just hell. There's so much I want to say—now. But I won't even be welcome at her funeral. I won't be able to publicly acknowledge that once I knew Lydia Dow, once loved her, and despite the mess we made of things, we were a part of each other's lives.

"I can't believe she's dead." Tears welled up and overflowed in Daniel's eyes, and he snatched at the napkin dispenser. "Damn."

Natalie looked out the window. The early morning traffic was increasing, the street noises growing louder. She turned back to her brother. "I have a lot more sympathy for her now that I've met her father. And Sarah, too."

"I'll say." Daniel blew his nose. "She was always a sweet kid—and she did worship Lydia. It's not her fault she was born of the silver spoon. It was good of you to go over there, Nat."

"Yeah, well, I have to tell you I wasn't exactly thrilled about it."

"I bet."

"In fact, six hours ago I was, like you, washing my hands of the whole bunch. But now—I'm just glad I've got an in. I'll call Sarah later." Natalie glanced at the clock behind the counter. "Jeez, it's six-fifteen." She yawned. The exuberance of their triumph at the courthouse was wearing off, and the vision of her firm mattress returned.

"Six-fifteen?" cried Daniel. "Already? Hey! I've got an eight o'clock class! Check, please!"

"Are you serious?"

"Yeah, I don't want to miss it. What's the matter?"

"Nothing. I must be getting old, that's all."

"Nonsense, you are just experiencing the side effects of incipient middle-class disease. Do you have time to give me a lift back to Bergenfield?"

"Sure. Do you want to get your stuff now? I could take it home with me."

"No, I'll just pick up my books, go to Paramus for class, then go back to Pete's and pack—boy, will he be glad to see me go. I'll be at your place mid-afternoon sometime. Damn, I work tonight, too. Oh, well. I'll manage—somehow."

Natalie smothered a smile and reached for the check.

Chapter Four

Natalie not only took Daniel to Bergenfield to get his books, but afterward drove him back to Bergen Community College in Paramus. Then she pointed the Volvo toward Haworth, heading for home and bed. Despite having quite a lot to think about, she was asleep by eight forty-five a.m.

She was awake again at one-fifteen p.m.

Not by choice.

The telephone, abandoned on the floor the night before, was ringing.

Natalie rolled onto her stomach, stretched out an arm, and grabbed the phone by the antenna. "Hello."

"Natalie? It's Sarah."

"Hi, Sarah."

"I guess I'm about the last person you wanted to hear from today."

"Actually, no. I was gonna call you later. Sooner. What time is it?" She looked at the clock. "Oh. How're you doing?"

"Better I guess. I really needed just to sleep. I got up around eleven. First I had another good cry. Then I got brave enough to go downstairs for something to eat."

"And?"

"I should have stayed in bed." Despite this denunciation, Sarah sounded more fretful than forlorn. "Something's come up. Otherwise I wouldn't have the nerve to bother you again.

Eric wants our lawyer to straighten out the financial situation. We haven't even planned the funeral! But he says it's been two months with nobody paying the bills and it has to be today. The lawyer said he'd come, but he insists that I meet with them. Eric says I'm going to inherit half under state law. I don't want to deal with it—today, tomorrow, or ever. It's just that…I suppose I've got to go through with it." Her voice faltered. "I'm such a coward…I thought I'd ask if you'd come over for some moral support?"

Natalie rubbed her eyes and rolled onto her back. "I don't know, Sarah. Won't your father go through the roof if an outsider is present at a family meeting?"

"Mr. Sherill told me on the phone—after I said I didn't want to do it—that he understood exactly how I felt, and he strongly recommended I have a friend present. Eric said it was okay with him. Of course he probably thinks I'll ask Harry. And I would, but—Harry is already so far behind at work. And I don't have any other close friends. I'm asking too much, aren't I?"

Natalie, fully awake, pulled herself up and sat cross-legged on the bed. "No, it's okay. I'll come. But wait a minute." She cut off Sarah's exclamation of gratitude. "I've got something to tell you first—and then you might change your mind."

The telephone went quiet so suddenly that Natalie thought they had been disconnected. "Sarah?"

"I'm here."

"Look." Natalie moistened her lips and pushed her hair behind her ears. "The police had Daniel down at the courthouse all last night asking him about your sister's death. They gave him a pretty hard time."

"Oh, no! Why? Oh—because he was here that night, before she disappeared?"

"Yeah—and because he has a record and makes a convenient suspect. Whatever. So I have a stake in this now—I'm not just a casual acquaintance helping you out of sympathy. Sarah, I honestly don't know what my answer would have been if Daniel weren't involved. But as long as my brother is a suspect in an unsolved murder case, my top priority is to make sure he gets a fair shake, and doesn't take the rap for something he didn't do."

"Well, sure!" protested Sarah. "I don't see—"

"Follow it through. To take the heat off Daniel, I'm pretty keen on making sure whoever did it gets nailed. Sarah, the day may dawn when it's a question of your family or mine."

"Oh."

"And on that day, if I know something that will help end this, I'm not going to keep it a secret."

"I wouldn't expect you to!" Sarah sounded indignant. "But I don't think it will come to that, do you? The police have been swarming around here all day, and they seem very serious. Don't you think they will do everything they can to find the murderer?"

"Of course," said Natalie. "But—I know my brother, and the police don't. Remember what you said to me the first time you called? 'I can't just stand by and do nothing.'"

There was another sudden silence, but this time Natalie waited until it reached its natural conclusion.

"I understand." Sarah's voice seemed distant. "You're stronger than I am. I couldn't do anything. Maybe you can. I won't stand in your way."

"Thanks," said Natalie.

"And besides—I never thought I would say this, but—I want to find out who killed my sister." A hint of menace crept into Sarah's voice, startling in its expectation. "I want him to pay, no matter who it is." Then her voice grew lighter and more immediate. "That's my top priority, too. So there's no conflict."

"I hope you're right," said Natalie. She promised to be there by three o'clock, and they rang off.

❯❯❯

Three county patrol cars, a beige sedan, and a limousine from Valentine's Funeral Home crowded the circular driveway at Castle Dow. Natalie snugged the Volvo against the fountain and headed up the walkway between the oaks. She was reaching for the buzzer when the door burst open and Eric Dow strode onto the stoop, forcing her to move backward so hastily that she missed the step and stumbled to the walkway.

"You've got the nerve!" He stared down at her with clenched fists. "Who the hell do you think you are?"

Natalie, straightening up, recognized the question as rhetorical, and knew that he had figured out exactly who she was. She lifted her chin and countered his angry gaze with disdainful eyes. "Would you please tell Sarah I'm here? Again."

"You deaf or just dumb?" His face twisted into an offensive caricature of disbelief. "Snooping around, taking advantage of an emotionally disturbed girl to try and disrupt a police investigation. You have no shame, do you?"

Hot anger brought Natalie's blood to a rolling boil. "You're going to lecture me on manners? That's a laugh!"

"You won't be laughing when they nail your brother for murder. Oh, yes." He bared his teeth. "When I heard they let him go, I gave them the whole story, and they're on to him now."

"You do exceed," said Natalie, her voice laced with condescension, "even my cynical expectation of the depths to which those who live lives of intolerance, selfishness, and ignorance can sink!"

He threw out an arm and pointing to the driveway. "Get off my property!"

Natalie, heart pounding, jumped unto the stoop only inches from his burly frame. She was tall, and their eyes were level. "But it's not 'your property' *yet*, is it!"

"Don't talk to me like that, young lady!"

"And you want 'your property,' don't you?" Natalie, propelled by gale-force winds of outrage, was conscious only of her need to defeat this horrible man the only way she knew how. "So you want a lawyer here, today, don't you? But, the lawyer wants Sarah—and Sarah wants *me*!"

A look of doubt crossed Eric's face. "You have no idea what you're talking—"

"Now, Eric!" They both jumped. "Your blood pressure! You mustn't get upset."

Rose had materialized from nowhere, a slight fluffy presence in a lemon-yellow pantsuit and pearl beads. She stood partially hidden behind Eric's rigid frame, one hand gently patting his right shoulder, the other tucked around his left elbow. "I'm so sorry, Natalie. I hope you understand that we're all under a terrible strain. He didn't really mean what he said." She smiled at Natalie, raising her pencil eyebrows and nodding her head a little.

Natalie, breathing hard, stared at Rose in bewilderment.

Fortunately, and possibly not by coincidence, Rose carried on without waiting for reply. "I think it's very sweet of you to want to help our Sarah like this. It's not an easy thing to be a friend in difficult times—I know. Sarah is meeting with the funeral director about the arrangements right now, and Mr. Sherill isn't here yet. You know lawyers—don't you? You just come on in and wait in the sunroom till we're ready. I'll explain to Eric that you're really doing us a favor. All right?"

Natalie looked uncertainly at Eric. His eyes were unfocused, and his flushed face showed no reaction to his wife's attempt to rewrite history. But it was clear his tirade was over.

As her emotions ebbed, her reason for coming resurfaced, and Natalie recalled what she was supposed to be doing, and why. "Whatever you say, Rose." She took a deep breath and let the muscles of her face relax.

Rose smiled broadly and steered Eric back through the foyer and into the living room. Turning to Natalie, she indicated an archway to the left. Natalie obediently retired to a small semicircular chamber furnished with a loveseat and armchairs upholstered in a pink-and-lavender-floral pattern.

"There are some magazines on the coffee table," said Rose. "Please make yourself at home." Then, a still-silent Eric in tow, she disappeared, leaving behind a whiff of her trademark coconut cologne.

Natalie unbuttoned her overcoat and dropped it onto a chair. She sank into the soft cushions of the loveseat and leaned her head back. *This wasn't the way to do it,* she thought, feeling the sting of self-accusation. *You won't get anywhere like this!* But what else could she have done? And what was she to make of Rose? Could anybody be that dense? Or was it subtlety—

"Good afternoon, Miss Joday."

Natalie's head came off the loveseat with a start.

Sergeant Allan frowned at her from the archway, as if, walking through the living room on his way out the front door, he had spotted her sitting there.

"Did I surprise you?"

"Oh, a little," was Natalie's grudging admission. Then, shaking off the last of her anger, she greeted him more cordially. "Good afternoon, Sergeant." He had changed from the gray suit of the previous night, and, with his trim figure and dark, clean-cut countenance, looked even more stylish in a three-piece number of midnight blue. "You're on the job twenty-four hours a day, I see. How do you manage to appear so..." She hesitated. What word—neither too trite nor too ingratiating—best fit the situation? "Well-rested?"

"I guess it goes with the job," he said, without reciprocal levity. "We're used to getting short shrift."

Natalie, gathering from his unmistakable tone that there was more behind his words than a comment on long hours, stared at him in confusion. He had changed not only his suit. His manner had grown stiff and wary, exactly like a policeman's.

He did not keep her long in suspense as to why. "You didn't tell me you were a friend of the family." He spoke from behind an authoritative mask of doubt and demand. "Or that you had come here last night to discuss the case. Why not?"

Natalie felt suddenly very frayed, and very alone. "You, too?" she said with exaggerated disappointment. "Just like old times."

The sergeant, having asked his question, waited for her to continue.

She looked into his watchful eyes. "Well, far be it from me to refuse to answer a question put by a law-enforcement officer in the course of his investigation." She knew her tone was too emotional, and steadied herself. "I didn't tell you those things because I am not 'a friend of the family,' and when I was here last night, it was not to 'discuss the case.' I only met Lydia two or three times, long ago, and we were never friends. Before last night I had only met Sarah once, also three years ago. I had, however, spoken with her on the phone in February. She called me looking for Daniel. She was trying to find out what had happened to her sister—remember? And I felt sorry for her! Yesterday afternoon, when I heard the news, I called her. *She* asked *me* to come here, and I came—totally unaware that my brother had been picked up and needed me."

She paused, and tightened her lips as she searched the sergeant's impassive face. "Today, however, I agree—the situation has changed. My brother is a suspect in a murder investigation, and although I have once again come here because Sarah asked me to come, you can be sure that I do intend to 'discuss the case' at every opportunity."

"I nonetheless wonder if Miss Dow understands your position," he persisted.

"I can only relate to you," said Natalie stiffly, "what she told me when I explained the situation earlier today. She said she didn't see any problem, since we both wanted the same thing: to find the murderer, no matter who it is."

Sergeant Allan furrowed his brow, taking his time to think it through. "I see." His expression smoothed. "I'm sorry, Miss Joday. I shouldn't have spoken to you like that."

Natalie, disarmed, ran a hand through her hair and made a self-conscious gesture of appeasement. "No problem." She felt slightly foolish at her display of emotion. "You can't compete with the full-time experts in false accusation," she added, thinking of Eric.

He stepped into the sunroom. "Did something happen?"

Natalie was startled by his question. Had she been that obvious? "Oh, nothing much..."

He seated himself, all attention, on a plush lavender chair. "When I first spoke, you said 'You, too?' Did you have an encounter with someone today?"

She hesitated.

"Miss Joday, you know that what happens in this house is my business now. Little incidents can be very important. I'm sure you—as a reporter—can appreciate that."

"Yeah." He was a policeman again, but now he was on her side. She shrugged. "You may as well know that while I get along okay with the daughter of the house, the vote for advancement to your friend-of-the-family status is unlikely to be unanimous. Eric Dow makes a habit of hurling verbal abuse at me whenever he sees me."

"What did he say?"

"Nothing original. 'Get off my property you so-and-so,' and 'I'll make sure your brother gets what's coming to him.' Like that."

"I see."

"Rose broke it up, and left me in here to recover. Wait a minute." It was Natalie's turn to put two and two together. "Was it Eric who told you I was here under false pretenses yesterday?"

"It came up while I was talking with him." The sergeant glanced through the archway, and then pulled out his notebook. "But he wasn't offensive about it. I'm surprised to hear he would speak to you like that—he was civil to me, exceedingly so. But," he shook his head, "I should have verified his interpretation before I spoke to you like that, particularly as it contradicted my own impressions."

His approach distinguished him from most policemen of her acquaintance, and Natalie, having recovered her bearings, was feeling generous. "Well, I can see where you might have been a little suspicious. He doesn't like me, and he really doesn't like Daniel."

The sergeant didn't look as though he needed any explanation on that point.

"Speaking of suspects," continued Natalie, "how's the investigation going?"

Sergeant Allan smiled at her. "You working a double shift, too?"

"Trying."

"Well, don't get too wrapped up in it."

"You mean you don't need any help."

"I mean I would hate to see someone like you, trying to do the right thing, get caught holding onto something too hot to handle. If I may speak frankly, obstruction of justice is messy, and I think you're better off leaving this one to the professionals."

She smiled at him. "Personally, I've always thought people who hide the truth because they think it will condemn them, when actually it's the one thing that will save them, deserve what they get."

"Miss Joday, have you ever thought that you have just one blind spot? I don't mean to offend you."

"You don't."

"I've dealt with a thousand loyal relatives, Miss Joday. My advantage is that I'm impartial."

"Really?" Natalie tilted her head back and blinked at him. Then she spoke without animosity or accusation. "And yet yesterday, when you wanted to talk to your suspects, you made a polite phone call to Harry Suter and asked him to drop by the courthouse at his convenience. You made sure he was home by supper time. Rose got interviewed in the luxury of her own salon. Even the mysterious second-cousin in the guesthouse was treated with kid gloves. But when you heard the name 'Daniel Joday,' you sent a patrol car and two plainclothesmen to invade his place of employment and haul him in—none too gently—talking in loud voices about parole violation and resisting arrest, with casual references to murder. I know that's the way it is in this world, Sergeant. I'm not even objecting—much. But I'm not willing to characterize the actions of the police—particularly when it comes to dealing with the haves and the have-nots—as impartial."

Sergeant Allan paid her quiet attention until she was done. Then he spoke, matching her detachment. "Five years ago your brother was convicted of a serious felony, Miss Joday. Law-enforcement officers do not always have the opportunity to review the ins and outs of the circumstances; we only see the list of priors, and read about the conviction. It has an effect on us, and it should. However, it is unfortunate if your brother was put in a bad light at work—that's something we try to avoid—and I hope it doesn't cause a problem for him. It won't happen again."

It was not what she had expected to hear. "I'll count on that." That sounded too unappreciative. "Thanks," she added. That sounded too humble. "I tell you what—you do what you think best, and I'll do what I think best. Is it a deal?"

"Miss Joday, it doesn't require a special deal to facilitate the inevitable."

Natalie turned his words inside out, seeking a hidden meaning. Failing in her quest, she looked into his eyes, but learned nothing from his cool and vigilant expression. It disturbed her that someone should read her so well—and yet disagree with her. She shook off the unsettled feeling he aroused and got back to the point.

"So, how's the investigation going?" she asked again, smiling this time.

Sergeant Allan reciprocated with a basso chuckle. "Not much progress yet, Miss Joday. We've got a lot of donkey work to do, and I'm not expecting a fast break with a case like this, where the actual crime took place such a relatively long time ago."

"Anybody ruled out?"

"You. Ex hypothesis."

"Why, Sergeant," mocked Natalie. "You're showing your partiality again!" She had meant it as a jest, but the sergeant broke eye contact and rose abruptly from his chair.

"I'd better get back to work," he said. "I take it you're providing 'moral support' for Miss Dow at the meeting with the lawyer?"

"Right."

"Good luck. Oh, and, by the way…we're off the record."

Natalie's eyes were all innocence. "Of course."

He passed under the archway, hesitated, and turned around. "A pleasure to speak with you, Miss Joday. I find your candor and—approach—extremely refreshing."

"Likewise, Sergeant. As you know, you are at the head of my top-ten list this week."

"I'm honored," he said, and bowed.

◇◇◇

Natalie spent another twenty minutes alone in the sunroom. She passed the time trying to work out the dynamics of the Dow family, asking herself how she would describe them if she had to write about them. It was an odd mix of personalities, full of contradiction. Lydia, although in control of the purse strings, had nonetheless been dominated by her father. Eric was obviously the type who liked to keep people in their place—a place of his design where they were permanently off-balance. Rose seemed able to defuse the most volatile situations, even when she was up against her domineering husband—surprising that Eric, in his mature years, had not picked someone easier to intimidate. And Sarah was cowed by everyone.

Rose finally came to retrieve her. The funeral director had departed, the lawyer had arrived, and the meeting would take place in Eric's basement office. Natalie followed Rose down a flight of stairs and into a chilly room heavy on black leather and golf trophies.

The lawyer, Mr. Sherill, was on the telephone, having usurped the position of power at Eric's desk. Sarah, her pale face half-hidden behind her loose hair, her slender frame lost in an oversized knit sweater, sat on a chair to the left; she mouthed a silent hello at Natalie, and mustered a smile. Eric, looking business-like and wholly non-threatening, sat on a chair to the right; he did not look in her direction, and Natalie concluded he was pretending nothing had happened. She and Rose seated themselves on a divan in the middle of the room.

Natalie, whose experience with lawyers was extensive, gave this one a critical once-over. He was round-faced and well-dressed. He had the look of a man who, if he did not smoke, neither did he jog; if he was not brilliant, neither was he incompetent. She pegged him as a well-established civil (as opposed to criminal) lawyer, who made a fat living catering to the peccadilloes of the upper crust. It irritated her that, besides being late, he was keeping them all waiting while he made phone calls.

Mr. Sherill hung up, and Rose introduced him to Natalie.

"Thank you for coming," he said in clipped accents. He studied her through his round lawyer's glasses.

"My pleasure," said Natalie. She had worn her black tailored suit with the white silk blouse, an outfit guaranteed to give nothing away, and thus perfect for meetings with lawyers and other fortune-tellers.

"Since it has proved unavoidable to commence proceedings so swiftly, I felt very strongly that Miss Dow should have someone here to support her during this difficult time." A hint of disapproval colored the lawyer's tone and expression. "The family, however, may be sure that I will not refer to any details of a private nature."

"We appreciate that, Arthur," said Eric. Natalie noted that his normal speaking voice was a pleasant baritone. "And I hope *you* appreciate that my fiduciary responsibilities have been greatly hampered by the uncertainties attendant to my daughter's prolonged disappearance."

Rose leaned over and put a hand on Natalie's arm. "He means she wasn't here to sign the checks."

"It's a sad fact, but true," continued Eric, "that fiscal obligation does not cease during times of family crisis. So it is for the well-being of the entire family that we file the necessary papers to straighten out the situation as quickly as possible."

Mr. Sherill was distinctly unresponsive. He opened his briefcase and flipped through a neat pile of files until he got the one he wanted. Natalie frowned. He was not likely to show the classic symptoms of catering to the gentry anytime soon. He was intent on something—that she could see—but he didn't seem to be getting enough pleasure out of being the center of attention, the man with the answers. Her skin tingled as she recognized the early warning signs of jurisprudential combustibility. She drew in as much air as she could, glanced once from right to left, and held her breath.

"Eh hem," said Mr. Sherill. He referred to his notes. "I must tell you that in December of 1992 Lydia Dow called me and asked a series of questions regarding her legal position vis à vis the property she had received from her mother. Later, we met at my office and she asked me to draw up a will covering the disposal of that property. Accordingly, I—"

"Wait a minute," said Eric. "She didn't have a will."

"I'm sorry, Mr. Dow, that is not correct. I myself—"

"She told me," said Eric, hands on the arms of his chair, half-rising, "she had no will!"

The lawyer pursed his lips. "Be that as it may, Mr. Dow, your daughter came to me and asked me to draw up a will for her, which I did do, and which I have here before me now, a copy having already been filed with the county."

Complementary expressions of suspicion and amazement crossed the faces of the senior Dows. The air sizzled.

"And?" crackled Eric.

"In short—" Mr. Sherill confirmed their attention with a sweep of his modest blue eyes. "The entire estate of Lydia Dow is left to her sister Sarah Dow, absolutely and without condition."

Natalie exhaled, and looked left. Sarah's eyes widened and then narrowed, and the corners of her mouth turned downward—but that was it. Natalie looked right. Eric's mouth had dropped open and his head had lunged forward in as clear-cut an exhibit of shock as Natalie had ever seen. Rose's cherry-red lips had disappeared into a thin line of displeasure, her eyes were dark and snapping, her nose wrinkled like a pug dog's.

Rose turned slowly to her husband, and secured the prize for First Able to Speak.

"You said," she rasped through clenched teeth, "she had no will."

"I can't believe it," gasped Eric. He turned to Mr. Sherill. "I've had control over my daughter's business affairs since she was 15 years old. She can't—cut me out!"

"I can guarantee you that there has been no error, Mr. Dow," said the lawyer. He pursed his lips again. "You used the term 'fiduciary' just now, but in fact any legal guardianship you exercised on your daughter's behalf ended over five years ago when she turned 21, at which time she took full possession of the property as per her mother's deed of gift. Since then, although you may have advised your daughter in financial matters—even taken over those matters—that arrangement was strictly a family one and carried no legal significance. The entire estate—this property, the summer home in Vermont, the complete investment portfolio, and Lydia's various bank accounts and CDs—now belongs to Sarah, and I have begun the paperwork to provide her with immediate practical control. When that is accomplished—say, within the week—the estate will once again be able to meet its financial obligations."

Natalie glanced around the room again. Sarah was still under-reacting. Rose had herself back under control, and was looking pink and blond and ladylike. "Now, Eric," she said in her normal voice, "never mind. It doesn't really make any difference." She reached for his hand and patted it supportively, and then turned around and looked cheerfully at Sarah. "As long as the money is still in the family, that's the important thing, isn't that right, Sarah?" Eric looked thoughtfully at Sarah; Sarah glanced nervously back at him, and then at Rose.

Natalie regarded Mr. Sherill with grudging admiration. No wonder he had insisted someone be there in Sarah's corner.

"I really think that's all we need go into today," he said putting his papers away. "Sarah, I'll have my assistant give you a call first thing next week, and perhaps you can come down to my office for a more in-depth meeting at a more appropriate time. No hurry." He shot another disapproving look at Eric. Then he turned back to Sarah. "Of course, if you have any questions, call me any time." He snapped his briefcase shut. "Any time."

There was a heavy knock on the door, and everybody jumped. In answer to Eric's impatient "Come in!" Sergeant Allan appeared, followed by two henchmen.

"Sorry to intrude," said the sergeant, not at all apologetic. His glance moved from face to face, stalling for half a second on Natalie's tense countenance.

"We have just finished," said Mr. Sherill, rising and moving around the desk.

"What do you want?" Eric asked without noticeable civility.

"I understand you are the registered owner of a handgun, Mr. Dow," said the sergeant. His eyes skipped from face to face again, this time ignoring Natalie.

"That's right," said Eric.

The sergeant moved over to Eric's side. "I understand you keep the gun in this room?"

"Correct. But it's perfectly safe. My office door is always locked when I'm not here."

"May I see the gun, please?"

Eric gestured to indicate his impatience, and went to sit at his desk, pulling a leather key holder from his pocket. The lawyer, betraying a streak of human curiosity, paused to watch.

Eric fitted a key to the bottom right-hand drawer and pulled it open.

Sergeant Allan moved to his side and made a warning gesture as Eric thrust his hand into the drawer. "I don't want you to touch it, Mr. Dow."

"Well, that won't be difficult because it doesn't seem to be here," said Eric.

Chapter Five

The sun was shining on the treetops as Sarah walked Natalie to her car. The oaks cast long shadows across the lawn, marking it off into narrow strips of light and dark. Behind them, the police battalion had completed its search of the house—and occupants—and had found, to no one's surprise, no gun.

Sarah reached the end of the walkway and stopped, eyes focused on the ground. She had shown few signs of life during the police search, seemingly lost in thought, far away. "So that's over with," she said.

Natalie squinted at her in the bright sunlight. "It wasn't that bad after all, was it? Mr. Sherill seems to be on your side."

"I meant the police have finished the search. They'll leave now."

Natalie shook her head. "They'll be back tomorrow."

Sarah pushed a lose strand of hair behind her ear, and shrugged.

Natalie patted her jacket pockets for her car keys. "Well, I'll see you."

As she looked up at Natalie, Sarah's expression changed. "I'm sorry." Abashed, she took a deep breath and put her hands in her pockets. "I never thanked you for coming. Because you were here, they couldn't corner me after Mr. Sherill left and give me the third degree. I know I haven't said much, but that doesn't mean I don't appreciate your being here. It's just—I don't feel very sociable today." Her gaze strayed again.

Natalie smiled. "I hear you." She moved away, squeezing between a couple of squad cars.

Sarah became aware of the jumble of automobiles in the circular drive. "Jeez, can you get your car out?"

Natalie could, and did—just in time to make room for Harry's Nissan, which at that moment appeared from among the rhododendrons. *Here to take the evening shift*, thought Natalie. She peeked in her rearview mirror. Sarah, head down again, had folded her arms across her chest, gripped her elbows, and hooked the toe of one loafer behind the heel of the other. Natalie returned her attention to the driveway, and inched the Volvo forward. Harry's face, glimpsed as the two cars passed on either side of the fountain, and thrown into stark relief by the harsh light of the setting sun, was drawn with strain, his eyes hollow with exhaustion. Natalie, greeting his lethargic wave with a nod, did not envy them their evening together.

At the front gate, she hesitated, suddenly unwilling to swing right and join the stream of traffic headed for Closter. Acting on impulse, she took advantage of a gap in the line of cars, and swung left. She drove up Closter Dock Road and turned left onto the highway dubbed Palisades Boulevard on county maps but always referred to by its more prosaic name, 9W. A short drive and a right-hand turn brought her to the Exit 2 on-ramp of the Palisades Interstate Parkway, and she was soon heading southbound in moderate traffic.

She kept her eyes peeled for signs of the crime scene. It was somewhere to the left, in the broad, woodsy median that separated the north- and southbound lanes of the parkway. She went past the gravel access road marked No Stopping or Turning, that cut across the median, linking the two highways. Around another bend she spotted what she was looking for: a deep valley, recognizable from the photo in the *Star*. Glancing at her odometer, she slowed, but the parkway was bounded by a low railing at that point, and she could not have pulled over if she had wanted to. She would have to go down to Exit 1 and come back. Natalie's foot went down on the accelerator, and the Volvo purred.

Ten minutes later, she was headed north on the parkway, the Palisades cliffs and the Hudson River close on her right.

When she was within half a mile of the crime scene, she slowed to 40 mpg.

Cars whizzed by. She passed the Alpine Lookout on her right, a semicircular area with twenty-minute parking and a spectacular view of the city across the river.

From her odometer she knew this to be the crime scene, although she could not see any sign of the police cordon. She crossed into the left lane, keeping her speed below 50 mph and ignoring the honking from cars whipping by on her right. Another 200 yards and she spotted the access road on her left. She nipped off the parkway and onto the dirt road where a parked car sat immediately in front of her. She hit the brakes and pulled hard right, sending up a shower of dirt and gravel. The Volvo skidded sideways and lurched to a halt inches from the back end of an unoccupied silver hatchback. The Garden State.

The engine was still purring. Natalie backed up, straightened the car out, and switched off the ignition. She sat still for a while, waiting for her heart rate to decrease, or for the owner of the other car to return. Her pulse returned to normal, but no one appeared. She got out and looked around. There was no sign of activity, police or otherwise, just a steady flow of cars whining by. She peered surreptitiously into the interior of the hatchback, but saw nothing more threatening than a broken dog leash and a purple gym bag on a backseat stained—judging from the overturned can—with spilled soda. *Car trouble*, she thought. She scanned the shrub-filled valley, twenty yards wide, between the two highways. There was no one in sight.

She walked toward the crime scene along the verge of the northbound highway. As the vegetation thinned, she left the roadside and dropped down into the little valley. She moved through increasingly heavy shadows, although far to her left the new leaves atop the trees guarding the cliffs were shining golden in the last rays of the sun. She came upon a cordon of DayGlo tape, strung from one spindly sumac tree to another. Ducking beneath it, she entered the crime scene.

Two semicircular tunnels ran under the south- and northbound highways. A trickle of water in a gravel channel ran between them. She walked to the tunnel under the northbound highway—its walls were made of concrete, and it was about six feet high in the middle. It was neither cobwebby nor dirty. She stepped inside and looked at the gray twilight at the other end.

Natalie could not imagine coming to this spot to murder anyone—especially in winter. Now that she saw the place, she knew that the murderer must have come with an already dead body, having previously decided where to hide it. Where would he put his car? Would the dirt access road have been clear of snow in February? She doubted it, especially given the fierceness of the winter they had had. More important, could he have been seen near the tunnel entrance? She looked behind her at the flow of cars, headlights already on, roaring southbound down the parkway. Wave after wave of beacons lit up the little valley and illuminated the tunnel. Would anyone have risked hiking two hundred yards down the snowy median with a body? The idea was absurd. She looked through the tunnel again. Maybe from the other side?

She moved into the tunnel, creeping along the trickle of water. Halfway through she saw, as a somewhat darker shadow, the narrow shelf in the curved side wall on which the body must have lain. She extended her arm to the back of the recess. It was empty, and about two feet deep.

A reedy voice echoed through the tunnel. "Having fun, Natalie?"

In a galvanizing split second, adrenaline radiated throughout her body, electrifying her fingers and toes. Looking everywhere at once, she became aware of a man standing in silhouette at the far end of the tunnel.

"Jeez!" She was suddenly aware of her pounding heart. "You practically scared me to death!"

"A thoughtless choice of idiom."

Natalie's thoughts spun helplessly. Surely the accent was English! The voice itself was smooth and languid—more amused than sarcastic. As far as she could tell, she had never heard it before—but how the hell did he know who she was?

"I hope I haven't frightened you too much—have I?"

She had two choices: she could skedaddle back the way she had come, or go forward toward her antagonist. She felt for her keys in her pocket, tightening her fingers around them so that the oversized ignition key stuck out between the middle and forefinger of her right hand.

That contact with her car keys brought the image of the Volvo to her mind, and she saw again the silver hatchback—she had been somewhat rattled when she had looked at it, but it had been a Subaru, hadn't it? Hadn't she seen a Subaru somewhere recently? Yes, in the Dow driveway! Only, in the dark it had looked white. There had been two cars parked beside the Volvo when she had left the night before. Two people had returned while she was with Sarah. One had been Harry, and the other… relief brought release from tension, and she almost laughed.

"Not at all—Graham." She walked down the tunnel.

"Aw." His voice choked with mock disappointment. "I suppose my accent gave it away! I would have tried to disguise it, but I find American accents so—inimitable."

"Actually, it was your car." Natalie emerged from the eastern end of the tunnel. She couldn't read his expression in the fading light, but she saw that he was slight, with fair, sleek hair and a long, drooping mouth. He wore a sport jacket over a light-colored sweater, and baggy trousers. His age could have been anything between 30 and 50.

"Well, that was clever of you," he said.

"Praise from Sarah's father's second wife's deceased first husband's second-cousin is praise indeed." She looked eastward over his shoulder and was surprised to see a trail disappearing into the woods at the top of the cliffs.

"Ah, now she grasps it," said Graham. "Come on. I'll show you what I've found."

They walked side by side to the woods. Natalie recollected that the Palisades Interstate Park was crisscrossed by hiking and ski trails. No doubt the tunnels beneath the highways were there as much for the access of hikers and skiers as for water runoff. And the Alpine Lookout was only a quarter mile away.

She looked at the trail. It went through dense trees, parallel to the highway. "Let me guess. It goes right to the lookout."

Graham folded his arms across his chest and touched a finger to his chin. "I've just been there and back. I make it that he parked at the lookout, and carried the body through the woods—they keep these trails packed down for skiers, you know. Not a bad plan—particularly as he must have done it in the dead of night." He stared at her face. "You've got a piece of dead leaf in your hair." He reached out his hand, but Natalie got there first, and, running her fingers through the soft brown curls above her forehead, removed several bits of dry leaf mold.

"Obviously, that means the murderer was someone who knew the area very well." He continued to stare at her. "And, even given that the trail would be open, I should think he would have had quite a struggle to tote her over that distance in the dead of winter. That points to a man, I should say. Now tell me, what secrets does the scene reveal to you?"

"The murderer had a car."

"Well, yes, but really—that goes without saying, doesn't it? I've been trying to reconstruct the crime, because, honestly, how many chances does one get in life to observe a murder investigation in progress? One has to use these opportunities for elucidation when they present themselves. Perhaps that seems cold-blooded to you—I realize how difficult it must be to keep an open mind—when your brother is one of the suspects."

Natalie tossed her head back. "I'm sure it can't compare with the strain of being a suspect yourself."

He reached out a hand. "I hope you don't think I'm in danger of being pushed over the edge by this!"

Natalie made no comment.

Graham laughed. "No, I suffer not at all, because I know I didn't do it, so I can enjoy the excitement of the investigation. You, on the other hand, must remain prey to nagging doubt and anxiety, fearing for your brother's future, holding your breath at the discovery of each new clue." He shook his head sympathetically. "But wait! If you really think your brother is innocent, then you must suspect one of us—even me! And that would mean… How awful to think you might be alone in the twilight woods with—the murderer!"

His desire to frighten her was palpable, but unfortunately this did not lessen Natalie's pulse rate. She fingered her keys and shifted her weight, but her voice remained steady—if somewhat flat. "At least if I disappear I'm sure they'll check all the tunnels in the park first thing."

"You display a dogged ability to maintain your cool." He doled out praise as princes disburse coins to the poor. "I wonder if Lydia was able to do the same when she faced her murderer. Probably not. She was a terrible actress, and hanging around the New Globe didn't help. That was one scene we can be thankful we didn't have to watch." He shifted his eyes, staring back at the tunnel, lips pursed and hands on hips. Then he smiled at Natalie. "We'd better be going before some punk steals our hubcaps."

Natalie, who never rejected good advice just because she lacked warm feelings for the person who gave it, agreed, and they walked northward along the edge of the woods. Away from the tunnel and out in the open, she regained her full faculties.

"Sarah says you write."

"When I am able. Which is not as much as I might wish—and this business has thrown me completely off schedule. Writing is a very transcendental experience for me, and if the ambiance is wrong…" He shrugged. "I'm afraid I couldn't do what you do—churn it out by the inch."

"Don't let it get you, not everyone can. What are you working on?"

"I'm doing an epistemological treatise on the major themes of post-modern society."

"Sounds fascinating," said Natalie. "Which, ah, major themes are you treating?" They were level with their cars now, but had to wait for the traffic to thin before crossing the northbound highway.

"Well, I'm trying to keep it down to three, since I believe that three is the root number of knowledge. Really, there are no numbers of any importance smaller than three."

Natalie blinked. She turned slowly to look at him, and found him looking at her.

He treated her to a supercilious smile. "I have conceptualized first, the Search for Reality, or, Reality/Meaning, and second, the Search for Happiness, or Happiness/Money, and third—the search for Power, or Power/Sex. Beneath these three core dogmas I, of course, touch on many other topics." The road cleared and they sprinted to their cars.

"Sounds epic. Have you got a publisher?"

"You have an appreciation of the business side of writing, don't you, Natalie? It is a pleasure to meet a colleague. I have a draft I'd like you to read. With your professional skills, you might be able to help me—I admit I don't spell very well."

"What a shame." Natalie glanced down at the car keys in her hand and regretted that they would be put to use only for their native purpose. "Tell me, Graham, how did you know who I was?"

He leaned against his car and crossed his arms. "I wouldn't deprive you of the simple pleasure of figuring it out."

Natalie nodded. "Okay. Off the cuff, you must have been scouting out the trails through the woods when I drove up, and recognized my car. It's been around a lot recently."

"Not bad for an impromptu effort," said Graham. "You show real promise. Perhaps we should work together in this investigation—you know, Holmes and Watson, Nero Wolfe and Archie Goodwin, The Thin Man and Asta."

"I'll be sure and touch base real soon," said Natalie with distinct insincerity. She got into her car and slammed the door.

She turned the ignition key, revved the accelerator, and put the Volvo into reverse. Graham laughed and waved good-bye as she backed past him, slammed on the brakes, and shifted into first. The Volvo's tires squealed as she roared onto the highway into a small gap in traffic.

Natalie turned off the parkway at Exit 2 and regained 9W, southbound. She shook her head. "What a crew." Racing past the top of Closter Dock Road without a glance, she took the long route home.

›››

As she entered her apartment, Natalie made note of Daniel's well-worn duffel bag and suitcase stowed in the living room behind the humidifier. Beleaguered by lack of sleep, she took the shortest route (via microwave and shower) to bed. By nine o'clock she was propped up on her pillows with the *Star*, checking the headlines and reading up on the murder. She was somewhat surprised to read that Sarah had been attending college in Florida since the previous September, and had been home for the mid-winter break when her sister had disappeared.

It was ten o'clock when, dozing over the crossword puzzle, she heard Daniel's key in the lock. She gave him a cheery "Hello!" to let him know she was awake.

His face peeked around the edge of her open door. "Are you alone?"

Natalie flung back the duvet to reveal the cat, sprawled out against her legs. Trick, thus disturbed, lifted his head, looked at her, and blinked: feline outrage. Natalie swept the duvet back into place.

"You make a lovely couple." Daniel took a step forward and stood in the doorway, holding a bag of groceries in each arm. "But what happened to the soccer player?"

"Spring training in Arizona," she said regretfully.

"And the French guy?"

"He had a habit of arguing at the bridge table." She shook her head in amazement. "Can you believe it?"

"Scoundrel," said Daniel. "Good riddance. Do you have room in your fridge for this stuff?"

"I have no idea."

Daniel wandered back into the kitchenette. Natalie refocused her attention on the paper.

She heard the refrigerator door open.

"Hmm," said Daniel. "Well, with a little rearranging…" Bottles scraped upon metal racks.

"What's a seven-letter word for 'kissable?'" asked Natalie.

"Pouting," said Daniel. "Natty, the cottage cheese keeps much better if you keep the top on."

"Throw it out. 'Pious,' five letters, noun, last letter T."

"Elect." There came the sound of a paper bag tearing.

"Good one. I thought it was 'godly.' But that means 'kissable' begins with an L. 'Pouting' must be wrong." She used her eraser.

"Lip-like." A cupboard door creaked open.

"Hyphenated." She stared nowhere for a moment. "Labiate."

"Nat, why are you still using skim milk? The rest of the world has lightened up and drinks two percent. I—good God!"

"What!" cried Natalie, dropping the paper.

"Oh, nothing…it's only raspberry jam." The trash bin popped open and something heavy was thrown in.

Natalie grinned.

"How 'bout some ice cream?" continued Daniel.

"Now?" She looked at the clock. "Gee, I don't know, it's a little late…"

"It's already soft."

"I don't know."

"Tin Roof."

"Daniel, you got my favorite kind of ice cream!"

"Of course."

"How can I refuse?" she purred. The freezer door swung open.

"It's the least I can do," muttered Daniel. "Or should I say, the *only* thing."

"No, you shouldn't. I didn't do a thing—just my earnest upstanding citizen bit. The sergeant was going to let you go as soon as you came up with a legal address. He just needed to fill in all the blanks on his forms. They didn't have a thing on you."

"Lucky for me. Speaking of The Situation, I called Evan this afternoon. I hope that doesn't bother you."

"He's your lawyer." Natalie picked up the paper again and focused on the answers to yesterday's crossword puzzle—which she hadn't done.

"So he is." Daniel appeared in her doorway, holding two bowls of ice cream at shoulder level. He went down on one knee at her bedside and presented her with one of the bowls. Then he slipped off his shoes and curled up in the hanging bamboo chair on the other side of the room. Pushing a toe against the bureau, he set the chair swinging, and dipped his spoon into the ice cream. "He told me I don't have a thing to worry about. But he doesn't want me to talk to the cops again unless he's there. Then he told me he's going away for a long weekend first thing tomorrow morning and won't be back in the office until Monday. Am I crazy, or is there a contradiction in there somewhere?"

"Lawyers thrive on contradiction. Lesser mortals in search of a straight and rubble-free path through life are severely tested by the challenge of remembering that."

Daniel arched his dark eyebrows and lowered his eyes, studying his ice cream. "He asked me to send you his regards."

Natalie contemplated her spoon. "I'm afraid I cannot return the salutation, Daniel."

"Just checking."

"Eat your ice cream."

Daniel ate, gave a deep sigh, and smiled at his sister. "Hits the spot, doesn't it?"

"To perfection."

But his smile faded as he ate, and a look of resignation took its place as his spoon scraped the bottom of the bowl. "One thing I have to tell you, Nat."

"Uh-oh."

"It's not that bad."

"Yeah."

"Just inconvenient."

"Promise?"

"You know I never make promises." He turned from her, and looked out the darkened window. "I've been laid off at the

A&P. I guess management didn't much care for the idea that one of their employees was hauled off for questioning in a murder investigation. Chuck said that given the givens it would be better if I laid low until this gets cleared up."

Natalie sat up in her bed. "They can't *do* that! You—"

"No, really, it's okay. Chuck was very decent about it. He gave me two weeks' salary—cash. If we're lucky it'll all be over by then and I can—"

"No." Natalie waved her spoon at him. "I mean they can't—push you out like that. I mean it's illegal!"

"It's not a big deal."

"It *is* a big deal!" Natalie stared at him in amazement. "Ask your lawyer! He may have fewer social graces than my cat, but he's a very good lawyer and he would love to tackle this one."

"Nat, would you listen to me?" Daniel uncurled himself and put his feet on the floor to stop the rocking of the chair. "I don't want to make a federal case out of this. I mean it. I understand where they're coming from. Chuck is a decent guy—what good would it do to cause trouble for him?" His tone darkened. "It's not like it's a *career*, Nat…it's being a stock boy at the A&P." He put his empty bowl on the bureau. "Besides, I can't afford the legal fees. I mean I could have called Evan last night—but frankly, the idea of increasing my already phenomenal debt to him by a dime makes me physically ill."

Natalie puffed out her cheeks and exhaled, her eyes downcast. "I don't understand why you always let people do this to you."

"And I don't understand why after all these years you're still asking me that question."

They looked at one another in silence, like eyes searching like for safe refuge, unwilling to harm, unable to heal.

Daniel stood up. "Look, I'm sorry it played out this way. But I figured I'd better tell you."

"Yeah. Thanks."

"Well, I've kept you up long enough." He retrieved his bowl from the bureau and took hers from her hands. "Good-night."

"Good-night."

Deserted, Natalie's righteous indignation melted into a pool of unholy doubt. She listened to the sound of dishes being washed, the kitchen light being switched off, and the unfolding of the living room sofa. She turned off her bedside light and rolled over. In the dark, she sought for a way out of this ancient dilemma, until, frustrated, she tried at least to reach a point where she could say to herself, *It's his life, not mine.* And when she got there, she nestled her cheek against her pillow, sighed, and let it go.

Chapter Six

Natalie was aware of the insidious assault on her senses before she was fully awake. Cool morning sunshine filtered through her lace curtains and dappled her pillow, an early Mozart symphony played softly in the background, and the intoxicating smell of smoked bacon drifted through her open door. The combination was so extremely pleasant that she was loathe to contemplate any action more sophisticated than a slow-motion stretch and yawn for quite some time. She reveled in the single person's guilt-free delight in knowing that for once somebody else was doing all the work.

"Natalie, breakfast is ready!" Daniel sang from the kitchenette.

She stretched one last time. "How do you know I'm awake?"

"You always wake up just when the bacon is done to a turn. How many pancakes do you want?"

"Oh, two."

"They're blueberry."

"Brute." She rolled out of bed and loped into the bathroom.

◇◇◇

As she finished breakfast, Natalie spared her computer a guilty thought for the first time in a day and a half. At any given time she had six to ten stories on her plate at various stages of completion, from outline to final copy, and the current assortment was growing staler by the hour. The niceties of her job included the freedom from regular office hours and the hard-won opportunity to pursue her own projects, but she still had deadlines to meet. Officially, her beat was the Haworth–Demarest–Closter trinity. Unofficially, she was often asked to cover the news in Harrington Park, Northvale, Rockleigh, Norwood, and Alpine, right up to the Rockland County border. She was connected to the *Star* offices by modem and fax, and had developed and maintained an excellent working relationship with her editor. She prized her autonomy but knew it came with a price. There were days when it was difficult to get motivated, and, thought Natalie as she stared at her tidy workbench, a cappuccino in one hand, this was one of those days. She entered her office—a sunny alcove that had been a second-floor porch before the conversion of the house into a duplex—flopped into her chair, and waited for the computer to boot. The sight and sound of Daniel humming Mozart as he did the dishes—rinsing everything twice—was some compensation.

The telephone rang.

Daniel dried his hands and reached for the phone, which was back in its cradle on the counter. "Hello. Just a second." He brought the phone to her with one hand over the mouthpiece. "I think it's Sarah."

Natalie took the phone, and Daniel turned away.

Sarah's lethargy from the previous day had disappeared. "I promise I won't keep you long. I just wanted to give you the update. And ask your advice about something."

What a beautiful voice this woman has, thought Natalie. *I wonder if she's still doing theater.* "I don't know about advice, but I'll be happy to listen."

"I'm assuming too much, I know. It's just that I promised Harry I'd ask your opinion."

"Well, that's different! I'm much better with opinions than advice. Where do you want to start?"

Sarah's voice bubbled with unaccustomed laughter. "Uh-oh, I've let myself in for it now."

Natalie smiled. "I take it you and Harry had a late night?" Her eyes followed her brother as he moved about the apartment. He had finished the dishes and was wiping down the counters.

"Actually, he went home early. We both needed to catch up on sleep. I mean, you can talk about these things forever, but what good does it do? I get upset, and then he gets upset because I'm upset."

"What happened?"

"I told him about the meeting with Mr. Sherill. And he couldn't believe Eric and Rose hadn't known about the will! He went on and on about it. What's the big deal? I told him I was sure they hadn't, but he said I always let myself be fooled by them."

"Well, if you were fooled, I was, too. I saw their reactions, and I agree with you."

"Well, then, so there," said Sarah. "I'm certain Lydia never told them. When people did things she didn't like, she didn't talk about it with them—she reacted. She didn't like debate. It can't be a coincidence that the will is dated December 19, and Eric and Rose were married on December 18."

"This past winter?"

"Unh-hunh. He eventually admitted they might not have known. But then he wanted me to call the cops to make sure they had the picture. He thought that'd get the police to focus on Eric and Rose instead of *me*. Then we had to go through it all over again because he couldn't believe Lydia hadn't told *me* about the will."

"He's probably worried about how you'd feel if you were seriously suspected." Natalie's words were reassuring, but into her mind came the memory of Sarah's underreaction as the lawyer told them about Lydia's will.

"I know. But really, I *was* surprised. Not that she left me the money—but that she didn't tell me. She always told me everything."

"Nobody tells their sister everything."

Daniel, mopping crumbs from beneath the toaster, straightened up and looked at her.

"Maybe. Anyway, Harry and I finally decided not to beat the subject to death, and he left. But the atmosphere around here is on fire. Eric and Rose had a huge blowup—I don't know why and I don't care. Last night the police took every car on the property away to run tests—looking for evidence of transporting the body, I suppose. Two policemen showed up again first thing this morning. Eric was politely but firmly asked to visit the courthouse again, and Rose just got called by the district attorney's office to go down. I phoned Harry to tell him what was going on. He thinks I should move out. This is where your opinion comes in."

"It's not a bad idea, Sarah."

"Do you really think so? But how can I walk out when everything is such a mess? It would be like abandoning my responsibilities! And now I've got all this financial stuff to worry about."

"You can do that from anywhere."

"That's what Harry said. I thought he was harping on his favorite theme."

"What do you mean?"

"Sorry, did that sound awful? It's just that this is a dead-end topic for Harry and me. He's wanted me to get out of here since—I don't know, since the opening of *The Children's Hour*. He wanted me to run off with him, get away from my family. We sat one night in the car freezing to death and talked it over for hours. He was very upset when I wouldn't go. But…I couldn't… just take off like that."

"Ah." Natalie's gaze drifted to the sycamore tree just outside the office window.

"I shouldn't be talking like this—it's not fair to Harry. It's just that every little problem has been magnified by what's going on." She sighed, and then cut herself short. "I'd better go. I've made an appointment with Mr. Sherill for this morning. I feel I can trust him. He was Mother's lawyer, you know, but he's stuck with us despite what she did. Actually, all this money being suddenly in my name makes me panicky. I think I should find out about making a will and things like that. By the way…" She was suddenly self-conscious. "Was that Daniel who answered the phone?"

"Yeah."

"Oh, I wasn't sure. Say 'hi' to him for me, okay?"

"Okay," said Natalie. They hung up.

"Sarah says 'hi.'"

Daniel draped the dishrag over the edge of the sink. "Well 'hi' back, next time you talk to her." He came and took the phone from her. "What's the latest?"

"Eric and Rose have been summoned down to the DA's office for further questioning."

Daniel raised his hands and eyes heavenward. "And I'm still here? Thank you, God." He returned the phone to the counter.

Natalie addressed her computer. Glancing at her notes from an interview she had conducted three days before, she began to type:

Norwood Business Down for the Count:
Are federal cuts partially to blame?

All Sorts of Sports, a privately owned retail store located at the corner of Broadway and Summit in Norwood, posted a Going Out of Business sign this week, attracting more trade than he'd seen in over a year, quipped owner Bernard Morris.

The telephone rang.

Daniel had settled with his books at the dining room table on the far side of the counter, muttering something about an overdue term paper. He had only to lean a little in his chair and extend a long arm to reach the phone, which he did.

"Hello." A curious expression crossed his face. "Just a second." He got up and brought the phone to her again. In answer to her look, he said, "Some guy."

"Natalie Joday."

"Hi, Natalie. So you've got the boy back where you can keep an eye on him. Was that his idea or the police's?"

"Hi, Graham, how are you this morning?" Natalie leaned back in her chair.

Daniel returned to the dining room table and flipped through a large book.

"Just fine. I was a little worried about *you*, though. I thought I'd better call and make sure you were okay."

"How sweet. But I'm just fine, too—thanks." Technicolor images from the previous evening paraded before her mind's eye. "I'm glad to hear you're still at large. I understand both Eric and Rose are at the courthouse."

"Yes, well, with the news of the will it's only to be expected."

"It must make your position rather—ambiguous." Natalie picked a pencil from the bouquet in the flowerpot and twiddled it between her fingers.

"Not at all! Why would you think so?"

Natalie scratched her long nose. "Well, I mean, to the casual observer, your relationship to the Dows must be a little difficult to comprehend. Particularly now that Sarah turns out to be the one in charge."

"Nonsense."

"I don't mean to alarm you." Natalie leaned back further, and put her feet up on the filing cabinet. "But it's possible the police might think *you* stood to benefit from Lydia's death. You don't have any income, do you? As a writer, you have to scratch a living however you can—I understand that, of course—but it might be hard for the layman to comprehend."

Daniel slid his glance sideways, watching his sister.

"People always think the worst, you know," Natalie continued. "Since you're so close to Rose, and since everyone thought Eric would inherit a pile if anything happened to Lydia, they might think that you and Rose were in it together—with Rose as the brains and you her cat's-paw. After all, as you said, it must have been a man who did the murder, and who else would Rose have turned to?"

Daniel leaned one arm across the back of his chair, nestled his chin in the crook of his elbow, and fixed his eyes on his sister's heart-shaped face.

Graham gave a little laugh. "I hardly think—"

"Oh, I'm probably worrying over nothing. After all, the DA's office didn't ask to see *you* again, did they?"

Graham hesitated—just an instant, but it was enough for her to know that the DA's office had called him, and for him to know that she knew it.

"Oh, dear," she drawled. "Sorry, Graham. Maybe it's just routine."

"No doubt. It is my understanding that they've asked everyone involved to go down—right?"

"Why, Graham, are you being foxy with me? Is that why you called—to find out if the DA's office called Daniel?"

"The thought never entered my mind."

"Well, you let me know if there's anything I *can* do to help," she said kindly. "Don't forget, we're partners in this investigation. Bye-bye." Natalie switched off the phone.

Daniel cleared his throat. "This is your rendition of drawing out the suspects." His voice betrayed what might have been a sneaking sympathy for the victim. "Would you call that investigation or inquisition?"

"I call it evening up the score." Natalie got up from her chair, crossed the kitchenette, and smacked the telephone back into its cradle.

"But," Daniel's face clouded, "if he is the murderer, I hope he doesn't decide to reestablish his advantage in a big way." He looked at her with concern.

"Yeah, I hope not, too," Natalie confessed. She went back to her workbench.

> ...Despite industry-wide increases in the sporting goods sector, Morris has experienced a 25 percent drop in retail sales over the past year. Other Bergen County sporting goods stores also report declining receipts, according to several county commercial associations. Morris believes that independent operators are unable to compete with chain stores, which absorb an increasing portion of the market share each year.

> With 30 percent of his business coming from schools, Morris has also been adversely affected by cuts in federal funding for education. Last week Morris lost one of his biggest accounts, the Norwood High School Fencing Team, to which he supplied

The telephone rang.

Daniel reached out and snapped it up.

"Helloo." His voice changed. "Oh, Sergeant Allan. Yes, yes, still here."

Natalie's heart sank—her brother's grateful prayer had been uttered too soon. Holding her breath, she fixed her eyes on the back of Daniel's head.

He sat slumped over, receiver against his ear, his free arm resting limply on the table. But suddenly his back straightened, his chin came up, and he turned to his sister with eyes glittering in wonder. Tilting his head, he lowered the phone, and said, "It's for *you*."

He got up and minced across the kitchenette, starting with a smile and ending with a grin as he handed her the phone. He did not go back to the dining room but leaned up against the refrigerator in an attitude of one prepared to be entertained.

"Hello," Natalie met Daniel's gaze squarely.

"Miss Joday?"

"Good morning, Sergeant Allan."

"Good morning. Or good afternoon," he said amiably. "How's the investigation going?"

"Slow. I've just been accused of bullying the witnesses. It gives me a whole new insight on the difficulties of your job."

Daniel smirked.

"Really." The sergeant sounded like he appreciated it.

"Yes. Speaking of which, how is *your* investigation going?"

"We're—proceeding. Perhaps you can help me with something."

"Of course."

"Can you give me a complete version, to the best of your memory, of your conversation with Eric Dow at the front door yesterday?"

"Sure. But why? If I may ask."

"After."

"Okay." Natalie thought for a moment and then reeled off the complete conversation in a noncommittal voice, using "I said," and "he said." As she proceeded, Daniel's smug expression grew serious, and a glint of anger appeared in his eyes.

Sergeant Allan let her speak straight through to the end. "Okay. Thanks. I got it."

"Are we on tape?"

"No, shorthand."

"Did I help?"

"I think so. Your encounter sheds light on the question of whether or not Eric Dow had reason to suspect he would inherit his daughter's estate."

"I see. Is the field narrowing?"

"Miss Joday—I know you realize this…intellectually…but will you please pause to consider that somewhere in this group of people there is a murderer? For example, I realize that Eric Dow was provoking in the extreme, but I question the wisdom of your counterattack under these circumstances."

"Yeah, well—habit."

"I understand. But murderers are the most dangerous people in the world. Getting on the wrong side of one is a mistake."

"Are you telling me to stay out of the way, Sergeant?"

"I'm…asking you…to please exercise above average caution, Miss Joday."

"I shall henceforth exercise extreme caution. Thank you."

"Thank *you*," said Sergeant Allan. They hung up.

"What was that about?" asked Daniel.

"I think I've just been warned not to go alone into any dark tunnels with Eric Dow. At least I think that was the point. I think he meant Eric." Daniel retreated to his books, and she turned back to her computer, thinking hard.

equipment.

Morris prides himself on carrying a complete line

> of sporting goods and accessories, stocking supplies not only for high-profile sports such as tennis, racquetball, squash, baseball, football, ice hockey, basketball, golf, bowling, and soccer, but less well-established sports such as billiards, Ping-Pong, darts, field hockey, lacrosse, the martial arts, shuffleboard, tetherball, hopscotch, and

The phone rang, and Natalie leaped from her chair and hurled herself across the room before Daniel had even moved. "Hello?"

"Hi, Natalie? Matt Eustis here. How are ya?"

"Fine, and you?"

"Nothing to complain of. Daniel there?"

"You bet." Natalie leaned over the counter and raised a provocative eyebrow as she looked at her brother. "It's for you."

He made a face at her and mouthed, "Who?"

She grinned. "Matt."

Daniel took the phone. "Hi, Matt."

Natalie wandered over to the cupboard and rummaged around for something to snack on. There appeared to be an alarming assortment of all her favorite treats.

"Back in town? Oh, yeah, bummer. No, we're all good buddies, so far. The sergeant in charge seems almost reasonable. No. No, I know. I won't. Okay. I appreciate that. Actually, I got laid off. No, they were very apologetic about it. That's what I thought." He glanced at Natalie. "Right, well—see you, uh, tomorrow? Thanks for calling. I will. Bye." Daniel switched off the phone.

"Is he back?" Natalie stood on the kitchen side of the counter.

"No, he called from Trenton. The police got through to him somehow."

"Proficiency in action. Does he think there's cause for alarm?"

"Doesn't seem to."

The telephone rang. As in a game of slapjack, Natalie and Daniel grabbed for the phone. The cradle skidded across the Formica and fell to the floor as Daniel brought the receiver to his ear.

He grinned at her, gray eyes twinkling. "Hello."

Natalie eyed him resentfully, rubbing her stubbed fingers.

Her brother held out the phone with a gesture of reconciliation. "It's for you."

"Natalie Joday."

"Natalie! At last! Where have you been? I try to call you all yesterday afternoon and evening. I let the phone ring twenty-five times! Nothing. I leave messages for you to call with half of Bergen County! I fax you! I email you! Desperate! Please call! Ginny! And *nothing*! And today I've been trying to call you all morning! But your damned line has been busy for hours! My God, the biggest story of my life, and my best and dearest friend has an inside track, AND SHE FALLS OFF THE FACE OF THE EARTH! How can you do this to me!"

"I'm terribly sorry!" Natalie's voice was filled with laughter. "What can I do to make it up to you?"

"*Talk* to me!"

"Of course! I—"

"But not now. I've got a hot interview in twenty minutes with the guy from the road crew who found the body. And after that—"

"Dinner tonight?"

"Great. I'll be in your godforsaken neck of the woods this afternoon, scoping out the neighbors. Is there anywhere affordable to eat in amongst the millionaires?"

"You know the Antlers on Hardenburgh?"

"I'll find it. Between seven and seven-thirty? And listen, get Daniel to come if you can, please. Tell him there's a companion piece here on how guys with records are treated unfairly by the cops. If that doesn't do the trick, bribe him."

"I don't think that's the right approach, Ginny. Daniel is remarkably lacking in venality."

"Well, you pick the approach. Just get him to come. I'm begging you—and you owe me!"

Natalie cupped the phone in her hand. "It's Ginny Chau, friend and colleague. She's on the case for the *Star*. We're going to pool our information tonight over dinner. She's dying for you to come. Want to?"

"Sure," said Daniel politely.

Natalie nestled the receiver back against her ear. "Okay, it's fixed. We'll be there."

"Brilliant! See you then!" They hung up.

"Ginny will know everything there is to know about the police angle," said Natalie. "She has more contacts than anyone else on staff."

"So far so good."

"Yeah." Natalie tossed her head, "We seem to be on the same side as the cops, for once. We might even be able to help out."

"I like that idea," said Daniel. "Particularly if it encourages them to keep off my back." He resettled at the dining room table.

Natalie went dutifully back to her computer. She looked at her notes, and then read the words on the screen. Disillusioned, she thumped her elbow onto the workbench, rested her chin in her hand, and typed with one finger:

blindman's bluff.

Chapter Seven

Ginny, a sight for sore eyes in black leather and a silver scarf, was in possession of the dimly lit Antlers bar when they arrived at 7:10. She expressed herself delighted to meet Daniel, offered him a petite hand and an expansive smile, and said cheerfully, "I heard the cops picked you up the other night. Clearly they have lost their grip."

"That's what I've always said!" exclaimed Daniel. "This must mean we're going to be friends." He returned her smile with interest and engulfed her hand in his. Ginny melted under this counterassault, and they stood beaming at one another, shaking hands long after simple courtesy required. Natalie rolled her eyes and herded them into the equally dim dining room, decorated in green and black and featuring a ceiling from which several hundred empty wine bottles were suspended. They critiqued the menu, placed their orders, and watched the waiter fill their water glasses and light the red candle in the middle of the table.

Ginny picked up her linen napkin and got straight to the point. "The fact is, we have a great opportunity here. We've each got a unique perspective on the crime, and we all want to answer the same question: Who killed Lydia Dow? The way I see it, it's just a matter of triangulation. Natalie? Now's the time for you to redeem yourself. Sing."

Natalie sketched her experiences with the Dows—stopping only once, to order a bottle of wine—starting with Sarah's phone call on February 11th, and then picking up the tale from the discovery of the body. Ginny scribbled in a black-encased notebook with a gold pen. She did not interrupt, although she got excited during the recital of the meeting with the lawyer.

"Unbelievable!" she said when Natalie had finished. "What luck! What did you do to deserve this? How come nothing like this ever happens to me? Actually getting invited to the reading of the will!"

"You forget I have not been wearing my professional hat during any of this."

"But by yesterday they all knew you had a vested interest in the case. And you've got Sergeant Allan, the prodigy of Homicide, calling you up and giving you tips!"

"He's a fan of my sister's," put in Daniel.

Natalie lifted her chin. "He didn't tell me anything I didn't already know."

"Baloney." Ginny took a sip of wine. "You don't know these guys like I do. He specifically tells you that he's checking up on the father's knowledge or lack thereof about the will. This is unheard of, I assure you."

"But I'm not a reporter on the case! He sees me as the sister of a peripheral witness. He knows I hate being involved, and that I hate Daniel being involved. So he's not afraid that what he tells me one day he'll read about in the paper the next." Natalie looked at Ginny and they shared a moment of spiritual communion. Then Natalie reached for her wine glass. "That's his mistake."

Their meals arrived, and there was a lull as the waiter organized Ginny's shrimp flambé. When he left, they picked up knives and forks and the thread of the conversation.

Daniel stabbed a French fry. "So what exactly is our position in terms of what's going to appear in print? I mean—"

"I won't quote you," reassured Ginny. "Either of you. I get a lot more mileage out of this type of situation by keeping my sources secret—and happy. Besides, insider information is often more valuable if you sit on it for a while, and then use it to root out the more deeply buried secrets."

Daniel's eyes twinkled. "So we won't get to read 'sources close to the investigation say such and such' and know it's really us?"

Ginny spoke with a tinge of regret. "Not this time." She popped a pink shrimp into her mouth.

"Speaking of sources," Natalie said, reaching for a roll. "I think it's time you told us what you've been doing. You're the professional—how does the case shape up in your eyes?"

Ginny, nodding and chewing, put down her fork and flipped to the front of her notebook. "Okay." She swallowed. "Enough of this could-mean-anything psychological stuff. While you have been floundering around in ambiguous relationships and fever-pitched emotions, I have been collecting facts!" She tapped her notebook with her pen. "Alibis, murder weapons, weather reports, autopsy reports, timetables, baseball scores..."

"Consider our breath duly bated," said Natalie. She reached into her shoulder bag for a notebook.

"First issue." Ginny's glittering eyes moved from brother to sister. "When did the murder take place? Lydia Dow was last seen by the stepmother, Rose Dow, at about 12:15 p.m. on the afternoon of Monday, February 8, when she left the family home without saying where she was going or when she would return. This, of course, is what the stepmother says in her statement to the police—there is no confirmation. There is no report of Lydia being seen or heard from again."

Natalie took a bite of her fish filet and made a note.

"On the other end," continued Ginny, "the sister is certain the murder must have taken place before six-thirty, the family dinner hour. Sarah says in her statement that Lydia would have called if she were going to miss dinner—but this seems to me to be a pretty flimsy basis for concluding that the murder took place before six-thirty, and I'm not inclined to pay much attention to it." Ginny grimaced at her vegetables and moved them to one side of her plate.

"I wouldn't write the idea off too quickly," warned Natalie. "Sarah describes Lydia as extremely conscientious—compulsively so—about things like that. She says Lydia always called—even if it was just a question of being late for dinner. Mary Dow, the girls' mother, took off twelve years ago—apparently walked out without a word of warning. As a result both girls were super-sensitive about letting each other know where they were." She sneaked a French fry from Daniel's plate.

"That's consistent with what I remember from when I was going with Lydia." Daniel slid his plate out of his sister's reach. "The first time I wasn't where I said I was going to be, when I said I was going to be there, no apology would do." He smiled sheepishly as the two women exchanged glances. "No, it wasn't just wounded feelings because I hadn't set the right priorities—she was really upset, panicky. It shook her."

"Okay, I'll buy it—for now." Ginny put down her fork and picked up her pen. "If we take the stepmother's word for it that she was alive at twelve-thirty, and if we go with six-thirty as the cutoff, that leaves a six-hour window in which the murder must have taken place. If the stepmother is lying, open up the window to between ten-thirty and six-thirty—and then find out why she's lying. If the sister is wrong about the six-thirty time limit, I think we can set midnight as the latest possible cutoff. The whole family agrees that she was never out after midnight in her life." She turned to Daniel. "Maybe you can throw some light on this."

Natalie smiled at her colleague's technique; so far they had not provided any details of Daniel's relationship with Lydia, but she had no doubt Ginny knew plenty from other sources.

"Was that how she was when you were going with her?" Ginny continued, cautiously echoing his choice of words.

Daniel raised his gray eyes and looked into a shadowy corner of the restaurant, where visions of the past danced in the candle-light. A translucent veil of sadness fell across his mobile face, and his smile was bittersweet. "Like Cinderella."

Ginny lowered her eyes, searching in her notebook for an empty spot in the margin where she could make a note. Natalie squeezed lemon juice onto her filet.

"Moving along," said Ginny, "this takes any possible mystery out of the evidence from the autopsy, which, because of the well-preserved condition of the body due to the cold temperatures over the past seven weeks, is pretty straightforward anyway. In terms of placing the time of death, it seems she hadn't eaten within four to six hours of the murder. With dinner ruled out, that could have been either breakfast or lunch and doesn't help us at all. In terms of what killed her: one .32 caliber bullet fired at point-blank range to the head—upwards from behind and below her left ear. The trajectory of the bullet eliminates the possibility of suicide. No explicit signs of a struggle, or of intent to rob—her handbag was found beneath the body—no sexual assault. Bullet recovered, no sign of the gun."

She flipped her notebook around and showed them two sketches of heads, one in profile and the other face front, with the bullet path represented by a dotted line, through each. Natalie leaned over for a better look. Daniel placed his fork on the edge of his plate and looked away.

Ginny flipped over the page of her notebook. "Sorry. That was insensitive. I don't mean to seem cold-blooded."

"It's not that." Daniel folded his hands and rubbed his thumbs together. "I know it's your job. It's—I don't think it's sunk in all the way that she's dead. Sometimes I forget, until..." He nodded at Ginny's notebook. "Then I remember, and it hits me all over again. But then I think, *somebody did this to her*, and I feel like I really want to see him or her pay for it. So don't mind me." He unclasped his hands and reached for his water glass. "Let's get on with it."

Ginny nodded. "Right. Let's go back to the timetable—because in addition to the parameters for the murder itself, we need to consider when the body was taken up to the parkway. Now this is where my interview with the road crew boys is particularly helpful. Here's the story."

She refreshed herself with a sip of wine. "To summarize what was a pretty convoluted interview, the road crew, according to their log, last inspected the tunnels in the park on January 29, during a three-day period when the temperature rose and there was a danger of flooding. They confirmed that the tunnel was unobstructed and moved on. Now, get this," she leaned forward irrepressibly. "A blizzard hit Bergen County in the early hours of February 9—the temperature plummeted and eighteen inches of snow fell over the next two days. In addition, because of the high winds and swirling snow, the eastern entrance to the tunnel was drifted over for a week or so."

"And the murderer must have used the eastern entrance, because the only safe place to put the car was the Alpine Lookout!" said Natalie. They huddled over an official Palisades Park brochure Ginny had, which contained a nice map showing the highways and trails, and considered likely places to park and the angle of the roads and the tunnels.

"Can we tentatively conclude," asked Ginny, "that the murderer must have hidden the body after dark—by necessity—on the night of February 8?"

"At least we can say it's highly probable," said Natalie.

"Blizzard or no blizzard." Daniel took a bite of salad and swallowed. "I can't imagine anyone keeping a dead body around the house for one moment longer than they had to—it had to have been that night."

"There are two crucial periods on February 8," said Ginny. "The afternoon, when the murder was done, and the middle of the night, when the body was hidden. We have to establish the whereabouts of everybody concerned. The police are focusing on the family, and everybody who was at that party the night before the murder. Let's see, where's my suspect list?" She flipped through her notebook with one hand and fumbled for an olive with the other.

"We'll start with the father: he wasn't at the party. He was out of town at—what—an import fair in Hartford. He drives back alone on the 8th, leaving Hartford after a late lunch and arriving at the family home around five p.m. No witnesses yet to substantiate either the time of departure or arrival. He says he did not go out again that night. But most of the time he was in his office in the basement, and could easily come and go through the back door—which is situated on a landing halfway up the basement stairs—without being seen." Natalie and Daniel exchanged impressed glances. "He makes an appearance at dinner—six-thirty to seven—and goes to bed at eleven, as per usual. I've got a man trying to pin down the exact time of his departure from Hartford.

"The stepmother: she's up and out of the house by seven-thirty a.m., on her way to an eight-to-nine a.m. exercise class in Tenafly at Homestretch Aerobics, Inc. You know them, Natalie—they take the half-page ad on page three of the sports section. She returns home between nine-thirty and ten, showers, etc., and is in the living room when Lydia leaves the house at twelve-fifteen. Goes out again at about two o'clock, to do some shopping at the Bergen Mall, stopping by to see a friend in Maywood on the way back and arriving home at six. Has dinner with the family—six-thirty to seven—and then dashes out to attend her weekly class in gemology, which is from eight to ten p.m. at Ramapo College in Mahwah. She arrives home at midnight—class ran late—and finds her husband already asleep. She says."

"Quite an itinerary," said Natalie.

"I'll say. Doesn't seem like she had much free time to be getting into any mischief, does it?" said Ginny.

"It only takes a second," said Daniel, sotto voce.

Ginny pounced on this comment. "You don't think she's telling the truth about where she was?"

"Let's just say I wouldn't eliminate her as a suspect just because she had a busy day," said Daniel. "Don't underestimate Rose Dow."

"Oh, I don't!" said Ginny pointedly. "I really don't. Now, your friend Sarah: her story is that she comes downstairs and the sisters have breakfast together from nine to nine-thirty in the dinette. Sarah says they had a heart-to-heart about her new boyfriend—girl stuff. She says Lydia seemed pretty much as usual. They had croissants and herbal tea."

"Where do you get your information?" asked Natalie admiringly.

Ginny twitched her eyebrows and continued. "After breakfast the sister goes upstairs to get dressed, comes back down about ten-thirty, says good-bye to Lydia, takes her car, and goes by prior arrangement to the New Globe Theater in Harrington Park to meet her boyfriend, who is the public relations director there. It was opening night for some show or other."

"You don't know?" quipped Natalie.

"Hey," said Ginny, "that's irrelevant detail."

"*The Children's Hour*," said Daniel. He shrugged in response to Ginny's surprised look. "Irrelevant detail is my specialty. Sarah mentioned it at the party and it stuck in my mind."

"Right," continued Ginny. "So the sister is with Harry Suter at the Theater in Harrington Park from a little before eleven till mid-afternoon, with time out for lunch at the Closter Diner. When Sarah arrives home around three, nobody is there, she says. She spends a couple of hours reading. She does not see her father when he arrives, due to the fact that her bedroom is on the third floor, and his is on the second. Anyway, by then she has retired to her bathroom to wash her hair and get ready for the opening night. Dinner, six-thirty to seven, check, then dash back to the New Globe for the show, where she was constantly visible. After the show she drives to the opening night party, arriving home at two a.m."

Natalie emptied the bottle of wine, pouring half in her glass, and half in Ginny's. "She drove her own car the whole time?"

"Of course. Just your average five-car family."

"Five?" asked Natalie.

"I include the mysterious Graham Bunch. He apparently lives in a little cottage separate from the main house."

"Surrounded by forsythia," said Natalie. The other two looked at her blankly. "I do detail, too." She removed a bone from her filet and put it in the ashtray.

"Forsythia." The tip of Ginny's tongue appeared as she wrote it down. "Right. Bunch says he slept late…till around eleven a.m., then fixed himself brunch, then went—are you with me?—to the Demarest Library, arriving at 1:25 p.m. and staying until their five p.m. closing time. Research. On a book." She looked at them closely to see how they were taking it. "A little shopping, home in time for, you guessed it, dinner with the family from six-thirty to seven. Isn't it nice to see traditional family values so religiously respected? That's what we need more of in this country! Says he did not go out again, which is a suspicious circumstance, because everyone says he is never home in the evenings, is up all night, and catnaps in the day. But like most of the others, this is impossible to check, because both the family garage and the company parking area—where Graham keeps his car—are so far away from the house you can't hear a car starting up.

"Which leaves the boyfriend, who I will include in the close family circle. He is a local boy himself, from Ridgewood."

"Ridgewood is not local," corrected Natalie. "Ridgewood is a foreign country."

Ginny, looking as if she thought Natalie was joking, glanced at Daniel, but he met her smile with serious eyes.

"I never ventured west of Route 17 until I was eighteen years old," he said, "not even to steal hubcaps."

"My God," said Ginny. "I never would have imagined. Let me rephrase my statement. The boyfriend is a foreign devil who went on the long march to Closter in 1990. He comes from a well-to-do family of the merchant class—Mom and Dad still own a hardware store in the Old Country." Ginny downed her last shrimp. "He's been doing PR at the New Globe for the past year or so. On to the day of the murder. He arrives at the theater in time for his ten-thirty rendezvous with the sister—apparently his hours vary widely from day to day and week to week—and spends the whole day at the theater, except for lunch, getting ready for the opening. He rushes home at five-thirty to change and have a quick bite, and is back at the theater at six-thirty. He has to hoof it both ways, since he had been having a problem with his solenoid, but it is only a ten-minute walk. He hitches a ride to and from the cast party with Sarah, arriving home around two a.m. And that's that."

The waiter appeared with a cart to remove their empty plates. Natalie grilled him about their coffee selection, eventually settling on a Sumatran blend. When she had released him, she nodded at Ginny to continue.

"Apparently the other couple at the dinner party at the Dow home had the good sense to leave on a trip to the Bahamas at seven the next morning—February 8th. So they're out of it. That's the suspect list. Except..."

"Except for me." A corner of Daniel's mouth curled in what might have been either humor or distaste. Ginny looked apologetic, but he shook his head. "You don't have to explain. You forget, Ginny, my sister is a reporter by profession, and a skeptic by nature. I accept your need to verify your facts from an independent source close to the events."

Natalie picked up her linen table napkin and used it to polish her teaspoon.

"Well, now that you mention it," admitted Ginny, "I'd appreciate your telling me where you were from ten-thirty on, and what you saw and all that. Your story is the one item I haven't been able to get a lead on. Honestly."

Daniel nodded his acquiescence, but Ginny held up a hand before he could speak. "First let me explain what you're getting into: I won't quote you without your permission, and I won't put a negative slant on anything you tell me in confidence. I want to do a 300-word update on the murder every day for the first week, but that doesn't mean I'm scrounging for angles. I'll protect your interests as far as I can. This does not, however, extend to suppressing facts as they become public knowledge during the course of the investigation, or after. When this case is solved, and you're in the clear, I'll do a major feature. But you'll see it before I print it."

"Look." Daniel shook his head, once, and then raised his eyes. "I'm for whatever helps the case. I've already told the police everything of relevance I know, and I don't mind telling you. I was living at my girlfriend's house in Cresskill at the time. On February 8th I was alone from ten-thirty to four. I went to the shopping district in Bergenfield for about an hour around lunchtime. My girlfriend got home from work at four o'clock. In the evening I left for work at seven-fifteen, and got back home at eleven-thirty. I walked. I don't have a car. That's it."

"That's pat," said Ginny.

"Practice," said Daniel. "I'm sorry I can't make it more interesting. What else?"

"What about this party…and the brawl?"

Daniel nodded and started in. He told Ginny much the same story he had told Natalie the previous morning, minus his personal feelings. "Sorry," he concluded. "I know it doesn't answer or even throw much light on the big questions. But I can't describe to you in strong enough terms how uninterested I was in those people and their problems. I really didn't want to be there—going there was a mistake, and it took all my energy just to be polite."

Ginny nodded as the coffee arrived.

"Well, let me ask you a couple of general questions," she said when the waiter had gone. "Had Lydia changed since the time you were together?"

"I didn't think so."

"Did you get any idea that she was in trouble of any kind?"

Daniel hesitated, then shook his head impatiently. "I've thought about this a lot. She gave no sign of any particular problem at the party. If there was any trouble—it must have been of her own creation. Or put it this way, if she was in trouble, it was because she wanted to be in trouble. She liked to overdramatize. Maybe something—got out of hand."

"You said she got hysterical when she realized there had been a fight. And yet, according to you, she couldn't possibly have known what it was about. Did she try to get somebody to tell her what had happened?"

"No. I don't know. Not that I heard. I didn't want to be there….I didn't want to get involved. I didn't want to know."

Ginny sighed, trying, unsuccessfully, to cover her disappointment. "Well, never mind." Comforting herself, she heaped three teaspoons of sugar into her coffee cup. "Let me give you the dope on the fight. According to the boyfriend, Bunch made some pretty crude comments about the younger sister—suggesting that he had slept with her before and he could again any time he wanted, since the competition was so negligible."

Daniel's eyes flashed. "Delightful."

"Bunch's version, although less graphic, is still pretty tasteless. He says he told Suter he was bored with Lydia's cloying style and suggested they swap sisters. When Suter got riled, Bunch fueled the fire by suggesting it was a good deal for Suter since he'd be getting the one with all the money."

"Harry's version sounds more realistic," said Natalie from behind her coffee cup. "I don't believe Graham would miss an opportunity to push to the limit."

"Well, at any rate, they both agree that Harry threw the first punch."

"Really?" Natalie was impressed. "Harry didn't strike me as the type to start anything violent. But then, he was dealing with the master of irritation." She took a sip of coffee. "I wonder if Graham would let anything important slip if I tried to pump him."

"Natty...." began Daniel.

Natalie waved him off. "In some highly public, nonthreatening location. Daylight only." Daniel looked away and shook his head, as siblings do. Natalie put down her cup and shook him by the forearm. "I won't do anything stupid. And he's such an egotist he might say more than he intends."

"Well—try," said Ginny. "Tactfully, if you can possibly manage it. What else?" She flipped through her notebook. Natalie turned over a new page in hers. Daniel looked from one to the other.

"How come I don't have a notebook?" he asked.

"You get to be a suspect," said Natalie. "The suspects don't have notebooks."

"Oh, well, all right," said Daniel, overpowered by her logic.

"The gun," said Ginny, ignoring them. "This is where it gets tricky. It seems that because the father's gun, which is a .32 caliber Smith and Wesson, disappeared, the police are more or less certain it was used for the murder. Well, duh. The father says his gun was kept locked in the desk drawer when not in use for over five years, and he doesn't remember using it since before Christmas. So who knew it was there?"

"I can tell you that," said Natalie. "The cops grilled everybody in the house when he found out the gun was gone. Sarah knew, but Rose said she didn't know."

"I wonder how securely that drawer was locked?" asked Ginny.

"Not very," said Natalie. "I looked. With a paper clip, or at most a nail file, I could have had it open in a minute."

Ginny raised her eyebrows. "You have hidden talents."

Natalie felt her cheeks catch fire. "I…uh…"

"Anybody can pick a simple drawer lock on the first try," cut in Daniel. "The real issue is, what about the door? That takes skill."

Natalie, her eyes on the opaque black liquid in her cup, nodded. "Eric said the door was always locked when he wasn't there." She raised the cup to her lips.

"There may have been a spare key the family had access to," said Ginny. "And with the father out of town, anybody at the dinner party could have snitched the key, or picked the lock—if they knew how."

"Don't look at me," said Daniel. "I'd never been in the house before, I was in the basement for all of about five minutes, and I didn't even know there was an office down there, let alone an office with a desk and a drawer and a gun." His gaze wandered to his sister. "I don't like guns."

"I know," said Natalie.

"Well, that's the picture," concluded Ginny. "Not pretty. But the question remains, who did it?"

Natalie and Daniel were silent. Ginny flipped her glossy black hair back behind her ears and answered her own question. "Well, here's my theory. The stepmother took advantage of the fact that the house had been full of people who would all be convenient suspects. She got the gun—somehow—in the middle of the night—remember, her husband was out of town—and committed the murder the next day, sometime between ten-thirty and three o'clock, when the house was empty. She hid the body in the trunk of her car—which she could do without fear of being seen since the garage is on the far side of the house from Bunch's cottage, and, on her way back from Mahwah that night, hid the body in the tunnel."

Natalie turned to a new page of her notebook, and wrote: *The Case Against Rose.* "Why?"

"For the money. Or what she thought would be the money."

"Oh."

"I told you I didn't intend to underestimate her," said Ginny, "and having heard Daniel's story about how she went for Bunch, I don't think she's afraid of violence. Remember what she said when she heard about the will! Don't you agree that's a reasonable motive?"

Natalie shook her head. "You haven't met her. Rose didn't strike me as the type who would risk that kind of a crime—murder."

"More psychology! I'll lay you two-to-one odds that this murder was committed for material gain, and not for emotional reasons! Anybody?"

"No takers," said Natalie.

"Gambling constitutes a parole violation," said Daniel. "Besides...."

"Yes? Go on, what's your idea?" Ginny held her notebook ready.

"It's not really an idea," Daniel hesitated. "The evidence, if that's what you call it, doesn't seem to point in any particular direction to me. But—I'll tell you what keeps me awake at night: I see a scene where Eric returns from his trip and goes down to his office, and Lydia comes home from wherever she was, and somehow—either he finds out, or she just tells him—but somehow he finds out I was there the night before and—and..." He stopped and shook his head, eyes downcast.

"Oh, come on!" objected Ginny. "I think you're stretching credibility there. Not to mention hogging all the blame." She grinned at him cheerfully. "That's the paranoia talking. Pay no attention!"

Daniel fiddled with the ashtray. "Thanks. Easier said than done, but I will try. Even so, I feel in my gut that it was Eric. For the money, if you like."

Ginny was not convinced. "From all I've heard about Eric Dow, he's a bore, he's a bully, and he's got a big ego problem. But he doesn't strike me as being devious enough to pull this off. It takes a particularly iniquitous subspecies of father to want to harm his own child, don't you think?"

She looked from Natalie to Daniel for confirmation, but sister and brother had gone mute. Nor would they meet her eyes, or each others'. Ginny shrugged.

"Okay. So let's hear your theory, Natalie."

Natalie frowned at her notebook. In the top margin she had written *The Case Against Eric* followed by half a page of bulleted notes. She turned a page and stared at its unblemished surface. "I think…it's all very interesting. I think we need to hear the other side of all these stories. I think somebody's lying."

"Of course!" Ginny grinned cheerfully. "That goes without saying. That's what makes it challenging. What we have to do is to find out who, and why. I'm going to tackle the stepmother's story—check out the times for her evening class. There's not much I can do with the afternoon alibi—that's a job for the police. My man will continue checking out this convention the father attended. And I must call the weather station at Teterboro Airport and confirm the time of that snowstorm."

Ginny lapsed into silence as she made a list of things to do. Natalie signaled for the check. The waiter brought it over quickly, and they paid their bill.

Natalie returned her wallet to her shoulder bag and stood up. "Why don't I do the New Globe? Maybe I can get a lead on Harry and Sarah's alibis." They retrieved their coats and walked outside. "And didn't somebody tell me Lydia used to hang around there, too? There may be people there that know something."

"Hey," said Daniel as they reached the parking lot. "What do I get to do?"

Ginny eyed him keenly. She was a striking-looking young woman and several years his junior, which did not stop her from sounding like a Dutch Uncle. "You get to stay out of trouble." She wiggled a forefinger at him. "There are more important things in life than getting a good story." To Natalie, "You never heard me say that."

Leaving them with this laudable sentiment ringing in their ears, Ginny hopped into her metallic-blue sports car, roared up Hardenburgh, turned left onto Schralenburgh, and disappeared. Natalie and Daniel climbed into the Volvo, swung over to Madison and up the back side of Tank Hill, arriving home within five minutes. They wound down from the excitement of the day with a jazz CD Natalie had bought the previous weekend, a game of Scrabble, and a Tin Roof nightcap.

Chapter Eight

At eleven the next morning, following three hours of steady work, Natalie fired off to her editor a couple of 400-word shorts and a 1,200-word mini-feature. Released by the knowledge that she had at long last filed, she headed for the New Globe Theater, a ten-minute-drive away.

She parked the Volvo in the vacant lot, stepped lightly up a wooden staircase onto a broad verandah, pushed open the main door, and wandered into the empty lobby. The entrance to the auditorium was locked. A quick look around turned up a door behind the box office, and, when her knock went unanswered, she turned the knob and peeked through the crack.

She found herself looking down a long hallway, directly into the face of a tall, older man walking briskly to her. She opened the door farther, mentally framing a polite query she never got a chance to use. He started speaking when still some yards away, as if time were a precious commodity and he already had plans for his daily allotment.

"Looking for someone?" He bore down upon her, showing no sign of slowing down.

"Yes, a Mr. Montgomery?" He was almost abreast of her. She fumbled in her jacket pocket. "I'm Natalie Joday from the *Bergen Evening Star*." She held out her press ID, panning to keep it in his line of sight as he breezed by.

The man stopped on the proverbial dime and spun around,

his arms flying outward as if from centrifugal force. "You want to see our public relations director. But he's out."

"No, I want to see Mr. Montgomery. I recently met Mr. Suter, and something he said prompted me to come." Natalie took a step forward and looked into his bright blue eyes. "I've been doing an in-depth series on cuts in government funding in Bergen County. I've just started looking into public funding for the arts. I want to work up something more sophisticated than the standard drivel about underappreciated artists and overstretched budgets."

"Oh, really? In what way—sophisticated?" His voice vibrated with an impossible suspension of doubt, longing, and challenge. Natalie thrilled to the combination, experiencing the awareness of infinite possibility that always came to her when she crossed the borders of the theatrical world. With his thinly disguised exigence and her own experience to guide her, she set forth on an extempore voyage of exploration.

"By discussing the effect of the shrinking sphere of live theater—if it is shrinking—on the quality of acting and technical talent, and on the range of shows selected for production."

His attitude was one of polite attentiveness—as if he were practicing to show an unruly audience how it was done.

"Further," she continued, "I think it's about time somebody broached the subject of the relative importance of the arts in human existence, by which I mean the proposal that they are an essential and basic mode of expression, not just a luxury to be indulged in if there's nothing more constructive to do." She raised an eyebrow.

A beatified smile illuminated his face, as if her words had unbound his heart. "Had a little to do with the theater, Natalie?"

Natalie returned his smile and tipped her head to one side. "Some. The first couple of years I was with the *Star* I reviewed high school and Little Theater productions in northeastern Bergen County. I saw *Tobacco Road* here in 1990. I don't remember you, however."

"No, I came on the scene in the summer of 1991. I'm Martin Montgomery, by the way. Please call me Martin."

"Happy to meet you, Martin. I guess by the time you got here my reviewing days were over."

"But how can that be?" His voice and manner oozed interest. His earlier attitude of no-time-to-spare had vanished. He had all day. "With your obvious grasp of the essentials, you must have been a natural."

"Oh, I enjoyed it, for a while. But the truth is I wasn't very good at it. My writing is too literal, for one thing, and for another I don't see why my preferences should be more important than anybody else's. Eventually I realized I prefer the objective struggle of putting a tricky story *together* to the subjective task of taking one apart. I'm at my best doing pieces that require a certain—oh, I don't know—a certain persistence to get at the facts."

"In other words, you're better at detecting than reflecting."

It crossed Natalie's mind that he might be psychic, but she decided he was merely...artistic. "I hope so," she said, meeting his twinkling eyes with another smile.

"Well, come into my office and we'll explore the amoral relationship between high art and high finance." Martin unfurled an elegant hand and led the way to a door emblazoned with a green and yellow wooden placard, upon which was written:

MARTIN MONTGOMERY
Artistic Director

Beneath this had been thumbtacked another placard, drawn in green and yellow Magic Marker on white posterboard. It continued:

...Business Manager
Typist
Switchboard Operator
Prompter
Painter
Doorman
Janitor

"We'll have tea!" he said happily, and ushered her in.

He switched on an electric kettle that sat on a purple velvet throne, and retrieved two moustache mugs from a papier maché mantelpiece. They indulged in almond biscuits from a stockpile in the filing cabinet and a quite exhilarating discussion about the utter inanity of the rigmarole entailed in "qualifying" for state and federal funding for the performing arts. They shook their heads in unison over the lack of imagination extant in nine-tenths of the theater-going public. From there they about-faced to endorse the concept of "educating the public," agreeing first and foremost on the debilitating effect of a lowest-common-denominator mass media on the country's theatrical palate. This naturally led to the topic of adapting modern marketing strategies to theatrical necessities. Natalie became excited about securing the good offices of the *Star* to help boost attendance at the New Globe and so save the theater from untimely demise. She filled a dozen pages of her notebook with ideas for ticket contests (*Name that Renaissance Playwright* and *What's My Next Line?*, etc.), a note to herself to contact the head of a dynamite jazz band she had heard was forming, and, most important, the skeleton of her "in-depth piece" on the demise of the theatrical world in affluent but culture-resistant Bergen County. Their personalities dovetailed agreeably; they were old friends within an hour.

As their excitement began to wane, Martin drifted into reminiscences of how different the theater had been in his salad days; how he had gotten his first big break; and how hard he had worked to become a theater manager. He reflected wistfully on those shows it had been his life's ambition to produce.

"Not that I don't like *The Sound of Music*—" He snuck a glance at the open door. "But, what about *Henry the Fifth?* Just once?" He sighed. "Well, everybody has to have a dream." He ran a hand through his thinning hair. "Listen to me soliloquizing!" He treated her to a sheepish grin. "What about you, Natalie? What do you yearn for in your secret soul?"

Natalie, lulled by Martin's comfortable persona, and caught off guard by the directness of his question, found her inner eye drawn down unfamiliar channels. Then she smiled and raised her chin with a shrug.

"I have pretty much what I want: a quiet life."

"But my dear Natalie!" said Martin in charming amazement. "For someone of your obvious talents and personality, surely that is aiming too low!"

"Low?" Natalie echoed the word with mock disbelief. "That's odd, because I feel as though I've been climbing mountains my whole life. That's how long it's taken me to get where I am, and I consider it something of an accomplishment! I wouldn't knock the quiet life until you've tried the alternative. I've got a job I like, a nice apartment, enough money for the first time to travel once a year, and a classic car I really love."

"But this is all material!" Worry lines appeared in Martin's forehead. "Didn't we just agree that there is more to life?"

"Yeah, there is. There's peace of mind." Natalie's emotions, loosened by the buffeting of the last 48 hours, churned, pushing hard to get out. "Martin, maybe you spent the summers when you were a kid getting up neighborhood shows, but I spent mine trying to keep out of sight, so that our snooty neighbors wouldn't find out how bad it really was around my house. I was constantly afraid they'd call social services down on us, and we'd be yanked out of there and maybe I'd never see my little brother again—that's if one or the other of us didn't get hauled off to juvenile hall. And while you were spending your post-college years interning with the circus, I was passing my days in the offices of lawyers I couldn't afford, and my weekends in one jail or another visiting the person I cared about most. While you were getting applause, I was getting either accusations or pity—and spending a lot of time trying to figure out which was worse. All I wanted all those years was for people to take me or leave me as who I really was."

Natalie brushed her hair back from her forehead. "I have that, now. So yeah, my life looks pretty damned good."

Martin's expression was sober, and his blue eyes glistened. "What happened with your parents?"

Natalie's glance slid away from his face with a barely perceptible shake of the head. "In a nutshell? Our mother was killed in a car accident when I was eleven. Our father couldn't keep a job; couldn't keep food in the refrigerator. Hell, he couldn't even keep a promise to a child."

"I'm sorry."

Her spine stiffened. "I'm not looking for sympathy!"

"Natalie! No one could ever think that!" Martin reached out and patted her hand. "You're a survivor, that's plain as day. But—I gather your brother lacked your resilience?"

Her gaze wandered down the line of posters from past shows that trooped across the walls. "He lacked something." She spoke in a flat, unemotional voice. "He started getting into trouble when he was thirteen. At first it was just endless, easily avoidable, stupid trouble. But eventually it was big trouble. He ended up doing 26 months in Sola Solita for armed robbery."

"Oh, dear..."

"He's not—" Natalie flashed a sudden, mirthless smile. "How can I say this without sounding like a jerk?"

"You're among friends—just say it."

"He's not—your average felon. He grew up with two sides—one consumed with dreams of creativity and achievement, generous and compassionate, and the other cheap and secretive and full of self-pity and resentment. With an uncrossable chasm in between. It's not that he was stupid—far from it. And he's a wonderful painter—used to do theater, too. But he didn't believe in himself, and he couldn't believe that anyone else did either. At a critical time he was...misadvised." Natalie's eyes grew sad, and her voice thinned. "He was twenty years old. He was desperate. He went into a liquor store, and yes, it was his intention to get whatever he could lay his hands on, by whatever devious means were necessary. But he'd never physically hurt anybody in his life, and he didn't intend to then. Only he didn't know that... the other man involved...had a gun." She spoke more quickly. "Don't believe he didn't know. The jury didn't believe it. Think I'm crazy to believe it—I wasn't around at the time, what do I know?" She slowed down again. "But his lawyer believes it. His parole officer believes it—hell, even the arresting officer believed it in the end."

"Well, that must mean something!"

"I guess." She gave a quick smile. "Anyway, cross off the next three years while he waited for trial, had the trial, and did his time after the conviction. But he's been out over three years now, and...he's been straight. It was very hard at first. Well, I can't really say it's easy now. But he has kept going, and he says nothing on earth will make him mess up again. He's in the Business Administration program at BCC, taking courses when he can scrape up the money."

"Trouble finding a job?"

"Yeah."

"I know how that can be. An old friend—a good friend—did some time. It was embezzlement; he siphoned fifty-thousand dollars from one of the biggest publicly funded summer stock theaters in New England. When he got out I offered to help him. But he went to Las Vegas to choreograph nearly nude chorus lines. No wonder we're underfunded."

"That must explain it." Natalie smiled, and, remembering her cup of tea, took a sip.

"It sounds like your brother's done better than most. But—Business Administration? Is that the right choice, do you think? Farewell to creative pursuits?"

"Right or wrong it was Daniel's choice. He feels very strongly about it. Says he wants something solid and practical in his life. Of course, that doesn't mean he doesn't have a lot more interest in his electives than he has in accounting and economics."

"Well, there he shows sense."

"You're one of a minority who think so. Cost Accounting: C-. Archetypes of Folk Art: A+. Anyway, he'll get his associate's degree this May—if things don't get out of hand."

"Are they likely to?"

"Well, of course you've heard about the discovery of Lydia Dow's body the other day."

Martin settled back in his chair and narrowed his eyes. "Yes, of course. She hung around here incessantly during our fall season last year—starting with *Little Foxes*."

"Really?" Natalie resisted the impulse to open her notebook.

"Yes…intense sort of girl…very sweet, of course, but—I always felt terribly sorry for her."

"Why?"

"She was never able to relax with another person, the way we've been able to today." They exchanged smiles. "You know I'm fond of acting—and of actors—but I think it's a good idea to be able to lay off it occasionally."

"I think I know what you mean. I met her a few times. She and Daniel were an item once—a few years ago. And in high school they took an acting class together. Did she act here?"

"No. Not even supernumerary. She belonged to the I'm Not Good Enough to Aspire league. She helped with costumes and props."

"Really."

"And your brother is mixed up with this somehow?" Martin folded his long arms across his breast. "Natalie, is that why you stopped by today?"

"Yes." Natalie felt herself blushing. "If I'd known you were going to be so damned nice I would have told you up front. Daniel was at a dinner at her house the night before she disappeared, and the police are checking out all the people who were there. I don't think he's very high on their list, but still—they really go over the top sometimes with the accusatory bit."

"So Harry was saying. You say you've met Harry?"

Natalie nodded. "I've spent some time with Sarah these past few days, and I've seen him a couple of times. He's pretty shaken up."

Martin's eyes widened and he puffed out his cheeks. "I'll say. It's a good thing we're more or less on hiatus this week. Frankly, he's a basket case. He's good at the finance end of things—a real detail man—but he lacks a knowledge of the theater, so he misses a lot of the nuances. You have no idea how timely your arrival on the scene is. If you can get this scheme of yours with the *Bergen Evening Star* going, it'll take up the slack a little. We're pathetically understaffed. It seems these days we can't organize anything properly—and not just since Lydia's disappearance threw Harry for such a loop. We've had a string of disasters this winter! There was the day the auditors showed up for their appointment and we discovered our accountant was on holiday in Australia. Australia! I thought our bookkeeper would lose her mind. She threatened to jump out of the flies during the third act of *Show Boat* if we made her meet the auditor alone. Then there was the fiasco on the opening night of *The Children's Hour*. We're trying to do dinner theater, and we seat one hundred and fifty people and discover we have no ice—and no milk or cream for the coffee. Ye gads!"

Natalie, suddenly very attentive, encouraged him to continue. "How did that happen?"

"Who knows?" He raised his hands skyward. "We were all in a panic to start with, because a big storm was predicted and we were afraid we'd be snowed out. Someone was supposed to call Garden State Farms before six p.m. to confirm delivery, but no one did. We put out an SOS throughout the cast and crew. Harry and Sarah dashed out and were able to buy—retail—enough milk and cream, but there was no ice to be found. Five minutes before we started seating, the leading man staggered in with a huge slab of ice which we dumped into the sink in the makeup room and beat into little pieces with a hammer from the carpentry shop."

It was clear to Natalie that Martin's sense of chronology ran from show to show, detached from real time as represented by the calendar, and that he had no idea he was discussing events that had taken place during the most critical period of the day of Lydia Dow's disappearance. To him it was just another story about how everything always went wrong in the theater, but somehow—magically—the show was saved in the end.

"What time do you seat when you do dinner theater?"

"Well, in that case it was seven-thirty, which may be all right for some communities, but it turned out to be a tad late for the

Bergen County audience. They want to be home by ten o'clock in winter."

"Was Lydia involved in that show?"

"Let's see. I think.... No. That was Sarah—she pitched in where needed and had a real feel for it. Nice girl. Much less in awe of the mystery of the theater than her sister. No self-confidence, though."

"Have you ever heard her sing?"

"No. She sings?"

"Like a goddess."

"I wouldn't have guessed. She seems content to play the role of Harry's girlfriend. A real trouper, though—she helped us out a lot starting with *Show Boat*. Like during the *Children's Hour* fiasco, we all stood there like dummies, stunned, but Sarah arrived and said, 'We can go buy milk, we have time—let's go!' She dragged Harry out practically by the scruff of the neck, shoved him into her car, and drove off! And you say she sings...."

Natalie could all but see the wheels turning in Martin's finely shaped head. "Maybe not just now..."

"Of course not. Poor kid. I haven't seen her much since her sister disappeared. I wonder if there's anything I could do.... Maybe I better give her a call."

"I'm sure she'd appreciate that."

The phone rang, and Martin answered it, making a face. Natalie, conscious that her unscheduled visit had been a long one, got up and collected her notebook and pen. Martin cradled the receiver against his shoulder and rose to bid her good-bye.

"We'll see you soon, I trust?"

"Certainly," said Natalie. "We've got to plan our long-term press campaign."

"Be still my heart. And don't worry too much about your brother. Things always work out in the third act—in the popular theater."

She turned to go, but Martin caught her hand, and she looked up at his gentle face.

"And about that other matter—a person can't live without dreams, Natalie."

She squeezed his hand. "I know."

As she closed the door, Martin resumed his call: "Now my dear Carl, I know your contract states that you will be paid weekly throughout the three-month period, but if you'll just look in section, you will find the definition of three-month period and see that it does specifically exclude the two-week break."

Natalie wandered back up the hall, trying to remember by which door she had entered. Fortunately, there was another placard in green and yellow on the correct door, saying Lobby—KEEP CLOSED. She went through and retraced her steps around the back of the box office and across the lobby, running straight into Harry Suter, just coming through the main door.

Harry, looking boyish in a sport jacket and jeans, walked quickly forward with an extended hand. "What are you doing here? Nice to see you." He shook her hand with a firm grip.

"I'm working on a story," said Natalie. "Nice to see you too. How's Sarah?"

"Not great. They've postponed the funeral."

"And how are you?" asked Natalie.

Harry squinted his dark eyes and looked at her uncertainly. "Do you really want to know—or are you just being polite?"

"Hey, we've got to take care of you," she said. "You're the only stabilizing factor in sight. Of course I want to know."

"You seem to be the only one who thinks that way. I'm coping, thank you. Trying to be there for Sarah. I don't know what more I can do." Harry's face fell. "This situation—it's eating us alive. I used to think we could face anything—together."

"That's asking a lot, isn't it?" Natalie was always irritated by overreliance on cliché. "I mean, how long have you two known each other?"

"It seems longer than it actually is—we've been through so much. We met at New Year's, just three months ago."

"Well, that partially explains it, doesn't it? You can't expect to be able to control what's happening. Nobody knows what the hell to do in a situation like this."

"You seem to."

"Don't you believe it!" scoffed Natalie. She had done enough talking about herself for one day. "So, you must have met Lydia before you met Sarah." He stared at her, thrown by her elliptical cut. "When she was here last fall. *Little Foxes*."

"Of course," said Harry, regaining his stride. "Lydia introduced us. She did tech for a show last fall, and brought Sarah to the New Year's Eve party here."

"What did you think of her—of Lydia?"

"Very beautiful, of course."

"And—" prompted Natalie.

"And, what?" Harry looked at her quizzically. "She had a screw loose. Is that what you want me to say?"

Natalie looked at him with a quizzical expression. "I don't want you to say anything, Harry. I just want to know what you thought of her."

"Sorry." Harry hooked his thumbs into his belt and regarded his boots. "I didn't mean to be offensive—it's just hard for me to admit that sometimes she was extremely difficult to deal with. The fact is I found her unpleasantly obsessive, and her moods highly erratic. Sorry, I don't like speaking ill of the dead."

Natalie pursed her lips. The ease with which both the Dow sisters were consigned to the handy pigeonhole of mental illness was beginning to get on her nerves. Even Harry, who had objected so strenuously when Eric had attempted to do the same thing to Sarah, had fallen into the trap about Lydia.

"Did she ever get any counseling?"

"I don't have any idea. Better ask Sarah—Sarah knew everything that went on."

"Not everything," corrected Natalie.

Harry stared at her. "Oh, you mean the will. I don't—"

A telephone rang in the box office. "Damn. I've got to go." A new set of worry lines encroached onto Harry's face. "But

I'm glad I've had the chance to say thanks. You've helped Sarah more than you know. And she's the most important thing in the world to me." He turned and dashed away.

Natalie went outside and hopped into the Volvo. She headed for Hackensack via Old Hook Road.

›››

About the time his sister was leaving the Harrington Park New Globe Theater, Daniel was shaking hands with his parole officer on the fifth floor of the County Building in Bergenfield. Matt Eustis, dressed in a checked flannel shirt and blue jeans, slightly plump, but staring down the gun barrel of 40, undaunted, was as upbeat as usual.

"Yup, I got a call from Sergeant Allan this morning. We had a real nice little chat. I explained to him that you're a reformed character and reminded him of his civic duty to remain uninfluenced by the minor detail that you've got an outdated rap sheet as long as his arm. Then he wanted to quiz me about the circumstances of your conviction, and I bent my rule far enough to allow as how you weren't the one with the gun." Matt didn't permit debate about the fairness or otherwise of the arrest, conviction, or sentence of his cases. His favorite phrase was, "the way it is now."

"Gee, thanks." Daniel settled into a chair next to Matt's overflowing desk. "How did he sound to you?"

"You mean did he sound like he seriously suspected you? No, he didn't. He filled me in on some details, and of course I've read up on the case in the paper. Apparently, since you didn't have any realistic access to the gun, or any imaginable motive even if somehow you had known the gun was there, you're not under serious suspicion."

"Great. So how was Trenton?"

"Horrendous." Matt's cheerful voice boomed around the room. "Rehab is out. Retraining is out. Education is out. Manual labor is making a comeback under the guise of 'enhancing work skills.' I expect the rack to be in common use by Halloween. The state legislature is introducing a bill to toughen up the parole system. Of course, it will never pass, since every county jail and state institution is already overflowing. But it just goes to show you the current trend. There are going to be senate hearings on the subject in Trenton. My union wants me to go and…listen, Dan, I want you to think about coming along, and testifying to the State Senate Committee about what the parole system has meant to you."

"Me?"

"Sure, you! Who else?" Matt's broad face was a study in enthusiasm. "Look at your case history. You do reasonably hard time. When you get out you survive your transition back into society without fucking up, you enroll in college and stick to your course of study over a period of several years, you work when you can, doing whatever you are able without being finicky, and—most important to the eyes of the average elected official—you haven't cost social services a dime since you hit the street! You're my star witness."

"Gee, I always wanted to be a star." Daniel's face crinkled up in disbelief. "Matt, are you crazy? Let me give it to you in chronological order: my girlfriend threw me out, I'm sleeping on my sister's sofa, I've got no job, and at last count I had 62 dollars to my name plus a student bus pass! I've got a term paper on macroeconomics in the 1990s due yesterday, plus final exams in five weeks—and I'm finding it increasingly difficult to study due to the presence of the police, who are breathing down my neck about the murder of an ex-girlfriend!"

"Well, now, take it easy. The hearings won't be until the fall. By that time you'll have your degree, and you'll be able to look for a good job, and find a place of your own. What's the problem?"

"Oh, God," Daniel leaned back heavily and stared at the ceiling.

"Hey, what happened to the guy who was going to make it, no matter what?"

"Get real, Matt."

"What aren't you telling me, Dan?" There was an edge on Matt's voice.

"You think it's all so easy," Daniel lowered his gaze and looked out the window.

"No, I said 'take it easy,' not 'it's easy.'" Matt studied Daniel's profile. "I know it's not easy."

Daniel, his chin jutting slightly forward, his mouth slightly open, stared out into the middle distance.

Matt moved to another topic. "How are things going between you and your sister?"

Daniel relaxed a little. "So far so good." He crossed his legs. "It's refreshing to be in a real home again after the trailer. Of course, there are two sides to everything: the damn telephone never stops ringing—remind me never to get a telephone—but it sure is nice to have electricity again."

"I bet."

"And of course Natty and I get along quite comfortably—I mean, after everything we've been through over the years, we know each other's quirks pretty well. She practically brought me up, as you know, and we have a lot of the same tastes."

"I take it you're not experiencing any repetition of the problems you had last time you stayed with her?"

Daniel shrugged. "That was then, this is now. I had just gotten out, I was hypersensitive about everything. No matter who I had been staying with I would have had trouble."

He buried his chin in the folds of his dark green sweater for a moment, and then looked up at Matt. "You know, you're right," he said in a more positive tone. "If I can just get through the next couple of months I'll be okay. It's just that…everything has fallen apart all at once. Of course, I know I asked for it." He stopped and looked out the window again. "Thank God for Natalie's unquestioning loyalty. I never would have survived if not for her."

Matt peered closely at Daniel. "Unquestioning loyalty? I'm not sure that's a compliment to your sister."

Daniel turned his head and looked at his parole officer in surprise. "I meant it as one."

"Really? The last time you stayed with her you found it very difficult to live up to what you perceived to be her extremely demanding expectations." Matt's penetrating eyes bore in on Daniel. "You said her view of you was unrealistic."

"That was then," Daniel repeated stubbornly. "What's the point of bringing it up?"

"And now?" persisted Matt.

"And now…Look, I fully appreciate how lucky I am to have the support of someone like Natalie, particularly after all I've put her through over the years. That's solid. It was hell for her in the bad-old shoplifting, dope-running days, when nothing she could say had any effect. And then when I turned on her—I'd give anything if I could undo that. For her sake, not mine. But as you keep telling me, I can't. So, yes, sometimes I do feel pressured. Is that what you want to hear? Sometimes I think it would be better if she didn't think I was such a great guy. Know what I mean?"

"Yes, I know what you mean, Dan." Matt tilted his head to one side. "You mean you don't think you deserve her confidence."

Daniel's face reddened, but he forced himself to smile. "Does anyone deserve what they get—good or bad?"

Matt leaned forward, resting his forearms on his thighs. "Dan, I've known you for a long time now, and we've talked over a lot of issues, and maybe, despite the odds against it, we've become friends. I'd like to think so, anyway. Maybe you've forgotten—or maybe you're focusing on all the negative things that are happening right now—but your parole is up this summer."

"I haven't forgotten."

"We won't see too much of each other after that. I know you're good and sick of being on the receiving end of other people's suggestions about where you should go and what you should do, but I'm going to say this now, because if you haven't learned how to hear it yet, after all you've been through, chances are you never will.

"Dan, you don't have to keep an ace in the hole to survive. You don't have to hold back because you're afraid people will think less of you if you tell them what you really think, or feel, or need. You'll never feel like people are relating to you the way you want until you can present yourself to them as you really are! Dan, life is just too short to go through thinking you'll straighten things out with the people you love, and who love you, at a later date. It's time now, Dan."

Matt's office resonated with the memory of his words, like the echo of ringing bells. Daniel sat motionless, not willing to meet his parole officer's gaze. He felt claustrophobic, and took a deep breath.

"Wow. Parole officer is too limiting a profession. You'd make a great shrink."

Matt Eustis leaned back in his chair, his intensity fading away with practiced swiftness. "I think you've got that backward, Dan." Then he stood up and extended his hand. "See you next month?"

Daniel arose from his chair and nodded as he shook Matt's hand. Then he turned and walked across the room, trying not to move with over-obvious speed. When he was safely outside, but before he closed the door, he swiveled around and looked back at Matt. He stood in the doorway, one hand on the doorknob and the opposite shoulder propped up against the doorjamb. "Thanks for the advice."

Chapter Nine

At ten that evening, Natalie and Daniel sat on opposite sides of the dining room table, a frayed Scrabble board in the demilitarized zone between them. A half-eaten pizza, assorted soda cans and glasses, and an Official Scrabble Dictionary had been deployed in strategic locations. Daniel won the first game 365 to 332 with a bingo (SNOOKER) on his second to last turn. Natalie won the second game 402 to 399 when Daniel lodged an erroneous challenge (NOME) and so lost his turn, enabling her to go out and catch him with minus 21 on his rack. They re-racked for the tiebreaker.

Natalie's afternoon at the *Star* had been productive. She had sold Byron Tollen, her editor, on the outline of the New Globe scheme, and then settled at an empty desk to turn that outline into copy, working steadily amidst the usual afternoon chaos. At one point, Byron, looking awkward but well-intentioned behind his horn-rimmed glasses, had found his way to her side to tell her how much he appreciated her Sticking With It despite the Family Problem. In his flat baritone, he told her he had been instructed by management to pass on a quiet reminder that they would (following strict *Star* policy) warn her before the appearance of any stories involving the misfortunes of the Joday family—at least five minutes before the paper hit the streets. Then he fled back to his office.

Later, she received a call from an excited Sandra Cappi, the Housepet Abduction Hotline guru, who wanted to Touch Base and bring Natalie up to date with the latest developments in the war against pet-napping. It seemed that both public interest in and financial support for HAH had soared since Natalie's original story appeared in February. Ms. Cappi was in possession of a stack of new case histories—which had meant an adjustment of all the relevant statistics. There were also three reports of pet abduction by intergalactic aliens intent on conducting unspecified "tests," the airing of which she feared would trivialize her organization, and a related rumor that substituted humans for aliens, but still involved the carrying off of pets for scientific experiment. She then recounted the exciting True Life Saga of one distracted pet owner who had chased a masked cat-napper down Cedar Road in New Milford, until the Napper, losing ground to his pursuer (who worked out thrice weekly at the Milford Gym), had jettisoned the cat (imprisoned in a vinyl gym bag). Thus disencumbered, the Napper had sprinted to his getaway car, whereupon the pet owner, owing to his concern for the well-being of his cat, had concluded his pursuit. He had, however, managed to catch a glimpse of the car as it had roared off down Charles Street, and was absolutely certain that it had been small and white. Surely that was enough for the police to become involved, wasn't it? And didn't Natalie think that a follow-up story was indicated? Natalie, putting the finishing touches on a doodle of a spaceship piloted by a basset hound, acknowledged that the Saga was exciting, and agreed to do a follow-up when the new statistics had been determined.

Late in the afternoon, Ginny swooped in to hear the Martin Montgomery report and fill her in on the latest about Eric Dow. It seemed that the import fair he had attended the weekend before Lydia's disappearance had been a very casual thing indeed. Although the group had certainly met at the Silverado Hotel, as per Eric's information, they were not registered as an Official Group by the hotel, which meant they had not requested the group rate (something unheard of in the hotel manager's experience). Nor had they utilized any of the hotel conference rooms, which could accommodate groups of 15 to 500, with a complimentary suite for the group leader. Ginny was thinking about going to Hartford herself to check out this suspicious situation. She had also managed to confirm Rose Dow's times at Homestretch Aerobics and the gemology class.

At 5:30 Natalie had closed up shop and headed for home. She had found Daniel *in situ*, wrestling with macroeconomic theory with her ancient stereo turned up very loud. Team Joday had compared notes, but reached no conclusion more significant than that pizza and Scrabble were called for. "Pepperoni and green peppers?" Daniel had asked. "Of course," Natalie had replied.

The third game of Scrabble was a test of patience. Finally, Natalie risked opening up a triple word score, playing the percentages by assuming that Daniel did not have the Y he would need to use it. Daniel, who did not, in fact, have the Y, countered by playing both his U's (UNCUT), and opening up a second triple word score, which he had every reason to believe he could use. Natalie, dazzled by the possibilities of the inviting board and on her rack (YASTERD), and fueled by the best pizza in Bergen County, smiled happily and tipped her rack face-up.

"STRAYED,'" she said. "One, two, three, four, eight, nine, eleven, thirty-three, eighty-three; and then, eighty-six, eighty-seven, ninety-three for MESSY."

Daniel slid all seven of his tiles onto the board in instant reply. "ACQUITTAL. One, four, fourteen, fifteen, sixteen, seventeen, eighteen, nineteen, twenty, sixty, one hundred and ten."

The doorbell rang. Daniel arose from the battlefield, brushed imaginary dust from his sleeves, and went to see who it was.

"Are you sure there are two Ts in acquittal?" asked Natalie dubiously.

"Are you challenging me?"

"I'm thinking."

Daniel smirked as he swung open the door, but his expression changed when he beheld Sarah standing on the threshold, her thin, white face bereft of joy, her burning dark eyes the outward testament of unrelenting inner pain. So arresting was her appearance that Natalie rose from her chair at the sight of her, more out of respect than alarm.

But Sarah had eyes only for Daniel. Since those two had last met, so much had happened that it proved impossible for Sarah to look upon him now and maintain her poise. Tears came to her eyes and she turned her face away, trying to hide her outburst behind the tangled curtain of her coppery hair.

Daniel went to her and putting his arms around her, drew her close to him and held her tight. She resisted for a moment, and then gave in, putting her arms around his waist and holding on as hard as she could, her face buried against his shoulder, her rough, tear-choked breathing muffled in the folds of his sweater. He laid his head against her hair, and as a loving parent with his grief-stricken child, patted her gently on the back again and again, saying softly, "There, there. I know, I know."

After perhaps a minute, Sarah relaxed her grip, took a long quavering breath, looked up into Daniel's tear-moist face and gave him a wordless nod. He smiled and loosened his hold, but kept one arm around her shoulders, as if unwilling to completely remove his protection and support.

Natalie, rooted by the dining room table and feeling terrifically out-of-place, swallowed the lump in her throat and bestirred herself. She retrieved a box of tissues from the kitchen and shooed Sarah and Daniel to the living room sofa. She placed the tissues next to Sarah and went to sit in her favorite green armchair. Sarah reached for a tissue, wiped her face carefully, and blew her nose.

"I'm going to have to buy stock in Kleenex." She gave an unconvincing little laugh. "Everywhere I go these days I leave a trail of tissues behind me like I'm playing fox and hounds."

"You're looking pretty rough," said Daniel.

"It comes and goes." Sarah sighed and bit her lip. "It was bad this afternoon. I was going through Lydia's room. The police finished with it this morning. I didn't like them in there—manhandling her things, going through her drawers, looking for secrets. It didn't seem right—she didn't hurt anybody. First chance I got,

I went in and took away all her personal things—things of hers that I can take care of, and love, the way she did. And there were these—" She opened her handbag, pulled out a packet of bulky letters, and held them out to Daniel. "I haven't read them—but the police probably have—they went through all her correspondence. I guess they're considered 'unimportant,' since they left them, but I didn't want anybody else to go snooping around and find them. I thought I should give them back to you."

Daniel accepted the letters in silence.

"And then there was this." Also from her handbag she pulled a five-by-eight photo in a thin silver frame. "I thought you might like to have it."

He took the photograph from her hand and rested it face up on his lap.

"You looked a lot different then," she said. "I hardly recognized you in February. You are so much more confident now."

Daniel looked up from the photograph.

Sarah gave him a shy smile. "Would you like to have it?"

He nodded his assent, and placed the letters and the photograph on the coffee table. "Thank you."

Sarah pushed her hair back from her face and resumed her tale. "In the end I had to stop. It was too much for me—just being in her room like that—alone." She sat leaning forward, placing her elbows on her knees. "I have to be careful these days...take care of myself. I had to get away—even if just for a little while. Dad and Rose were downstairs in the living room—arguing again. I couldn't face them—I've never seen Rose like this. I slipped down the back stairs and out through the back patio. Pathetic, I know." She leaned forward, resting her face in her hands.

"You're welcome any time," said Natalie.

"Just go slow." Daniel spoke with the clarity that comes from personal experience. "Don't let anybody push you. You'll pull through."

"I'll try," promised Sarah, resurfacing. "I'll be okay. But what about you, Daniel? Are you okay? Are the police still giving you a hard time?"

"Nope. Not so far, anyway. What about at your place?"

"Dad said he thought he had convinced them he was out of it."

"And Rose?"

"They went through her room and everything in it. She refused at first, but Sergeant Allan said he'd get a search warrant if she liked, and Dad got really angry at her for refusing, because it made it look like she had something to hide. In fact, he told her—right in front of me—that if she knew anything she'd better tell now, because if he found out she'd been lying to the police he'd throw her out of the house. He said if she didn't know anything she should do what the police said and shut up."

Natalie caught Daniel's eye.

"They've been at it off and on ever since," continued Sarah with ebbing emotion. "I try and stay out of it."

"What about Graham?" asked Natalie.

"They searched the cottage, and his car too—they're looking for the gun, I guess. What they talked to him about I don't know, because of course he wouldn't say. But I know what they asked me about."

She hesitated, looking first at Daniel and then at Natalie, and then back down at the tissue in her hand. "They wanted to know whether Lydia or I had ever been 'romantically involved' with Graham. What got me was the way they asked, you know? I could tell somebody had said something."

"Not necessarily, Sarah," said Daniel. "Sometimes that's their crass technique to get at something they think you are reluctant to tell—by making you think they already know. It doesn't bother them that it hurts like hell if they're wrong."

"Maybe, but it sure sounded to me like somebody had said something. Talking to them is so unreal!" She flopped back against the cushions of the sofa, and wrapped her arms around her upper torso. "They seem to know everything about us. Things I don't know myself. It scares me. Of course I told them there was nothing between me and Graham. But as for Lydia, all I could say was I had no idea. I mean, I didn't think so, because she always told me she didn't like him. But I'm not as certain as I used to be. I've learned a lot of things from all of this...things maybe I didn't want to know. I thought I knew Lydia better than anyone—she was my sister and we were a team—but I know now she didn't tell me everything. Besides—" She picked at the loose folds of her green-checked flannel shirt. "She had a good reason for not telling me about Graham, if something was going on."

She raised her sad eyes to Daniel. "She always held me responsible for telling Dad about you, you know."

Daniel shook his head. "I didn't know—and that's not my understanding of what happened." His eyes were full of trust. "I don't believe you would ever intentionally have done that."

"Oh, not intentionally, but in a way it really was my fault. I was too young to realize it wasn't all just an exciting, romantic game that Lydia was playing. I wasn't careful enough. One day Dad found a note or something you had written to Lydia. She had left it in a book in the dinette. I guess he saw from my reaction that he'd found something he wasn't supposed to see, and that I knew about it. He really went for me. It was—awful. I tried to keep the secret, but he can say the cruelest things, and I just couldn't take it. I'm not as strong and determined like Lydia was; I can't shout back at him the way she could. I just crumble. I tried not to say too much, but I said enough. I'm sorry, Daniel." She hung her head.

"Don't feel that way, Sarah," said Daniel. "Please."

"But," she choked out the words, "if I hadn't screwed up, maybe everything would have been okay between you! Maybe you would have stayed together, and been happy. Maybe she'd be alive today!"

Daniel looked helplessly at Natalie. She met his gaze with a blank expression. To date, comforting explanations about the impossibility of assuming guilt for the actions of others had been her exclusive province, but this time she was a bystander. Daniel turned back to Sarah.

"Don't say that, Sarah," he urged. "Please, don't even think that." He groped for words. "You can't think that way, it doesn't work. You never hurt Lydia. I don't believe you've ever hurt anybody! Look, your father had already found the note. He would have found out everything else sooner or later. And besides—" Suddenly he found his way and his words came more easily. "Even if he hadn't found out—we couldn't have gone on like that much longer...in secret, with all that pressure. In a way, Sarah, it was just what you said—exciting and romantic. But then we started to argue. Pointlessly. Like you said—she could argue and fight and—I couldn't. I couldn't take it." He swallowed hard. "It's not my way. I guess that's what happens when you fall in love fast and assume it's the answer to all your problems, because for a little while you feel so good. Sooner or later—probably sooner—we would have gone our separate ways."

Sarah had lifted her head, her eyes transfixed on his anxious face. Her expression had grown more hopeful as he had spoken, as his words offset her fears and diluted her unhappiness.

"Really?" she asked in a small voice.

"Really," said Daniel. "Please let it go, Sarah. Please."

She looked at him, trying to believe it, trying to imagine that she could do it, trying to convince herself that things would be better if she could.

"I'll do my best." She looked at him, and then at Natalie. "I'd better be going."

"You don't have to," said Daniel.

"Please, stay," said Natalie. "We've got pizza."

Sarah shook her head. "Better not. I don't want to be reported missing." Registering their blank looks, she added, "Didn't I tell you? Dad has decided that I'm in some kind of danger. Like, I'm supposed to be the next victim. I've been told to stick close to home, and file an itinerary if I go out. He's bought a new handgun and is trying to get me to learn how to use it. I really hate it. But...if he found out I'd left without telling him, he'd go through the roof. I know I shouldn't let him have so much control over me. I'm such a coward. I told you—"

Daniel reached for her hand. "You don't need to explain."

Sarah looked at him swiftly, a look full of questions unasked and unanswered, and clutched at his hand. Natalie wondered if it was time for a discreet exit.

But Sarah stood up, and Daniel's hand slipped away. She collected her things, pulled on her shapeless overcoat, and departed. Brother and sister stood in the open entryway and watched her descend the staircase, climb into her car, and back carefully out onto Haworth Avenue.

As Natalie closed and locked the door for the night, Daniel retreated to the dining room table and picked up a half-empty can of soda. Natalie retrieved the box of tissues from the sofa. Her eyes fell on the photo. With a voyeur's glance at her brother, she picked it up and stared at it.

It was a picture of Daniel and Lydia, taken in the medieval garden of the Cloisters on a sunny day in spring. They were seated side by side on a stone bench, looking into each other's eyes as if there was nothing else in the world of any importance to see. Behind them, framing their happy faces, was a wilderness of quince trees in full bloom. Lydia's hair, a golden version of Sarah's auburn cloud, rippling loosely about her shoulders. She was leaning back on her hands, her print dress falling over her knees in graceful folds.

The Daniel of the photograph was as far removed in appearance from the brother she had been playing Scrabble with as the yearling colt from the Derby winner. He looked impossibly young, and painfully thin. His hair, long and thick and curling, was swept straight back from his square forehead and bound in a ponytail that fell awkwardly over the collar of his beige work shirt. But the camera had caught the life in his eyes as he looked at Lydia, and the joy in his wide smile as they shared some long-lost lovers' jest. Natalie's eyes searched the photograph for its secret, because she could not remember how long it had been since she had seen her brother looking so happy.

"Did I really look like that?" Daniel had approached her silently, soda can in hand, and stood gazing at the photo over her shoulder.

"Evidently."

"God, I look so conceited. Mr. Innocent."

"That's not what I see," said Natalie quietly.

"Maybe you're only seeing what we wanted you to see," said Daniel coldly. "Trick photography."

Natalie looked at him. "Did Sarah take this?"

"I don't really remember. She might have. Sometimes we three went places together—at first. Later Lydia didn't like Sarah tagging along. It comes back to me now, seeing this photo, hearing Sarah talking like that." He turned and walked away in sudden emotion. "Did Lydia have to blame her sister for our mistakes?" He drained the can, placed it on the table, and stood with his back to her.

"Maybe she realized that Sarah had a bit of a crush on you." Natalie replaced the photograph on the coffee table and walked around the table to face him. "And felt a little threatened?"

Daniel's voice betrayed no surprise. "Sarah's feelings were always transparent. I suppose that's why people take advantage of her so easily." He looked over his shoulder at his sister. "You know I never underestimate your powers of perception, but that was a long time ago—how did you know?"

"She told me she had a crush on you."

"Ah. I never mentioned it to Lydia. I hoped she wouldn't notice. Wishful thinking. I should have known better. That was one of the reasons—" He hesitated.

Natalie sat down at the table. "One of the reasons you broke up?"

"No, I was going to say, one of the reasons I didn't like her very much after I got to know her." Daniel sat down with a grimace. "That sounded just as awful as I thought it would. But it's true. Lydia was as manipulative as they come. If she didn't get what she wanted, first she pretended it wasn't happening, then she tried to force people to act the way she wanted, then she tried to deny she ever wanted anything, and if that didn't work she looked for a handy place to lay the blame. No wonder they got along: Sarah was happiest taking all the blame, and Lydia was happiest being blameless."

"And no wonder you and Lydia got along," said Natalie. Daniel blanched, and Natalie reached out a hand across the table. "Sorry! That was incredibly thoughtless. I—"

"Don't worry about it. It's true, after all, though painful. At least I got the hell out." Daniel knit his brows. "That combination—Lydia and Sarah—was trouble. You could sense the potential for disaster whenever they were together. They were both so pretty, so artistic, so lonely. At first, fresh on the outside, I was so intoxicated with freedom I couldn't believe my luck—and I believed in the Castle Dow fantasy that love would conquer all. Later, I started to wise up. Toward the end, I began to be drawn into a situation I didn't fancy. Not that Sarah ever did anything overt—she was way too timid for that. But look, Sarah was very sweet, and when things started to fall apart, I admit it crossed my mind that maybe I'd fallen for the wrong sister. But I didn't pursue it. I was already in way over my head with their father. Besides, I think Lydia would have killed me if I'd shown any interest in Sarah. Talk about sibling rivalry. I had had enough of scenes." He sighed.

Natalie picked up one of the glossy wooden Scrabble tiles. "Sometimes these things have a way of working out. She's more grown up now. Maybe you and she—"

"No." Daniel lifted his eyes to Natalie's, and in his set face there was no doubt or regret. "If she had been then the way she is now…or if I were now the way I was then, it might have been possible. But I don't want the same things now that I wanted then." He nodded at the photograph, lying abandoned on the coffee table. "That's not me anymore, Nat."

Chapter Ten

Early the next morning Natalie emerged from her bedroom wearing a Harvard Law sweatshirt and fuzzy slippers. She was enchanted to behold a spandy clean kitchenette (pizza boxes and empty cans miraculously absent) featuring a primed coffee-maker and a fresh apple Danish artistically presented on her Washington Monument plate. A note from Daniel lay folded beneath her waiting coffee cup.

"Dear Natty," it ran. "We were out of milk, so I borrowed your car to run downtown and get some. The Danish were irresistible. I bumped into the trash collectors on my way back. They would like to remind you that it is now municipal law to use animal-proof garbage cans, and suggest that you invest in those steel spring contraptions that go from handle to handle over the lid. But is this really the best option? I thought the raccoons had worked that one out years ago. The A&P is having a sale this week on polyply garbage cans with child-proof snap-tight lids, your choice of olive or tangerine. I can still use my employee discount, so let me know. I'm off to the BCC library for the a.m.—should be back early. Will pick up something for dinner. D."

Natalie turned on the coffee-maker and the radio, and wandered into the living room with the *New York Times*. Things were suddenly looking good, and she wondered if her concerns had been exaggerated; Daniel was not under serious suspicion and would probably get his job back soon, just as he had said he would. She stretched out on the sofa to read the paper, tease the cat, and wait for her coffee to brew. Noting the tidiness of the living room, she thought to herself: *the perfect house-guest... bedclothes and personal belongings tucked out of sight, does the dishes, and is frequently somewhere else.* She opened the paper to the sports section and yawned.

◇◇◇

The apple Danish consumed, the breakfast dishes virtuously done, Natalie, on her third cup, sat at her desk incorporating Byron's suggestions into the New Globe Theater piece. When the phone rang she thought it would be the Globe's theatrical maven, calling with the answer to a question she had posed about doing a companion editorial on civic responsibility for the arts.

"Natalie Joday."

"May I speak with Natalie Joday please?" It was a cool and unknown female voice.

"Speaking."

"I'm calling for Arthur Sherill, Miss Joday. Mr. Sherill would like to see you in his office. Do you have any free time this morning to stop by for half an hour?"

"In reference to what?"

"I'm sorry, Mr. Sherill did not say."

"I see. Will anyone else be there?"

"No. Just you. Would eleven o'clock be suitable?"

Natalie hesitated long enough to fight back the urge to say something rude, a reaction that an imperious attitude always aroused in her. "I'll try and make it," she said, none too graciously.

"Thank you, Miss Joday." The unknown gave Natalie an address and phone number in Teaneck, reconfirmed the time, and hung up.

Mystified, Natalie stared out the window above her desk. "What is it with lawyers?" she asked the budding maple trees. "They think all they have to do is whistle." She turned her attention back to the computer, determined to finish the New Globe piece before she left for her appointment.

›››

It was eleven-twenty when Natalie introduced herself, without apology, to Arthur Sherill's aloof assistant. After a hushed exchange on the phone, Natalie was told "Mr. Sherill will see you now," and ushered through an oak door into an airy, old-fashioned (wood and wallpaper as opposed to steel and concrete) office. Natalie took off her overcoat, adjusted the collar of her red silk blouse, and shook hands with Arthur Sherill, who came out from behind his desk to do the honors.

"I appreciate your stopping by on such short notice." He released her hand and poked at the bridge of his eyeglasses. "Please have a seat." Natalie slid into a leather chair, and Mr. Sherill returned to his desk.

"This is a little unusual, I know, but Miss Dow asked me to speak with you as soon as possible." His hesitation invited comment, but Natalie restrained her curiosity. "Miss Dow met with me yesterday and asked my advice about drawing up a will. I recognize—and sympathize with—her need to feel secure in an extremely confusing and frightening situation. I offered to represent and counsel her to the best of my ability. Perhaps it is not unwarranted to say to you, her friend, that I took the same approach with her sister. In that instance my counsel was insufficient to prevent an abdication of control over her financial affairs. I found that Lydia had no head for figures, and was not interested in the particulars of financial management. The end result was that, due to disgracefully poor investment strategies, the Dow Estate is considerably smaller than it was when Lydia inherited it."

Natalie's eyes narrowed. She could hear Ginny's *I told you so*, already.

Mr. Sherill folded his hands. "Perhaps it is because I am loathe to repeat this failure that I am willing to bend over backward to accommodate Sarah's ideas—so long as they are constructive and will enable her to better understand the responsibilities inherent in the possession of significant assets. I am not an advocate, you see, of young women leaving their financial management to others."

He paused again, but Natalie had long ago learned that the best way to handle lawyers was to remain noncommittal until they got to the point.

The lawyer smiled. "Sarah has asked me to discuss naming you executrix of her will. Legally, it is not necessary to inform the nominee of this, but Sarah does not want to impose such a burden upon you without asking your permission. She asked me to put the idea before you—and I promised I would, for the reasons mentioned. Naturally I tried to reassure her about her concerns—after all she is only twenty-one, and at the beginning of her life. But, given the death of her sister, I can understand her sense of urgency, and, as I said, I do not want to discourage her from playing an active role in all aspects of her inheritance. She has given me permission to discuss the details of her financial plans with you, including her intention to sign over a significant portion of her estate to Henry Suter, in the event of their marriage."

The lawyer put a hand on his breast. "For my part, let me add that I have no objection whatsoever about your nomination, and would be happy, for Sarah's sake, if you accepted, thus allowing her to move ahead on this issue. My hope is that this might begin a dialogue concerning the more pressing financial matters she will be facing from now on. So please feel free to ask me any questions you might have." He sat back in his chair and folded his arms.

Natalie contemplated the seascape that hung on the wall above Mr. Sherill's head. Assorted reasons for this meeting—some more unrealistic than others—had occurred to her, but this had not been one of them. "Let me ask you this. You said you would represent Sarah as you did Lydia. Don't you represent the whole family?"

Mr. Sherill shook his head. "Eric Dow has used another lawyer, or rather, several lawyers, over the years. Of course, it has been necessary to work with him on many issues, beginning back in the days when I was the Sole Trustee, before Lydia took control of the estate. But I have never represented his interests."

"Then how did you become involved?"

"I was Mary Dow's attorney for many years prior to her… departure."

Natalie's eyes widened.

The lawyer spoke with casual frankness. "Naturally Eric Dow was…upset…at his wife's removal in that decidedly unorthodox manner."

"Naturally."

"For several years we were on opposite sides of the fence, legally speaking. Later on, we were able to work together without incident, if not without a certain resentment."

"And Lydia chose to retain you when she inherited?"

"Yes."

"I'm a little surprised—I've gotten the impression she was pretty much under Eric's thumb."

"To a point. She hired my services out of a sense of duty to her mother. She was very stubborn. Her family was everything to her, which meant that of necessity she had to live with certain contradictions. Thus, although she was dominated by her father, she never ceased in her loyalty to her mother, nor did she cease hoping that her mother would someday return. Since I remained Mary Dow's man of business in this country, Lydia saw me as a link to her."

"Wait a minute." Natalie raised her hand. "You have remained in communication with Mary Dow?"

"Of course. Our communication has not been frequent, but we correspond several times a year, mostly by fax. Currently she uses a business service in Jaipur."

"And the rest of the family—Lydia, Sarah—were all aware that you were in touch with her?"

"Oh, yes."

"Really. I got the impression…" Natalie paused to reorder her thoughts, and realized that something didn't make sense.

"What's the story here?" she asked. "Sarah seems to think her mother was a nut-case who ran off with some man without a thought for her family. What really happened?"

Mr. Sherill stirred, frowning in lawyerly reticence. "The story is not a secret, Miss Joday. There were extenuating circumstances. But perhaps you'd better ask Sarah that question." He folded his hands together and placed them on top of the desk.

"I have," said Natalie promptly. "Or rather, she told me the story unasked the night they found Lydia's body. But what she told me doesn't seem to fit with what you've been saying." She tucked in her chin and turned her gray eyes on the lawyer. "Look. Sarah was only nine at the time, and I'll bet the family never once talked about it rationally in the twelve years since. She has only a vague idea of what occurred, and apparently none at all of why. Lydia may have retained her affection for their mother—and maybe that was because she knew the facts. But Sarah despises her mother—and maybe it's because she doesn't really know what happened."

Natalie threw up her hands. "You know, Mr. Sherill, everybody, including Sarah herself, keeps telling me she has emotional problems, but I'm beginning to think she's done remarkably well considering what she's grown up with, and in comparison to the rest of that crew. You'd think with all their resources, somebody would have thought about getting some good family counseling, so they could put some of this stuff behind them. Hasn't there been enough of the hush-hush stuff?"

Mr. Sherill met her frank look with his round blue eyes. "A valid observation, Miss Joday. All right, I will speak about what happened, in a general way, as one friend of the family—or rather, a friend of Mary, Lydia, and Sarah—to another. I will not, of course, enter into the realm guarded by attorney–client privilege."

"Certainly not."

The lawyer leaned forward over his folded hands. "From the very first Eric Dow was quite a philanderer—pardon my old-fashioned way of putting it—and he always had a ferocious temper. It was my assessment that his simple strategy was to strike the first blow—before anyone had time to mount an attack against him. The more vulnerable he felt, the fiercer the attack. His biggest defense against having his affairs found out was to make sure he kept Mary as off-balance as possible. For example, a favorite trick of his was to accuse her of infidelity, with anyone he happened to think of—the pharmacist, her travel agent—"

"Her lawyer."

"Mmmm. Mary would then spend all of her time trying to prove herself faithful to him, and could not, of course, herself believe that a man who would take such a virtuous stance with regards to her would ever himself—misbehave. Eventually, however, he became involved with someone too close to home."

"Who?"

"Mary's sister. Well, that was the proverbial last straw. When her own sister, overburdened with guilt, finally told her what was going on, Mary believed it. But she couldn't cope with it, and had what we used to call a nervous breakdown. She was hospitalized for some time, but it didn't help. In the end, she did exactly what Eric Dow had always accused her of doing—ran off with a young nobody college student from India. Of course Eric felt completely vindicated. The thing was ludicrous, but Mary was, by that time—beyond caring."

"What was she like?" asked Natalie.

"Sarah reminds me a lot of Mary—Mary in the old days, before she found out what she had married. She was the sort of young woman it's a pleasure to help out. Later, something just—broke. Nothing meant anything to her anymore...not even her daughters, apparently. She drank heavily. What she's like now, after twelve years of living the bohemian life all over the world, who knows?"

The lawyer took off his glasses and held them in one hand. "I remember the day she came and told me she was leaving. The state she was in...And she wanted the impossible! I tried my best to carry out the spirit of her intentions within the practicalities of the legal framework, but—in recent years, I've wondered if I did the right thing.

"I said just now that Lydia never ceased to hope for her mother's return. Mary unwittingly contributed to that hope by insisting on adding a very unwise and legally meaningless addendum to her deed of gift. In it she said her purpose in giving everything to Lydia was to keep the estate intact and out of Eric's hands—and thus safe for her possible return, at which time she anticipated that Lydia would simply hand the whole kit and caboodle back to her."

"I wondered why Sarah was passed over."

"She included a rambling paragraph to the effect that Sarah 'would receive her share eventually.' Also legally meaningless."

Natalie's eyes flashed. "Not to mention completely insensitive to the needs and feelings of her children."

The lawyer met her look. "I could not make Mary see it in that light. Nor, for that matter, could I, Lydia."

"I see," said Natalie. "And what happened to Mary's sister?"

"She died of a drug overdose almost ten years ago. Such a tragedy. Mary refused to come back for the funeral." Sadness tinged the lawyer's voice. "She said…she said she did not have the courage."

A chill ran up Natalie's back, and goosebumps appeared on her arms.

Mr. Sherill sat for a moment with his head bowed, then he replaced his glasses and looked up. "So that's the picture, Miss Joday. Now, about the matter of the will?"

Natalie did not need to think about it. "I'm sorry, Mr. Sherill. I must say no. Apart from whether or not I would agree to take on such a commitment in principle, I feel it would be inappropriate, given the circumstances. Perhaps you are not aware that my brother is peripherally involved in the murder investigation?"

"No, I didn't know that."

"Well, he is. I don't want to agree to anything that might prove prejudicial. But I shall certainly talk with Sarah about what you have told me…and strongly recommend that she name you executor, and so resolve the issue." Natalie stood up and reached for her overcoat.

Mr. Sherill also rose. "I understand, Miss Joday. We all do what we can in our own way." He smiled at her—unleashing a surprising set of dimples which transformed his dour, scholarly face into a vision of down-home good nature. Natalie, somewhat astounded to discover that she had developed a healthy sense of camaraderie with this man, shook hands with warmth, and left.

As she passed through the outer office, she found the haughty assistant serving a cup of tea to the next appointment—a massive woman dressed in a dark-red, full-length skirt, a heavy shawl with an exotic pattern in purple and black, and hiking boots. One hand dragged at a wisp of gray hair that had fallen over her eyes, the other grasped a tattered knapsack. She looked like the archetypal bag lady, as far removed from the upper crust clients Natalie had assumed Arthur Sherill would stick to as it was possible to be.

Natalie realized as she left that she had misjudged the lawyer and felt ashamed.

⟩⟩⟩

Ginny, not one to let the weekend keep her from a story, spotted Natalie and waved her over the minute she entered the newsroom. "Police ballistics report." She held up a fax.

"How did you get that?" demanded Natalie querulously.

"Never mind. The police found out that, while at the family summer home, the father often indulged in a little target practice in the cow pasture. So they sent up a team to dig bullets out of trees. Seems he used to tack the targets on the trees. This is no way to treat a tree—why didn't he use hay bales? But they've got a perfect match with the bullet that killed Lydia. So that's that: it was the father's gun. You are not sufficiently thrilled. What have you uncovered?"

"Just had a very interesting meeting with Sarah's lawyer."

"Sherill?"

Natalie pulled up a chair and sat down. "Yeah."

"And?"

"He filled me in on Mary Dow."

"Who's that? Oh, the mother. She's not a suspect."

"I know, but all of this goes back a long way. At least, if we are taking this as a family murder."

"I think the use of the father's gun settles that point."

"That's what I mean. When I first met Sarah, and she told me about Lydia, she talked about their mother and the money angle, as if the connection was obvious to her. Eric married Mary for her money, but Mary thought he really loved her."

"And?"

"And those two girls grew up in that environment: arrogant, brutish father; weak, unrealistic mother. Then, without any warning as far as the girls were concerned, Mary up and walks out of their lives and never looks back. No wonder Sarah thinks familial love is supposed to hurt like hell."

"Here's a thought!" Excitement danced in Ginny's eyes. "Has she been heard from? What if the mother was murdered too!"

"Sorry," said Natalie, employing professional irony. "She's still alive. Mr. Sherill is in communication with her." She hesitated. "Not face to face, though—she lives overseas. I didn't ask if he's actually spoken to her on the phone."

"This needs to be checked out," said Ginny, encouraged. "No wonder Sarah can't stand the mention of her. What mother abandons her children like that? Don't you think it's more likely that she was done away with?"

"I think that if Eric Dow had murdered Mary, it wouldn't have been so that Lydia could inherit."

"True." Ginny grinned sheepishly, and then grew pensive. "I wonder what the mother would have thought of the way the older daughter let her father have the management of the estate. Damn! Now you've got me doing it. The *fact* is she ran out on her kids. The husband may have deserved it...but the kids? Didn't she care about what happened to them, what they must have gone through?"

"Some people are too wrapped up in themselves to notice," said Natalie. "Some people can justify anything by saying they just tried to do what was best."

"Maybe. Well, I'll leave the speculation to you. I want the facts! Why did she leave? Was there somebody else?"

Natalie hesitated, then shook her head. "That sounds more like gossip than speculation. Even if other people say that was part of the reason, how do we know there wasn't something else far more important? No comment."

"Okay, be that way. I forgive you." Ginny never pressed her sources when they said no. She just waited them out. It was her most devastating tactic.

There was a commotion over by the mail room. A plump elderly woman, carrying a large canvas book-bag with *Give a Hoot—Don't Pollute* stamped on it, had backed hastily out of the mail room and bumped into a tall metal rack stacked high with paper products. The rack teetered, spilling a shower of number 10 envelopes and note pads onto the floor. Ginny and Natalie (along with the other twenty people in the newsroom) feigned instant attention to nonexistent work. An anemic-looking young man dressed in a bright yellow coverall bounced out of the mail room and confronted the woman, who struck a pose of terror. Across the length and breadth of the hushed office, he was heard to say in a shocked tone: "Now look what you've done!" The woman put a hand to her mouth, then bent over and hastily gathered the fallen supplies, mumbling, "I'm so terribly, terribly sorry!"

When he saw she had finished, the young man stalked back into the mail room. The woman scurried across the cluttered newsroom to the exit, frequently backtracking, with the self-absorbed concentration of a white mouse in a maze. Natalie ducked her head and appeared very busy indeed as the woman dodged past her chair. As she disappeared, twenty amused glances were exchanged.

The woman was the *Star* advice columnist, known professionally as "Louise," in accordance with her weekly column, entitled "Ill at Ease? Ask Louise!" In real life she was the great aunt of a major *Star* stockholder. Said stockholder saw no reason why a lack of identifiable talent or experience should prevent his seventy-one-year-old relative from pursuing a writing career if she wanted to. Byron, when presented with a *fait accompli*, had smiled nervously but reckoned it was one of those situations that would work itself out over time. So Louise had started her advice column with minimal fanfare the previous summer. All had gone well (if without color) until the unmuzzled tongue of Rudy, the mail room doyen, had let it slip at the Christmas party that Louise had, in fact, never received any mail. With 20–20 hindsight, the underappreciated gossip-mongers in the mail room and print shop had agreed that they had always known she was writing all those silly letters herself.

The senior writing staff had condescended to raise a collective eyebrow in support of this theory. Cynical and analytical alike had long been amused not only by the passé conservatism of Louise's advice, but by the admirable consistency of style with which the Ill-at-Ease wrote.

Louise, made aware that her secret was out, retreated, then set about battling back. Shortly thereafter, mail had begun to arrive for her. She made regular forays into the mail room, demanded her mail of Rudy, marching away, head held high. Rudy, his reputation on the line, had been stymied but briefly. After a month he let it be known that although letters had begun to arrive for the old lady, it sure was a coincidence they were all postmarked in Oradell. Louise lived in Oradell.

"Have you heard the latest?" Ginny spoke in an undertone, glancing sideways to make sure that Rudy, who had begun his afternoon rounds, was out of earshot. "Now the letters are all mailed from different post offices, and the envelopes are always different, and different colored pens are used to address them. It must take her all day!"

"You go, Louise," said Natalie gleefully. "You show that little—" She stopped as Rudy, going from desk to desk with his trolley to pick up the outgoing mail, turned their way. She stared at him rather guiltily, but he smiled at her as he passed.

"Hi, Miss Joday. Gee, how's your seriously awesome brother?" Rudy never read the paper.

Natalie rolled her eyes heavenward, which Rudy appeared to accept as sufficient reply. He moved on in good humor. *Man, woman, or child,* thought Natalie, *they all swoon before Daniel.*

"Joday! Call for you! Line six!" Without really recognizing where the voice came from, she went to an empty desk, punched up six, and spoke.

"Natalie Joday."

"Natalie? It's Sarah." Her usually melodious voice was tight and flat.

"What's wrong?" asked Natalie.

"It's Rose! The police actually came here and took her away—they wouldn't say what was happening or anything! They didn't even give her time to change! She just had to go! Right then, and they wouldn't say why! It was awful!"

"Yeah, bummer isn't it?" said Natalie coolly. "Did they arrest her?"

"What? I guess so—isn't that what being arrested is?"

"Not necessarily. Did they handcuff her, or read her her rights?"

"N...nno," faltered Sarah. "They just said she was wanted at the district attorney's office for questioning."

"Well, then relax, they haven't arrested her yet."

"But their whole manner had changed. That means something's happened, doesn't it?"

"Yeah. Did she say anything?"

"Not a word. It was spooky. She was totally calm—almost like she was patronizing them. Natalie, do you think she did it?"

"Sarah, honestly I have no idea. But look, you can't let stuff like this hit you so hard; you've got to prepare, because no matter who did it—it's going to be a blow when it comes."

"I know, I know!"

"Is anybody there with you?"

"No—well, Graham may be at the cottage, I don't know. Eric went with Rose, followed them in his car, I mean."

"I wish you weren't there alone, Sarah. Isn't Harry coming over?"

"Why should he? Am I so utterly helpless I don't know how to lock a door?" Her anger burst forth like lightning through a darkened sky. "Doesn't anybody have anything else to do besides protect me from my own shadow?"

"Okay, okay. I'm sorry, Sarah. I just don't think this is the time to get careless."

"That's what people have been telling me my whole life! 'This is a difficult time; it's just for a little while; later you'll get to be a real person.' But later never comes!"

As Sarah spoke, there hove into Natalie's field of view a pair of uniformed county officers. They weaved their way slowly and inexpertly across the newsroom. From the moment she saw them she never doubted they were looking for her. Ginny had spotted them too. Natalie caught her eye, and the two women stared at each other.

"Sarah, I've gotta go. Sorry. I'll call you as soon as I can." She could see their faces now, clean-cut, uncommunicative, confident.

"Okay. Is something wrong?" Her voice was filled with concern, her anger disappearing as quickly as it had come.

"I'm not sure. I've gotta go."

She hung up the phone and rose slowly as the two officers, glancing briefly at each other, came to a halt at her side.

Chapter Eleven

"Natalie Joday," said the shorter of two.

"Yeah?"

Ginny glided to her side.

"Sergeant Allan from County Homicide sent us over to ask you to come down to his office at the courthouse, ma'am."

"Why?"

"He would like to have a talk with you, ma'am."

She ignored their passive attempts to get her to move. "What about?"

"I really couldn't say, ma'am," said the officer. But he had no difficulty in conveying the impression that he could, in fact, have said, ma'am, had it not been his self-righteous duty to maintain the very highest standards of confidentiality. It came to her that the gratuitous belligerence of the average peace officer was strikingly like that of the average law breaker. What was it that had ever made her think that Sergeant Allan was different?

She gave a disdainful snort, and opened her shoulder bag to root for her car keys.

"You don't have to go if you don't want to," said Ginny. "I can call—"

"No," said Natalie. "I'm going. I wouldn't miss this for the world."

"I'll come with you."

"No, thanks." She found the keys.

"We'll take you down in the squad car, ma'am," said the taller of the two.

Natalie closed her bag and threw it over her shoulder. "You may follow behind me, or you may ride with me, but I'm driving my car." She turned her head and addressed Ginny. "I'll either call you or come back here after."

Ginny, her black eyes wary, but also very, very curious, nodded.

Natalie swept her eyes around the hushed newsroom. Twenty questioning faces were turned to her. She pushed her hair back and squared her shoulders. Twenty pairs of eyes watched, as, followed closely by the two officers, she strode across the room and out the door.

It was a brief drive up Union Street to the courthouse, but the long walk from the parking lot to the main entrance, along the vast hall and up two flights of stairs, made the trip seem epic. When they reached Sergeant Allan's cramped office, they found it empty. After a whispered consultation, the two officers left her there alone.

Forty-two and a half minutes later Natalie heard the sound of running footsteps, and Sergeant Allan burst through the door with an armload of folders and a guilty expression.

"Sorry I took so long!" He dumped the papers onto his desk and watched helplessly as the six uppermost folders shifted and slithered across the smooth surface and onto his chair. He turned back to Natalie. "I got tied up." He took a closer look and backtracked. "Have you been waiting long? Did anybody offer you…?"

Natalie rose from her chair to address him as near to eye level as she could get. "What exactly," she asked with razor-sharp enunciation, "were you thinking, when you sent those two goons to my place of employment?"

"I thought we need to talk. There have been developments in the case that you—"

"Developments that made it impossible for you to contact me yourself if you wanted to talk to me?"

"Damn it, take it easy! I couldn't come myself. I've been tied up all morning. I had to testify before a Grand Jury on another case and the assistant DA—"

"And the telephones are no longer functioning in Bergen County?"

His head snapped back as if he had been struck. "No, I—" He stopped himself, recovered his poise, and made a calming gesture. "Look, is it possible you're overreacting? I don't work alone, you know. I was stuck downstairs waiting to testify, and I figured it would save time if I told Maxwell to go and ask you to stop by. I told them to extend my apologies and explain that I was busy." He saw that her anger was unappeased. "All this because I kept you waiting?"

"Sergeant Allan, if you ever, ever again, want to speak with me, about anything, *anything*, you can God-damned-well tell me so yourself, and not send a pair of no-necked licensed bullies to do it for you."

"There's no need—" He closed his mouth tightly and glanced to one side. When he looked back at her, his eyes were narrow and his jaw set. "I don't need to give you any special treatment."

Natalie treated him to a sarcastic smile. "So I'm a suspect now?"

"Of course not, damn it. But this is still a murder investigation—"

"I don't care if it's World War Three!" Natalie slammed a fist onto his desk. "You have no right to use your civil authority for mere convenience. Or were you trying to intimidate me?"

"Wait a minute!" He raised his hands, palms outward. "Trying to intimidate you! Good Lord, I was trying to do you a favor!"

Natalie's eyes flashed. "If you want to do me any favors, you're going to have to work harder than this!" She clenched her teeth. "I don't consider hauling me over here to tell me you've picked up my brother again to be much of a treat!"

Surprise washed over Sergeant Allan's face, checking his anger. "How did you know that? Did Maxwell tell you? Is that why you're so upset?"

"No, Sergeant. Nobody told me one single damn thing. *That's* why I'm upset."

Curiosity replaced his surprise. "Then how did you know?"

"Sarah called and told me you'd picked up Rose, and so when the boys showed up with your message, it was pretty clear that there had been a break in the case. And since you sent for me, it must involve Daniel."

Sergeant Allan's dark face smoothed. "I see."

"Don't you carry any memory at all of our discussion at the Dows'?" Her angry, earnest eyes bored into Sergeant Allan's cool, guarded ones. "With regard to invading places of employment?"

He paused, and stood silent before her, his lithe frame motionless beneath his loose brown suit, his thoughts unreadable behind the angular planes of his face.

His mouth and eyebrows twitched in unison. "My apologies," he said with professional cool. "I hope this won't make things uncomfortable for you at work."

"It won't," snapped Natalie. "I'm a black belt at explaining why there are police crawling all over my life. Fortunately, I'm not in the tenuous position at my job that my brother was at his. But the principle is the same."

He started to say something, closed his mouth, and looked her in the eye. "You expect a lot from people, don't you, Miss Joday? Very well. I can promise you, if there is a next time, I shall certainly come myself."

"Thank you," said Natalie. She took a deep breath, trying not to betray her shakiness as her anger ebbed away.

"Will you please have a seat?" He gestured to the chair at the front of his desk.

Natalie was glad to do so. It came to her, in the backwash of her anger, how annoyed Ginny would be with her for alienating a solid contact.

Sergeant Allan removed the folders from his chair and sat also. "Do you think we can talk about this calmly?"

"I hope so." Natalie folded her hands in her lap. "That's why I came."

◇◇◇

He took a minute to put his papers away and make a quick phone call. Natalie eyed his profile surreptitiously as he was thus employed. He had an aquiline nose, as suited a man in his line of work, and she noticed he wore a slim gold chain around his left wrist. He went about his business without pretense, and made no attempt to downplay her criticism. This was a sign of professional self-confidence, she thought, and highly preferable to the sort of institutionalized superiority she was familiar with.

She felt it to be her responsibility to show him there were no hard feelings. "Nice office. Now that I finally get to see it."

"Thank you." He pulled his chair forward, and folded his hands on top of the desk. "I assume your brother will tell you what has happened, so I see no reason not to, in the hope that you will continue to lend your insight. Please be clear as to my motives: I want to solve this case, Miss Joday. I want to find whoever committed this murder and get him or her off the street."

"You don't need to sell me on the idea that murderers should be caught." Natalie raised an eyebrow. "I'm a believer."

"That is obvious." He raised an eyebrow in his turn. "But sometimes, in the course of digging around in an investigation like this, we uncover details we weren't looking for. Sometimes the facts can be unpleasant."

"No kidding. But always less unpleasant than a stupid lie."

"You are very idealistic, Miss Joday."

"Sergeant, I wish you could shake off the idea that I am inoperably myopic when it comes to Daniel. You have been very delicate." She sighed shortly and swallowed. "Consider me forewarned and spit it out."

"All right." He fixed his eyes on her face. "As you know, we do extensive cross-checking of minute details in an investigation like this. Looking for little things—things that start the cracks that eventually split the case wide open. In due course we got around to Rose Dow's shopping spree on the afternoon of the murder. She had lost the receipts for the items she had purchased, but the details were on her credit card. We went to the stores in question at the Bergen Mall and got their copies of the receipts, which include the time of purchase."

"Ah."

"She had stated she shopped from about two-thirty to four. But all of the receipts were between three-fifty and four-thirty p.m. When asked to explain this discrepancy, she said that she had given us false information and would like to correct her statement. She said the essence of her story was true—she had left her home shortly before two, but had been too embarrassed to tell us that she had not gone directly to the Bergen Mall. At first she resisted telling us the story, saying that it had nothing to do with the case, but in the end we made her understand she had no choice. Finally, she stated that she had gone to see your brother in Cresskill and had remained there from shortly before two until just past three."

"Oh," mouthed Natalie silently.

"Yes." Sergeant Allan cleared his throat. "Naturally, we immediately sought out your brother for corroboration. He was distressed, but made no attempt to deny the meeting. He confirmed the times and stated that he had not been expecting her visit. He refused to comment on what she was doing there or what happened, sticking to it that it had nothing to do with the case. You don't seem very surprised, Miss Joday. Has he already told you about this?"

"No."

"I ask because I believe he would have told you if he had told anyone."

"This doesn't sound like the sort of thing one tells one's sister, does it?"

"No, but I wish he had." He shook his head, unclasped his hands, and pulled his notebook from his jacket pocket. "I don't like it, it's so—pat. It's the most hackneyed reason in the world people give to explain why they didn't tell the truth about where they were." He fell silent.

Natalie eyed him for signs of further revelations, but his bolt appeared shot. "Is that it?" she asked cautiously.

"Isn't that enough?" His eyes narrowed. "You sound relieved. Why?"

Natalie did some quick thinking. "I thought you were going to tell me they had been arrested." She averted her eyes from his searching look.

"They may yet be, Miss Joday. It's not solely up to me, as you know. At the very least they'll be at the DA's office for a while, until we can…do more checking." Sergeant Allan made a gesture of frustration, and tossed his notebook onto the desk. "I can't arrest someone for murder based on something like this. Even though they both lied. But the DA's office—What I need to find is an independent witness to confirm what time Rose Dow really left home."

Natalie pinched her lips together and concentrated on a crack in the linoleum to the left of her feet.

A gentleness came to the sergeant's eyes as he looked at her, and the firm line of his mouth wavered. "I'm sorry about this, Miss Joday."

Natalie's chin flew up, and she caught the tail end of his look in the dusky recesses of his eyes. She thought he was pitying her, and she didn't like it.

"Why?" she asked disdainfully. "Adultery isn't a capital offense—yet. Is it?"

"No, Miss Joday. But I'm trying to tell you I'm not necessarily buying the idea of the romantic tryst." He paused to let that sink in, with its implications. "His activities between ten-thirty and two remain unaccounted for. You've invested a lot of time and faith in your brother. If things turn out badly for him… You see, up until today, there was no real hint of a case against him. No possible motive. But now…"

"Yes, I've worked that one out too." Natalie stood up. "Now comes the part where you start collecting evidence to support a case that Rose and Daniel were in it together for the money. How's this? Rose took the gun from Eric's desk while he was out of town and gave it to Daniel the night of the dinner party. Daniel, drawing on his well-documented experience with firearms, did the deed, at some point prior to two p.m., I presume. They had a celebratory rendezvous in Cresskill. That night Rose hid the body on her way home from gemology class. Good luck finding your independent witness. But may I make a suggestion? Perhaps you should take another look at your case histories. Do you know, for example, that my brother, his conviction for armed robbery notwithstanding, has never held a gun in his hand?"

"I know he has told you so."

Natalie's expression was one of mock apology. "Oh, I forgot. I am the innocent sister, admired for her loyalty but dismissed for her blindness. I lack objectivity: the police specialty."

"Miss Joday, I realize you care a lot for your brother—"

"Gee, you are a detective!"

Sergeant Allan leaped to his feet. "Damn it! Do you have to be so offensive?"

"Do you have to be so patronizing?"

They stared angrily at one another.

Sergeant Allan checked himself. "I am not patronizing you. But when I say something that upsets you, you lash out at me as if it's my fault. You don't like the police, do you?"

Natalie did not hesitate. "No, I don't. And I have good reasons. Bitter reasons. I've seen you sacrifice your humanity on the altar of the Solid Fact. You support your prejudices against the people who need you most with unbiased statistics, and the dutiful jury of our peers—carefully schooled to exclude all else as inadmissible—is duly impressed. 'Sixty-two percent of felonies are committed by high school drop-outs. Eight out of ten home-coming convicts are re-arrested within the next year. Once a thief always a thief.' You know everything there is to know as long as you can attach a number to it."

Natalie's face twisted, tears welling unwanted but unashamed in her eyes. "Is this all there is to life? Don't you have room for anything besides lifeless facts that can be learned by rote? For the interplay of feelings, of joy and sorrow—for a little compassion? Can you, with all your obvious intelligence, possibly believe that this clerical hogwash is enough? That because you know a person's income, or their address, or how much their house is worth, you actually know them? It scares me sometimes! Who am I to you? 'Natalie Joday, phone number 555-5999, residence 128 Haworth Avenue.' Do you really think that this sort of stuff tells you anything? 'Graduated high school 1982. Moved back to Haworth four years ago.' What was the rest?" she demanded passionately. "I'm sure you have it memorized!"

An eerie, unsettled expression took possession of the sergeant's face. "Graduated college 1987; twenty-nine years old; one brother; one focus; two clear gray eyes that see through me as if—"

He stopped himself, and for the second time in less than a minute they stood staring, face-to-face, in silence. But what a difference! The atmosphere, already electrified by Natalie's unleashed emotions, had, without lessening in intensity, taken on a completely different charge. She lowered her eyes. Amidst the myriad thoughts and feelings threatening to overwhelm her, she was galvanized by a swift shock wave that ran through her body and left her overworked mind reeling and her cheeks burning. Her anger and fear, so all-consuming moments before, evaporated. She was left feeling empty and alone. Damn him! She jerked her chin up—but he had turned away, and was rubbing the back of his neck with his hand. He looked surprised at something.

"Sorry." His voice sounded surprised, too. "That was—unprofessional. I hope you can—Will you accept my apology?" He faced her squarely again. His eyes were clear, but his lips were drawn into a thin, embarrassed line.

"Yes."

He shook his head back and forth. "I don't usually; I mean I've never—" He exhaled loudly, puffing out his cheeks. "Look, I can take myself off the case if you feel—"

"No." Natalie waved the offer away. "I'd just as soon somebody with brains was on this case. Look, I'm sorry too."

"You didn't do anything."

"I shouldn't have unloaded all that on you. You were right. I am fully aware that you personally have treated Daniel well, and that this is what he gets for lying to you. Look, I don't really believe all policemen are rotten just because I've met some lousy ones. When calm I am perfectly willing to admit it's a sore spot with me." She shook her head in bewilderment, struck suddenly with the absurdity of the situation. "I think I'd better go." And then she winced to hear the cliché.

Sergeant Allan stepped around his desk to open the door for her. "No doubt your brother will phone you if—Well, if we decide to arrest."

"No doubt."

"Has he been in touch with a lawyer yet?"

"Yes. Unfortunately he's mountain-climbing in France this weekend."

"Really? Who's that?"

"Evan Braedon," said Natalie with admirable detachment.

"Champion of justice for the disenfranchised. Well, I suppose lawyers can afford to take ski weekends in Europe."

"Don't get me started on lawyers," said Natalie, and was gone.

›››

Natalie headed back to the *Star* office, but as she slowed to turn left across traffic and into the staff parking lot, she realized she had no stomach for the questions of her colleagues. Nor, despite her promise, did she want to talk things over with Ginny. Not now. Not given the knowledge that it was only a matter of time before all hell broke loose. She was back in the midst of the turmoil, tempest-tossed and in danger of losing her way, and old wounds forgotten in the sunshine throbbed again in the storm. What she wanted to do was—just drive. So she continued down Hackensack Road, heading south at a crawl, not minding the traffic since she had nowhere to go.

Daniel and Rose? From everything he had said, she had taken it as given that Daniel had no use for Rose Dow. Was this another "distinct impression" she had been intentionally left with? Could it be that her own opinion had been transferred gratis to her brother? What was it he had said to Ginny at dinner the other night? *Don't underestimate Rose Dow.* Surely his emotion had been one of honest distaste...Emotions...She had challenged Sergeant Allan to deal with emotions—well he had certainly taken her up on that one!

To hell with Sergeant Allan! Think about the case. But was this going to complicate matters? Would he continue to keep her informed? He was obviously very ethical, quite—Forget him! Forget about everything. Think only about the case.

Natalie turned the situation over in her mind, and looked unflinchingly at the underside. If there was something going on between Daniel and Rose, wouldn't it be the natural cover-up—considering Lydia's death—for them to feign dislike of one another? But seriously, Rose was not Daniel's type at all.

Daniel's type. She crossed the Hackensack River on Cedar Road and cruised slowly around the residential back streets of Dumont. At the junction of Washington and Madison Ave she spotted a pay phone. Suddenly seeing her way, she pulled the Volvo over, jumped out, stepped into the booth, and grabbed her address book out of her shoulder bag. After a moment's consultation, she dialed.

"Lodi Community Center."

"Hello, may I speak with Dr. Elias, please?"

"One moment please." Natalie waited. "I'm sorry, Dr. Elias is not in the office today. May I take a message?"

"No thanks, I'll call again."

Natalie hopped back into the Volvo and rested her arms on the steering wheel. She looked across the street and realized that fate had brought her to within half a mile of where she most wanted to be. Starting up the car, she pulled back into traffic and headed toward Cresskill. Within five minutes she found herself on Beacon Street. She parked the car and went up the front walk of a cozy little house, its lower portion faced in colored sandstone, with freshly painted green clapboard above. She snapped the door knocker smartly a couple of times, admiring a brass door plaque that read "R. Elias" in a flowing script. She was gratified to hear an answering rustle within, followed by the opening of the door.

A tall, sepia-skinned woman in her early thirties stood before her. Her thick, waving hair, pulled back severely from her forehead and bound by a tortoise-shell clip at the back of her head, fell in cascades onto her shoulders. Her dark, intelligent eyes showed surprise—surprise and pleasure—at seeing Natalie standing on the stoop.

"Natalie! Nice to see you. Come in." She stepped back from the door.

"Hi, Rebecca." Natalie walked into the comfortable gloom of the living room. "It's been too long."

"It has. Take a seat."

"Thanks." Natalie sat on the pillow-laden sofa, going suddenly limp.

Rebecca looked at her with a clinical eye. "You look exhausted. This business with Daniel, I suppose."

Natalie smiled weakly, relieved she wasn't going to have to be delicate. She had always felt that she and Rebecca could have been quite good friends—had they not shared a mutual caution about developing a close relationship. They were each burdened, after all, with the notoriety of being the respective "other woman" in Daniel's life.

"Yeah," she said. "I wondered if you knew about that."

"I had the police around a couple of days ago."

"Really!"

"Checking up on his alibi. And asking a lot of impertinent questions."

"That is my cue to admit I have a couple of impertinent questions myself, if you're willing to answer them."

Rebecca drew her legs up onto the seat of her chair, and wrapped her arms around her knees. "That's the difference though, isn't it? The police just ask their questions. You ask if you can ask. I suppose you have a good reason."

"I think so."

Rebecca nodded. "I suppose he's standing in his own light again."

"Yeah."

Rebecca nodded again, puckering her lips in an expression of chagrin. She was not a classic beauty (her chin was rather long and her nose had a bump on it), and she was dressed in day-off-at-home attire chosen for comfort, not looks, but she was the kind of woman who, sooner or later, inevitably attracted attention. Just sitting there she was enthralling.

"Let me save you some time," she said. "I'll tell you everything I told the police." She raised a finger. "And there's a bonus. The questions they asked were superficial—times and dates and phone numbers. But they got me thinking—looking at it again in the light of what's happened. And I've remembered certain things: how I felt; what I thought—things they didn't ask about. I'll save that for afters." She rested her chin on her knees. "How to begin?"

"Daniel moved in in January," prompted Natalie, "and for a while everything was fine, and then one day..."

Rebecca smiled, and took up the story. "And then one day—one night—I came home from my Sunday night seminar in Lodi and stopped off at the A&P, figuring I was early enough to give Daniel a lift home. But he wasn't there—he had traded nights with a friend. Okay, it was unusual he hadn't mentioned it to me, but no big deal. I went home, and he was here by 11:30. He said he'd been invited to a party. It didn't seem to have anything to do with me, and I didn't quiz him. I don't like to look for trouble—enough comes along all on its own. Well, it came along real fast. I went to work the next day—Monday—February 8th, right? The day everybody wants to know about. At about two-thirty in the afternoon I gave Daniel a call from work. He was here. I told him I was coming home early and asked did I need to pick up anything for dinner. He said no. I got home at around four o'clock. We were here together until he left for work at seven or so, and, after he got home from work at eleven-thirty, we were here together all night. Two days later Daniel and

I had a serious fight, during which we discussed—among other things—the fact that the party he had been at Sunday evening was at the home of an ex-girlfriend. As a result of this fight we agreed it would be best if he moved out. He did. This is exactly what I told the police. Strictly speaking, those are the facts in full. All that's missing is what really happened."

Natalie's thoughts strayed to Sergeant Allan, and she heard the echo of her angry words and saw in her mind the look on his face.

Rebecca released her knees and shifted around to sit sideways on her heels. "Because the fact is I knew when I called he wasn't alone. I could hear it in his voice when he answered the phone—guilt. I was also quite sure I heard a noise in the background, and then a sound as though Daniel had covered and uncovered the mouthpiece with his hand. He was—not himself. Just as well he didn't need me to pick up anything on the way home, because I really wasn't in the mood.

"I walked in the door and was hit by the smell of perfume. *Not very subtle*, I remember thinking. Coconut cologne. Daniel was in the kitchen, starting dinner. He had a batch of scratch brownies ready to come out of the oven. I presume, since it was too cold to leave the windows open, he had been trying to smother the coconut smell. It didn't work. The house just smelled like coconut brownies. I went into the kitchen.

"I'd never imagined he could be like that. He was wrecked. Shattered. If he had painted the words I DID IT in capital letters across his forehead he couldn't possibly have aroused more suspicion. Whatever had happened, it had not been pleasant. He wouldn't—no, he *couldn't* talk. I *demanded* is I guess the word, to know what was going on. For a long time I couldn't get anything out of him. It was grotesque. The brownies burnt, and then the house reeked of burnt coconut brownies. Finally, cold or no cold, we opened the windows to let the smoke—and the coconut—out.

"It was the next morning before he could admit that there had been anyone in the house. Then his story was that it was someone he had met at a party, and that she had tracked him down, and that nothing of a sexual nature had happened, and nothing was going to happen, and that she was just a trouble-maker. 'What party?' I asked. When he didn't have a quick answer, I suggested that he had perhaps met her the previous Sunday evening. Well, we went around about that one another day or so. He had told me about Lydia previously, and now he told me that the party had been at her house. I suggested that it had been Lydia who had come over, but he denied it. He assured me that the party was a disaster, that he wished he had never gone, and that it was his dearest hope never to see any of those people again. He said he had only gone because he wanted to prove to himself that things had changed in his life, and that he was a worthwhile human being who didn't need to be ashamed of who he was, or who his ex-girlfriends were. He then undermined this happy theory by admitting the reason he hadn't mentioned the party to me was because he thought I might be upset because he was seeing an ex-girlfriend."

Although Rebecca's tone remained detached, the strain of reliving those days, even in shorthand, was showing on her sculpted face. She took a deep breath and continued. "That was as much as I ever got out of him. Until the minute he left, he insisted that the woman who had come over was not Lydia, but he wouldn't tell me who she was or where he had met her or what had happened. The last words out of his mouth as he went out the door were: 'Whether you believe me or not, nothing happened.'" She fell silent, brooding in the growing darkness.

Natalie, witness to the pain still alive in Rebecca's eyes, experienced a strong desire to deliver to her brother a swift kick in the shins. "But you didn't believe him."

Rebecca came out of her reverie with a start. "Oh, don't get me wrong, Natalie! I believed him, all right. It wasn't that! Whatever happened, it wasn't about sex. Forgive me if I've given you the impression that I wanted to end it because I thought he was cheating on me. No, I knew…and I mean *knew* that there was no one else. Wrong psychological profile. No." She reached out an arm and turned on a light. "What I found unacceptable was the way he shut himself off; the way he said 'Everything's fine, trust me,' when clearly everything was not fine. I had thought he was past that, but I was wrong. Daniel is a sweet man, but the victim role is killing him—because he thinks people are going to think he's guilty, he feels guilty and goes on the defensive. That gets old. You know."

"I know."

"It was a very difficult decision—and not least because he thought he was being unfairly accused. Again. I tried to explain that wasn't it, that it was something more important, but—he didn't see it. Well, what could I do? I can't live my life like that. And it's all so stupid. The party, hey, we all make second-rate choices, but when that woman showed up here and I called? Why didn't he just say, 'Look, Reeb, I'm in trouble. There's this weird woman here trying to compromise me.' I mean, I may not know who she was, but I know she was no amateur. I know she was trying to get Daniel into trouble somehow, and I know that he fell right into it.

"Coconut cologne?" Rebecca spread her arms wide apart in general appeal. "Great balls of fire! Is anyone so stupid in this day and age to carry on like that in someone else's house and then leave the place drenched with distinctive scent? She probably waited until Daniel left the room for a minute and then dumped half a bottle onto the carpet! The next day I found a brooch—really tacky, by the way—shoved down between the cushions on the sofa. Now I call that overkill. National statistics prove conclusively that 98.2 percent of all articles of clothing or other personal effects left in people's houses are left intentionally. We're talking well-documented fact! But Daniel didn't get it. He missed a lot when he was in the slammer, and he didn't learn much from his romance with Lydia either. It never occurred to him that he was being set up, when in fact it was so obvious! Who rustles papers thoughtlessly in the background while her lover is on the phone with his girlfriend? Hey, I always hold my breath and cross my fingers when in that situation, don't you? I'll say she was here to make trouble! This takes someone accustomed to getting away with murder!"

"This takes Rose Dow," said Natalie. Rebecca looked at her questioningly. "Lydia's stepmother."

"Thank you." Rebecca covered her heart with her hands. "I'm glad to know who she is at last. Now I can follow through with a little plan I have to send her a quart of coconut cologne for Christmas with a note saying 'Just to replace the bottle you so unfortunately spilled while visiting my house.'"

"I'll give you her address."

Rebecca laughed, then shook her head. "It would be comic, if only—Why didn't Daniel see it as comic, Natalie? We could have had such fun making up coconut jokes. I know he got—you both got—nothing but mixed signals when he was a kid. And prison is the best institution ever devised to eradicate dignity and a sense of self-worth. Is it pride? Immaturity? Was he hurt that bad?"

"I don't know, Rebecca. His pride is pretty much shot to hell. He's got an immature streak, and, yeah, he was hurt that bad. But still, there's something else. Because he's not that stupid."

Rebecca leaned over the arm of her chair. "That's it. That's what I felt—this is all so stupid, and you're not stupid, Daniel! We had a nice thing going, I mean we'd been hanging out together for a year before he moved in. I knew him pretty well. Not as well as you, of course," she added considerately.

"Oh, I'm sure you knew him better than me," objected Natalie. Then she grinned. "Well, differently anyway."

Rebecca laughed. "What I liked best about him was that he wasn't hung up on trying to fill the role of being the Man Around the House. He was fun to live with; he wasn't possessive. And you know—" She spoke as though sharing an astounding fact. "He's very domestic, really."

"I know!" Natalie echoed her tone. "He's been at my apartment like three days, and the place is spotless."

"And he seems to like it, that's the thing. I mean, I figured we'd have trouble because I was making so much more money, but it never phased him. You know we split expenses proportionally."

"Oh yes, that's a good plan."

"Of course, he has trouble saving money—but then he's never had any worth saving, so how's he to know? And what he does buy, whether just for fun, or for showing off, is always wonderful, even if not expensive—particularly jewelry."

Natalie nodded vigorously. "Have you seen his collection of earrings? He has this habit of leaving them on the sink."

"Oh I know!"

"And I'm always scared to death I'm going to knock one into the damned drain!"

"You know the little ruby one?" asked Rebecca. "That's my favorite."

"I love that one!" exclaimed Natalie. "I admit to larcenous impulses whenever I see it!"

Rebecca let out a peal of laughter, in which Natalie joined.

But their laughter was short-lived, as remembrance of the way things were replaced the image of the way things might have been.

Natalie stood up and reached for her coat. "Thanks for telling me all this."

Rebecca stood up too. "Is he really in hot water?"

"Scalding. And—it could get worse. I'm not sure if the police have picked up on all the ramifications, but it's only a matter of time."

Rebecca opened the door. "I'll never believe he had anything to do with it."

Natalie looked at her gratefully. "Have you spoken with him since he left?"

Rebecca shook her head, then gave Natalie a wistful glance. "I still miss him, you know. But what can I do? I can't change him. And I can't take him like that."

Natalie stepped onto the front stoop. "He says he's changed."

"Then why did all this happen?" asked Rebecca. "If he had changed that would mean he would be able to avoid being dragged into situations like this. In a way, this is just like the robbery. You said before that it takes a Rose Dow—someone used to getting away with murder—to try and set a trap like this. Well, it also takes a Daniel—someone willing to be used—to get caught in it. And since he's let himself get shafted again, it means he hasn't changed." Rebecca shook her head, regret etched on her face like scrollwork.

Natalie left her standing in the brightness of the doorway, and turned to the dark street, heading for the only place left to go.

Chapter Twelve

Natalie arrived home shortly after eight p.m. to find Trick meowing for his supper. The apartment was otherwise silent, and she was in no mood to disturb the stillness with TV, FM, or CD. She felt herself being dragged back into a life of alternating fear and anger, and wanted only to dig in her heels and stop the slide. She dumped her coat on a chair and walked to the back of the apartment, stepping over Trick, who had thrown himself onto the floor directly in her path.

In the kitchenette she found signs of hasty departure. A brown paper grocery bag sat on the counter, a damp spot darkening its lower reaches, a can of black olives beside it. Natalie peeked inside the bag. It was full of assorted goodies: green grapes, fresh spring rolls, Earl Grey tea. She identified a squishy carton of raspberry sherbet as the cause of the dampness.

Under the can of olives was a scribbled note: "Hi. The police have arrived to take me in for further questioning. Don't worry, okay? There's a box of cat food in the bag—we were out. I'll call Evan's office if I run into trouble. Sorry. D."

Trick threw himself bodily at her legs with enough force to make her knees buckle.

"Just a minute!" she snapped. Then she sighed and rooted in the bag for the cat food, pulling it out from beneath the sherbet. Glued to the box by pink froth was a sticky register tape. As she peeled it off, blue ink stained her fingers. She looked at the slip of paper with distaste, and her eyes focused on the total: $32.71.

"Maaaannnnng!" said Trick.

"Jeez, cat, you're worse than having a kid!" Natalie aggressively popped open the box with her thumb and filled the cat dish to the top. Then, having no appetite for food, she put away the groceries. She roamed aimlessly into the living room and stood by the picture window with folded arms.

◇◇◇

At 11:05, Natalie, lying on the sofa under a Navajo blanket, heard footsteps on her staircase, and the long-anticipated sound of a key turning softly in the lock. Something deep within her—something existing apart from more complex considerations of right vs. wrong, society vs. family, and honesty vs. falsehood—cried out in blessed relief as Daniel Joday stuck his head into her apartment. She wanted to leap up and throw her arms around him and tell him how much she loved him and how outraged she was at what was happening. But—

"Hi," was what she said.

"Hi," was what he answered, and came inside.

Daniel appeared no more altered by the day's events than by his recent night at the courthouse. His chalk-gray trousers and dark-green shirt were neat and fresh, his broad shoulders were square, his hair was soft and gleaming, his face showed neither pallor nor flush. Yet as he passed through the living room and into the kitchenette, Natalie looked for her brother behind his unruffled facade and could not find him. A barrier she had thought long-dismantled had been reconstructed, and he had taken refuge on the far side.

To her mind came unbidden a picture from a distant past—a clear cold winter's day, and the Big Hill at White Beeches. She heard the swoosh of well-waxed iron runners skipping over hard-packed snow; she felt the bite of a wind that numbed her thin cheeks and brought icy tears to her eyes; she heard her own high-pitched little-girl voice calling above the wind, "Hold on tight!" as they approached the Big Bump; she felt her brother's skinny little-boy arms tighten dutifully around her waist, and his chin dig into her shoulder for extra purchase. A sudden wrenching, and then they were sailing, flying through the air, defying gravity. Then came the jolt, the shock, the wobble—they had made it! They danced in the drifts like snow-sprites, shrieking with joy, and then raced back up the hill to have another go, and another, and another, all afternoon long, and then home for hot chocolate.

Daniel returned from the kitchen with a root beer, and sank down into the green armchair. He drank deeply, as if he had not a care in the world, as if he were not sitting on a time bomb. Natalie watched him in silence, willing him to speak.

"This is very good for a generic brand." He rubbed his thumb across the beads of condensation. He looked at Natalie. "You want one?"

"Sure." She spoke lightly, but her heart sank. This was not what she wanted. This was not what he had said he wanted. It was as if they were teenagers again, reprising old roles that neither had ever asked to play. Natalie realized, with a sudden clutch of fear, that she did not know what to do.

He got up and fetched another can, brought it to her, and resettled himself. The silence grew oppressive.

At length Daniel sighed a let's-get-this-over-with sigh, and arched his eyebrows. "They decided not to arrest, but they're not very happy with me."

"They don't like being lied to."

"I didn't exactly lie to them." Daniel lowered his eyebrows and tilted his head. "They never asked me if I'd seen Rose. It may be a technical point, but not mentioning something nobody asks you about is not the same as an outright lie." He looked away. "Of course, they drew their own conclusion about what she was doing there. Not that they care about anybody's morals. They just want to know where she was."

He looked at her. "You think I've let you down."

"Me?" Natalie moved her head backwards retorted in surprise. "This has nothing to do with me."

"Oh, come on," said Daniel skeptically, "I know you better than that. First you think I shouldn't have let Rose into Rebecca's house, and then you think if I did let her in I should have told everybody about it way before now. Look. My encounter with that…creature…was something I thought I'd never have to mention to anyone. Is it so terrible to want to avoid being humiliated when you haven't done anything wrong?" His expression soured. "Not that anyone would believe me anyway."

"Oh, come on," said Natalie, skeptical in her turn.

"I mean it! You get this 'Oh, Danny' look in your eyes that makes me feel about two feet tall." He glanced at her warily. "It's there right now." He turned away.

"If it is, it has nothing to do with Rose!" countered Natalie. Then she calmed herself, unwilling to let her emotions get out of hand, wanting to think clearly. "Daniel, I do not give a damn what happened between you and Rose, and I have no difficulty in believing that she was up to no good. Further, the police 'conclusion' is not necessarily what you assume it is."

She put it as clearly as she could: "Look. For the record, I want you to know that I think you are perfectly capable of running your own life. What happened between you and Rose, whatever it was, is none of my business, and under ordinary circumstances no one would care whether you wanted to talk about it or not. I'm truly sorry for you that it's come out into the open like this. But it has, and we've got to look as objectively as possible at what this means to—"

"You should hear yourself!" Daniel leaned way forward, his arms tight against his breast. "You are so in control—so rational! You always are. Don't you get it by now that I don't work that way? I'm not as good at 'running' my life as you are at 'running' yours, Nat! I can't keep up with you—you're a hell of a pace setter, and I don't stand a chance. But you never seem to notice when I'm falling behind. You make it sound so easy: define the problem, identify a solution, implement the plan. But what if I can't do that? What if I can't see it in black and white the way you do? What if the pressure of trying to live up to what you want me to be makes me want to quit trying?"

Natalie felt the sting. "What *I* want *you* to be?"

"Yeah." Daniel leaned back and took a sip of root beer. "Maybe it would help if you could ease off on the idea that in spite of all the rotten things I've done, I'm really this wonderful guy, and bound to achieve greatness now that I've got my head screwed on straight. Don't you see it just adds to the pressure, and makes me realize how ridiculously far I still have to go?"

"Wait a minute." Natalie was affronted. "You know damn well you go out of your way to make me think you're a wonderful guy!"

"What? What are you talking about!"

"I'm talking about being the world's most perfect guest! I'm talking about the way you do all the housework and carry out negotiations with the trash collectors. And of course there's the daily barrage of Tin Roof Sundaes, apple Danish, blueberry pancakes, and God knows what all else at a volume that would normally do me for a year! What am I supposed to think but *What a wonderful guy*?"

Daniel's voice was distant. "Did you ever think that maybe I do all that because I know you expect it, and I'm trying to please you?"

"Sorry, that one's too complex for me." Natalie's eyes flashed. "I figure people generally do pretty much what they want—if they're lucky enough to have a choice. Even if it involves spending every last dime they have on frivolities."

"You're welcome," said Daniel.

Natalie slammed her untasted root beer on the coffee table with a thud. The air was heavy with their silence, but this time Natalie knew there was no point in waiting for Daniel to break it. "Tch. Well, here we are again."

Daniel stared at his hands. "Maybe we never left."

"I refuse to accept that."

"Then what are we supposed to do?" burst out Daniel. His voice grew more quiet. "What am I supposed to do?"

Natalie's eyes narrowed. "Damn, it, do what you want—the same as everybody else. But would you please try and realize that at the moment all you are doing is increasing suspicion against yourself."

"So what else is new?"

"Is that what you want?"

"No!"

"Then try something different! Before it's too late."

"How?" he asked, in a voice that defied answer.

Natalie set her jaw. "Don't lie to the police."

Daniel tried to brush it away. "I thought we agreed I hadn't lied."

"No." Natalie's voice was tight. "I'm not referring to the fact of your meeting with Rose. I'm referring to something else, which the police haven't noticed—yet. The hole in your story."

Daniel's face was a mask. "What are you talking about?" he chided.

Natalie looked downward. "I was hoping you'd tell me."

"How can I when I don't know what you're referring to?"

"Fine. We'll do it your way." Natalie swallowed hard. "You told the police that Rose appeared unexpectedly at Rebecca's house, right?"

"Right. I told you, I had no idea she was coming, I—"

"How did she find you, Daniel?" Natalie looked up at him, her eyes boring into his. "How did she know where you lived? Neither the address nor the phone number was in your name, and you never gave them out. You asked me not to give them out, and I didn't. Sarah didn't know where you were or what your phone number was—that's why she called me in the first place. You told Ginny and me the other night how relieved you were that none of the Dows knew where you lived, or what your phone number was, or where you worked. So if you didn't invite Rose, or tell her where you were living, how did she find you?"

Daniel moved his lips, but nothing came out.

"I tried to think of an innocent explanation," continued Natalie relentlessly. "But I couldn't. So all I know for sure is that there's more to it than either you or Rose are telling, even now. Well, as I said it doesn't matter what I think. But the police—if they, that is *when* they, figure out that you're *still* covering up, they'll have every reason to assume that it must be something major—they'll assume you're covering up a murder."

Daniel's face flushed, the mask broke, and he stared at her aghast. "Wait a minute!" His voice was raspy. "You think—you think I did it!"

Natalie made her hands into fists and slammed them on her knees. "That's not what I said!"

"Jesus Christ!" said Daniel. "But you think I *might* have done it; you think I *could* have done it!"

"Danny!"

"You really don't know me at all—you really don't!" He sprang up from the chair. "You think I'm capable of doing something so utterly—"

"Great! Just great!" Natalie, caught between her pain and anger, was on her feet too. "Five minutes ago I am a dough-brained big sister who thinks Little Danny can do no wrong! Now I don't trust you blindly enough to realize you couldn't possibly do the murder! Terrific! Which is it? Shit! I can't win, can I?"

Their eyes met and for a split second Daniel wavered, and she saw it and held her breath. Then he lowered his glance and turned away.

"That's your problem, Nat," he said woodenly. "You're always trying to win, and I'm just trying to keep ahead of the jackals. I'm surprised you didn't point out the oversight to the cops—that would have been more characteristic."

Natalie's eyes were steel. "You pig-headed idiot."

Daniel shrugged. "No matter what anybody thinks, I know I didn't do it and that's what matters. It's my life, as you keep telling me. So I'll do what I want, as you advise. I don't owe you—or anybody else—anything."

"Say it a little louder. I'm not sure you've convinced yourself." She placed her hands on her hips and held her chin high.

"I gotta get out of here."

"Do what you want." She threw up her hands. "I have my own life to lead. You taught me that, long ago."

Did he hesitate for just a moment before walking away—to see if she had more to say? But she made no move, no sound.

He moved quickly around the room. He grabbed an extra sweater from his duffel bag, retrieved his coat, opened the door, and disappeared into the night.

In the sudden silence, Natalie could hear the pounding of her heart. It was like the ticking of the bomb her brother carried with him as he walked through the darkened streets. She tried to breathe, but the air seemed to catch painfully in her throat. She tried to collect her thoughts—she needed to be able to think clearly, now more than ever. But she could not think. She could not even guess. Instead, her mind turned unbidden to a picture of delicious cold clean snow during a White Beeches winter day long ago; she heard the shouts of children playing; she felt her feet fighting to control the direction of the sled against the chattering of the runners on the icy patch. She heard herself whispering, "Hold on tight!" and she heard her brother's voice answering in childish protest, "I'm holding on as tight as I can!" as he tightened his arms around her.

Chapter Thirteen

Natalie put in a restless night filled with disjointed dreams through which she wandered in ceaseless anxiety, surrounded by ever-changing faces that brought her no comfort. After a solitary breakfast, she made her long-delayed call to Ginny Chau. The exchange of information that two days before had seemed so beneficial was now a distasteful obligation she had to force herself to fulfill.

"Ginny Chau."

"It's Natalie."

"Natalie! Thank God you've called. I was getting worried. We heard they picked up Daniel yesterday. Is he okay?"

"No. Have you been filled in on the details?"

"Some. The stepmother, right? Well, now we know why Daniel warned us off her. I told you that woman was trouble. Just the type who would think that putting the moves on her stepdaughter's good-looking ex would add some zip to her afternoon schedule. We haven't been able to get a lead on what tipped the cops off, though."

"I can tell you that—on background." Natalie related the story of the Bergen Mall receipt hunt.

"It's irrelevant, isn't it?" Ginny sounded skeptical. "Charge card receipts, mysterious rendezvous. This doesn't have anything to do with the case, does it?"

"The police don't seem to think so. They let Daniel go."

"Lucky. What a fool he was not to have told them about it in the first place. I mean it might be embarrassing for him, but this is a murder investigation, which is no time to prevaricate. You'd think he of all people could have worked that one out."

"You'd think," said Natalie. Ginny had such a way with words.

"Silence only makes him look guilty of something worse," continued Ginny. "And it's not like the cops are out to get him. Sergeant Allan plays fair."

"Is he married?"

"Who?"

Natalie's diction was immaculate. "Sergeant Allan."

"Um...." Ginny's internal hard drive emitted an almost audible whir. "I'll find out." She put Natalie on hold for no more than thirty seconds and then was back. "I'll have that for you in a couple of minutes. Listen, let me fill you in on the latest with the father."

Natalie poured her second cup of coffee and went to the sofa with her notebook. She flipped it open to Eric's page.

"We've finally got a line on this import business he runs." Ginny grew confidential. "Orlando—do you know Orlando? My leg man? He's a genius—well, either that or he's psychic. He's been checking out the father's import store—*Asia Fantasia*—in Westwood. Anyway, he found out that the shop may be selling exotica from the Far East all right, but its financial setup is strictly backyard. Dow doesn't seem to have a single legitimate international connection. He only handles small batches—shipments is too strong a word—of goods brought into the country as regular luggage, either by himself, by world travelers looking to cover their expenses, or by enterprising foreign nationals. Strictly penny ante. Most of the stuff in the shop's been there for years...not that it's not nice stuff—showy. But that's just it—it makes him look like an international businessman, when he doesn't even have an import license. The turnover is minimal. He has no employees other than a clerk in the shop. The Malaysian national who currently works for him is an industrious young woman who came as a student to do pre-med and is quietly overextending her visa for a few months to squirrel away some extra cash."

"Sounds like a cover for something."

"I'll say. Orlando is checking out a possible drug connection. That's the most likely explanation, don't you think?"

"Why? We haven't heard a hint about drugs from anybody. Actually, I was thinking of something closer to home. I can just see Eric keeping up appearances with a fancy import store that never makes a dime—but which provides a handy cover to travel anywhere he wants to go—just to hide the fact he's been living off his daughter for the past twelve years."

"But would he do away with said daughter just to continue to hide that fact?" Ginny sounded like she didn't buy it. "That's the point. And if he did it—when did he do it? Apparently, he was telling the truth about his times—his alibi is pretty tight up to the six-thirty deadline. No way he could have had the time to do it—unless you think he did it when Sarah was right there in the house."

Natalie choked on her coffee in her haste to speak. "Wait a minute! We set six-thirty as the latest for the murder because we agreed that Lydia would have called if she were going to be late for dinner, right? Well, what if she did call to say she'd be late—what if she called when Sarah was in the shower, and what if Eric answered the phone! He could take the message that she was going to be late—say, after eight—but not pass it on! He was alone in the house from seven-thirty to midnight. If Lydia came home between those hours he could shoot her, hide the body and the car—and have a good alibi!"

"Of course!" said Ginny eagerly. "We'll have to completely rethink this, allowing for the idea that somebody might have taken a call from Lydia. Just a sec." Ginny's voice was replaced by a Chopin etude, and Natalie looked out the window at the dark gray clouds rolling slowly in from the east.

The music ended abruptly on an unresolved chord. "Natalie? No, never married. Twenty-eight years old. Graduated Rutgers 1987—Summa Cum Laude. Lives at 19 Woodfield Road in

Washington Township, with his parents. Phone number 555-3874. First name, Geoffrey."

"Thanks."

"Any service. You'll fill me in if anything breaks, won't you?"

"Of course." Natalie made it sound as light as she could.

"I'm sure it'll work out okay—about Daniel, I mean."

"To hell with Daniel," said Natalie. As she hung up a gust of wind came up from nowhere and the shutters rattled against the outside wall.

>>>

Several hours later Natalie picked up her cat and cuddled him in her arms. "This day is going to be endless, Trick." She had tried to work at her computer, but could do no justice to her simple tales of the community in which she had been born and bred. So she had given up, unwilling to do work she knew would have to be redone, and not by nature a masochist. The sight of Daniel's textbooks gathering dust on the credenza distressed her, but she had not been able to bring herself to dump them somewhere out of sight.

Trick purred for a while and then squirmed to get down. Natalie, dressed in jeans and an I Love New Jersey sweatshirt, moved restlessly from one room of her tiny apartment to another. This inactivity was alien to her nature. Half a dozen times she felt the urge to phone someone—anyone, but she never got farther than an outstretched hand, immediately withdrawn. She did not want to risk being drawn into discussion of the latest developments in the murder. She had no stomach for speculation about what Daniel and Rose had been doing the afternoon of the murder. Ginny's easy assumption—or had it been reassurance—that Rose, attracted to Daniel as wasps are to wine, had sought him out for casual sex, was not convincing, because it did not answer the key question of how Rose had been able to find him. Natalie wanted nothing more than to discover what had been going on—but how could she ask a single question without giving it away that Daniel was still keeping something back? It seemed to Natalie that, like the low clouds gathering outside her window, events were coming to a head impelled by forces beyond her control; all that was needed—for the patient and the impatient alike—was to wait for the storm to break.

And yet the urge to reach for the phone remained, because much as she did not want to discuss the case, she did want to talk about what was happening to *her*. The memory of her fight with Daniel raced through her mind like a toy train on a circular track. The encounter had frightened her with its unexpectedness, and with its familiarity too. As violent storms churn up the earth, it had uncovered and revivified the fossil record of the worst years of their relationship, which she had thought long dead and gone.

But what could she do if Daniel was determined to hold back the truth? And yet, knowing the pitfalls of old, why had she been unable to keep herself from ending up in this helpless situation? She couldn't get a grip on it. She needed to talk with someone; someone who had a sense of proportion; someone who had done their growing up and wasn't afraid to discuss the facts. But she had always been such a loner, despite her outward sociability and hard-won status as upstanding member of the community; she had always kept her family problems to herself, bottled in a volatile compound of fear and shame marked Do Not Open.

She leapt from the sofa in frustration. She really must try and keep busy. There was but little, she acknowledged sarcastically, to be done in the way of straightening the apartment. It was with a sense of relief that she hit upon the unoriginal idea of fixing something for lunch so that she might have the mindless pleasure of cleaning up afterward. But when the last dish was put away, inspiration failed, and she collapsed on the sofa and succumbed to fretful worry.

⋄⋄⋄

It was two-fifteen in the afternoon when Natalie heard footsteps on the stairs. She swung her legs off of the sofa, sitting upright—the same position she had been in the night before when Daniel had come home. This time, it would be different, she told herself. But instead of a quiet scraping of a key in the lock, the doorbell rang.

Natalie got up and advanced to the front door. As was her egocentric habit, she guessed to herself who it might be. Sarah, perhaps, or the sergeant? Her heart leaped; if it was the sergeant, come himself in fulfillment of their agreement, he would not be bringing good news. She opened the door and found herself zero for two.

Rose Dow stood in the entryway, her tense hands clutching a white patent leather purse, exuding an aura of tragedy and eau du coconut.

The sight of her cleared and invigorated Natalie's mind like the rush of a cold, strong wind. She had never felt more sure of herself than when she ushered Rose silently into her scrupulously tidy living room.

As Rose walked past her, Natalie regarded her with detachment. She wondered if it were vocation or avocation that led to Rose's habit of appearing unexpectedly on doorsteps. Well, this time, whatever her game—and Natalie was quite certain she was playing one—she was in for a surprise.

Rose was the picture of an overwrought woman heroically clinging to courage. Her powder-puff hair had an over-teased look and her pink lipstick was smudged on her parted lips. Fear glinted in her eyes and she teetered unsteadily on old-fashioned high heels. It suddenly struck Natalie, whose lower income bracket had not prevented her from finding a first-class hairdresser, and who had read the surgeon general's report on knee and leg damage resulting from the wearing of any heel higher than an inch, that this caricature of feminine middle-age was barely forty. Why on earth did Rose go out of her way to look and act older than she was? The better to match her stodgy older husband? The better to fit the part of wicked stepmother? The better to gain the confidence of the unsuspecting? Those little-old-lady blue eyes, well-schooled in ignorance—The better to see you with, my dear! Natalie pressed her lips tightly together. In her life she had known many fakers and cheats, but they had tended to be distinguished by lack of money and seediness of lifestyle. It had never before occurred to her that the upper classes she had so uncritically envied might contain their fair share of con artists, distinguished from their less well-off counterparts only by ratio of success.

"Natalie." There was a quiver in Rose's tight little voice. "Forgive me for bursting in on you, but I didn't know which way to turn! I think the police are following me. That's why I thought of you. You're so intelligent. And you have so much experience dealing with the police." She blinked her pleading eyes. "I admit, I've been taken care of all my life. I'm not used to making decisions. Especially when it means I might get someone else in trouble. But I can't go to Eric about this!" She hid her face in her hands, her shoulders shaking.

Natalie, alert to the subtext of her performance, said nothing.

Conquering her emotions, Rose flung her hands to her sides and stood tall in a show of bravery. "I'm sorry to break down like this. May I have a drink of water?"

Natalie's eyes were wary slits. The room was filled with her personal property—not to mention all of Daniel's belongings—in plain view and easily accessible. In her youth, Natalie had once picked her father's room clean in less than a minute using a similar ploy. What possible use Rose might have for pocketing something Natalie did not speculate, but she wasn't going to give her any opportunities.

"Sure, Rose," she said obligingly. "But you must sit down, you look…upset." She steered Rose into the green armchair—the only one visible from the kitchenette—and waited until she sat. She kept on talking as she went for the water, looked back over her left shoulder and kept her eyes on Rose.

"Yes, it's just *awful*, isn't it," she said fatuously. "What I wonder is, how much longer can this go on? I mean, the strain is just…*awful*, isn't it, Rose? Ice?"

"Please don't trouble, my dear." Rose's eyes traveled quickly around the room, but she stayed put. "What were you saying? Oh, yes. You're right, of course. It can't go on much longer. I mean—" She paused dramatically as Natalie reentered the living room with the glass of water. "*I* can't go on any longer!" She put her hand to her throat.

"My goodness, Rose, what are you saying?" Natalie handed her the glass. Her gray eyes, hard and narrow, met Rose's blue ones, soft and wide.

Rose wrinkled her brow and took a deep breath. "It's about—why are you making me say it when you know? It's about—Daniel!"

"Do tell."

"You're angry with me." Rose ducked her head so that her narrow chin touched her lime-green coat. "I can't blame you, knowing what you must think. And at my age."

Natalie sat down on the sofa. "Please don't think I'm one of those self-righteous types who will hold that against you, Rose. I like younger men myself."

Rose winced. "You have a right to be sarcastic. I did a terrible thing; I betrayed your brother! I told the police that Daniel and I were together for a personal, private, reason." She turned her head to one side and stared at the floor. "But I have to tell you the truth—it wasn't what you think, between me and Daniel! You mustn't be angry with your poor brother. Nothing, nothing at all happened! You've got to believe me!"

Her protestations were delivered with an absence of sincerity that served to solidify the impression she was lying, which Natalie found quite intriguing since she was quite certain that Rose was—for once—telling the truth.

How could anyone, least of all her brother, well-schooled in deception, have failed to recognize such calumny at its earliest appearance? It leapt to Natalie's mind that something must have been preoccupying her brother's thought processes. But later would do for that analysis. For the moment, she evinced no reaction, determined to force Rose to continue without any indication of audience reaction.

Rose took a sip of water. "Sometimes—I'm sorry to say this to his sister, but I want you to know everything—sometimes

I think it would have been better if something had happened. At least that would have been explainable—even though my husband would have killed me." Her tone had changed. She was talking to a confidante now, telling secrets too-long hidden. "Eric is so suspicious—and really a violent man. I understand now why his first wife left him. I know he's looking for something to get on me. He watches me all the time. Listens to my phone conversations. I think he's having me followed."

Natalie raised her eyebrows quizzically.

Rose gave a definite nod. "You're not married, my dear, so maybe you don't understand how simpatico two people can be. He's my husband. He knows when something's wrong, and of course he's so jealous. He knows I've been keeping something from him. At first he thought there was something between Graham and me. I've had to ask Graham to leave the guest house as soon as possible—and it isn't fair, because he's such a pussy cat, really. I thought that would satisfy Eric. But it hasn't, and now with this story about Daniel, it's happening all over again—only worse. My first marriage was a nightmare, and I always swore I'd never get involved with anything like that again—the suspicion, the fights, the pain. But we always repeat our mistakes, don't we? There's no escape." She took another sip of water.

Natalie, in a throwback to her career as a theatrical reviewer, noted that Rose had set the scene nicely. "What's your point, Rose?"

"I'm sorry." Rose took another quavering breath. "I'm rambling, aren't I? This is hard for me. I'm not very good at keeping secrets. I only hope I'll get some relief if I tell someone—when someone else knows."

"I have no doubt you will," said Natalie.

"You give me hope." Rose held her breath a moment for maximum dramatic impact, and then let it rip. "The truth is, I didn't really stay in the house until two o'clock the day Lydia disappeared. I left around one, to do some shopping. I went downtown to Bergenfield first, to pick up a prescription at the pharmacy. That's when I saw Daniel. He—he was inside the

Maverick Diner on Cameron Road in the last booth. He—" her voice caught. "Oh, Natalie, I'm so sorry! He was with Lydia."

Natalie's face was as mask-like as Daniel's had been the night before, when she had told him what he had not wanted to hear. Beneath the mask, her heart and mind reeled from the blow, little sustained by the conceit of having seen it coming.

Rose's face was tearful, anxious, watching. "They were sitting on opposite sides of the table. I—maybe it sounds silly, but—I am—was—her stepmother, and I was concerned." Again she was the old-fashioned mother-protector, claiming her involvement by right. "Frankly, I had been shocked to see Daniel at the house the night before. Eric had told me about their earlier involvement, and about Daniel's history with drugs, and his imprisonment, and I knew he would never have allowed Daniel in the house. Of course, I thought that was too harsh, but in light of what's happened, I can't help wondering if he wasn't right.

"Lydia was a very vulnerable girl. She tended to see in people only what she wanted to see. Daniel was so charming at the party, so at his ease, that I thought there might be something going on between them. When I saw them at the Maverick, I knew it was true. I'm sorry to say this to you, because I know it must hurt you and I don't want to do that, but I was worried for Lydia. She had not been herself, and I was afraid Daniel might have involved her in something that would lead to trouble. I knew I had to protect Lydia somehow. I had to find out what he was up to. I waited for him to come out of the diner, and when he did," she gasped, "I followed him!" She shot a guilty look at Natalie, as if she couldn't believe herself capable of being so underhanded.

Her words gushed faster and faster. "He was walking. I got in my car and kept some distance behind him." Her chest rose and fell in practiced exaggeration, an accomplishment, Natalie noted, guaranteed to impress the opposite sex. "I'll never know how I did it—through all that traffic, and without being spotted. When he got to his house, I parked the car around the corner. I had to wait a while to get up my courage. Then I went and knocked on the door.

"He was surprised to see me, and very nervous. I thought at the time it was me that made him nervous, but later, after Lydia disappeared.... I tried to be straightforward with him. I explained that Eric was still adamant about Lydia having nothing to do with him, and how shocked I had been to see him at the house the previous evening. He was very brusque with me, almost rude. He said there was nothing between him and Lydia anymore, and he had come to our house just to see an old friend—that was his expression: an old friend. He said he had another girlfriend now and that was all there was to it. I told him I hoped he was telling me the truth, and I left."

Rose closed her mouth and allowed herself more composure. She crossed her legs, and her narrow shins lined up in silken parallel beneath her canary yellow skirt.

"Of course, I didn't tell Eric about it. Why would I, when my concern had been to keep him from finding out about Daniel and Lydia? There were more important things to think about, what with poor Lydia's disappearance. And then, when her body was discovered, I honestly thought it was best to keep silent—I didn't want to besmirch her memory." She shook her head sadly, then, as one to whom a thought occurs, raised a finger. "But then I started thinking—why hadn't *Daniel* told the police about his meeting with Lydia? What was *he* trying to hide? Should I speak out? My original reason for not telling didn't exist anymore, since Eric had found out Daniel was at the party.

"And then—yesterday. You know about that. The police were awful. They thought—everybody thought—well, you know what everybody thought. I could hardly bear it, I was so ashamed! But my first instinct was not to make trouble for Daniel. So I told them I went straight to his place when I left my house.

"But—what if the police find out about me being in Bergenfield earlier than I said?" Fear crept into her voice, and worry lines appeared on her white forehead. "Those receipts—it's indecent the way they pry into your personal affairs—but what if they check with my pharmacist, and his records show what time I was in his shop? How can I explain what I was doing without telling them I saw Daniel with Lydia the very day she disappeared!

"It's such a dilemma. *I* have nothing to hide—But if I tell, I just know Daniel will be in serious trouble." She tilted her head from side to side as she spoke, hesitating after each phrase, as if thinking aloud. "Of course, the staff at the Maverick will be able to verify my story. I just don't know what to do. I don't have a *reason* to keep quiet about what I saw."

Her head came to a rest and she looked deeply into Natalie's eyes. "That's why I came to see you, my dear. I'm just sure you'll be able to suggest something, some *reason* for me to keep this from the police. There must be a solution...some...compensation? Don't you think so, Natalie?"

Rose Dow blinked at Natalie, deferring, as she had done at their first meeting, to the younger woman's superior intelligence.

There was a long pause, during which Natalie, with pursed lips, thought it through. The scent of coconut cologne had begun to permeate the apartment.

She stirred in her chair and cleared her throat. "This is such a shock. I hardly know what to say, Rose. It's hard to take it in at once. Now let me see if I understand this. By the way, Rose, how did you find out where I live?"

"Oh!" Rose's cheeks flushed and she lowered her eyes. "Daniel mentioned it."

"I see. That sounds just like Daniel. And one other thing I was just wondering about. You said you followed Daniel home in your car—you know it's over three miles from Bergenfield to Cresskill, Rose. It must have taken quite a while. Why didn't you stop and give him a lift once you were out of town if you wanted to talk with him?"

"I guess I didn't think of that," said Rose earnestly. "I guess I had it in my mind that we needed to talk somewhere very private, where we wouldn't be seen by anyone."

"I see. I thought it was because you didn't want him to know you were following him. Either that or because you wanted to make sure you found out where he lived."

"Oh, no!" Rose was horrified. "I just thought there might be a scene, and I didn't want to it to be out in the street with strangers passing by." She touched the tip of her tongue to her upper lip. "Do you think the police will be *very* upset with Daniel for not telling them about this?" She went on to answer her own question, in case Natalie hadn't worked it out. "I suppose the fact that he has a criminal record works against him, doesn't it, Natalie?"

"I guess it does, Rose," said Natalie. She was suddenly tired of the game. She had heard what she wanted to hear, and it remained only to rid herself of this…creature. "Well, Rose, what's next? I believe you were talking about compensation?"

"Well…" Rose grew suddenly reticent.

"I believe financial compensation is the norm in situations like this—is that what you had in mind?"

"Financial?" Rose look startled, as if it were a completely new concept. "Perhaps that's the answer. You know we really don't have much money of our own now. I just knew you'd think of something, Natalie."

"How much do you want to keep your mouth shut, Rose?"

"Oh! It sounds so sordid when you put it that way," objected Rose. "I hope you don't think that of me, Natalie."

"That's the least of it, Rose. You'd be amazed at the scope of the things I think of you." Natalie's voice seethed. "I don't think I've ever met anyone with quite your appetite for causing pain. I guess it's your way of gaining the upper hand. You started in on me the minute you met me, didn't you, Rose? Sitting there in the dinette plying me with tasteless decaf and conversation about the evils of the criminal element and the leniency of the courts. At the time I thought your choice of topic was accidental, but I realize now you damn-well knew who I was, and who my brother was, and that he'd been in jail, and you brought the subject up intentionally."

"I wasn't thinking!"

Natalie was not interested in her problems. "Now that I know *how*, I know *why* you showed up at Daniel's that day. You went to threaten him with exposure to your husband, didn't you? Just like you're trying to get at me by threatening to expose him to the police. I don't mind sharing with you that I feel almost honored that you're hitting me up for money. I take it as a sign that I'm coming up in the world. But Daniel—Was that wise, Rose? Surely a woman like you—with your many resourceful methods of information gathering—knew he hadn't been as fortunate as I had, and didn't have any money to speak of. Or, was there some other form of 'compensation' you were thinking of getting from him?"

Rose stood up—bounced up—her chin pushed defiantly forward, her expression one of wounded pride. "I can't believe you would speak to me like this. I thought you would see I was trying to help you!"

"Oh, come off it, Rose," said Natalie with a bored air. "Why on earth didn't you tell the whole story to the police yesterday if it wasn't that you were still hoping to make capital out of it?"

"You're forcing me to make a choice I don't want to make. How can you do this to your brother? Don't you care for him at all?"

"Go away, Rose. Go home to your husband." Natalie stood up and moved to the door.

"I'm not going home!" Rose stood up defiantly. "I'm going straight to the police. I did my best, but you—you're inhuman! I thought you would want to protect your brother. I gave you your chance. Now I'm going to tell the police everything!"

Natalie, one hand on the doorknob, turned around. Rose was standing several feet away, waiting—waiting for Natalie to climb down, waiting for Natalie to come to terms, waiting for Natalie to give in to the inevitable.

Natalie wrenched at the knob with her right hand, and gestured to the open door with her left.

"Go right ahead," she said forcefully, and demons fled from her in droves.

Rose, head held high, whisked out the door without giving Natalie a glance. She went down the steep stairs in her high heels, clutching at the cedar handrail. She stood by her car and fumbled for her keys. Only when she had the car door open did she look back. Her face was twisted with anger, pinched by selfishness, and her eyes were filled with hate. Then she slipped into the car and drove away.

Natalie, possessed of what she had most wanted to know, went straight to work. She sat at the dining room table with her notebook, jotting down an account of Rose's visitation, writing until the notebook was full. Then she got a new notebook, and with only a moment's hesitation, wrote across the top of the first page *The Case Against Daniel.* Below that, to the left, she wrote, *Timetable*, and then *8:00 a.m. - BCC class.* She worked for an hour, flipping through her notes again and again. When she was done, she stared at the page for several minutes. Then, with a deep sigh, she stood up, and walked over to the picture window.

Despite the cold, she opened the window an inch to purge the last of the coconut scent from the air. An icy blast whistled through the crack and sent shivers up her arms. The rain had begun to fall.

◇◇◇

At four p.m., Natalie gritted her teeth and called the Dow residence. She was relieved when Sarah—a withdrawn, belligerent Sarah—picked up the phone. When she asked what was wrong, Sarah informed her in a sullen voice that Rose was at the courthouse. Again.

"Eric took her down to Hackensack with some lawyer he dug up. I don't know the details, but Eric says she was still hiding something. He told her she had to come forward now rather than wait for the police to worm it out of her."

"That sounds reasonable," said Natalie, quite truthfully.

"We've postponed the funeral again."

"Oh, I'm sorry."

"Don't be. I'm getting used to it. And there are compensations. With everybody out of the house all the time I'm getting a chance to hear myself think. She's dead; I know it; I hate it; I can't change it." She took a deep breath. "I just need time—and closure. By the way, I talked to Mr. Sherill about the will."

"Oh, I'm sorry I didn't—"

"Never mind." For the second time, Sarah was uncharacteristically curt with her. "It was a dumb idea to involve you. I had to tell Mr. Sherill to hold off for a while anyway. When I told Harry what I was planning, he point blank refused. In fact, he found the idea highly offensive. Well, pardon me. So I'm dropping the whole thing. What's happening with you?" Her tone changed. "How's Daniel?"

"I'm okay. Look, there's something that's bugging me that I wanted to ask your help on."

"You don't give up, do you?"

"Do you want me to?"

"No. Ask."

"Everyone except me knew Lydia. And I get a different picture of her from everyone I talk with. Honestly, Sarah, sometimes things begin to make some sense—but Lydia doesn't seem to fit in anywhere. I'm asking myself, what was going on in her life that made somebody want to kill her? We must have missed something. I'd like to try and get a handle on her. For myself. I'm sure the police have already checked this, but…did she keep a diary or anything? Scrapbooks? A journal? People reveal a lot when they write, whether they mean to or not, and I'm used to dealing with the written word."

"No. The police asked, and I looked everywhere, but, no."

"Okay. But, you told me once you had received a letter from her. It must have been while you were at college. Were there letters?"

"Letters? Yeah, she wrote a few. But the police searched her room. Oh, they would be in my room, wouldn't they? I've got them somewhere."

"Would you mind very much if I took a look at them?"

"I'm past caring about a little thing like that."

"Thanks. Maybe I can come pick them up? Is the coast clear?"

"Positively barren."

"I'm on my way."

❯❯❯

The rain had settled down to a chill and steady drizzle—heavy enough to need windshield wipers, but not enough to allow those wipers to glide smoothly across the glass. The resultant squeaking would have been annoying in much less harrowing circumstances.

Natalie, with the story of Daniel and Lydia's meeting foremost in her mind, took an extensive detour through downtown Bergenfield. She headed for the southwest side of town, and cruised the Maverick Diner four times, peering in the windows as well as she could from the car. She saw nothing of note. There was no pharmacy anywhere nearby.

She was crossing West View Drive for the fourth and last time when her eye caught sight of a familiar figure standing on the sidewalk in the rain. He was coming out of a narrow yellow brick building, which housed *Ageless*, the New Age used-book store on the ground floor, and Fairlawn Research, Inc., dealers in rats and mice for scientific research, on the top two. It was Graham, carrying a large black umbrella and wearing a tan cap and hound's tooth trench coat. Natalie drove past him, pulled into a gas station, swung around the pumps, and inched back out onto the street. She was crawling along about fifty yards behind him when Graham came abreast of the Maverick. He stopped and stretched to his full height to peer into the side window.

"Well, well," said Natalie to herself, "my fellow sleuth hot on the trail again. I wonder where he gets his information." She passed by him when his back was turned, and sped away.

❯❯❯

"I found those letters," said Sarah as she met Natalie at the door. She held them out—half a dozen sky-blue envelopes addressed in black ink with a wide-point calligraphy pen. Natalie took them and put them in her shoulder bag.

Sarah had not invited her in, but Natalie had another item on her agenda. "I need to talk to you, Sarah."

Sarah acquiesced and they sat down in the living room. The house seemed unnaturally empty, echoing the drumming of the rain and the buffeting of the wind.

Natalie spoke without preface. "Rose came by to see me earlier today. She saw Daniel with Lydia in Bergenfield on February 8th. She said she would tell the police if I didn't make it worth her while not to."

Sarah's eyes widened, her pupils expanding and then contracting like a cat that spots a sudden movement. "That's blackmail."

"Right. I don't know how much of what she told me was the truth and how much of it was self-serving nonsense. But I'm sure the salient point is true."

Sarah slumped back in her chair and pushed her hair behind her ears. "Did she overhear their conversation?"

"She says not. Says."

"I didn't think she could be so—What does Daniel say?"

"Daniel took off last night. I have no idea where he is." Their eyes met, and Natalie knew that no further explanations were needed.

Sarah stood up abruptly. "Let me make you a cup of tea. It's freezing outside, and you're all wet."

Natalie put a hand to her forehead and found it moist and hot. "I guess I could use something."

They went to the kitchen, and Sarah set the kettle on a back burner. "It might not be true, Natalie, about Daniel being with Lydia. If Rose would try to blackmail you, she must be capable of anything."

The two women looked at each other again.

"She might be trying to throw suspicion on Daniel," continued Sarah, "just to protect herself."

"No," said Natalie. "I'm sure the meeting took place. She went out of her way to tell me there were unimpeachable witnesses. People like Rose don't mess with the basic facts. They color and camouflage them to make them appear to support their personal interpretation, but they don't change them. Besides—well, there are other things that don't add up. Listen, you know when you stopped by the other night? How did you get my address?"

"From Lydia's address book. She kept it by her phone—the same place I got your phone number. I had a vague idea where you lived—I went by your house a couple of times with Daniel and Lydia. But I couldn't exactly remember."

"Where's Lydia's address book now?"

"With the police. I copied the address and phone number into my own address book back in February.

"Where's your address book?"

"In my room. Why?"

"Because my address is not included in my phone-book listing."

"I see," said Sarah. "Maybe I'd better think about getting a lock on my door." She turned away and opened a cabinet.

Natalie went to the dinette to look at the theatrical programs on the shelf above the picture window. They were arranged in chronological order. Some of the programs were old and faded: *Hello, Dolly*, and, even older, *Twelve Angry Men*—Daniel had been in that as a high school freshman. She leafed through some of the more recent programs. The last one on the shelf was *The Children's Hour*.

As Sarah appeared in the dinette, there was a tap on the door. The two women looked up to see Harry's face at the window. Sarah frowned as she put Natalie's tea on the table, then went and unlocked the dinette door. Harry entered hurriedly, shedding his raincoat and giving Sarah a quick kiss on the cheek. Natalie noticed he barely made contact.

"Hi," he said huskily. "Glad you're here, Natalie. I hate to think of Sarah being in this big house alone." Sarah, behind him, rolled her eyes and went back into the kitchen.

"The roads are terrible," Harry continued. "I'm afraid they'll ice over tonight if the temperature drops any more." His face was pasty white, and his eyes puffy from lack of sleep. He glanced around at Sarah, rummaging in the kitchen cabinet for another teacup, then leaned over to Natalie and spoke in a whisper. "Eric called me. He and Rose are at the DA's office, and he thought I'd better come over and sit with Sarah. What's it all about?"

Natalie shrugged, and turned her attention to *The Children's Hour* program.

Sarah returned. "We're out of Summer Lemon, Harry. What do you want, Herbal Festival or Apple Autumn?"

"Anything, it doesn't matter."

"Well then, choose one!"

"You choose one, it doesn't matter!"

Natalie frowned at a page in the program. "I thought Lydia wasn't involved in *The Children's Hour*."

"She wasn't," said Sarah.

"Her name's listed as a member of the production staff."

"Ask Harry, he does the programs." She approached him with both hands behind her back. "Pick a hand."

"Left," he said absently.

"Well?" asked Natalie. "Did she help with the show?"

"Apple Autumn." Sarah turned and went back into the kitchen.

"Uh, yeah," said Harry, struggling to concentrate. "Early on she did some stuff."

"No, she didn't," sang out Sarah.

"Before you came back from college!" said Harry in exasperation. "Then when you came back she dropped out."

Sarah appeared with Harry's tea, and thumped it down in front of him. Hot water slopped over the lip of the cup, running down the side and onto the table.

The atmosphere was chilly in the extreme. As far as Natalie could see, the battle lines had been drawn: Sarah had refused to leave her home, so Harry had come to protect her from harm; Sarah didn't want to be protected, she only wanted to be alone, but Harry thought it was his responsibility to keep her company.

The phone rang and Sarah fled to the hall.

Harry looked helplessly at Natalie, dropping the facade of confidence he had assumed for Sarah's sake.

"I don't know what to do."

"About what?" Natalie spoke rather querulously. He was starting to sound like her brother.

This thought brought her up short. She had not before noticed the similarity between Harry and Daniel that Sarah had spoken of. To be sure, they were both appealing, considerate men of the sort that are deemed sensitive and nonthreatening to women. But! Harry's life was focused and stable where Daniel's was adrift at sea, Harry was financially secure where Daniel was broke, an upstanding citizen where Daniel was.... Natalie shivered as insight came to her. Perhaps it was not Harry's positive characteristics that had led Sarah to make her comparison.

"About everything!" A touch of panic cracked Harry's voice. "About Lydia! About me and Sarah! What am I supposed to do?"

Natalie remained silent in the face of Harry's appeal. Daniel had not appreciated her answer to that question, and she had no reason to suspect that Harry would either. She was of an age, she suddenly felt, when she should be able to identify a rhetorical question when she heard it.

Sarah reentered with an emotionless face and sat down at the table.

"That was Eric. Rose has been arrested for impeding the investigation. He's on his way home. Alone."

"That's my cue." Natalie rose. "Call if you need anything."

"We'll be fine." Harry's confidence seemed to come from nowhere. "Everything's going to be just fine."

"Right," said Sarah sarcastically. "You see? I don't have a thing to worry about with Harry here to take care of me."

Natalie looked at a Sarah she had never seen before. *People do change*, she thought, *not because they want to but because change is forced upon them.* She turned up the collar of her coat and disappeared out into the rain.

Chapter Fourteen

Daniel Joday curled his fingers around the chain-link fence. He peered through the diamond-shaped openings at the blue water of the Oradell Reservoir, watching wind-swept ripples run to the swampy shore and scatter against the reeds. The morning quiet was broken only by the sounds of nature: shore birds called to one another from the marshland in a melodic augur of spring, some unknown burrowing animal rustled through the heavy bracken behind him, and a steady wind billowed the boughs and bent the supple trunks of the tall pine trees.

Unable to think of anyone who might put him up for the night, or—more precisely—anyone with whom he was in the mood to negotiate, Daniel had turned to his childhood for refuge. There survived an undeveloped wilderness behind the golf course in the northwestern corner of town, an anachronism in compulsively house-beautiful Haworth. "The Desert" they had called it, when, as children, he and Natalie had run wild among the evergreens, built fortresses in the sandy soil, and toasted marshmallows over campfires in the twilight. It had been their enchanted forest: a place of certain comfort in contrast to the instability of home; a place where differences from school friends and neighbors vanished, equalized by the power of imagination; a place to read and act out tales of adventure far beyond their years, with fabulous plots of travel, fame, and heroism. Daniel had made his way through the darkness without misstep to a small lean-to constructed of yellowed pine boughs, hidden in a protected dell in the heart of the wood. The sand, interlaced with pine needles, had made a comfortable bed, and, bundled in his sweater and greatcoat, he had not been cold. Most important, he had been alone, and free.

In the early morning he had wandered through the forest solitude, reexploring the trails, crossing Lake Shore Drive (at its western extension one of the few remaining dirt roads in Bergen County), and walked along the southern shore of the reservoir. He tried, unsuccessfully, to find the trees on which he and Natalie had once carved their initials. But he did find the spot where the fence ran between a spur of red sandstone on one side and a mighty pine on the other, by means of which they had regularly risked their necks, clambering over the three strands of barbed wire at the top of the fence, to reach the forbidden marshland beyond. He felt as though he were traveling through an alien, less-complicated world.

But as the morning passed, he had been drawn back unwillingly to the present. He heard the morning bustle at the nearby power company, and he realized he was hungry.

He uncurled his fingers from the fence with a sigh and walked to Sunset Avenue, headed for Oradell.

He ordered the set breakfast at a shabby diner on Orchard Street. It was all he could afford, which left him with only odd change in his pocket. He lingered as long as he dared and then wandered over to the Oradell memorial park, adrift in moody cogitation.

What if he had chosen to defy Eric—defy Lydia, too, for that matter? What if he had married her and taken her away from that failure of a father? He could have made her happy, or, if it were indeed impossible to make another person happy, and she had rejected the opportunity, he at least could have been happy himself, because it must be nice, after all, to be rich beyond one's WD. Wouldn't it have been a good thing to be able to pay off his debts? Did it make sense to hold the fact that she was rich against her? Had not Lydia been so in need of love, of companionship, of nurturing? Hadn't he been so himself? Did it really matter that they had such a different way of viewing life—when in the end they both wanted the same things from it? Would it not have been heroic to rescue her from her thorn-hedged castle? Or would it have been merely unprincipled—taking advantage of the weaknesses she, all trusting, had revealed to him? And how the hell was he supposed to tell the difference! How could he ever predict the reaction of other people to what he did? He contemplated the plaque commemorating Wally Schirra, a local boy who had made good, then turned away with a scowl. It had been his bitter experience that whatever he did was bound to be perceived as wrong. Better learn to devote more time to looking after Number One.

Acting on that decision, he took a bus to Ridgewood (at least he still had his bus pass), and made his way to a private research lab he knew of which operated a blood bank. They were always thankful for a pint of AB negative, the one legal tender he happened to have in abundance. An hour later he hit the street again, a ham and cheese sandwich and a glass of milk in his stomach, and a twenty in his pocket. Feeling better, he went down to Graydon Park and blew fifty cents on a copy of the *Star*. He avoided the crime page, flipping instead to the Sports Section, and then to Entertainment. He was amused to spot his sister's byline above an article lauding the accomplishments of the Harrington Park New Globe Theater and promising that Great Things were in the offing for the Upcoming Season. He shook his head in amazement.

Natalie: managing to get her copy in while the world was falling apart all around her; placing her bets on the outside chance that the news of collapse was only a rumor. Level-headed—that was Natalie. She had saved his neck countless times with her clear thinking and determination. Indeed, though he had once pushed her cruelly away, she had returned to stand by him during his darkest days. And yet—it had always annoyed him that she could be so…unemotional…so practical, and that she expected him to be so, too. Crisis after crisis might disrupt his life like collapsing fault lines in an earthquake zone, razing to the ground everything he had ever managed to build—but his sister never seemed to appreciate the gravity of the situation. He knew what she would say: "You don't have to let this happen! Didn't you see this coming? It doesn't have to be the end of everything. Life goes on."

Life goes on. Daniel frowned into the middle distance. Well, to be honest, that had proved true. For many years he had thought—had been quite certain—that his life was over. But somehow it hadn't ended. He had survived prison, and he had survived on the outside without—for the first time in his life—messing up. Yet once again he was possessed by the old feeling; he was quite certain *this was it*, that there was no escape from this one. But was it true? Was his life ending? And what was he doing while Natalie wrote her copy and placed her bets? Stealing a few precious hours of peace before the axe fell? Or merely—wasting his time. In fact, wasn't it absolutely true that life was going to go on? And on…and on. No matter what he chose to do?

What he chose to do. Could there possibly be any choices for him? Natalie, returning from her year overseas when he had most needed her, had told him that having choices was the real freedom. Was he that lucky?

The wind picked up and sent a blast of cold air through the park. He turned to the Help Wanted section and scanned the Unskilled Labor columns. Dishwasher, stockboy, clerk in a music store—that looked promising. The wind ruffled the pages of the paper, then tore it from his grasp. It was getting cold, and, yes, there were scattered drops of rain. Music store, in Saddle Brook…that was something he should look into. It was getting too cold to stay in the park; he had to keep moving. He could take a bus down Paramus Road to Saddle Brook and fill out an application. Yes, answering job application questions—that was always fun. Particularly when he got to the one about "Have you ever been convicted of a felony?" Maybe he should answer "Not really, because the first time I didn't know what I was getting into, and the second time won't happen for a few more days."

"You're shit, Daniel," he whispered. "And there's nobody left who doesn't know it."

The rain fell in torrents, and Daniel, teeth chattering, jumped up and raced to the bus stop, running to warm himself, or to lose himself. He climbed soaking wet onto the first bus that came along and shouldered his way down the narrow aisle. The bus lurched forward and he fell heavily into the back-most seat.

It was getting late—almost four o'clock. The desert was out of the question in the rain, and besides, he needed a change of clothes. And his books…Jesus, he had forgotten all about class tomorrow morning. Better face it and go back to Natalie's for his stuff. Maybe she wouldn't be there—she and her inquisitive eyes—she was usually out in the afternoon. Better go quick while there was a chance she wouldn't be there. Better wake up and figure out what bus he was on and what bus he needed to take next. Better start thinking about where he'd go when he left Natalie's.

He hadn't found an answer by the time the second bus had dropped him off at Chestnut Bend. The rain was lighter now—little more than a mist really—but the wind was icy. He walked down Schralenburgh with his collar up around his ears, his arms crossed over his chest, and his hands tucked up out of the cold. He turned left at the top of Tank Hill and hurried down to Number 128. No sign of Natalie's car. He experienced a swift surge of what he took to be relief. He clattered up the stairs and used his key.

Inside, the silence was oppressive; he felt as if he had no right to be there; he felt like a thief. Moving quickly, he got his suitcase from behind the humidifier, opened it up on the sofa, pulled out a change of clothes, and went to the bathroom. He took a quick shower, shaved, and put on his pants. He was scooping his various toiletry items (and earrings) into a little drawstring bag when the phone rang. He jumped.

What to do? He came barefoot out of the bathroom and looked at the kitchen clock: 5:15. The phone rang again. It obviously wasn't for him—nobody knew he was there. Or could it be Natalie, guessing he had come back and trying to reach him? The third ring. Daniel edged into the living room. The phone was on the coffee table just where Natalie had left it after she had called Sarah. The fourth ring. The cat, having made its appearance while Daniel was in the shower, had taken the open suitcase as an invitation, and nestled down amongst Daniel's sweaters. Five. What if it was the police? He crept up to the coffee table, sat down slowly, and rested one hand on the receiver. Maybe whoever it was had given up. Six. He picked up the receiver.

"Hello?"

After a brief hesitation, a surprised child's voice said "Daddy?"

"Sorry." Daniel felt a wave of relief. "Wrong num—" He stopped.

"Daddy?" It was a little girl's voice.

"Gayanne?" he whispered.

"Hi…"

Fireworks exploded behind his eyes. "Gayanne…."

"It's me, Daddy. Are you surprised?" Her piping little girl's voice was at once bright, excited, anxious—and too old.

"Yes, really surprised." He must try to sound calm, so that she wouldn't suspect how his soul reeled at the sound of her voice. "Are you okay?"

"Oh yeah, I'm fine!" But then she faltered. "Is it all right that I called, Daddy?" She sounded so anxious, and it hurt him terribly that she should have to ask.

"Of course! It's my fault. I should have gotten in touch with you before now. I…I wasn't sure…your mother…would like that, though." How could he say that? His stomach sickened with self-loathing. She would hate him forever for this.

But her voice was all sympathy and understanding. "Well, Daddy, I thought maybe you might feel that way."

Had he thought this a child's voice? So sensible, so caring. Dear God, she reminded him of—

"So I thought I'd better just call you," she was saying. "I talked it all over with my friend Jennifer—you don't know her but she's way cool—and she agreed it sounded like a plan. You know, today is my birthday, Daddy, and I thought maybe you didn't know I wanted you to call, so I thought I'd try and call you. I wanted to surprise you." Her voice trailed off, losing confidence again. "Daddy? Is something wrong, Daddy?"

"No!" gasped Daniel in quick denial. "No!" His stomach churned again—was this the best he could do? What in God's name was he supposed to say? "I mean—yes." He somehow caught his breath. "I'm so very happy that you wanted to call me. But," the words came slowly from some place deep within him. "I'm also feeling terrible because I didn't try and call you, for your birthday. Happy Birthday, sweetheart. You're nine years old."

"And you'll be twenty-seven next week."

Daniel gulped. "That's right." He tried to think. "Does your mother know you're calling?"

"No. But it's okay, Daddy. I'm not living with Lara now. She was pretty sick this winter. Well, not sick really—you know what I mean. She's living in supervised housing in Maywood, but it's no children allowed. I'm staying with Marie and Don now, so I'm perfectly okay."

"Who are Marie and Don?"

"They were our neighbors where we used to live. They're really great. When they asked me what I wanted for my birthday I said I wanted to make two long distance calls, and they said okay! Isn't that nice? I was going to call Aunt Natalie and ask her what your number was, and then call you, but there you were!"

"How did you know Aunt Natalie's phone number?"

"You just have to find out the area code and call information. I knew where she lived, because she always sent me a Christmas present and a card when I was littler, and a birthday card too. But we've moved so many times since then, I don't get the cards anymore. I'm glad she hasn't moved. Daddy? Do you still paint sometimes?"

"Yes…"

"I'm learning! I got acrylics for Christmas, and today I got some new brushes and an easel."

"That's wonderful. Gayanne, is everything all right, are you really all right?"

"Oh, yeah." But all at once her lilting voice quavered with every word. "Only, don't you ever want to see me, Daddy?"

Daniel tightened his fingers around the receiver. Did he want to see her? Had he ever wanted anything else? No matter that he had not been aware of it five minutes before. He wanted, needed to see her, with a blinding passionate unbearable need. And he knew—he heard it in every syllable she uttered—that she needed him too. His head swam, his empty arms ached.

"Oh yes!" he said passionately. "Yes! I want to see you so much!" This then, was what truth felt like.

"Daddy, couldn't I come stay with you? Couldn't I? I'd try and not be too much trouble—and I don't need very much, so it wouldn't be expensive, only the plane ticket." She spoke with nervous delicacy. "And sometimes we could do things together, Daddy, like paint. We could go for walks in the woods and set up our easels. Wouldn't that be fun, Daddy? I'm sure we have a lot in common, Daddy. I think I'm more like you, Daddy."

Daniel clutched at his head. "Oh dear God, I—"

But she didn't want to hear it. "I've got it all figured out, Daddy. I talked to Mrs. Kimura, my social worker. She said she wanted to talk with you, Daddy. Please, Daddy? Please?"

Daniel's breathing was quick and shallow. What was he supposed to do?

He grabbed for the pad of yellow paper and fumbled among the old newspapers on the coffee table, looking for the pencil. "Give me your phone number, sweetheart."

She gave him the number, her sensitive voice trembling with excitement.

"Do you need anything?" asked Daniel. "Do you need money?"

"No. But—will you call me back, soon?"

"Yes, I will."

"When?" Her voice quivered again, awash with her child's need for certainty.

Daniel closed his eyes. "Tomorrow. Have you got school? I'll call you tomorrow evening."

"Really Daddy? Promise?" Her excitement was like an explosion; he felt its impact; his heart and mind staggered from the concussion. "Promise?"

"Promise," he said. "I promise, Gayanne."

"Wow!" She was in ecstasy. "You know, Daddy, it sounds funny when you call me Gayanne. Nobody does anymore. I like it."

"Nobody calls me Daddy, either. I like it too. I like it a lot." He choked up and could only sit in agonized silence while she chattered on.

"Everybody calls me just plain Anne now. Don calls me Sunshine sometimes and I kind of like that. We're going to the movies tonight after my party. I want to see *Fantasia* again. Jennifer says it's dumb me wanting to see a movie made a million years ago, but I like it.

"Well, I guess I better hang up, Daddy. I can't believe I found you so quick. I want you to be sure—in case you didn't know, I love you, Daddy."

Daniel cradled the receiver against his arm, bowing his head down, tears streaming sideways across his cheeks. He tried to take a deep breath, and it shuddered through him uncontrollably.

"I love you too, Gayanne," he said. "I love you."

She said, "Good-bye, Daddy," in her little-girl voice, and then a dial tone blared in Daniel's ear.

"Oh my God, my dear God." He held the receiver in both hands and looked at it. "My own dear child." Three thousand miles away clinging to a telephone, tracking down her thoughtless Daddy. Wants to live with her worthless Daddy, who has nothing to give her, no money, no job, no home, no God-damned telephone—and proud of it! Thank God Natalie had a phone. Natalie, putting her rotten childhood behind her at the earliest opportunity, never letting anybody tell her she couldn't do what she damn-well wanted, plowing through life, always busy with something, but managing to remember little details—like Christmas, and birthdays. Oh, he remembered sometimes too, but always too late to do anything about it. Or so he had told himself. Cruel man. Cruel, thoughtless man. Blind to a loving glance, deaf to a passionate plea. But he had heard it—three thousand miles away but still as plain as day: "Help me, Daddy, help me." God, what help had he to give?

He pictured in his mind a rainy, wind-swept day, and a crowded airport gate. He saw himself standing quite still, choked to immobility with pent-up emotion. Then he saw a little girl—tallish, or plump, curly haired, or in braids—he saw her looking about her for someone, outwardly bold but not quite hiding a sensitive inner fear. He saw himself go up to her, and heard her say, "Daddy?" and he took her, so big and so real, into his arms, and she froze onto him and snuggled a soft cheek against his face, and said again, with certainty this time, "Daddy!"

The picture was so real it took his breath away.

And then he saw another scene, even more real because of its inevitableness; he saw her again, waiting by a telephone, waiting for a call that would never come, waiting until the waiting sealed up her heart with its unremitting pain; waiting while he looked the other way, or tried to pretend it wasn't true, or told himself, *She's better off without me.*

"Oh my child," he sobbed. "How can I do that to you?"

With a cry as if he had been struck, Daniel leaped off the sofa, stumbling in his haste to find shirt and shoes. Grabbing his overcoat, he flung himself out the door and down the stairs.

The rain fell in sheets; it beat against his head and trickled down his collar, but he was numb to mere discomfort. He strode up Schralenburgh, all the way to Old Hook Road, possessed. He turned left and walked to Westwood. It was fully dark. The streets were crowded with rush-hour traffic. Headlights and streetlights reflected off of wet surfaces everywhere and made a kaleidoscope of dancing dizzying lights.

A car pulled out of the stream of traffic and up onto the curb with a thump just in front of him, glancing against his legs. He staggered back and fell, rolling across the wet sidewalk. He lay stunned for a moment, then, realizing he was unhurt, pulled himself to his feet. His heart thumped wildly, but before he could escape, the passenger-side door opened in front of him, blocking his way. A man leaned over and said to him, in commanding tones not to be denied:

"Get in!"

It was Eric Dow.

Chapter Fifteen

It was pouring rain and very cold when Natalie arrived home. She slid out of her raincoat, hung it on the coat rack, and turning, spotted Trick asleep in Daniel's open suitcase. Her eyes swept around.

"Daniel?"

A brief tour confirmed that the apartment was empty. It also convinced her that not only had Daniel been there, but that he had left in a rush. The evidence was clear—an uncharacteristic pile of wet clothes in the middle of the bathroom floor, an open toiletry bag, and the pad of paper and the pen next to the telephone. Had he been talking to the police? Or to someone else. She picked up the pad of paper and looked at it, then turned away.

She put a cup of soup in the microwave. She threw Daniel's wet clothes into the washing machine, and shoved the toiletry kit into the bathroom cabinet. She evicted Trick from the suitcase, closed it, and replaced it behind the humidifier. Despite this erasure of all traces of his presence, Natalie was unable to dispel from her mind the images of myriad disasters her brother might be facing at every tick of the clock.

But wherever he was, Daniel was on his own, and she could not help him by worrying about it. Instead she steeled her mind and heart to her self-appointed task. Sitting at the dining room table with her soup at her elbow, she spread the tools of her trade—notebook, pens, and paper—in a semicircle before her.

She stacked Lydia's letters in chronological order and placed them at the top of the arc. She opened the notebook, smoothed back the first page, and wrote, *Who could possibly want to kill Lydia Dow, and Why?* Selecting a loose piece of paper, she printed, *Lydia—Chronology from Sept. 92.* She picked up the first letter.

September 10, 1992
Dearest Sarah,

How are ya—settled in yet? I bet you've adjusted better than I have! I still can't believe you're gone. The house seems so empty without you. I know, I know—it had to happen sometime. But I miss you at every turn.

The weather has been damp. I tried to work yesterday in the garden—time to get the flower beds ready for winter! I can hardly believe another year is passing. Can another winter really be around the corner? It makes me so sad to think that all the flowers I have loved are dying.

Father is really anxious about you, worried that you won't have a good experience at college—he's so concerned about you. Isn't that nice? I know you think he doesn't care, but really, he wants only the best for you. I know sometimes he's too demanding, but it's because his expectations are so high. I want people to have high expectations of me—how else can I do my best?

I am longing to hear from you. Write me soon and tell me everything. And remember what we talked about, i.e. MEN.

I love you!
I miss you!
Lydia

October 1, 1992
Dearest Sarah,

I got your letter today! I read it four times—although I admit I skipped the part where you GOT ON MY CASE.

Okay, okay, I know I promised to get a job or something, and I will, really! These things don't happen in a minute.

Actually I'm thinking about getting involved in theater again. I went to see Arsenic and Old Lace *down at the New Globe, and got to talking with one of the ushers. She said they're desperate for help—so, Lydia to the rescue!! OKAY?*

You're right, I know, I need to get out more. Things are really oppressive around the house sometimes. What really upsets me is, now that you're gone, this sort of automatic pairing off occurs whenever we're all in the house together, like around meal times. It's so clearly Father & Rose and Graham & Lydia. Yuch. There's nothing much more I can do about the Father & Rose part, but it's driving me crazy having to pretend that I even like Graham. I mean, he is everything I detest! He is so rude, and he always seems to be laughing at me. When he's nice it's a condescension—and he never tells anybody what he's really doing—he prefers to talk in riddles.

I know that Rose thinks it would be a great idea if he and I got together—well, I suppose it's only natural for her to think so. She thinks there's something wrong in a woman my age being alone, and I admit I agree with her there! But!?! Father just plays into her hands, too—Rose will say something like, "Lydia was just saying how she wished she could get out more. Why don't the four of us go bowling... we'll play teams!" Father will say something like, "I didn't know you liked to bowl, Lydia," and then I'm on the spot—I can ruin it for everybody else, or I can go along. Great.

Well, write me again soon. What do you mean you don't have a boyfriend yet? I don't believe it!

Love,

Lydia

October 21, 1992

Dear Sarah,

Hello! Are the trees turning down where you are? Is the sun glinting on the maple leaves like liquid fire? I hope so! Can anyone doubt the existence of God on a day like this?

I sat in my window last night and watched the stars for the longest time, so long that I thought I could see them turning overhead, following their eternal courses. I imagined I was on a distant world, looking up at an alien sun, in a far-off tower high up in the mountains, tall, wooded mountains with secret paths

The telephone rang, and Natalie came back to Earth with a jolt. She leaned over to the counter and picked up the receiver.

"Natalie? Ginny."

"What's the news?"

"Not great. This is your official call to warn you we're running a bulletin concerning the arrest of Rose Dow in the late edition. Just got it in."

"And?"

"Yes, and. And there's an APB out on Daniel. That's in too. Front page."

"I see. Thanks for letting me know."

"Anything I can do?"

"Not right now. There's a lot happening, but I've got to hold off a little while longer. Sorry."

"I'll live."

"Right." They hung up.

Natalie sat for a moment, letting it sink in. The rain beat down hard on the north side of the house. Her thoughts wandered to what must be happening, somewhere out there. To her unwilling mind came the memory of that horrible night five years before when she had learned that Daniel, blind with fear after learning of the DA's decision to go for a felony indictment, had jumped bail. Good-bye chance for leniency; good-bye bail deposit; good-bye already heavily mortgaged family home. Poof.

Wrenching her mind to her task, she forced herself to pick up the letter she had been reading. Her eyes swam as she tried to find her place.

wooded mountains with secret paths that only I knew.

I feel so alive these days! The autumn is so beautiful! I feel as though I know what it must be like to be immortal, for a little while.

I just know if I try hard enough I can live the kind of life I want to live! Yes, I want my life to be filled with beautiful things, I want magic, and mystery! What's wrong with that? In the past, I've experienced little pieces of what I want, so I know it's out there, the dream. The real thing does exist, and if I find it, I'm going to hang on to it!

You sounded so tired on the phone the other day. I know it was late, but still—I worry about you so much. I just want you to be happy! I want that more than I want my own happiness. I know it sounds silly, but I would do anything to keep you safe. I wish I could be there for you, to help you through the difficult times. Well, that's what big sisters are for, isn't it? I can't be fully happy unless you are happy! So you've just got to be happy!

Write me soon,

Love,

Lydia

November 10, 1992

Dear Sarah,

Is it warm down there? Here it's Indian summer. I don't think there's a place in the world as beautiful as Bergen County—it's a bower all year long.

I had a long talk with Graham the other day—I know, I know, I said I couldn't stand him. Well, somehow these days he doesn't seem so intimidating. Actually it all started when I got so mad at him—he was really being a jerk, dropping sly little hints about Dad and Rose—that I finally let him have it. I told him he wasn't really impressing anybody the way he always acted like such a big shot, and that nobody likes a person who is so secretive! I thought that would make him run away with his tail between his legs, but it didn't. He got all serious—it was as if a mask had been ripped away. He said he didn't mean to be so secretive, only he had learned through bitter experience that it was a mistake to tell people everything, because it could only work against you in the end. He told me he had lost someone very near and dear to him because he had been foolish enough to want to tell the world about it, and then people had worked against him to try and break them up, because he had a lot of enemies. I asked him point-blank if he had been involved in something illegal, and he said "No, no way." I believe him about that, somehow. If you get hurt, really deeply,

The phone rang and Natalie snatched at it.

"Hello!"

"Natalie? It's Rebecca Elias."

Natalie's heart gave a bound. "Hi." Was Daniel with Rebecca?

"I just got a call from a friend at the DA's office." Rebecca made no attempt to hide her distress. "What's going on?"

"I wish I knew."

"Is Daniel there with you?"

Natalie's heart sank. "No. I don't know where he is, Rebecca."

"Damn. How can he just disappear like this? He's got to come forward!"

"I know…I know."

"Speaking of police—" Rebecca's tone changed from concern to amazement. "There are two coming up my front walk. My God."

"Looking for Daniel." Natalie went over to the window and peeked down at her driveway. "They're covering all the bases."

"I'd better go let them in. Call me when you know something?"

"I will."

Natalie hung up the phone and glanced at the clock—almost seven o'clock.

She looked around at the litter of paper and notebooks. Suddenly her task seemed stupid. With all hell breaking loose around her, why was she sitting there reading these inane letters and making careful notes of dates and incidents? Probably she had just kidded herself into thinking there was a point to the exercise. But she went doggedly on, fighting her feelings of futility and the impulse to panic.

> *If you get hurt, really deeply, you have to learn something from the experience. It seems sad, because I believe we should always be completely honest with the people we love, but, you know, I believe Graham is actually right—sometimes it's better to keep some things to yourself. Not lie, of course, it's always wrong to lie, but as Graham says, keeping your mouth shut is not lying!*
>
> *Anyway, our talk improved our relationship, so I don't dread running into him anymore around the house. That's something, isn't it?*
>
> *Father has been off on a business trip (with Rose) this week, and although I miss him, it's been great having the whole house to myself. The feeling of freedom is really wonderful. Someday I really want to have a home of my own, to fix up the way I want it, and to take care of! Someday soon.*
>
> *I can't wait to see you at Christmas. It's only a little over a month away. Sometimes I worry that maybe you've changed—but I know things will never change between us!*
>
> *I love you!*
>
> *Lydia*

> *December 2, 1992*
>
> *Dear Sarah,*
>
> *Look what I found! Father and Rose are away for the weekend—they're really acting like a couple of teenagers—and I was cleaning up in Father's office, and found this wedged behind the filing cabinet. I've photocopied it so you'll know I'm NOT MAKING THIS UP!*
>
> 6th June, 1981
>
> Dear Twinkie—
>
> Well, here I am in Jaipur, being showered with favors, flowers, and adoration by the local peasants. I am madly in love with a mysterious and gorgeous

Sikh from the north—we are flying to Katmandu for the weekend—or maybe for the summer.

By now you must be familiar with the disposition of my estate. I hope you think, as I do, that you've gotten your fair share.

Love and kisses to the little girls, and remind them Mama will be back one day, when she's fully recovered from fifteen years of Papa.

Try and remember to keep your sodium intake below two grams per diem.

Must dash—

Little Mary

Can you believe it? All these years, and Father never passed on her message to us! Those were her words of love for us and we never got to hear them! I don't think I can ever forgive him for that. Do you think it's possible that she has been in the country—and he kept her from seeing us? The way he's acting these days I would believe almost anything!

Why must life be like this? You think everything's going better than it ever has before—and then you find out something and it just explodes!

Please write and tell me what you think of this.

Lydia

Natalie read and reread the photocopy of Mary Dow's letter, and then did the same with Lydia's remarkable critique. She took a sip of her long-cold soup. Was this creditable? Could Lydia have read her mother's letter and somehow ignored the anger packed in every word and focused only on the throwaway greeting to the children—which Natalie read as a clear attempt to cause the father pain, far removed from thoughts of maternal affection?

With this horrifying example of warped filiality for contrast, she saw in high relief how central to her life the childhood memories of her own mother's love had been. Was it possible that she, Natalie, had only imagined those moments of bliss and comfort; the sense that she was loved unconditionally for exactly who she was? No, she surely had not imagined that! She had not had to. But Lydia—it was no surprise that Lydia had grasped at any hint of maternal affirmation. How she must have hungered for the most basic element of human happiness, and how she must have feared rejection.

She wondered suddenly if Arthur Sherill had gotten word to Mary about her daughter's death. The answer was obvious. The lawyer prided himself on providing the best of service to his clients. But what would Mary Dow have the courage to do?

The doorbell rang.

Natalie shoved the letters into the top drawer of the credenza and went to answer the door. She opened it, and was flabbergasted to see Graham standing on her doorstep shaking the raindrops from his oversized umbrella.

"Hello, Natalie." There was a sulky smile on his rubbery lips.

Natalie's grip tightened on the doorknob. "To what do I owe the honor?"

"Now there's no need for you to take up an attitude. I thought we were a team. Are you going to let me in or am I still in the doghouse?"

It was a good question, particularly when so expertly presented as a personal challenge, because at the best of times Natalie did not like to back down. Besides, she had him pegged for a coward. She glanced at the clock—it was seven-twenty—and made a quick calculation. With a toss of her head she moved aside for him to enter instead of slamming the door in his face and throwing the bolt. She thought of Sergeant Allan, and knew he would not approve.

"Thank you." He divested himself of his raincoat. "Lovely weather, isn't it? Reminds me of home."

"Was Rose's first husband English?"

"No, very American."

"Then how come you're English?"

"I'm his English cousin."

Natalie, one point down, waved him to a chair. "What can I do for you?"

"I think it's more a case of what I can do for you."

"Oh, good. That takes less energy and is more fun."

Graham laughed, and crossed his legs comfortably, displaying an expanse of mauve sock below his black trousers. "I wish I had some idea what it is you have against me."

Natalie sat on the sofa. "What makes you think I have anything against you?"

"In fact, I'd like to help you."

"Okay, help me. Who gets to decide what constitutes help, you or me?"

"You." Graham was completely at his ease in Natalie's comfy green chair. "Would you like to know what Harry really told me during our famous fight the night of the infamous dinner party?"

Natalie paused, and he smiled. Two points down. She looked at the clock, and then back to the amused eyes of her guest.

"Sure! What?"

"That's not how we play the game, Natalie. First you tell me something."

She tried to keep it light. "What do you want to know?"

"You tell me what Rose has on your brother, and how it relates to Lydia's murder."

Natalie's brain whirled. What was this! Why was Graham trying to find out about something the police had known for two hours and which would be splashed all over the newspapers by morning? Was it possible he didn't know Rose had spilled the beans? Or that she had been arrested? Just possible, she thought, and mustered her wits.

"Okay, I'll tell you." She tried to make it sound like it was a tough decision. "But first you tell me about Harry."

"Oh, I can't do that."

"All right, I'll go first. Rose came here this afternoon to blackmail me—"

"Oh dear." The facade was nearly perfect. There wasn't a hint of surprise on his flexible face. His green eyes were hooded and amused, his mouth was curled in its habitual smile—only a little red scratch on his chin, the sort Natalie was wont to receive from her cat, marred the picture of complete, insolent control.

"You see," she continued, "Rose had seen Daniel—doing something. Okay, your turn. What were you and Harry fighting over?"

"Hmmm." He tilted his head. "I guess I can trust you."

It's my reputation for honesty, thought Natalie.

"Here it is," continued Graham. "Our Harry knew about Lydia's will. Your turn."

"Wait a minute, how do you know he knew?"

"Nope."

"Okay," Natalie licked her lips. "Rose saw Daniel having lunch with Lydia the day she disappeared."

Graham's eyes glowed. "So that's why she wanted to know about the diner in Bergenfield. And about you. Now isn't our collaboration paying dividends!"

"Your turn. How do you know Harry knew about the will?"

"Well, I confess I was toying with him—just a little. About his relationship with Sarah, you understand. We were discussing the pleasures of marrying into the Dow family, and I commented that, despite the clearly superior attractions of the younger sister, I would nonetheless prefer the heiress to the ingénue. Perhaps I said something rather…ribald. Men do that sort of thing in private, you know. Or perhaps you don't know, but you can take my word for it. He said if anything happened to Lydia, the money would come to him, via Sarah, and not to me. Well, of course this served only to annoy me. Naturally I remarked that if anything happened to Lydia we would know at whom to point the finger. He became rather violent."

"Unh-hunh."

"Of course this sort of private talk always seems very crude when taken out of context. But he had been quite nasty about my honorable intentions toward Lydia, and I was annoyed. I never could resist a verbal dogfight, but I never meant it to get physical. Now tell me how Rose found out this tidbit about Lydia and your charming brother?"

"She *said* she spotted them by chance in Bergenfield. Somehow I didn't believe her."

"No. You're such a skeptic, aren't you Natalie?"

Natalie smiled at him benignly. "I assume she followed Lydia when she left the house. I take it from your lack of surprise this is not the first time Rose has attempted to put her private knowledge to financial gain."

"Hardly. I believe it's an addiction. That's what I'm told, anyway. Hard to give it up once you've started. I've always felt rather sorry for her. As if she had alcoholism or something. Of course, she must have blackmailed Eric Dow into marrying her. I can't imagine anyone actually wanting to marry Rose, can you? But then you're a woman, so perhaps you don't see these things."

"Possibly not." Natalie looked at the clock: seven-forty-five. "I wonder…might one posit that Rose has practiced her hobby on you?"

"Good heavens, my sweet Natalie, Rose may have you in her clutches because of your all-too-vulnerable brother, but whatever do you imagine anyone could find to blackmail someone like me?"

In the ensuing pregnant pause, Trick stalked into the living room to scope out the visitor. He focused his large eyes on Graham, blinked once, and then scurried away as if he had been stung, nails scraping noisily as he belted across the kitchen floor. Natalie, although intent on her conversation with Graham, was so surprised by this unusual behavior on the part of her sociable cat, that she paused to wonder what on earth could have caused it.

In that instant she saw it, and the seeing was like a line of dominoes tipping one another over until they all lay flat: out all hours, silver car that looked white at night, dog leash, gym bag, research lab, scratch on the chin.

Natalie's eyes opened wide. "Son of a bitch!"

"I beg your pardon?"

Natalie sprang up from the sofa. "You son of a bitch." She made it personal this time. "Reality/Meaning my eye! You're the pet-napper! That's what Rose had on you! I bet she's been bleeding you dry! And that's why you're so keen to get something on her."

Graham seemed puzzled. "I wish I knew what you were talking about." But then his voice darkened, and he rose out of the chair. "But I advise you—strongly—not to go sharing your fantasies with anyone else. You wouldn't want that little item about Daniel and Lydia to get out?"

"That's the time we fooled you," said Natalie. "Where've you been, Graham? Rose has nothing on me, and neither do you. After I kicked her out she went straight to the cops and told them everything. They've known all about it for hours."

"Fucking..." He took a step toward her. "You really irritate me. It would be a real pleasure to shut you up." He took another step.

She backed up into the kitchen. A voice in her head told her it had been a mistake to let him in. Then another voice told her he was just trying to scare her—and it was working again. Finally a third voice suggested she start thinking about what would be the best weapon to grab. Her pulse raced but time stood still.

The doorbell rang.

Natalie's heart leaped.

Graham hesitated.

"All I have to do is scream!"

He backed away, hands raised.

She edged toward the door, heart thumping, never taking her eyes off him. He looked ugly—brutal and ugly—but he did not make a move. She yanked open the door.

"Good evening, Miss Joday." Sergeant Allan stood in the entryway wearing a funereal expression. Natalie, her heart still in her mouth, could not speak. "I thought I'd better come myself." Then her expression registered, and his face was transformed. "What's wrong?"

Her hands and voice were shaking with an extraordinary mixture of fear, embarrassment, and outrage. She took his arm, pulled him into the apartment, and pointed at Graham. "That man—"

Sergeant Allan gripped her elbow, and looked Graham up and down.

"What are you doing here, Bunch?" he challenged. He looked and sounded every inch the policeman, for which Natalie was heartily grateful.

Graham managed a weak smile. "We were trying to make some sense out of this despicable case—a case you don't seem able to solve. I'm afraid we've had an argument about it."

"He's…he's—wait a second." Natalie detached herself from the sergeant's grasp, hurried to her office, and pulled a folder out of the top drawer of the filing cabinet. "It's all in here," she said—steadier now—as she returned to the sergeant's side. "He's been involved in a pet-snatching ring operating in Bergen County since last summer. Since just about when he hit town, in fact."

The sergeant looked at her skeptically. "I read an article in the *Star*. Did you write that?"

"Yeah. Look, you've got to check his car again—and this time look for animal hairs and stuff, not human."

"You have no cause to justify another search of my car," said Graham. "I absolutely forbid it and if you try it I'll have you before the Police Ethics Committee for harassment."

"There is cause," said Natalie. "Eyewitness evidence. Mine." She tapped her chest with her forefinger. In a low voice, she told Sergeant Allan about the gym bag and the dog leash she had seen in the back of his car, and about the midnight chase of the cat-napper, observed departing the scene of his crime in a small white car. The sergeant looked unconvinced at first, but his expression changed when she reached the conclusion of her tale. "And I saw him not three hours ago coming out of Fairlawn Research, Inc. in Bergenfield. They breed rodents for laboratory experiment, but maybe they deal in untraceable dogs and cats as well. There's a rumor going around that the missing animals are being sold to research labs. I understand there's quite a high-paying black-market trade. Graham was probably getting his orders, or picking up his pay."

Sergeant Allan moved. He stuck his head out the door and called to an invisible colleague below in the rain. There was a blur of activity: two uniformed officers thundered up the stairs; Graham was read his rights and arrested on suspicion of theft; when frisked, five one-hundred-dollar bills were found neatly folded in his back pocket.

"Been to the bank, Bunch?" asked Sergeant Allan.

"Could be."

"We can check up on that for you. Friedman?" One of the officers came forward with a pair of shiny handcuffs; Graham put his hands behind his back; the officers took him by the arms and led him silently from Natalie's apartment. The door closed with a snick.

Natalie went to the liquor cabinet above the credenza and pulled out the first bottle she laid her hand on. She poured a drink, sat down at the table, and took a swallow. "I told him all I want is a simple life."

The sergeant greeted this expressive but incoherent statement with a puzzled frown. "I guess things have been pretty rough."

"You don't know the half of it." She took another swallow. It was Campari. "You want a drink?

"No, I—Regulations."

"Well, sit down, why don't you?" Natalie gestured to a chair.

The sergeant sat across from her, looking terribly serious, and very out of place. It made Natalie want to laugh.

"Don't look so solemn," she said reproachfully. "Your entrance was right on cue." But his expression didn't change, by which she knew that she was not going to like whatever came next. She gulped down what was left in her glass and frowned. She hated Campari. She poured herself another glass, and looked at the sergeant with a sigh. "I realize you're here because...Have you found him yet?"

"No. You don't know where he is?"

"No. He was here this afternoon while I was out, but he left before I got home—which was around six p.m." Her eyes wandered to the stack of textbooks nearby.

"There have been some developments."

"Yeah, I know. I had Rose here this afternoon."

The sergeant shook his head in disapproval. "You seem to attract all the suspects."

"My payback for sticking my nose into the investigation, no doubt." She took another drink. "She told me a simple story in words of one syllable. She didn't mention that when she threw herself on your mercy?"

"No."

"What a surprise." Natalie leaned her elbows on the table. "Look, I'll tell you about it and maybe you can give me some advice. When Rose was here this afternoon, she tried to blackmail me, and I want to know my options." She retailed the salient parts of the visit. The sergeant took hurried notes, glancing at her frequently with mingled incredulity and indignation.

"What I want to know is," concluded Natalie, "can I press charges? Or, if, as I suspect, she was blackmailing other people—Graham, whoever—isn't that a criminal offense?"

"Yes." The sergeant pushed his notebook to one side. "I'll see what the DA thinks when I get back to the office. Blackmail of this kind—besides being a felony, is also an attempt to impede a murder investigation."

"I never thought of that!" Natalie, charmed, took another sip. "I'd love to see Rose get half of what's coming to her."

"If she does, she'll be unluckier than most, but still luckier than some," he said.

Natalie was surprised by his equivocacy. "I'm sure you'll do your best to nail her."

Sergeant Allan said nothing, and there was an uncomfortable pause. Natalie looked at his lean face. His dark, slanting eyes were closely set on either side of that hawk-like nose. He appeared to be thinking. Her eyes slid downwards, across his neatly tailored shoulders and along his arms. His hands rested lightly on the table. They were large, loosely jointed hands, with slender, arcing thumbs.

His fingers twitched, and she looked back at his face, all innocence. "Was there anything else?"

"I'm afraid so, Miss Joday." He laced his fingers together. "I must ask you some questions. About your brother."

"Oh." Natalie was brought up short. "Right. Go ahead."

"Can you give me a description of what he's wearing?"

Natalie's chest tightened. He meant to ask her *those* kind of questions: short, unambiguous, purpose-built. She looked at the duffel bag peeking out from behind the humidifier. She swallowed. "No. He changed this afternoon. I don't know into what."

"How about a coat or jacket. Can you tell which one he took?

"Yeah." Her words came ever slower.

"I know this is difficult."

"He took his heavy wool coat, charcoal gray, three-quarter length, buttons down the front, wide collar."

"Thank you. Did your brother have a set of keys to your car? Did he have them in February, I mean?"

She looked up into his eyes, and the seconds ticked away in silence.

"Yeah."

Sergeant Allan set his jaw. He reached into the breast pocket of his jacket and pulled out an envelope. "I have a warrant to take in your car." He put the envelope on the table.

She nodded. Her keychain was in the pocket of her jeans. She pulled it out, and struggled to remove the car keys from the communal ring.

The sergeant spoke in quiet detachment. "I want to tell you something I probably shouldn't." Natalie, her attention focused on the recalcitrant key ring, did not look up. "Things are looking pretty bad for your brother right now—holding back information, taking off when he said he wouldn't—you know that as well as I do. Finding him and getting the story about the meeting with Lydia is now our top priority. However..." His tone changed. "Despite the accumulating evidence, despite the fact that he's lied to us repeatedly, I don't believe he did it."

Her heart leaped, but not from relief. She looked up. "You worked out the timetable."

"I keep making the mistake of thinking I'm bringing you news." A smile danced across his face. "And you said you didn't do numbers."

"I never said that. I said—never mind what I said. If you're convinced he didn't do it…"

"I am. Compared to some of the other suspects in this case, your brother has begun to look like a model of upstanding citizenship and discretion."

"Be still my heart." She took another drink.

"In fact, it seems to me like he's being set up—but by whom I don't yet know."

"I can tell you that." Natalie finally liberated her car keys. "But it won't help solve the murder."

"Why not?"

Natalie stretched out her arm and slid the keys across the table. "Don't you get it? He's being set up by himself."

"Himself?" The sergeant looked at her quizzically, and then looked at her again.

Natalie could have spent an hour studying his gaze. "Yeah. It's his fatal flaw. He just can't seem to see that by running away from problems, by refusing to talk about them, he makes them worse."

Sergeant Allan's brow furrowed. "Do you think it's as simple as that? Have you considered—Maybe he doesn't understand that virtue is not the absence of fault. Maybe he doesn't see that everybody has greater and lesser problems, makes major and minor mistakes, and lacks the judgment to distinguish between the two. He runs not because he is afraid of failing but because he thinks he has already failed. And maybe he doesn't ask for help, as you or I might do, because he doesn't understand that the people he cares about, and who care about him, aren't going to condemn him when he blunders."

Natalie dropped her eyes, her face warming. "I've never condemned him."

Sergeant Allan reached out his hand and touched her fingers. "I'm not talking about you." His voice was full of compassion. "It wasn't your responsibility." He withdrew his hand.

"I practically brought him up," whispered Natalie.

"He needed something you couldn't give."

Her thoughts moved sluggishly through her overworked mind, wrapping around his words and incorporating them laboriously into her consciousness. As the sense of it spread, she felt a deep-bottomed stillness in her mind, and knew he was right.

In the wake of this healing calm came the coincident realization that she was drawn to this man by a heady mix of emotional and intellectual attraction. Exhilarated by the surcease of the day's conflicts, and liberated by the alcohol that warmed her blood, Natalie was in no mood to be logical.

She slid one hand, palm up, fingers open, across the table until her arm was at full stretch. She framed a question with her face and looked up at him.

He returned her look, and in his eyes she saw a light as of fire reflected on dark windows. Then he drew a soft breath, and the light was blown out. He smiled at her; a smile of intimacy, affection, and regret. He reached for her hand, held it for a moment between both of his, and then released it.

"Time to go," he said gently.

Natalie, her mouth pulled slightly to one side, nodded.

He stood up, and she stood too.

"I want to solve this case." It was a statement of the obvious, but she understood why he made it. "I want to work out why this happened."

Natalie walked around the table. "That's been on my mind too." Again and again during the long day she had forced herself to focus on the problem at hand, and somehow she did so now. "Why would anybody want to kill this woman, and in such a violent way?"

The sergeant showed an equal ability to focus. "Apart from the money angle, we haven't turned up a thing. But money as a general motive does not get us anywhere, since it works equally well against practically anyone in the case."

Together they headed for the door.

"I almost forgot," said Natalie. "Graham says Harry knew about the will *before* the murder. Whether you believe him or not is up to you."

"Tell me."

She repeated her entire conversation with Graham. Sergeant Allan, heedless of his notebook, never took his eyes off her.

After relating the facts, Natalie observed: "Of course I don't think Graham would have told me the story about the fight if he had realized the implication—"

"Because if Harry knew about the will—"

"Then so did Graham," finished Natalie.

"And who else, I wonder?" He looked at her, eyes troubled with a concern he could not hide. "You've got to be on your guard from now on. This case is making you enemies left and right."

"Yeah!" Natalie was in whole-hearted agreement. "A lot of good it does to have an unlisted address. I bet Rose peeked in Sarah's address book to find out where I lived, and then either Graham did the same, or got it directly from Rose. Or followed her. It's clear he's been playing her both ways. And equally clear they both thought I was fair game."

"Perhaps you should be a little more careful when unexpected visitors call."

Natalie raised an impenitent eyebrow. "I was perfectly safe."

His eyes widened. "Oh, really?"

"Of course. I knew you were on your way." She spoke with calculated nonchalance. "You sent someone to see Rebecca Elias, looking for Daniel. If you were checking her place I knew you would be checking mine, since this is where he was supposed to be. And I, shall we say, counted on it, that you would be the one who did the checking. You said you'd come yourself the next time. This is the next time."

His eyes were suspicious, but the smile was back, playing around the corners of his mouth. "Goodnight, Miss Joday."

"Goodnight, Sergeant." She closed the door after him and slid the dead bolt home.

❯❯❯

Alone again, Natalie took a long, hot shower, donned her pajamas, and propped herself up in bed with a cup of herbal tea, her notebooks, and Lydia's letters. The evening's events had vented much of her pent-up frustration and emotion. She was relaxed and thinking clearly again—clearly enough to appreciate the sergeant's discretion, and even to be a little surprised at her own presumption. Nonetheless, and despite the physical distance between them, she was keenly aware of him, knew he was moving in tandem with her, pondering the same questions, sifting through the evidence for the same answers. A part of her saw things from his perspective now.

It was ten o'clock when she picked up the last letter:

December 12, 1992
Dear Sarah,

The wedding is next week. When I called you, I know I said it wasn't for sure, but then I found out just how helpless I was to stop it. I was stupid to hope I could get in touch with Mother and that she would come back, and they would get together again, and we could be a family. I suppose it's stupid to feel that our father is being unfaithful, but that's the way I feel! Like it's something obscene.

I hate it when I feel this way—desperate. I don't know why people do the things they do—I can't believe how selfish people are. Why can't we all just live peacefully together? I believe in seeing the good in people. But I feel as though I've been beating my head against the same wall all my life.

No, I am not interested, as you said in your letter, in Graham! This is just what I mean! Just because we're friends now, you leap to conclusions! Can't a man and a woman be just friends anymore? Besides, he is not my type at all! You know that!

I wish you were here, Sarah! Maybe you could talk Father and Rose out of this—I want to do something, but I don't know what. I just want to be happy, is that so terrible? But always, always, always, something seems to happen to ruin everything!

I'm sorry to write like this to you. I don't want to upset you. Please you be happy. We were so happy as children. Until that terrible time when Mother left. You were young then, so you don't remember it clearly, but I do. Sometimes I wake up in the middle of the night and remember, even now. Since then I've always tried to protect you, and I always will.

Love,
Lydia

Natalie stared at the pale blue paper, but in thought she was far away, hurled back through time to early childhood, when the Jodays had been a two-car family, when going to a fancy restaurant was a weekly ritual, and August meant fishing in Maine. Change had been slow and inexplicable at first, as when a room darkens in response to an unseen cloud passing across the sun. Later it had been swift and unequivocal, beginning with the spring day on which a rock thrown up by passing traffic on Route 17 had shattered the windshield of her mother's car, causing her to lose control. The car had spun into the guard rail, flipped over, and crashed into a stone retaining wall. It was in flames in seconds, they said, and Natalie had spent many a white night in the dark days after wondering if her mother were conscious enough to realize that her seatbelt latch was broken and inoperable.

She came back to the present with a jolt. Drawing a breath, she wiped her eyes, and downed the last of her tea.

She turned off the light and settled back onto her pillows. Lydia Dow was dead. Natalie had at last formed a vivid image of her, but was it really—could it possibly be—accurate? How had it ever transpired that Sarah had been the sister tagged as "the unstable one?" The Lydia of these letters was removed from what was going on around her by a wall of denial, and utterly lacking in judgment. To Natalie, who depended for her living and her peace of mind on seeing with a clear eye, Lydia's interpretation of events was frightening. In fact, of all the people connected with the case, Lydia seemed the one most primed to do something desperate. Yet she had ended up the victim.

And her brother had been the last person to see her alive.

"Where are you, Daniel?" she whispered aloud. "Please come back. I have to tell you something." She lay for a long time awake in the darkness, listening to the rain.

Chapter Sixteen

With an eerie sense of doing exactly the right thing, Daniel got into the car. Eric stepped on the gas, and the sedan spun off the sidewalk and onto the road with a jolt.

Outside, bright lights whirled in the rainy darkness: street-lights, car lights, shop lights, kaleidoscoping around them as they drove through the darkness. Inside, Daniel had Lydia's father in profile—large head, thick neck, and powerful torso. They had met only once before, but the memory of that encounter had galled him through the intervening years without relief: the startling appearance, the deft violence, the debasing words. He had often pictured what he would say, or what he would do, if they ever met again. He had wondered what he would feel—hate, fear, anger, intimidation, panic? Now that the moment had arrived, he felt only regret.

Eric drove in silence along the length of Old Hook Road, through downtown Closter and on up Closter Dock Road, through the gate and onto the driveway of Castle Dow. A shower of white crushed rock rained onto the lawn as he took the curves too fast. He swung around the fountain and pulled into the garage behind the house. He got out of the car without a word and walked across the lawn to the house.

Through the rain-mottled window Daniel watched Eric's retreating figure. Taking a deep breath, he got out and followed him. Floodlights illuminated the walkway and the glistening shrubbery with a cool white glow. They entered the house through the back door, went down a short staircase to the basement, and along the dark hall to the office.

Eric switched on the lights and settled into his black leather throne behind the desk. Daniel lowered himself onto the chair that Sarah had sat in at the meeting with the lawyer, and unbuttoned his dripping coat.

They eyed one another.

"You've gotten yourself into quite a fix, haven't you?" said Eric, in a fatherly tone.

"That about sums it up," agreed Daniel.

"You don't have a very well-developed sense of self-preservation, do you? Suspect in a murder investigation, lost your job, lost your girlfriend, lying to the police, on the run. Your problem is you've got your head up your ass."

"Thank you," said Daniel. He dried his face on the inside of his coat sleeve. "Your analysis is flawless, but I must in all fairness to my other benefactors admit that you are not the first to have noticed."

Eric's broad face twisted. "Smart mouth, too! It must run in the family." He regained control, crossing his arms over his chest. "Well, I'm in it up to the neck, myself."

"Really? That's news to me."

"It is, eh? Suspected of bumping off my daughter for her money? Wacko kid controlling the family purse strings? Wife in the joint because she held out on the cops? That sound like a picnic to you?"

"I guess not," admitted Daniel.

"You guess not." Eric narrowed his eyes disdainfully. "That's because you don't know jack shit about responsibility! You don't know about trying to raise two daughters all alone; trying to keep your family together; wanting nice things for your kids, and keeping the predators away! What the hell do you know about being a father?"

Daniel shook his head and looked at the floor.

"Nothing, that's what," continued Eric. "And people like you never will. I do the best I can to protect my family! And right now the only thing that counts is the one daughter I've got left. Thank God she had the sense—more sense than her sister—to pick somebody who knows right from wrong like Harry Suter instead of a jailbird like you! He'll protect her, when his turn comes. But right now it's my job to shelter her from anyone that tries to fuck her over.

"And speaking of getting fucked over…" Eric uncrossed his arms and leaned forward across his desk. "That was some cheesy story about you and my wife."

"I assure you…" Daniel tightened his fingers around the arms of the chair. "Any entanglement with your wife was the last thing on my mind. Nothing happened."

"What are you, stupid?" Eric's eyes and mouth were open wide. "Don't you think I worked that out?"

Daniel stared at him.

"Boy, you do have a talent," said Eric. "What. You think anybody with shit for brains couldn't figure out there was something a lot more complicated going on than a quick game of poke the floozy? Not that you wouldn't have saved me a hell of a lot of trouble if you'd just taken the bait and screwed her. But she's not your type, is she? You like a little personality, right?"

"I beg your pardon?" Of all the conversations he had carried out in imagination with this man—

"Here's the way I see it." Eric drummed his stubby fingers on the black desk and squinted with one eye. "I've got something you want—and that's money. And you've got something I want—and that's power over my wife."

"Believe me," said Daniel, and of this he was certain, "I have no power over Rose."

"Sure you do. You just don't know it yet. You need me to explain it to you."

"I'm telling you, if anything, she's the one with the power over me!"

"What—you worried about her telling the cops she saw you and Lydia skulking around the Maverick Diner?"

The words hit Daniel like a blow.

"Don't bother to deny it." Eric grinned at him. The cops know the whole pathetic story. You'll have to deal with that on your own. I can't help you there."

Daniel struggled to keep on top of a tidal wave of panic. "I see."

"But you and Rose at your sweetie's place, that's her word against yours. Most people would just as soon believe something juicy happened."

"But you just said you didn't believe it!"

"I know what I said, you dumb fuck! Do I have to spell this out? I thought you were a pro!" Eric's eyes protruded and his lips tightened in frustration. "I'm telling you it might be in your best interests to change your story."

"Change my story to *what*?"

"To say that something did happen, God-damn it!"

Daniel's eyes widened and he leaned forward in the chair. "Why!"

"To get that fucking bitch out of my—my daughter's—life!"

Came the dawn. "Oh," Daniel sat back with his mouth open.

Eric ogled him impatiently. "Well, you got a full dose of her, didn't you?"

"Uh, yes."

"Then you should understand my problem. She's got my balls in a vice."

"I'm starting to get it."

"Okay, so what's your problem? Let's cut the crap and talk bottom line. What do you say to ten thousand bucks to swear on a stack of Bibles that you bounced the mattress with my wife?" His little round eyes bored into Daniel's contemplative face.

Daniel said nothing.

"What are you worried about?" Eric let his impatience show. "It doesn't implicate you in the murder. It makes you look like a stud to all your pretty-boy friends. And if that's not enough incentive, it makes me look like a horse's ass to all my friends. Don't tell me that doesn't get you all hot and sweaty! Or, if you're too prissy to enjoy kicking a man when he's down, think of the money. There must be something worthwhile you can do with that kind of dough."

Daniel thought.

"That's more like it," said Eric, with satisfaction.

"Wait a minute." Daniel held up his right hand. "There must be an easier way to get out of your marriage. Not to mention cheaper."

"That shows what you know. Okay, I don't mind telling you. I got a guy who tails Rose when I'm out of town. Half the time the son of a bitch loses her, but that day he got lucky. I knew all about Rose following you home two months ago. I knew there was no hanky-panky. My guy had binoculars."

"Jesus."

"Surprises you, eh? Well, I knew about your little rendezvous with Lydia too, but I couldn't mention it without giving it away that I was having my wife followed. I've been biding my time, and today was my day. Rose went to your sister's place this afternoon—you didn't know that? Well, I followed her and confronted her when she came out. She tried to get out of it, but I forced her to go to the cops with the whole story, and didn't have to give away my hand."

Daniel was only half listening. "What was she doing at Natalie's?"

"She wouldn't tell me in so many words, but I know Rose, and my guess is she tried to put the squeeze on Little Miss Self-righteous. She knew sister-dear would do anything to keep poor misunderstood brother from going to jail again. I wonder how much she got out of her?"

"You're a fool if you think she'd get a dime."

"Sensitive, aren't we? Sensitive enough to turn away from ten Gs? Okay, okay. Don't get me wrong—I feel sorry for your sister. Every time I see her, she's out of control. What's her problem, anyway?"

"You don't know a thing about us," said Daniel. "You haven't got a clue."

Eric shrugged. "Whatever. Back to business. You've got the picture now. What've you got to lose? All you have to do is say Rose showed up at her boy toy's door, did her little coconut dance, and you ended up in the sack. Big deal. Nobody will find out it's a lie—who would believe that *you* would ever stoop to doing business with *me*? It's a sure bet. What do you say?"

Daniel cocked his head and pondered Eric's proposition. He felt unusually focused. He probed his emotions, searching for the old fears. He tried to remember what it had felt like to be dumped into an ice chest in front of a Fourth of July crowd, but the memory had vanished.

In the distance, the front door slammed. Footsteps crossed the living room overhead, and Rose Dow called out, panicky and insistent:

"Eric! Eric!!"

He stood up and pointed a finger at Daniel. "You stay put. I'll come back when I've got rid of her and we'll settle our deal." He grinned, pulled a hundred-dollar bill out of his wallet, and dropped it on his desk. "Here's an aperitif!"

He strode out the door, closed it. Daniel heard him calling, "Coming Rose!" as he hurried up the stairs.

"Son of a bitch!" muttered Daniel, unwittingly echoing his sister's sentiment from across three towns. Shaking himself, he rose, opened the office door stealthily, and crept up the stairs. Standing in the hall, he heard whispers coming from the sunroom. He tiptoed across the living room and stood, back against the wall, just outside the archway.

"You don't have to pay the entire twenty thousand, you idiot." Rose's voice conveyed her biting impatience. "You pay ten percent to a bondsman and he pays the full amount, and keeps a percentage."

"I'm sure you know all about these things, Sugar Plum."

"Don't be so crude, Lovey."

"Where the hell am I going to get even two thousand dollars?"

"You'll think of something—you always do."

"That was before—things are more difficult now."

"Oh, yes." Her words were venomous. "You mean before—in the days when Lydia never noticed how you siphoned off her money for your business trips and your party girls!"

"Shut up!" hissed Eric.

"Oh, don't worry, I won't tell your little secret—as long as you remember to toe the line! I hope Sarah is smart enough to keep her guard up when you're around. We wouldn't want what happened to Lydia to happen to Sarah—would we."

Eric's reply was a wordless growl. There was a rustle of clothing.

Daniel had heard enough. "Excuse me." He stepped into the archway. "I'm just going to let myself out." He pointed over his shoulder at the front door.

Rose, hair flattened by the rain, the harsh lines of her face unsoftened by makeup, stood like a statue in the middle of the room. Eric stood beside her, his hands clutching her wrists.

"Thanks for the offer, Eric," said Daniel. "Maybe next time. Nice to see you again Rose, you're looking well. Possibly jail becomes you."

"You'd better get a move on, Danny-boy," snapped Rose. "The police are crawling all over Bergen County, looking for their new prime suspect."

Daniel bowed. "Thanks for the warning."

"You'll regret this, punk." Eric let go of Rose's wrists and raised a fist at him.

"I sincerely doubt it," said Daniel. He made a broad gesture with both arms. "Hey, why am I still standing here chatting? You'd think I'd learn." He turned and walked out the front door.

Outside, he crossed the luminous semicircle thrown by the porch light, and raced across the darkened yard through the rain. Reaching the cover of the rhododendrons, he slowed and moved cautiously through the dripping leaves to the wall. At its base he paused. The police might well be watching the house; should he risk slipping out the gate, where he might be seen and picked up? Or should he try to scale the wall, hazarding the broken glass with which it was topped? Opting for the latter, he headed west, keeping the wall on his left, until he came upon a utility shed built against the bricks. He clambered onto the roof, took off his coat, and laid it over the rough edges of the glass. He sighted a likely landing place in the ditch by the road, climbed gingerly onto the top of the wall, leaped, and rolled. Getting up, he found a sturdy branch, and used it to retrieve his coat. He waited for a break in the traffic, crossed Closter Dock Road, and moved like a shadow under the cover of the rain-soaked trees.

⋄⋄⋄

Natalie awakened with a start. Trick had left his station at the foot of the bed. In her sleep, she had heard the familiar soft thud as he had leaped to the floor. But she had heard something else too.

There it was again, a soft scratching noise—coming from the direction of the kitchenette—then another thud. She looked at the clock: one-thirty a.m.

She slid out of bed, thinking of the sycamore tree which grew so close to the office window that Trick used it as a causeway in summer. It was conceivable that someone less welcome might have had the same idea. Her tennis racket was leaning against the wall by the door, waiting to be re-strung for the summer season. Grabbing it, she tiptoed to the bedroom door.

She heard the latch of the office window click open, and felt a draught of cold, moist air slide through the house. She slipped behind the open bathroom door, then peeked cautiously across the kitchenette to the office.

Someone eased through the window and onto the filing cabinet, stretching out long legs to avoid banging into the computer.

Trick jumped onto the workbench and arched his tail above his back; she could hear him purring. The intruder reached for him, and Natalie, tightening her grip on the racquet, came out from behind the door.

The man turned and said "Natty?"

Chapter Seventeen

Did I scare you, Natty?" asked Daniel guiltily.

"Oh, no. I was just practicing my top-spin backhand." She took a couple of swings for verisimilitude, then flipped the racket into a corner. "Jeez, Daniel, I almost had a heart attack! Haven't I asked you a million times to use the door?"

"Sorry! But there's a cop staking out your driveway."

"Oh, well, that's different." She went past him into her office. "What did you do to my window?"

"Don't turn on the light. Your window's fine. Master craftsmanship."

"I'm impressed. So is it craftsman-like to close and latch the window behind you? What if you needed to beat a retreat?"

"Well, it's raining. Your computer might have gotten wet. I didn't want to get arrested for disrupting the flow of vital news throughout greater northeastern Bergen County. I'm on parole, you know."

Natalie inspected the window latch. "Where do you learn these things?"

"You pick up lots of useful skills if you get around enough."

"I think these are words of deep wisdom. In fact, it's crossed my mind several times lately that I ought to see about sharpening some of *my* life skills!" She paused, put the backs of her hands on her hips and pouted. "I've had a tough day!"

Unable to keep up the banter a moment longer, Daniel went to his sister and put his arms around her, dropped his tired head on her shoulder with a voiced sigh, and patted her on the back. "I know, dear Natty," he said softly, "I know…"

Natalie locked her arms around his waist and closed her eyes. They stood like that for a little while, rocking slowly back and forth.

"I'm getting you all wet." Daniel's voice was muffled.

"Never mind. I've been wanting to do this for a long time. I don't know what I'd do if anything happened to you. I'm so glad you're all right!"

Daniel released his hold on her a little.

"Me too," he said. "Sorry I'm late. I came cross-lots, because I knew the police would be swarming, and it took forever."

She stepped back and helped him out of his sopping coat. "How did you find out they were looking for you?"

He brushed back his dripping hair with his wrist. "I'll tell you—"

"Better get changed first," she interrupted. "No point in dying of pneumonia."

"Actually I'm dying of thirst—got any Cherry Coke?"

"Certainly. Hungry?"

"Of course."

He took a shower while she made grilled cheese sandwiches for him and a pot of Arabian mocha for herself. They moved through the apartment in semi-darkness, knowing that a light would attract the attention of the policeman outside. At length they gravitated to the living room sofa, where they sat facing each other cross-legged in the gloom. There was a comfortable familiarity in the tableau. They had often sat so in bygone days—spinning tales of future glory, or baring their troubled souls—talking till dawn, with no one to say them nay.

Natalie sipped her coffee while Daniel spoke of his encounter with Eric and Rose, pausing only for an occasional bite. When he had finished the story, he asked her about the visit from Rose. She told him everything, and, when pressed, did not spare the details. Daniel, a half-eaten sandwich forgotten in his hand, listened spellbound.

Natalie concluded her tale with a characteristic shrug. "I think we now have a clear picture of Mama and Papa Dow. What a pair—bribery and blackmail."

Daniel shook his head, the self-reproach that dragged at his face visible in the colorless light. "I let you in for that. It's my fault."

"You may have left the door open for her, but you can't take responsibility for what she did once she walked through."

But Daniel was not in a mood for excuses. "No. You're looking at this as an isolated incident—and you know you can handle Rose Dow any day of the week. But look at my life as a whole—don't you see the pattern? Mile after mile of open doors.

"I'm sorry you had to go through that. I'm sorry I wasn't here, where I should have been. We must have missed each other this afternoon by about ten minutes. If I had waited a little longer—but I just couldn't stay." He shook his head from side to side.

Natalie thought back to the open suitcase, and the signs of hasty departure. "What happened?"

Daniel rocked his head ever more slowly and in ever widening arcs. "I got a phone call."

"From who?"

He looked at her in mute misery.

She whispered the name. "Gayanne?"

"How did you know?"

"The look on your face. The impression of the phone number you wrote on the message pad: it was a California area code. Besides—it's her birthday."

"At least one of us remembered."

Natalie brushed the remark aside. "How is she? Where is she?"

"San Diego. And she was—wonderful!" Daniel's voice took on a shy eagerness that Natalie had not heard in years. "Still a little girl, but autonomous."

"I hear that happens eventually."

"Yeah. As you know I haven't seen her in three years—since I went to LA right after I got out. She still seemed like a baby then—what I was able to see of her. But now! She has ideas, feelings, dreams."

"I can't wait to talk to her. Get a chance to know her a little. But—how's Lara?"

"Not good, from what she said." Daniel popped open his second Cherry Coke. "Gayanne isn't living with her now. Lara's in what sounds like a halfway house somewhere. But get this. My daughter—my nine-year-old daughter, said to me, her father, 'Lara'—she calls her Lara—'was sick a lot this winter...well, not exactly sick, you know what I mean.' Subtle, wasn't it? That's some astute kid. I may be dense about some things—for instance I seem to remember believing Lara when she told me she was clean—but I got the hint. I should, since I've known Lara for—what is it—ten years now? I got the picture all right. Whatever it is this time—crack, Jack Daniel's, dope—it doesn't matter. What matters is, Nat, she is not able to take care of our daughter, who is living with strangers. This is wrong. Somebody has to do something about this. I have to do something about this."

Daniel leaned to his sister and spoke in the slightest of whispers, though there was no one to overhear. "I want her, Nat, I need her. She begged to come and live with me. I could have begged her to come. I want her with me. I know—Jesus—it's a pipe dream. But I'll do anything I can, I'll do anything I have to do, to get her."

He spoke slowly, as if discovering one by one the perfect words for what he wanted to say. "It's as if lately I've been living in a darkness that no one else seemed to notice. Then I spoke with Gayanne and a light went on, and now I can see too. I know what to do."

The skin on Natalie's arms tingled.

He spoke as if to himself. "I must redeem the time. And I'd better start now. Nat." He reached out and touched her knee. "Everything you said last night about me was true. I'm so sorry."

"Daniel..." Natalie took his hand, and peered eagerly into his face. "I'm the one who should be apologizing. Everything I said was pointless, and everything you said about *me* was true."

"No—"

"Yes! I knew you'd made a mistake, I knew you were in doubt, I knew you were scared—but I didn't care why! I knew you didn't trust your own reactions enough to guide you, but I still blamed you for not handling the situation better!

"Daniel, I need to tell you what I should have done last night." She squeezed his hand, and then let it go. "I should have thrown my arms around you the second you walked in the door and told you how much I loved you; then I should have decked you for holding out on me, and demanded to know what the hell was going on! Anything else was—illogical!"

Daniel ducked his head and smiled briefly. "I wish you had—but I'm not sure it would have made any difference. Because the truth is I did keep things back, just as you said; I did try to blame you for my problems. What you said was true."

"But what you said was true too."

Daniel gestured with his empty hands. "Maybe we were both right?"

In his words, Natalie caught a glimpse of one of the elusive facets of truth. She looked out the window. "I wonder…Is it possible we've never really understood how we affect each other?"

"I don't know. I thought we had worked all this out after the robbery."

"I thought so too—that's what makes this so scary. But—you were down and out then, and you needed me so much. It was natural that I led and you followed. It's different now—we're on more equal footing." She looked at his troubled face. "Now we need each other."

Daniel raised self-mocking eyes. "You need me?"

Natalie tipped her head back and made a noise halfway between a laugh and a cry. "Does the Earth need the sun?"

In the gray light, Daniel searched his sister's face in wonder. And the tide that had been so long against them turned, carrying them into calmer seas.

◇◇◇

At length Daniel spoke. "Nat. We had an agreement to share everything we knew about the case. If it's not too late, I'd like to tell you the whole story."

"It's not too late." She picked up her empty coffee cup. "Which leads me to ask, is it too late for me to mention how pissed off I was when I realized you were holding out on me?"

"It's not too late," said Daniel. "Because it gives me a chance to apologize for being a jerk."

"Apology accepted."

He paused expectantly.

She poured herself another cup of Arabian mocha.

"That's it?" asked Daniel.

Natalie shrugged. "I don't know, I'm new at this. Better just start and we'll see what happens."

"Okay." Daniel collected his thoughts. "Well, you know the story up through the night of the dinner party. That was straight, and complete. I got home that night and—as I said—devoutly prayed that I would never see any of those people again." He raised his eyebrows over downcast eyes. "I counted my blessings that I had met someone like Rebecca who, unlike Lydia, looked at the world head on, and saw problems and difficulties as natural phenomena and not as portents of doom, to be feared—or hidden.

"But I had forgotten one thing. I told you how I had used my early morning class as an excuse to leave the Dow house, right? Well, I forgot Lydia knew I was attending BCC.

"The next morning, I got a message in class—it must have been around 9:45—telling me I had an emergency phone call in the office. It was Lydia. At first I was angry—I had finally had it with her, and started to tell her so. But she said something horrendous had happened. And she sounded different, more blunt than I had ever heard her. She was upset, but controlling it; she didn't beat around the bush. She said she knew by the way I had looked when I had left the night before that she was the last person I wanted to hear from. 'But, I need your help,' she said. 'You're the only one who can help me now.' She asked me to meet her."

He gave a little laugh. "Of course what I should have said was 'I'm sorry, I can't help you.' How could I have believed that she had changed overnight? Looking back I can see all the danger signs. No, that's not true. I saw them at the time—but I thought it would be cowardly to run away. I thought she was in trouble, so I had to consider what was best for her. I thought it didn't matter that I didn't want to go, that the best thing was to meet her and listen to what she had to say and help her straighten out whatever it was, and then, if I was lucky, maybe she would leave it at that and wouldn't call again." He laughed again. "Right."

›››

They'd agreed to meet at the Maverick in Bergenfield at 12:30. Lydia wanted it to be somewhere out of the way, and that suited Daniel just fine. She got him to promise to keep it a secret and they hung up. Just like old times, Daniel thought. He went back to his classroom to catch the end of the lecture. Then he checked a couple of books out of the library and took the bus home. He tried not to think about Lydia for the rest of the morning—why borrow trouble? He kept busy—did the laundry; vacuumed; started his homework.

A little after noon he headed for Bergenfield, taking no pleasure in the journey. Sitting on the bus he tried to cheer up by remembering that being there for people when they needed you wasn't always fun and games. He told himself, "For once I'm the one who's being turned to for comfort and advice, I'm the one going to the rescue."

Lydia was there when he arrived, sitting in the last booth in the back, next to the bathrooms. Although it was lunchtime, the diner was nearly empty. A couple of off-duty policemen sat at the counter shooting the breeze with the waitresses. Daniel sidled past them and made his way to the back. He sat down across the table from her, glad the waiting was over and anxious to get on with whatever it was.

He greeted her cordially, asking how she was. Lydia, sitting bolt upright on the edge of the blue vinyl seat, mumbled a reply he did not catch. She wore a simple print dress. In her lap she held—gripped—a floppy, multi-colored handbag made of woven straw. Her knuckles were white.

›››

"She looked stoned, Nat," whispered Daniel in the dark. "Her pupils were dilated and her eyes were huge—an other-world look. But I couldn't believe she was really on anything; she had always despised any kind of substance abuse—used to patronize me for having ever, even in my misspent youth, done any drugs, and look where it got me, etcetera. I've thought about it a lot since then—was she using? But even though it would explain a lot, I just can't believe it."

Natalie looked skeptical.

"I know what you're thinking," said Daniel. "Lydia Dow, exercising her penchant for overdramatization. Well, that's what I thought too. And I really did not want to be there to watch it play out. I thought if she ate she might feel better, so I picked something from the menu real fast and got our order in."

›››

Daniel had made small talk while they waited for their food to arrive. What his plans were; when he would finish school; what he wanted to do after that. But he was unable to draw her out. Nor could he rid himself of his own discomfort. Growing desperate, he asked if she'd been doing any acting.

"I'm surprised you of all people would ask me that," she said.

"Why?"

"I thought you knew theater is a waste of time and effort." Her face was scornful, and it hurt him. "A place where people hide from reality."

Daniel tried to change the subject. "The family getting along okay?" he asked—and instantly regretted it.

"What family?" she burst out bitterly. "I've got a father who drove my mother away—no, first he drove her crazy with his promiscuity and then he drove her away. I've got a mother who deserted her children, who ran off to have a life of fun and irresponsibility in every rat-infested corner of the world she could crawl into. I've got a jackal for a stepmother. I've got a sister who's such an emotional ruin she can't think of anybody but herself, and doesn't stop to wonder if what she does might hurt anybody else! And me? I must be crazy, because I always try to do the best I can by them all; try to keep my sister from hating my father; try to keep my father from bullying my sister; try to take my mother's place, to keep it safe and sound for her. And now it's too late. It's too late! If she had only come back long ago we might have had a chance—but she destroyed everything."

She rambled on and on, far removed from him, talking to people who weren't there about things Daniel knew nothing about. Even when she looked at him, he felt that she wasn't really seeing him.

The waitress came with their food, and in her presence Lydia sat like stone, staring into the air above Daniel's head. Getting ready to say whatever it was she had come to say, he thought. When the waitress left, Daniel started on his hamburger, glad of an excuse to lower his eyes.

But Lydia did not touch her food. Eventually, her staring got to him, and he stopped eating.

"What?" he asked, although he dreaded the answer.

"I need to get rid of somebody. Permanently. Do you know anybody who can do the job?" There was no emotion in her sky-blue eyes.

◇◇◇

Even over the distance of time the memory overwhelmed him; he choked, and looked up at Natalie with a face blanched in pain. "Nat…she was asking *me* if I knew somebody who could *kill* somebody. Me! That's what she wanted my help for; that's what she thought I would be good for!" He buried his face in his shaking hands.

"Oh, Daniel!"

"No. Not yet." He removed his hands from his face and took a breath.

◇◇◇

Daniel had stared at Lydia. This could not be happening. And if it was, what then? What was he supposed to do?

She did not wait for him to figure it out. She gave her head an impatient toss, and her voice grew insistent. "Well, *do* you?"

Daniel felt his anger surging out of nowhere, regardless of the consequences. "No!" he shouted. "What a vile thing to say!" He remembered how she had made him feel the evening before—and other times, when they had been together—like he was supposed to know all about the mysteries of the criminal underworld—romanticizing it. It made him ill. "You think committing a crime is some exciting game people play. Like in *Deathwatch* or *Mousetrap*! Well it's not! It's hell! And then one way or another you pay, and pay, and pay!"

Her expression remained haughty, detached. Her eyes got so huge he could see the veins showing around the edges. For once in her life she spoke without emotion. "You're wrong, Daniel. I know exactly what I'm doing. I'm going to do something for myself for once, since nobody will help. I thought you would understand because of all the things people have done to you, but I was wrong. If you won't help me, I'll have to help myself."

Her white face remained calm, as in uncanny slow motion she pulled her handbag up onto the table, opened it, and pulled out what was inside.

›››

"Nat," said Daniel, his voice shaking, "she had the gun."

"Ah," said Natalie, and light shone in the dark places, chasing away the last of the shadows.

"My God." Daniel spoke quickly, unaware of the epiphany that was taking place at the other end of the sofa. "I'm sitting there in the Maverick Diner in Bergenfield, New Jersey, trying to mind my own business and be a good guy, and someone I used to honestly care about turns out to be from another planet and starts waving a gun around under my nose! Jesus Christ! Just sitting there at the same table with her and that gun was a fucking parole violation!"

His voice grew louder, and he gestured with his hands. "I mean, what is this? Some gothic horror plot-twist that's gonna haunt me till I die? People I think I know are gonna meet me somewhere, then pull out a gun and do their best to attract attention? And there's nothing I can do about it? Nat! I will never forget how I felt the day of the robbery—when Rick pulled out the gun. Sick—sick to death! I had never dreamed things could get so out of hand. And there was Lydia, holding—and I felt just the same. This can't be happening again—I can't believe it!" His voice changed, lashing his words with cynicism. "Nobody else is going to believe it either." Tears gathered in his eyes, visible as little stars of light, reflections of the street lamps outside the window. "Nat, I'm sunk."

"No," she said. "Not by a long shot. Go on. Tell me what happened next."

"Yes. Okay." He breathed more slowly. "I lost it completely is what happened next."

◇◇◇

Daniel had lunged across the table, trying to close the stiff flaps of the handbag over what Lydia had revealed, shoving the thing back into her lap. Glasses, ketchup and mustard bottles went crashing in every direction, rolling to the floor and down the aisle. The waitress rushed over. There ensued a scene in which she tried to reorganize the table, while Daniel sat shaking and trying to breathe, with Lydia like stone again, the handbag back on her lap.

When the waitress left, Lydia began to speak. But Daniel could not bear to hear another word. He struggled out of the booth. She tried to stop him, grabbing for his arm, but he shook her off and half ran out the door.

◇◇◇

"I walked home. I couldn't take the idea of standing around waiting for a bus, and then riding on it in close proximity with other human beings—people who might turn out to be toting machine guns they wanted to show me. Besides—I needed to walk.

"I got home—Rebecca's—at two. I about had time to take my coat off before the doorbell rang. My God, Nat, when I saw Rose standing on the stoop I thought I was done for. I couldn't figure out how she found me. It wasn't until much later I realized she must have followed me from Bergenfield. But at the time—"

◇◇◇

Rose's pink and white face, nestled in a luxuriant fur collar, had conveyed her attitude of disapprobation. Her narrow lips were pulled back at the corners, and her eyes, as they searched Daniel's shell-shocked face, had a reproachful cast.

Daniel gripped the doorknob tightly, trying to steady himself amidst a sea of conflicting thoughts and questions. What was she doing there? From his swirling mind leaped one clear thought: He didn't care why she had come, he wanted her to leave.

"Aren't you going to let me in?" She asked it as if she had a right to expect entry.

"No," said Daniel, the lesson learned at last. "I'm not."

Rose's eyes flashed dangerously. "I suggest you reconsider." Her words were sharpened by a threatening edge. "Unless you want the whole world to know what you've just been doing!"

The veil on her threats was spider-web thin. In his fertile imagination, Daniel heard the snick of keys turning in steel locks as his parole was rescinded, and had a vision of broad-shouldered detectives asking him how he had learned everything he knew about making a hit.

"You'd better let me in."

He stepped back in soul-searing surrender, and Rose, aloof in victory, stepped into the house, walked to the middle of the living room, and turned around.

"I'd like to know," she asked, "just what you think you're doing."

Daniel, in the absence of hope, fell back on old habits. "I was getting ready to make dinner."

"Don't try that with me!" She used the familiar parental tone. "I saw you and Lydia—having lunch together. I know what's going on!"

Daniel shrugged to show his disinterest—but unseen, his pulse rate soared. "About what?"

Rose wrinkled up her face in a condescending smile. "I know Lydia's been seeing someone all winter. Don't bother to deny it was you!"

Hope was reborn in Daniel's breast. He had unthinkingly assumed that Rose had spoken with Lydia about what had happened. Was it possible that Rose didn't know the details of his meeting with Lydia—only knew they had met—and had leaped to this wild conclusion?

"I'm afraid you're mistaken." His kept his voice and manner artificial. Then he sidled up to what he wanted to know. "Where did you get that idea?"

Rose gave a snort of impatience. "She's been preoccupied all winter, and when you showed up last night so chummy I knew it had to be with you. I know your type! Then I saw you through the diner window just now!"

"You're making a mistake," said Daniel, more sure of himself. "If we seemed close, it was only because we've known each other a long time."

"I know that. I know all about your history." Rose gave him the once-over with a critical eye. Then she softened her approach. "You have to understand that I'm just looking after Lydia's best interests. She has a tendency to fantasize too much, and we worry about her judgment." She seated herself on the sofa. "You might not realize how protective Eric is of his daughter."

"Possibly a little overprotective," ventured Daniel.

Rose sighed. "He's a volatile man, I admit. I don't know what he'd do if he found out about this. Such a temper...You don't want him to find out that you've been seeing Lydia, do you? He could make things difficult for somebody like you if he wanted to. I'm telling you this for your own good. I don't think you can afford to get into trouble."

Daniel, in the midst of his turmoil, identified the direction in which she was headed. A wave of fear hit his already harrowed soul.

"Look," he said desperately. "We're not seeing each other. We're not going to see each other." He looked at Rose with increasing emotion. "In fact, I think she's nothing but trouble and I don't ever want to see her again!"

Rose was offended. "I wonder what Lydia would think if she heard you say that? Maybe I better just go tell her what you think about her, and see what she has to say about you!"

Daniel grew queasy at the prospect. "No—why do that?" He tried to make it sound casual, and knew by the flash of Rose's eyes that he had failed.

The telephone rang, and Daniel, not knowing which way to turn, picked it up.

"Hello?" His voice was tense with suppressed fear.

"Hi, Danny," said Rebecca. "I'm between clients. What's happening?"

He stared at the phone. "Nothing," he said.

⟩⟩⟩

Daniel shook his head in self-reproach. "I didn't handle that conversation very well. You can imagine what Rebecca must have thought."

"I can imagine what *you* must have thought."

"Yeah. Anyway, Rose was there for almost an hour altogether, throwing out insinuations left and right. Eventually I told her to do whatever she damn-well wanted—not that I was able to stand up to her in any way. I just figured it didn't make any difference, since I was a sitting duck. Then things got a little sticky. In the end I had to forcibly detach her, one finger at a time, and drag her to the door. And that's it. That's what happened. That's the whole story."

Daniel leaned his head back, throwing a forearm over his eyes. He sank more deeply into the sofa and stretched his legs out before him, feet on the floor. It was a pose of exhaustion, but also liberation.

Natalie looked at her brother in mute sympathy. She was emotionally drained from merely hearing what he had gone through that day; what it must have been like to live through she could not guess. And yet…how hard it was for him to find his way along a path which to her seemed so clearly marked. How he struggled at every step, at every decision, always taking the long way around; always traveling alone! She heard the echo of Sergeant Allan's voice in her head: *Not because he is afraid of failing, but because he thinks he has already failed.* Her eyes misted over and her breath caught.

She uncrossed her legs and wrapped her arms around them, resting her chin on her knees. "Now I understand why you never called Sarah back. That bothered me. It wasn't like you."

"I know." Daniel spoke from behind the crook of his arm. "I was horrified when you gave me Sarah's message. There was no way I was going to phone that house. For any reason. Ever."

"I can see why."

"My mistake was I should have told you I was through with the Dows. But at the time you called, Rebecca and I were arguing about Lydia, and about what had happened, and I was already committed to my 'nothing's wrong' story, which turned out to be the end of us. That was another bitter pill." Daniel's voice took on a bitter cast. "Knowing that someone like Rebecca would think I might prefer someone who walked in off the street. Jesus. But I couldn't tell her what Rose was really doing there—couldn't make it make sense, I mean—without telling her about Lydia. And I couldn't do that—I wasn't strong enough to do that. So Rebecca thought the worst."

Natalie nudged her brother's thigh with her toes. "I went to see Rebecca yesterday."

Daniel's arm came away from his eyes, and his head came off the back of the sofa. A fleeting look of half-smothered eagerness and half-remembered happiness lit his face.

"Is she okay?" he asked. He frowned. "How did she seem?"

"She was fine. She was—she doesn't think you saw something in Rose you didn't see in her, Daniel."

Daniel shrugged. "Well, you could have fooled me. She was sure upset about something."

"Of course she was upset!" Natalie raised her hands. "Good night! On the one hand, you couldn't hide the fact that there was something going on, while on the other, you wouldn't tell her what the hell it was. That's not fair, Daniel. Also—brother—it doesn't work. If you are going to keep a secret, the first rule is you can't let anyone know you have it."

"But I couldn't tell her about Lydia and the gun!"

"Why, not?" Natalie stressed both words. "Do you really think telling her the truth would have been more unpleasant than what happened when you didn't?"

Daniel thought it through. He looked questioningly at his sister.

"Call her," said Natalie.

Daniel threw his head back against the sofa. "Why? Realizing my mistake doesn't make it go away. It's too late to explain now. It's over—at least for Rebecca."

"Oh?" said Natalie. "Call her."

"You may think it's not too late, but you...She...Is there something you're not telling me?"

Natalie shook her head and held up three fingers.

Daniel eyed his sister dubiously. "My respect for your powers of deduction has grown considerably of late. I've always known you were sharp—none better—but...You don't miss much, do you?"

A vision of Sergeant Allan's extraordinary behavior at the courthouse flashed across her mind. "I don't know about that; sometimes I'm surprisingly slow on the uptake."

"You're being modest."

"Well then, trust me on this one. You told me you had changed, that you wanted different things from life now. Well, I believed you, because I knew how you felt about Rebecca, and she sure is a different type entirely from a Lara or a Lydia. Call her."

Daniel opened and closed his mouth. "Okay. If you say so. Assuming I ever get the opportunity. And I will try to remember that sins of omission—my favorite kind—carry their appointed penalty." He sighed. "Which reminds me—I'm in a hell of a mess."

"Momentarily." Natalie's tone was one of reassurance. "Just until the police work out who did it."

"But don't you get it? Since Lydia brought the damned gun with her, anybody she met—not just the family—could have done it." Daniel's voice edged toward desperation again. "She had been bewitched by some melodramatic idea that she was an avenging angel, and was wandering around Bergen County playing the part to the hilt. Somebody was using her for something, and she walked right into it. It's the ultimate in self-destructive behavior, isn't it? Providing the weapon for your own murder."

He looked at Natalie with a drawn face. "I know you believe I didn't do it, Nat, and I'm grateful for that. But do you really expect anyone to agree with you? To me it looks awful! I had the means (I actually *saw* the gun), the opportunity (I was the last one to see her alive), and for motive, they'll think up something—either I had a deal with Rose, or maybe I was involved in some criminal activity that Lydia found out about and I silenced her so she wouldn't tell on me. I don't see a way out of this!"

Natalie was unsympathetic. "You need to develop objectivity, Daniel. You had no means: when you left Lydia, she still had the gun. You had no motive: you hadn't seen Lydia for almost three years, and you had only met Rose the night before, so how can it be suggested let alone proved that you were involved with either of them? Most of all you had no opportunity: Lydia was alive when you left her—presumably the waitress at the Maverick won't have completely forgotten that scene—and your alibi, from Rose, not to mention Eric's detective, and then Rebecca, is rock solid! You were only a suspect if you did the murder around midday, and now we know Lydia was alive at two o'clock. Granted, you were alone in the house between three and four, but—get real—it may only take a second to pull a trigger, but you had exactly one hour to a) find Lydia, b) do the murder, c) hide the body somewhere, d) get home, and e) bake a batch of brownies—from scratch, no less—before Rebecca got home. As soon as I heard Rose's story and worked out your timetable I knew you were in no danger. Not even the police can screw this one up." Natalie leaned forward and belted him in the shoulder with the back of her hand. "You've been sitting on your own alibi!"

"Oh," he said. "Shit."

"Exactly. Y'know..." Natalie grew reflective. "If you're gonna be a father, you're gonna have to learn to keep one step ahead of the game—any nine-year-old worth her salt will walk all over you if you carry on this way."

Daniel's rueful expression shifted instantly to one of eagerness. "I wish you could have talked with Gayanne, Nat. I think she has a bit of your practicality in her. She was so down to earth! I liked it. I've always had a horror of her growing up to be an upper class New Milford snob—like Lara used to be before she discovered crack. I needn't have worried. California is a long way from New Milford, and I don't think Lara's parents have relented or given her any help." Daniel brought one leg up underneath him and sat on it. "Natalie, did you know, my daughter has her own social worker? Takes you back, doesn't it? Remember Mrs. Moochy? She had great toys, I remember. I must have been about twelve."

"I remember," said Natalie. "She was very sweet, wasn't she? I wonder if she realized how much I lied to her? Never mind that. Tell me more about Gayanne."

Daniel was glad to do so. "In a way, we sounded like two long-lost friends catching up on the news; then in another way, it was like we'd always been together and now—for the first time—we're apart. And I don't want us to be apart. I want us to have a home, and for me to have a job, and her to go to school. And, God save me, I want to have a telephone so that my daughter can call me when she needs me. But how can I possibly do it?"

"You'll make a wonderful father."

"Make?" Daniel shook his head. "You forget, I already am a father. A lousy father. Just like the kind I swore I'd never be; just like the one I had." Daniel thrust his chin forward. "Well, I want to be a better father. I want my child. I want her to know I love her, no matter what." He lapsed into thought-filled silence.

Natalie rested her arm along the back of the sofa and laid her cheek against her shoulder, brushing a wayward strand of hair out of her eyes. It filled her with happiness to hear Daniel speak so, to think he had found his way at last. But it made her wonder too, because, after all, she was not sure she could say as much for herself. And as she looked again at her brother's dream-swept face, she found the strength to dare, because if he had found the courage, couldn't she? Her eyes wandered out the picture window, where the cloudy sky reflected the bright lights of Haworth, filling the world with a luminous glow.

They sat silent again for a while, wrapped in their separate thoughts, both for their separate reasons unwilling to end this quiet interlude. All that had to be said had been said; there was no predilection in the Joday clan for pointless repetition or empty words of comfort; both knew the time for conversation had ended, and both knew what must come next.

It was Daniel, as indeed it had to be, who, after some minutes, broke the silence.

"Well." He put his hands on his knees. "I guess I better call the police." He sighed. "I don't want to approach the guy downstairs—he'd probably get excited and shoot me. I'd rather salvage what's left of my pride by surrendering willingly. I don't suppose your sergeant is on the job at this hour—more's the pity—I would prefer him to any of the others."

"Why don't you call him at home?" suggested Natalie ingenuously. "I suspect he might well come."

"I beg your pardon?"

She thanked the darkness as her cheeks grew warm. "I have his home number."

"I see." Daniel pursed his lips and nodded. "You know I may not be in your league, but I am not totally devoid of perception."

"Don't be silly, what are you talking about?"

"Unh-hunh," said Daniel agreeably. Then he grimaced. "I made you look bad in front of Sergeant Allan, didn't I? You told him you trusted me to stay put—and I left. I'm sorry, Nat."

"You told him you wouldn't leave the county," said Natalie. "You haven't left the county, Daniel."

"Yeah, so tell me you weren't worried that I would."

Natalie looked away.

Daniel stood up slowly, stretching his tired limbs and running a hand through his hair. "Well, no point in waiting—I've had it with that tactic. I noticed in the bathroom mirror this afternoon—my hair is starting to go gray. Stress will do that, I understand. I feel as though I haven't even got my life started yet, and here's my hair going gray."

Daniel went to find the phone, while Natalie got her notebook and located Sergeant Allan's phone number in the gloom. They returned to the living room together and sat side-by-side again as Daniel dialed. Trick, aroused from his slumber by all this untoward nighttime activity, came over and jumped on the sofa between them. Natalie reached out a hand to him, and he tilted up his head so that she could access his chin.

"Hello, may I speak with Sergeant Allan, please?" Natalie slipped her hands around Trick's midriff and pulled him, purring loudly, onto her lap. "Hello. This is Daniel Joday speaking. I'm sorry to disturb you at home, and in the middle of the night, but I understand your people are looking for me, and rather than call the station, I was hoping you could—I'm at my sister's. Yes, she's right here." Natalie leaned forward and rubbed her cheek against Trick's silken head. "No, everything's okay. Yes, I'll tell you everything. Can you possibly—? Thanks, I appreciate it. Okay."

Daniel turned and held the receiver out to his sister. Natalie took it from his hand.

"Hello?" she said, and realized how much she looked forward to hearing his voice.

"Are you all right?" He did not sound sleepy at all.

"Sure. Are you?"

"Yes. I'll be there with a squad car in half an hour. By the way, your car was clean. I'll arrange to bring that too."

"Thanks."

He hung up, and Natalie sat staring at the receiver.

"I'd better get some stuff together," said Daniel. "Damn. I'll miss class tomorrow morning. Well, nothing to be done about that. I'll take my books—they usually let you study in county." He wandered around the darkened flat, packing books and pens, along with a change of clothes and other personal items in the duffel bag. He put the bag ready by the door. Then he came back to the sofa, where Natalie still sat, petting Trick, holding the phone.

"What else am I supposed to be doing tomorrow that I'm not going to be able to do?" he asked himself. As he sat down he remembered. "Oh..." His body sagged, his head dropped forward.

Natalie put the phone down and turned to him, and Trick jumped off her lap.

"Gayanne...She's expecting me to call her tomorrow night. I promised. And I'm going to be in jail." He wrapped his hands around his head, trying to keep away the image of the child waiting by the silent phone. "Everything I touch turns to sand."

"This is a house of mirrors." Natalie's tone was detached, cool. "It multiplies fear; it strangles thought. But it doesn't accurately reflect the situation."

Daniel raised his head.

Natalie paraphrased the sergeant's words as well as she could. "We all have to learn how to tell the big problems from the little ones. And we have to trust ourselves to wait long enough to figure out which are which before we panic. If you can't tell the difference yet, get the opinion of somebody you trust—but don't assume the worst. Odds are it's not that bad."

Her words resonated with his own recent thoughts, and he felt himself calming down. "Okay," he said, trying it on for size. "It's not the end of the world. Maybe if I explain to the cops, they'll let me call her. I'll tell Sergeant Allan—that's my best chance. Or...if he can't help, Evan will be back later this morning. They'll let me call him, and I can explain it to him, and he can call her and—" He frowned. "That's cold-blooded, though, having my lawyer call her." He looked at Natalie. Surprise lit his face. Surprise at the simplicity of it. "Would you call her if I can't?" He gripped her arm. "She trusts you. Tell her—something. Tell her I can't..." He shook his head and closed his eyes. "Tell her what's happened." His eyes opened. "Tell her the truth. Tell her I'll be out soon, and I'll call her as soon as they let me use a phone."

"Of course I will, if—if you're still in jail."

"No fear of that," said Daniel wryly. "After the way I've acted, alibi or no alibi, they're not going to let me out until they solve this case."

"Well..." Natalie's eyes narrowed and the line of her mouth hardened. "That's what I meant. When the case is solved."

He eyed her quizzically, but she had turned her head and was gazing out the picture window.

"Look," she said, "the rain has stopped. I can see the stars."

>>>

The faint wail of sirens broke the pre-dawn silence, as police cars streamed past White Beeches unseen. The wail grew louder and rose in pitch as the cars came out of the trees and rounded the corner at the top of Haworth Avenue, then swelled in swift crescendo as they roared over the railroad tracks to the bottom of Tank Hill. It became an intolerable scream as the cars raced up the hill and bumped into the driveway of Number 128.

There was a squeal of car brakes and the slamming of car doors, and then there was the ringing of the doorbell above the crackle and jargon of a police radio, and insistent, spinning lights invading the house and streaking across the walls in painful bursts of blue and red which would not go away.

Chapter Eighteen

Upon retiring in the quiescent early morning, Natalie, accepting the inevitable, brought the phone with her to bed. Thus, when it began ringing some hours later, she had but to roll over, crack open an eye, and pick it up.

"Yeah," she slurred.

"Natalie? Hi! It's Martin! Did I wake you up?"

"Hi, Martin. Yup. What time is it?"

"Ten-thirty. Late night, Natalie?"

"Yeah." She ran her tongue over her lips and swallowed. "What can I do for you, Martin?"

"Aha! The question is what can I do for you?"

"What?"

"Wake up, Natalie, and listen to this! Your scheme has taken off like gangbusters. This morning our PO box was flooded with responses to the contest, and last night I had a meeting with your jazz ensemble, and they're definitely going to make the New Globe their base."

"That's great, Martin."

"But listen to this! I also got a call from *the* personal secretary to Zizi Morgan-Bassouni—you know her."

"No, actually…"

"Oh, my dear, she's the widow of ex-Senator Mitchford "Mitch" Morgan-Bassouni. He's the one who was censured in the Sixties for conflict of interest because the Senate Committee he chaired recommended the awarding of an astounding number of government contracts to companies he was on the board of directors of. Big scandal, major sensation, and it all ends with a bang when Mitch takes the quick way out by drinking a quart of turpentine and expiring in Zizi's bejeweled arms. Curtain. He made his fortune in paint products, you know."

"Good heavens." Natalie rubbed her eyes.

"*Well!*" continued Martin. "Imagine my astonishment when her secretary calls me, and *he* says Zizi read about our struggle to preserve the capital A Arts in Bergen County, and was touched, and so he would like to meet with me to discuss possible funding beginning in the 1994-'95 season! Of course I won't get to meet 'herself'—she's been a recluse since the turpentine episode in 1969. But—get this—*she likes the classics!*"

"Martin, that's great."

"You're the one who's helping to make my dreams come true, Ms. Joday! Now etiquette demands that I return the favor. Are you ready to talk turkey?"

Natalie stretched, and tucked her free arm under her head. "Actually I've been thinking about what I want to do with my life."

"I'm so proud of you, Natalie! Well? You're keeping me in suspense."

Natalie laughed. "Okay. I was thinking of world travel for starters. France. Greece. Japan in autumn. And the sound of the South China Sea has always fascinated me. And all of Africa, of course."

"All—of—Africa," he repeated, as though taking dictation. "Next?"

Natalie blinked. "I want, I guess—a more challenging job at the paper. And someday I want to own a house, with a yard big enough to play no-boundaries croquet. And I want to win a regional bridge tournament next year. And—I'd like to get my pilot's license."

"Now we're making progress. But Natalie, this is still too prosaic! Use your imagination."

"Oh, is that what you're after?" Natalie, resting the phone against her shoulder, clasped both hands behind her head. "Well, in that case, I want to win a Pulitzer Prize before I'm forty, and I want to be constantly pursued by all the best-looking young men, who will tell me how astoundingly clever I am, and whose hearts I will break one by one, although of course I'll feel very badly about it—for a while." She crossed one leg over the raised knee of the other and made circular patterns in the air with her foot. "And I want to be world-famous in my field, and—yes, I want to make a million dollars, and be stinking rich, and then I want to retire to lead an eccentric existence on a seafaring yacht, from which I will run my empire by satellite communication, accompanied—when scheduling permits—by my one true love, preferably a concert pianist or an international tennis star." She stopped herself. "Is that enough for starters?"

"I'll get right on it. You know I play a little piano myself—"

"Oh, Martin," said Natalie, grinning.

"Just wanted to get my name on the list early. So. We have a lot to talk about. Any chance of your stopping by today?"

"No. I'm sorry." Natalie's smile faded. "There were a lot of developments in the murder case yesterday."

"I guessed from what Harry said. He's just left to be with Sarah—seems they hauled off her father *and* her stepmother first thing this morning and she's in crisis."

"That means the cops have a full set. My brother was arrested last night—this morning."

"Oh, no," said Martin mournfully. "I'm sorry—sorry to be rattling on about trivialities."

"You didn't know."

"Natalie, isn't there something I can do to help? I meant it when I said I'd be happy to do anything for you—and not just because of your articles. Because, well, we're friends, Natalie—family."

"Oh, Martin, could you call me up every morning and tell me that?"

"You bet," he said.

"You're something, you know that? But unfortunately there's nothing—although. Maybe—Martin, y'know, Daniel, my brother—"

"I remember."

"Well, he's given the police his whole story now—a little late, maybe, but as soon as they verify it, they'll let him go with a rap on the knuckles for being a jerk. But being a jerk is a far cry from being a murderer. Martin, he needs a good job—real bad. Would you be willing to meet him, after this is all over, and see if you could do anything for him, or if you know anybody who could?"

"Well, Natalie, I'd like to help him out. But I've got to tell you honestly we don't have any openings for salaried jobs right now. Maybe if our finances improve."

"I understand. But—you're the sort of person who wouldn't hold his past against him. Besides, he's got experience doing theater, and he'll have the damned business degree. Couldn't you meet him, just in case? You never know when something might open up."

"And that's true too. Of course! I'll talk with him—see what stuff he's made of."

"Thanks, Martin."

"The pleasure, my dear Ms. Joday, is mine."

She switched off the phone and threw her head back against the pillows. As she stared at the ceiling, vivid images from the previous night appeared in her mind's eye.

Sergeant Allan had come in unescorted and had then sat in her living room for a few minutes as if paying a formal call. He had been subdued, deliberative. Daniel had explained, in a calm and unambiguous way, about his desire to have access to his books, and his need to make a long-distance phone call that evening on a personal matter of extreme importance. Sergeant Allan had said he didn't see a problem with the books, but that the phone call was more difficult. He would, however, see what he could do. The sergeant had searched Daniel's tired eyes and pale face for traces of lingering equivocation. He seemed at last satisfied there were none. Preliminaries attended to, he had read Daniel his rights, frisked him with clinical detachment, and pulled out his handcuffs. At that point he had hesitated, looking back and forth between the strained faces of brother and sister. "I guess we can put these on outside," he had said. Daniel had shot him a grateful look. Then Sergeant Allan had pulled Natalie's car keys out of his pocket and held them out to her. "It's downstairs," he had said. Their eyes had met as she extended her hand, and time had slowed to a crawl. She had taken the keys from him, and lowered her hand to her side. He had looked away, and time had resumed its accustomed pace. The two men had turned, passed through the door, and she had closed it. It had been an almost apologetic arrest.

With a sigh Natalie threw back the covers and slid out of bed, fully awake and ready to face the task of the day.

As she prepared for her departure, she grew more and more preoccupied. She heated up a cup of last night's coffee in the microwave. She brushed her teeth and ran a comb through her hair. She dressed in chinos and a t-shirt. She ate half a bagel and drank the coffee. She fed the cat. She put away the loaf of bread that sat on the kitchen counter. She pulled a bulky, rust-red sweater over her head. She replaced her car keys on her keychain and headed out the door to confront Lydia Dow's killer.

◇◇◇

Natalie drove through the elegant streets of Haworth and Closter, past the large wooden houses and landscaped yards, at an obedient 35 mph. It was a drive she had taken many times. But for the first time in her life, she had no sense of isolation from her neighbors.

In her youth she had been alienated from the community in which she lived, not only by her anachronistic hand-to-mouth existence, but by the secrets she had been forced to keep about it. At the age of twenty, her last reason for staying obliterated by what she had viewed at the time as a permanent rift between her brother and herself, she had packed her bags and left the area for what she thought was an equally permanent good. Out in the world, she had learned that economic hardship was nothing to be ashamed of. Later she had justified her decision to return by saying, "I belong here as much as anybody," a statement of fact in which defiance played as much a part as catharsis. But now she knew she had been drawn back for a different reason: her need to learn—in the one place where she would fully believe it—that she and her family held no monopoly on burdensome secrets.

She eased her foot off the gas and signaled left as she neared the entrance to Castle Dow. Then she came to a stop in the middle of the road. The gate was closed.

Car horns blared. Shoving her foot down, she shot across traffic and edged the car into the ditch beneath the high brick wall. She got out, locked the car, and put her keys in her pocket. She walked over to the intercom, which was attached to the brick gatepost at eye level, pushed the button, and waited.

The day was sunny and cool, with a steady breeze that ruffled her hair. Hands on hips, she peered through the gate at the house, but could see nothing but rhododendrons, forsythia, and oak trees. She pushed the button again, several times. There was no response. She pursed her lips.

She backed up and squinted up at the brick wall. It was about eight feet high. Bits of glass, imbedded in cement, were visible at the edge of the cornice. She walked over to the gate and gave it a shake. It was over six feet high, made of sturdy steel bars, spaced four inches apart, reaching to within a couple of inches of the ground at the bottom, with pointy spikes at the top. Recessed runners imbedded in the pavement on the other side of the gate made a pattern like butterfly wings. She ran a hand over the locking mechanism. There was no keyhole.

Natalie looked around. She wondered if the police had the house staked out. There were no parked vehicles in sight. She pushed the intercom button again, shouting, "Hello!" several times.

She shrugged.

Standing close beside the steel bars, but facing the gatepost, she reached up with both hands and grabbed the last two spikes. Leaning backward, she walked her feet up the bricks until she was able to find purchase for her left foot on a narrow hinge, about four feet off the ground. Shifting her weight forward, she reached back with her right foot, and rested it on top of the intercom. She bounced a little, testing its sturdiness. Shifting her weight back onto her right foot and adjusting her grip, she pulled her left knee up under her chin, and slipped her foot onto the top bar of the gate, between two spikes. Then, balancing cat-like, she removed her right foot from the top of the intercom, slid it between the spikes, and sprang down to the ground.

She landed lightly on the pavement, knees bent to lessen the impact. She straightened up, and turned around just in time to see a beige sedan, followed by a squad car, pull into the narrow space on the other side of the gate.

She experienced a moment of supreme indecision, and then Sergeant Allan got out of the sedan. Her choice made itself, and she stepped up to the gate. Her heart was pounding, whether from her exertion or her sense of being discovered, she knew not.

"Hello," she said. The wind coming from behind her blew her dark hair into her eyes.

"Hello," he said, nodding. He turned around and looked at his two colleagues, and then back at her. "What are you doing?"

"I was just—coming to see Sarah." She nodded, and he nodded back. "But the gate, here, was locked." He nodded. "Nobody answered the intercom, so I thought—well…" She closed her fingers together and arced her hand through the air.

He nodded.

"So," she took a deep breath. "What are you doing?"

"Coming to see Sarah," he said.

She nodded. "The gate's locked."

He pulled out his cell phone and dialed, put the phone to his ear, and turned sideways. Her eyes wandered to the road, and then back to the pavement beneath her feet.

"No answer," he said, pocketing his phone. "She may be out."

"Sarah?" scoffed Natalie. "Out?"

"People do leave their homes occasionally, especially when they have a good reason."

"Yeah, but—"

"Did you expect to find her here?" He was watching her closely. "Have you heard from her today?"

"No." Natalie chose her words carefully. "But Martin Montgomery at the New Globe told me Harry had come here to be with her. Harry seemed to think it was a crisis—his word. I was concerned, so I thought I'd better come over. She has no one else." She looked in the direction of the house, and the wind whipped the hair back from her face.

"Hold on a second, please." He stepped back for a consultation with the two officers, and made several more phone calls. Natalie clasped her hands behind her back.

He came back to the gate. "No report of her anywhere." He sounded neither surprised nor concerned. "I've checked at the courthouse and with her lawyer—he's been looking for her too." He squinted over Natalie's shoulder. "I've got the okay to proceed onto the grounds. My men will keep an eye on things here." He looked at the gate.

Another consultation between the three policemen resulted in the backing up of the squad car to the gate. The sergeant took off his jacket, stood on the trunk of the car, and, supported by the other two, got one foot on the locking mechanism in the middle of the gate, and then the other on the top bar. The gate wobbled, the policemen wobbled, and the sergeant leaned forward precariously. Natalie sprang forward and he released his hold on the spikes and grabbed her outstretched hands.

"I've got it," he said. He brought his other foot up, using her to balance himself, and leaped down.

"Ta da," said Natalie.

His eyes flashed, but she turned away, walking to the edge of the pavement. There was but a single purpose to her thoughts this day, and all her faculties were in thrall to that focus.

The sergeant tucked in his shirt, put on and buttoned his jacket, and regarded her impatient profile. "Okay." Authority and resignation mingled in his tone. "You're here. You're her friend. This is no time to quibble about the definition of trespass. Let's go."

They walked side by side along the driveway, gravel crunching beneath their feet. Natalie spotted a loose stone, which sat like an egg above the rest, and kicked it bouncing on ahead of them.

"That was quite a statement your brother gave," said the sergeant. "I almost thanked him for getting me up in the middle of the night to hear it. Incidentally—resourceful of you, managing to get my home number."

"You're not the only one on good terms with my night editor," said Natalie. She espied the egg-shaped stone, and, sneaking up behind it, kicked it again.

They rounded the first bend. The sergeant's eyes swept the grounds. "By the way, I stopped by to see your brother on my way here."

She turned to him, brushing her hair out of her eyes. "And?"

"He's...studying."

Natalie's imagination distilled from his words a high-resolution image of her brother, reclining in thoughtful nonchalance on a bunkbed beneath a barred window, concentrating on the finer points of macroeconomics. She looked back up the driveway and smiled.

"I know he's out of it," the sergeant continued. "But I can't spring him until the DA gets over his pique. As I said at our first meeting, we need him where we can find him, and he's lost his credibility. It could be a while."

Natalie's face remained impassive. "You picked up Rose again."

"Yes. The DA took her actions personally. It seems her lawyer pulled some pretty sensitive strings to get bail set so fast and so low yesterday. Somebody high up somewhere looks bad. The DA's anxious to get a deposition from you. He's going to try and dig up enough evidence to indict."

"For blackmail."

"Yes."

"And Eric?"

"He's being questioned by the prosecuting attorney from Serious Fraud. They've subpoenaed his financial records. Siphoning off money from somebody else's trust is a no-no, even when it's your daughter's. Your brother's testimony will be key. Dow may be indicted too."

"For embezzlement?"

"Yes."

"And Graham?"

"We're going to pursue prosecution for grand theft."

Natalie whistled. "That cuts away a lot of the dead wood."

"Yes, the field is narrowing."

"That's not what I meant," said Natalie. "Just because they're all in jail for something else doesn't mean one of them didn't do the murder, as you very well know. The murderer may already be safely behind bars."

"That's one way to get the perpetrator off the streets, but it's professionally unsatisfactory, as *you* very well know."

They rounded the final bend and walked around the fountain. Harry's Nissan sat alone in the designated company parking area.

"Sarah keeps her car in the garage," said Natalie.

"I know," said the sergeant. They walked to the garage. Through the open doors, they saw the cars of Sarah, Eric, and Rose.

"We've still got Bunch's car," said the sergeant. He led the way across the yard to the front of the house.

The door stood half open beneath the peaked roof. The sergeant undid the button on his jacket as he stepped onto the stoop. Ignoring the doorbell, he called out "Is anyone here?" There was no answer.

Turning to Natalie, he said, "You stay here. Keep your eyes open and call me if you spot anything."

She blinked. "Don't you have a partner?"

He looked over his shoulder. "Maternity leave."

She stood on the stoop and watched him cross the living room. He moved quickly through the rooms on the ground floor. Then he disappeared up the stairs. Natalie turned and studied the pink and purple flower beds.

The sergeant reappeared after a couple of minutes. Heading back to her, he spotted the control box for the main gate in the foyer. He popped open a little panel, pushed a couple of buttons, and shook his head.

"Operates by a four-digit code, but I don't know what it is." He snapped shut the panel, turned, and walked out the front door and past her without a glance. When he reached the oak trees in the front yard, he stopped.

Natalie threw an anxious look over her shoulder and hurried after him. "I don't like this. Something must be going on. Something must have happened to Sarah."

He turned half away from her, put his hands on his hips, and scanned the sunny yard. "Or, she's trying to leave town."

Natalie watched the wind buffeting the sergeant's trousers. "You think Sarah killed her sister."

"I think it's a possibility," said the sergeant. "And if she's bolted..."

"All the cars are here."

He shook his head. "We'd find her real fast if she took a car. Public transport—such as it is in this county—is a better bet."

"So where's Harry?"

"Possibly helping her get away—whether he knows it or not."

Natalie raised her eyebrows. "Have you requested a warrant?"

"No. Not yet. But I've reexamined her testimony."

"And you found something?"

"Not yet. But the whole picture changes if you take out her version of events."

Natalie leaned back against a tree, her hands behind her hips, one knee slightly bent. "Such as?"

"Such as, Sarah says she didn't know about the will—contrary to the belief espoused by the rest of the family that the sisters always told each other everything. But I think she did know about it—because Harry knew, and who else could have told him but his girlfriend? And what about this, Sarah says Lydia wasn't in the house between three and five o'clock, and that there was no phone call from her—but this is unsubstantiated. Lydia might have been at home the whole afternoon for all we know. Again, Sarah says her sister was perfectly normal at breakfast that day, but in fact, the evidence suggests the sisters had a major confrontation at the breakfast table—oh, yes, I picked up on Lydia's anger toward Sarah in your brother's story. Again, Sarah had access to the gun. There may have been a spare key that nobody knew about, or she might have picked the lock—she had all the time in the world alone in the house that afternoon. It's motive, opportunity, and means—staring us in the face all along."

"You think she did it for the money."

"She got it, didn't she? Money is the most common motive for crime. It all adds up."

"Yes, it adds up," agreed Natalie. "Perfectly." She raised her head and ran a hand through her hair. "You think it was premeditated?"

"She's been in therapy off and on for ten years. You didn't know that? She's also a talented actress."

He looked at his watch, glanced around the lawn again, and looked at Natalie. "Let me try this out on you. Point out the flaws, okay?"

Natalie eyed him warily. "Okay."

The sergeant came closer to her side. "Sarah gets home around three, as she said. The house is empty. Lydia has told her—so like Lydia—that she'll be home promptly at—say—four. Sarah goes downstairs and gets the gun. She waits for her sister by the garage. Lydia arrives home. Sarah shoots her and hides the body in the trunk of her car. Later that night, on the way home from the opening night party, after she drops Suter off, she hides the body under the parkway. She goes home.... What?"

"Daniel's testimony," said Natalie. "What was Lydia doing toting the murder weapon around and trying to hire a hit man? Are you gonna tell me after all that's happened you still don't think he's telling the truth?"

"No. I know he's telling the truth—but how far does that go? You've been insisting since the day we met that he doesn't know a thing about guns—except that the very sight of one gives him the heebie-jeebies. I grilled him about the gun he saw in Lydia's handbag. He has no idea what caliber or make it was: single-action, revolver, semi-automatic, large, small, new, old—it could have been a bazooka and he wouldn't be able to identify it. Believe me, his testimony will not stand up in court. We have no way of proving, based on your brother's story, that Lydia Dow had possession of the murder weapon."

"But that scene at the Maverick still took place. Don't you have to fit that in somehow?"

"Lydia lived in a fantasy world. She was trying to get involved with your brother again, and picked the most dramatic way she could think of to get his attention. Unfortunately his reaction wasn't what she had anticipated—what fantasy is when you play it out in real life—and her little drama had the opposite effect from what she wanted.

"Furthermore, I think Sarah learned of her sister's plans for your brother at breakfast that morning. I think she made her move that day because she saw an opportunity to throw the blame on someone else—your brother. I told you I thought it looked like a setup. I think Sarah has been the manipulator all along, playing helpless to make sure she got what she wanted—even if it meant getting away with—"

The sergeant's head snapped to the right, his eyes focusing on something beyond the oak trees. Natalie turned to follow his glance, and, as the sergeant brushed past her shoulder, spotted Harry hurrying across the lawn.

"Mr. Suter!" called the sergeant. Harry's head came around, wandering a little until he spotted them in the shade of the trees. He took a step forward, stopped, looked behind him, then came toward them again, breaking into a run. As he neared them, they saw the cast of immediate fear on his perennially anxious face.

"Have you found her?" He placed his hands on his hips and breathed hard. His hair, blown by the wind and damp with sweat, had fallen onto his forehead and stuck there.

"Wasn't she with you?" asked the sergeant. Natalie felt the change come over him as he switched from analyst to operative.

Harry shook his head, looking back and forth between the sergeant and Natalie. "I searched the whole house. Twice. She didn't leave anything—" He drew his thumb across his damp forehead. "I mean, there's no note."

The skin on the back of Natalie's neck tingled.

"And why would you think there would be a note?" The sergeant's unhurried, professional attitude contrasted sharply with Harry's barely controlled panic.

"She called me. At work. She was—she could barely speak. She said—I'll never forget her voice—she said 'It's time, Harry. Time to end this, one way or the other.' I knew what she meant. I told her not to do anything; to wait for me; that I was coming right over. She hung up on me. I came as fast as I could, but I'm afraid—"

"It's eleven-forty. How long have you been here?

"I don't know!" He could not hide his impatience at the sergeant's interruption. "Three quarters of an hour, maybe a little more. I searched everywhere. I think we should go—"

"Where did you just come from?"

"What? What difference does it make?" Harry's voice edged up a further notch in pitch and volume. "I went through the guest house! Before that I checked the garage. Does it matter?"

"And where were you going when I first spotted you?"

Exasperated, Harry raised his hands, fingers outspread. "I've been trying to tell you!"

"Please try and stay calm," said the sergeant in his cool voice. But Natalie noticed that the muscles of his neck and jaw had tightened.

There was a silence, broken only by Harry's breathing. He lowered his hands. His eyes sought out Natalie. "Last night she was talking about...she said she wished she were dead. She talked about the cliffs....There's a path that runs eastward through the woods to the Palisades. The cliffs there are four hundred feet high."

Natalie's skin tingled again.

But the sergeant's tone grew sharp. "This path through the woods.... If it leads to the cliffs, it must cross 9W somewhere near the top of Closter Dock Road, right?"

Harry nodded, still looking at Natalie.

The sergeant's eyes narrowed and he shook his head. "There's a bus stop right there." He reached for his cell phone again and walked a few paces away.

Harry moved closer to Natalie. "I was going to call you. There was a bad scene last night, after you left. She went off the deep end."

"About what?"

"About nothing! About that play! Whether or not Lydia worked on a show. She said Lydia had lied to her. She went nuts! If she—"

"Harry," Natalie spoke in a voice that made him listen. "I don't think you should underestimate Sarah anymore. I think you'd better watch out. For yourself."

One look, and then he turned his head away from her, and closed his eyes.

The sergeant finished his call and came back to them. He looked at Harry. "Where's this path you're talking about?"

"The main path runs about fifty yards behind the property. There's a little path at the back of the yard leading to it." He pointed, and took a few steps. "I'll show you."

"Just a second." The sergeant turned to Natalie, placed a light hand on her elbow, and steered her a few paces away. "I had my people check the bus schedules," he said in a low voice. "She may have taken the eleven a.m. bus into the city. If she went by this path Harry's talking about, there will be footprints."

Natalie nodded.

"I've called for backup," he continued. "Say fifteen minutes." He looked at her in uncharacteristic doubt.

Natalie met his gaze. "I'll wait here. When your people arrive, I'll show them which way you went."

His eyebrows twitched. "That would be helpful. But *stay* here, okay?" He fished a moment in his inside pocket and pulled out a card. "Here's my cell phone number." He turned from her and went to join Harry.

Natalie retreated to the front stoop and folded her arms across her chest, flicking at the card with a forefinger. She watched the two men cross the lawn, skirting the pool at the north end of the property. The contrasts between them, inward and outward, were pronounced: Harry, impatiently seeking the woman he loved, afraid of what he might find, but desperate to reach her in case it was not too late; Sergeant Allan, moving steadily along the trail of a fleeing murderer, eyes searching everywhere for signs of her passage, his mind on bus schedules and escape routes. She marked the spot where they disappeared into the woods.

She turned quickly and entered the house. What she wanted was a vantage point, and she headed for the landing at the top of the first flight of stairs. She slid into the cushioned seat that nestled in the bow of a three-sided window. From there she had a view of the entire back property, from a glimpse of the car park on the left to the Japanese garden on the right. For Natalie knew that Harry and the sergeant were both dead wrong in their conclusions—because someone had been there to close that electric gate after Harry's arrival, and that someone could only have been Sarah.

Sarah must have known that Harry would come if she called; must have therefore wanted him to come. The locked gate showed that she wanted to be alone with him, because she must have waited until she saw his car before closing it. Then why had she disappeared? She must have meant to avoid him. But why? Natalie refused to believe Sarah had fled—there had been no time for her to catch the eleven o'clock bus if she had also been the one to lock the gate. Then where had she gone? Natalie had no idea, but she concluded that Sarah would not have gone to such lengths to get Harry there, only to leave without seeing him. Therefore, regardless of Harry's search, she had not gone far.

Despite her careful reasoning, it took her breath away to see, after only a minute of waiting, a sudden movement behind the little Japanese pagoda. Stunned, she watched a slender figure in faded dungarees and a gray sweatshirt materialize out of nowhere and sprint across the grass, the bright sun glinting off her coppery hair. She was carrying something—something small but heavy—in her right hand.

Natalie's fingers pulled at the window latch, but it was locked. Helpless, she watched Sarah disappear into the trees on the eastern edge of the lawn—not using the little path to the north where the men had gone. In a flash, she realized Sarah was taking a shortcut to the main path, and would no doubt gain the path to the cliffs well ahead of the sergeant and Harry. Natalie sprang from the window seat and flew down the stairs. With quick strides, she raced across the lawn, conscious only of the wind roaring in her ears. She headed for the spot where Sarah had entered the woods. Reaching the trees, she melted into the shadows as quietly as she could.

She slowed to a fast walk, eyes searching for signs of a trail. The ground was rough and damp, covered with leaf mold and spring wildflowers. She moved farther into the woods, and finally spotted a small, heel-shaped depression in a muddy hollow between two tulip trees. As expected, Sarah was headed northeast. Natalie took the most open way, stepping carefully and trying to keep her bearings. Minutes ticked by, and her pace slowed, as she opted for silence rather than speed. She spotted another footprint, and her eyes widened as she saw the groundwater still oozing into the heel mark. Heart pounding, she picked her way through a stand of mountain laurel, and was rewarded by a glimpse of gray sweatshirt all but hidden by the heavy underbrush. She inched forward, crouching low.

Sarah was kneeling behind the massive trunk of a fallen oak tree, looking westward. Her arms were outstretched, and her hands, resting on the tree trunk, were clasped together. It was a stylized attitude of prayer, but in her folded hands she held a .357 Colt magnum.

Natalie crouched lower still, her fingers brushing the top of the undergrowth. Pulse racing, she moved as quietly as she could across the damp carpet of rotting leaves and woodsy groundfall. With the wind in her face, carrying the sound away from Sarah, she managed to creep within half a dozen yards without attracting her attention. Then she saw what Sarah saw.

Sergeant Allan and Harry were walking toward them along the path, about seventy-five yards away. The sergeant was taking his time, bending down frequently to examine the ground and shaking his head. Harry, impatience in every gesture, was urging him on. The two men stopped and fell into animated discussion.

Sarah nestled the butt of the revolver against the tree trunk and settled herself down, sighting along the short black barrel.

"Sarah."

Sarah jumped, and twisted around in surprise, bringing the gaping muzzle of the revolver to bear on Natalie's midriff.

Natalie, transfixed, was surprised to hear her own voice saying "Would you mind pointing that somewhere else?"

Sarah blinked, looked down at the revolver, and said, in grotesque parody of her customary diffidence, "Sorry." She lowered the gun.

Natalie, revivified, moved swiftly to Sarah's side, and knelt beside her in the damp undergrowth. Natalie put both hands on the gun, made sure it was pointing downward, and gently pulled it away.

Sarah winced, resisting. "You don't understand." Her voice was a symphony of emotions, her face tormented behind her windblown hair.

"Yes, I do," whispered Natalie. There was no time for anything but the truth. "I know what I'd want to do to anyone who killed my brother." Her face spasmed.

Sarah looked at her in amazement, then in appeal. "Then let me do it!" she pleaded. "Let me do something at last!"

Natalie shook her head. "You'd be throwing your life away."

"I don't care," whispered Sarah.

"Lydia would care," said Natalie. "All she wanted was for you to be happy. That's the catch. You can't help her by destroying yourself."

Natalie pulled gently again. Sarah's fingers slipped from the gun, her hands falling lifeless onto her lap. She raised her face, exhaled, and closed her eyes.

Natalie's hands shook as she cracked open the cylinder and upended the gun, catching the falling cartridges in her palm. She could hear the voices of the searchers, coming closer. She shoved the cartridges into her pocket. She undid her belt, and pulled it out of the first three belt loops.

Sarah had opened her eyes, and watched with a puzzled expression as Natalie poked the belt through the trigger guard of the gun. Then she ran the gun along the belt until it lay against the small of her back.

"Okay, here's the plan." Natalie re-threaded the belt though the loops. "If they find it, I'll tell them what happened. Until then, it's none of their business. I found you in the woods, period." She drew the belt tight and buckled it.

Sarah's face hardened. "I'm not going to let him get away with this."

"I'm with you." Natalie yanked her sweater below her hips as far as it would go. "But let's come up with something better than luring him here and shooting him, okay?"

Sarah looked her in the eye. "I wanted him to go to the cliffs, so I could push him over. The gun was just insurance—until you arrived and I had to improvise."

"Reasonable." Natalie shoved her hair behind her ears. "But if you were trying to make it look like an accident, you never should have closed the gate."

Sarah, still staring at Natalie, pushed her rippling hair away from her face. "Why are you helping me?"

"Because I like you, Sarah." Natalie stood up. "I liked you from the first, when you told me how you felt about your sister—exactly the way I feel about Daniel." She held out her hand. "Come on. Let's end it."

◇◇◇

Natalie pulled Sarah up, and they picked their way through the underbrush to the path. Harry and Sergeant Allan stared at them, the one with relief, the other with displeasure. Harry hurried anxiously to Sarah's side. He reached for her shoulder, seeking to soothe and caress.

At his touch, Sarah threw up her arms in explosive violence, knocking his forearm away and striking his face with the side of her hand. He stumbled backward with a cry, and she went after him with clenched fists and sharp elbows, emitting short sharp gasps with each swift blow. Harry, hands over his face, went down, and she would have gone down on top of him, had not the sergeant gotten his arms around her, pinning her against his body. Natalie, superfluous, stood by with arms half-raised, mouth agape.

Sarah struggled and kicked heedless of pain or injury, but the sergeant handled her skillfully, forcing her to her knees to counter her kicks, locking one arm behind her back. Then he had his cuffs out, and one narrow wrist was pinioned. He captured her other hand as it clawed for his face, twisted it down, and slapped the second cuff home.

Unable to move, Sarah continued her attack in the only way left.

"Murderer!" she screamed. Her mouth stretched wide as she clung to the final syllable. "Murderer!" She screamed it again and again, upright on her knees, hands behind her back, wild hair whipping in the wind.

Harry regained his feet. Blood trickled from a cut on his forehead. He looked at Sarah, incredulous. But as comprehension came to him in all its ramifications, his face was transfigured: despair was followed by fear, and then came desperation. His head and shoulders wavered back and forth, then he turned and fled, sprinting wildly along the path to the cliffs.

Sarah fell silent, sank back on her heels, and watched him until he disappeared around a bend in the path.

Sergeant Allan, caught flatfooted, stood motionless behind Sarah. Then he looked at Natalie, and doubt laid siege to his face. Suddenly he grimaced, spat out an expletive, and bounded away, racing after Harry with swift, ground-eating strides.

Natalie also sprang into action. Leaving Sarah crumpled and pinioned in the mud, she bounded into the woods, heading due east. She ran low to avoid the tree branches, keeping her eyes on the undergrowth as she scrambled for secure footing. Suddenly the ground fell sharply away before her, and she slid out of control down a rocky outcropping ten feet high, landing on her feet by sheer luck. Recovering, she passed through a dense thicket of hawthorn, sweeping the branches aside with her arms as she ran. When the foliage thinned, she caught a glimpse of Harry through the trees to the left, coming down the more gently sloping—but longer—route of the path.

She burst out of the trees and onto a little bank. Her feet sank into the soft earth and she stumbled, sprawling head first across the slippery leaf mold of the path. Harry was only a few yards away, running hard. She heard the rasp of his breathing. With no time to get up, she raised her legs and arms, trying to block his way, or slow him down. Faltering only a little, he jumped over her, and almost made it, but his trailing leg touched her outstretched hand. He spun his arms, hung as if suspended in midair a moment, and then fell forward heavily.

Before Natalie could move, the sergeant raced past her, slid onto his knees at Harry's side, grabbed a wrist, and twisted his arm around behind his back. Harry flinched and gasped in pain.

The sergeant frisked him thoroughly and without ceremony. Then he spared a glance at Natalie.

"You okay?"

"Yeah." She took in air by the lungful, and edged her hand around to the small of her back. Then she stood up, pulled her sweater down, and looked at the muddy wreck of her chinos.

"Doesn't anybody in your family ever stay put?" asked the sergeant, glancing up again, glaring this time.

"I don't think so," said Natalie, still trying to catch her breath. "I saw Sarah from the house, and figured I'd better collect her." She looked back and forth between the two men. She felt very strange.

The sergeant released his grip on Harry's wrist and rolled him over. Harry's arms flopped helplessly; his eyes were empty, uncomprehending.

The sergeant stood up. He came and stood at Natalie's side, looking over her shoulder. "I gather I am supposed to conclude that he killed Lydia?"

Natalie nodded.

"So he could marry Sarah and get at the money?"

Natalie shook her head.

"He just wanted to kill her for the fun of it," said the sergeant sardonically.

"He didn't want to kill her." Natalie took a final, deep breath, and looked the sergeant in the eye. "It was Lydia who wanted to kill him."

Chapter Nineteen

"And may she forgive me for not finishing the job." Sarah had come up the path behind them, arms bound, pale face streaked with dirt. She looked at Harry with hot contempt.

Harry stirred, trying to raise himself on one elbow.

The sergeant took a step toward him, pointing a 9 mm Beretta, which seemed to have sprung into his hand from nowhere. "Don't move."

Harry froze, then closed his eyes. "I'm not going to do anything. I shouldn't have run. I panicked." He opened his eyes and looked up at the sergeant. "Please take the cuffs off her."

The sergeant looked at Sarah's livid face, then back at Harry's defeated one.

Harry, interpreting his looks, gave a short, ironic laugh. "Don't you get it? I'm telling you I did it! Arrest me, not her. I shot Lydia." He waited expectantly, and then made the laughing sound again. "You don't believe me. You think I'm covering for her. Well, you'll have to believe me when I tell you what happened. She came to my apartment late in the afternoon—"

"Wait." The sergeant held up his hand. "We're not going to do this. We're going to go back to the house, and I'm going—"

Sarah shoved past Natalie and confronted the sergeant, her slight figure and disheveled face taking on extraordinary presence in the force of her passion. "I have a right to hear what he has to say!"

The sergeant shook his head. "He has a right to remain silent."

"It doesn't matter," said Harry. "She knows I did it. There's nothing left to hide. This will kill my parents, but if it's come to where you think she did it, do you think I can remain silent? I want to explain. I—"

"Wait." The sergeant spoke with the full might of his authority behind him. "This violates section four twenty-two—"

"Sixteen, forty-four, three, two, one," said Natalie.

The sergeant fell silent. He raised his head, as though listening. Above him, the budding treetops danced in the wind, and the sunlight glinted on the fresh green leaves. He looked eastward along the path, in the direction of that not-too-distant spot where Lydia Dow's body had lain hidden.

He looked at Sarah, and his expression grew soft. "Okay," he said. Sarah's lips moved. He looked at Harry. "I'll read you your rights, and then if you want to make a statement, I won't stop you." He glared at Natalie. "You're a reporter—I'm going to want a full statement from you corroborating everything he says."

"Okay." Natalie tried to gather her wits. Things seemed to be moving very fast, and it was disorienting.

The sergeant replaced the Beretta in his shoulder holster. He took Sarah by the arm, turned her around, and freed her hands. Then he went and knelt beside Harry, put the cuffs on him, ran through the Miranda warning, stood up, and stepped back, reaching for his notebook.

Sarah wrapped her fingers in the end of her sleeve, and wiped at the dirt on her face. She looked down at Harry with cold expectation. "Now tell me."

Harry, sitting in the mud, had been looking at his shackled hands with a dazed expression. But at her command, he raised his face and spoke. "I left the theater that day, February 8th at five-thirty. I went home to get dressed for the opening. She was in my apartment when I got there—"

"How did she get in?" snapped Sarah.

"She had a key."

"You were lovers, weren't you?"

Harry averted his head. "Yes."

"I knew it. I was too cowardly to face it for days. But I knew it last night. And I knew what you had done. You should have seen your face." She clenched her fists, and the sergeant put a hand on her shoulder. She shook him off, her eyes never leaving Harry. "Why didn't you tell me?"

"I wanted to!" Harry looked up briefly. "But—it was a secret. Lydia's secret. Last fall we started meeting at my apartment. I gave her a key. She told me her father mustn't suspect; that he would make trouble if he knew we were seeing each other. I didn't think it made sense, but I went along with it, because she insisted. Later, I was glad nobody knew, because I realized we had no future.

"Things started to go sour around the time Eric and Rose got married. She was angry at them, and then she got angry with me when I tried to help her. She didn't want help. She wanted them stopped, and was furious because I wouldn't do anything about it. What could I do? I didn't even understand what the big deal was! I tried to ease out slowly, and hoped she would get the picture and do the same. Over the holidays I said I had a lot of family commitments, and I was able to avoid her."

A look of revulsion came to Sarah's face.

Natalie, suddenly feeling shaky, located a half-buried boulder on the bank, and sat down.

Harry flinched under the spell of Sarah's accusatory gaze. "I didn't want to have a big scene," he explained. "I thought it would work out. And then I met you. You were so nice, and fun to be with, and really helpful. I never thought there would be a problem; you were only supposed to be around for a little while, and I didn't expect to—Lydia stopped coming to the theater, and I hoped it was because she had realized it was no good and was pulling back too.

"Only—she wasn't. She still had her key. She kept showing up at my place; I'd come home and find her there, like everything was okay between us. It was incredibly awkward. She had dreamed up an explanation to cover the situation—supposedly we had decided to see each other only occasionally, and not at the theater, because that was too open, and we needed to maintain secrecy. I couldn't just kick her out, could I? I tried to be as discouraging as I could without hurting her. I kept hoping she'd get fed up and stop."

"Did you try refusing to have sex with her?" Sarah treated him to a sarcastic smile. "Or changing the lock?"

Harry's face crumbled. "No, but—that was before things got so serious so fast between you and me. After that night when you and I—well, I realized I had to do something quick." Harry looked up at Sarah and his voice grew defensive. "I tried to convince you to come away with me! I tried to make you see that you were living in a madhouse! But you wouldn't even think of 'deserting your family.'"

Harry wiped his mouth with his hands and looked down again. "I tried to avoid Lydia the next day. The famous dinner party that Sunday? There was nothing wrong with my car—I just didn't want to go. But Lydia came and got me. I tried to tell her on the drive over here that we were finished. I tried. God—what an awful night. Outside I managed to stay calm, but inside I was dying. I didn't want to make a scene. But I did anyway—didn't I? The way Graham talked about swapping sisters—I was sure he knew something, and I just erupted. Everything I did led to disaster.

"The next day was the opening. After what had happened the previous night, I wanted to tell you about me and Lydia. But then we got so busy, I just let it go. Then in the afternoon you left.

"When I went home Lydia was there. I thought at first it was just another of her routine visits, that she had convinced herself once again that everything was just fine between us. I tried to tell her—

"She wouldn't listen. She called me names. Screamed at me. Accused me of a million sins. I got angry. I shouted at her to get out. But she wouldn't go."

Harry's voice was very low, his expression one of remembered amazement. "She stood in the middle of the living room. She said I had destroyed her life, but she was going to make sure I never hurt anybody—never hurt Sarah—again. It happened so damned fast. She pulled out the gun, and held it with both hands, and pointed it at me." He raised his shackled hands and pointed into the trees.

"I was on the other side of the room from the door. The only chance I had was to make a lunge at her, and hope I got there before she pulled the trigger. I couldn't wait to see if she was just acting a scene or really meant to do it. I jumped, hurling my body at her and reaching for the gun. We fell to the floor together, me on top of her. She let go of the gun as she twisted around. I had it in my hand, and I tried to point it away, but when she jerked out from under me, my elbow hit the floor, hard. The gun went off.

"It was an accident. I didn't ever want to hurt anyone." He stopped abruptly, and closed his eyes.

Sarah exhaled briefly. She looked at him sitting in the middle of the muddy path. The twist of her lip, the arch of her eyebrow, and the disdain of her eye bespoke her sovereign contempt. Throwing back her head, she turned abruptly away and walked back up the path to the house, an erect figure in gray beneath a mass of ruddy hair.

Harry watched her go, but, as the sergeant helped him to his feet, he turned to Natalie.

"I never dreamed things would get so out of hand, I swear. You believe me, don't you?"

Tears sprang unwanted to Natalie's eyes. "Yeah," she said, but it was not Harry she was thinking about.

Chapter Twenty

Later, Natalie sat alone on the back patio of Castle Dow, feeling dazed but content. The need for focus had come to an end, and the events of the past week, clear at last in their entirety, were sinking in. She was in no hurry.

They had returned to the house to find a couple of uniformed officers on guard. Sarah had explained how to open the automatic gate, and disappeared upstairs. Half a dozen squad cars had raced up the driveway and were now crammed in the *Company Parking*. Harry had been carted away without fuss. County police wandered about the house and grounds in groups of two or three, not doing much. A team from social services had arrived and hastened upstairs.

An officer—the tall one she had met at the *Star* the other day—interrupted Natalie's reverie. "The sergeant would like to see you in the dinette, Miss Joday, to take your statement." He was a picture of politeness. "If you'll give me your keys, I'll bring your car around."

"Oh." Natalie, remembering their former encounter with some embarrassment, stood up hastily and put her hand in her pocket. Then she froze.

"Something wrong?" asked the officer. "Did you lose your keys in the tussle?"

Natalie came back to life. "No, no." She fished her keys carefully out from amongst the cartridges from Sarah's gun, and handed them to the officer. "Thanks."

He left with a tip of his hat.

She went around the house and knocked on the door of the dinette. She could see the sergeant inside, sitting at the table. He got up and came to the door. They looked at each other through the diamond-shaped panes, reflecting one another's inscrutability as if the window had been mirror instead of glass.

The sergeant opened the door and Natalie entered.

She looked around. They were alone. "How's Sarah?"

"They say she's doing okay." There were dark circles under the sergeant's eyes. "Angry, aloof, bitter—but in control. They think she's past the worst of it. She's strong, isn't she? If she were as crazy as I thought she was, she might have tried to kill him when she found out, and wouldn't that have been an unholy mess."

"Indeed."

He gestured for her to sit.

Natalie slid carefully onto the front edge of a chair. There were paper and pens in front of her on the table. "You want me to do my statement?"

"Not exactly…" He reached out a provocative hand, and slid the writing materials out of her reach.

Natalie's pulse soared.

He sat down opposite her with a sultry smile, placed his elbows on the table, and intertwined his long fingers. "I want you," he said seductively, "to tell me how you knew."

"Oh!" Natalie started to lean back for support, thought better of it, and folded her hands on the table in front of her instead. "Is this standard department procedure?"

"No." He raised an eyebrow. "Professional growth."

She blinked. "Well then, I don't think I exactly *knew*. But I can tell you what I thought."

"That's what I want."

Natalie felt distinctly off kilter. "Where should I start?"

The sergeant, eyes searching deeply into hers, slowly leaned across the table. Her heart melted. "How did you figure out that Lydia wanted to kill Harry?"

"What? Oh." Natalie gathered her wits. "Well, I knew she wanted to kill somebody, because that's what she told Daniel." She looked at him querulously. "Why did you—and Daniel too—assume she didn't mean what she said? I'm not saying she would have gone through with it—I guess we'll never know that now—but that hit man stuff was pretty dramatic, even for Lydia. So the question became not who wanted to kill Lydia, but who did she want to kill—and why?"

The sergeant folded his arms and leaned back in his chair.

Natalie got into the swing of it. "It wouldn't have been so confusing if only Daniel had returned Sarah's call. If he had found out in February that Lydia was missing, he might have come forward with his story way sooner—he may be an expert at hurting himself, but he doesn't do things that put other people in danger. Don't you think, if you had heard his story from the first, you would have spent more time trying to discover why she wanted to kill someone, instead of why someone wanted to kill her? And the picture would have been clearer, because you would have realized immediately that both Daniel and Rose were out of it. As it was, seven weeks passed without anyone knowing it was Lydia herself who had taken the gun from her father's desk."

Natalie turned her head a little to one side and raised a finger. "But Daniel didn't call Sarah. Why not? Not because he knew Lydia was dead—if that had been the case he would not have dared to arouse suspicion by not returning the call. No, it was because he was—quite understandably—too terrified to have anything to do with anybody named Dow.

"Sarah, by the way, was correct in her conclusion that Lydia was dead—her reasoning was sound, too. Lydia would never have left without telling Sarah. It was not part of her character—her theatrical character.

"Everybody mentions Lydia's theatricality when they talk about her. Lydia was always playing a part. I think that was because she had no idea who she was, or how to get what she wanted. I think, growing up in this house, with a father who twisted the truth to suit his own selfish ends, and a mother who tried to cover up the unhappiness of her private life by constantly excusing her husband's actions, and pretending everything was fine, that Lydia never stood a chance at learning to deal with what she was feeling, or who she was. By the time her mother ran away, she was ready to carry on the tradition of covering up for her father; of telling her sister everything was going to be fine."

The sergeant flipped over a hand. "But why should it have been any different with Sarah?"

"Sarah was still a child when her mother left. She knew exactly what she felt—and she thought having your mother run out on you hurt like hell. And having a father who intimidated you and belittled you was awful too. She didn't play the game. She complained when things went wrong, she cried when she was hurt. This aroused the contempt—and fear—of those around her; she was labeled emotionally unbalanced, because she dared to have—and show—her real emotions.

"Lydia, out of touch with her feelings, was attracted to surface patterns—dramatic situations that gave her emotional release. Daniel, for example, was a great source of drama. He was gentle, lonely, hurting—but not so much that he wouldn't sympathize with her problems—he was artistic, and totally nonjudgmental. As an added bonus he had a dark past she was able to romanticize. Their relationship was full of intrigue and romance. Perfect!"

The sergeant frowned. "It sounds rather superficial to me. Nothing to build on."

"Exactly. Lydia's tactics were only good for the short term. She dabbled with the occasional job, the occasional love affair, the occasional artistic pursuit. But nothing lasted very long—how could it when her interpretations of what was going on were so off-base—and then she would run home to the familiar, sick environment. Sarah, on the other hand, however guilty she might have been made to feel about it, wanted out. And she made it too. She went away to college.

"It's hard to reconstruct what went on when Sarah was away last fall. Most of the witnesses to Lydia's last few months are either congenitally incapable of giving an objective account, or have warped the story to their own benefit. One thing we know, Rose and Eric decided to get married. Well, actually," corrected Natalie, "I presume Rose threatened to tell what she knew about Eric embezzling his daughter's estate. Her price for silence was marriage, and, one assumes, a piece of the action."

"You'll never be able to prove that."

"Happily, I don't need to." Natalie grinned at him. "I'm only telling you what I thought. I believe Lydia knew all about Eric's embezzlement. Her lawyer attributed Lydia's refusal to take an interest in her investment portfolio to not having a head for figures. But Daniel assured me she was a whiz in math and finance. Mr. Sherill was sure she didn't understand even the basics about her investments or financial management. No doubt it suited her to appear so to him. She was inured from infancy to the practice of glossing over her father's aberrations. To have done otherwise would have meant betrayal, and that was not in her character.

"But when she heard about the marriage plans she was devastated. This to her meant that her mother—twelve years after the fact—must be accepted as really and truly gone. It didn't bother Lydia in the slightest that Rose had been living in the house for the past two years, on apparently reasonably good terms—by Dow standards—with everybody. No, it was the idea of a *marriage* that upset her so much. A marriage was not going to conveniently evaporate if her mother fulfilled her promise and returned. Therefore she had to face the fact that her mother was not going to return. Lydia was distraught."

"Do you think she confronted her father about it?"

"No. She didn't confront him about the money, did she? That wasn't her technique for dealing with problems. But she made a symbolic gesture of revenge on both counts—probably without even admitting to herself what she was doing—by making a will. That was her mother's money—and Rose wasn't going to get it, ever."

The sergeant's expression grew sour. "Rose…She did nothing but cause confusion in this case from day one—and unlike your brother, she didn't even have a good excuse."

"Rose was in her element at Castle Dow. She could spend her time—when not improving mind and body with her various classes—divided between listening in on other people's telephone conversations, snooping through personal belongings, and otherwise looking for opportunities for personal advancement. She got Graham, whoever he is—I'm sure you'll have fun working it out—moved into the cottage on the estate, where he had free rein to try and woo Lydia and thus secure an even greater piece of the action. Then, sometime early this year, she found out about his pet-nabbing scheme, and I bet she decided she deserved a share of that. Their relationship suffered. Graham could have left, but that would have meant losing his chance with Lydia, not to mention the free meal ticket. Of course Graham didn't stand a chance with Lydia, because he wasn't Lydia's idea of someone to fall in love with, being alarmingly self-satisfied, egotistical, and sarcastic. Graham and Lydia did eventually strike up a friendship of sorts, no doubt because he knew exactly how to reinforce her preconceptions, and because she lacked the judgment to see what he was doing."

"We're getting off the track a little here, aren't we?" asked the sergeant.

Natalie smirked at him. "You sound like my editor. Okay, okay. The most important thing that happened while Sarah was away was that Lydia started helping out at the New Globe. Lydia began with *Little Foxes* in October, and was involved, albeit in a minor capacity, with every single show up till *The Children's Hour*. For that show, Lydia signed up before Christmas for props, but after the holidays she faded away."

The sergeant leaned forward with a stern expression and demanded, "How do you know this?"

Natalie wondered if this was how he looked at his suspects during a grilling. "I've checked through the production credits in the programs of all the shows last fall." Natalie waved at the row of theatrical programs on the shelf behind her. "I've also talked to the theater manager. And yesterday, Sarah gave me a few letters from Lydia."

The sergeant eased back in his chair, probing the inside of his cheek with his tongue.

"You'll get a lot out of them," said Natalie smoothly. "They give you a feel for Lydia—they are riddled with examples of her misconceptions and absurdities, and her severe mood swings. One key letter suggests that Lydia was rationalizing her decision to keep something from Sarah. But what was her secret? That's what I wanted to know."

Natalie licked her lips. "Here's how I worked it out. After her initial reference to the New Globe, Lydia never mentioned it again. Why not? She was there all the time, the programs prove it! She knew Sarah would be glad to hear she was doing something. So why not write about it? There had to be a reason for so glaring an oversight."

She made a steeple with her hands. "When Sarah first goes to college, Lydia is morose, upset, lonely. But starting with the next letter after she mentions the New Globe, she is soaring, happy, alive again. She writes, 'I felt for a little while that I was immortal.' Almost word for word the way she once described being in love with Daniel. Rose told Daniel she thought Lydia had been involved with someone over the winter. Rose had a nose for that sort of thing, although she had the wrong person in mind. The only question was, who was the right one?

"It had to be someone who was 'her type,' someone kind, and sensitive, and vulnerable. Someone like Daniel—superficially. Sarah once told me she had been attracted to Harry because he reminded her of Daniel. I didn't get it, because they don't look alike, and well, because I took Harry for a choirboy. It took me a long time to realize the similarity was there—more deeply rooted than I had thought."

"And what Sarah reacted to, Lydia might have reacted to."

"Exactly. Lydia met Harry in mid-October, and he was precisely her type—sweet, kind, considerate, involved in the arts, a little lonely. Perfect! But this time she was going to make it work, she was going to take extra precautions. In the past, other people had interfered. This time, nobody must know."

"Not even Sarah?"

"Sarah had blundered once before," explained Natalie. "She helped Eric find out about Lydia and Daniel. It wasn't her fault, but Lydia, melodramatically—cruelly—always blamed Sarah for it. So this time, not even Sarah would know the story." She leaned forward and raised a finger in triumph. "And *that's* why there was no mention of the New Globe in her letters!"

The sergeant gave her an admiring tip of his head.

"Everything was just fine—for a while. Lydia was happy—it's fun to be in love, fun to share secrets with your lover." She smiled at the sergeant, feeling in control of herself again. "You said earlier, who more likely to have told Harry about Lydia's will than his girlfriend, but—

"I had the wrong girlfriend." He nodded his head slowly, gazing absently out the window. "Lydia told him about it, in secret, of course."

"Yeah. But things had already begun to go wrong—how could it be otherwise with no third act curtain? Lydia had no skills for coping with problems other than pretending they didn't exist, or declaring them insurmountable. And Harry started displaying his true Daniel-like characteristics—couldn't say no, didn't want anybody mad at him, couldn't tell her the truth if he thought it would hurt her, thought it would all work out. Blah, blah, blah."

"And Sarah came home and walked right into the middle of it."

"Lydia must have been so glad to see her. She took Sarah to the New Year's party at the Globe. Sarah went—and met Harry." Natalie's face grew sad. "Daniel at least had the good sense to see it coming and avoid that situation. Harry didn't. Sarah started helping at the New Globe too—you can't have too many volunteers at an impoverished theater, you know. She and Harry grew closer."

Natalie sighed. "We know how pathetically badly Lydia handled the situation. I don't doubt she saw what was happening between Harry and Sarah. It must have been awful for her—she knew Sarah would never do anything to hurt her intentionally—but she didn't have the resources to confront the situation. So she tried to fight back. She met Daniel by accident, and invited him to her house, telling him how Sarah had grown, how happy she'd be to see him. Lydia, of course, had known all along about Sarah's crush on Daniel. She hoped she would be able to divert Sarah's attention from Harry to him. Well," Natalie shrugged apologetically. "It's the sort of thing that happens in the theater."

The sergeant drew in a deep breath. "On Sunday night Lydia was still trying to make things work out, but by Monday noon she had decided to commit murder. What happened?"

"Just a little thing; just the speaking of a few honest words that had the power to destroy a thousand illusory ones." Natalie brought a hand to her face and rubbed her chin. "Sarah came downstairs around nine and she and Lydia had breakfast. Sarah said Lydia was as usual. But what was usual for Lydia? She was always either up or down; her moods could change in an instant. Anyway, the important thing is, Sarah told Lydia she was in love with Harry."

Natalie spoke with detachment, but her expression was grim. "Sarah went upstairs and left Lydia alone with the inescapable fact that the man she had been having an affair with, and had been trying to hang onto, had just slept with her sister. That the man she loved and whom she had convinced herself loved her was in fact in love with her sister. There was a pattern for you with a vengeance—more deeply cut than she could stand. For wasn't that *exactly* the cause of the final breakup of her parents, and the reason for her mother's departure?"

The sergeant lifted his head, a sober expression on his angular face.

Natalie shivered. "Can you imagine how she must have felt? Lydia, with her inbred horror of repeating her mother's perdition? Can you see what it must have done to her? The fabric of her life must have disintegrated like a cobweb in a flame—and she had no one to turn to for help."

"Her rage and sense of betrayal must have been incredible," said the sergeant.

"Yes. At first she would rail against everyone, against her father for cheating on her mother, against her mother for leaving, against Sarah for unwittingly humiliating her. But mostly she would focus on Harry, who had betrayed both her and her sister."

"Harry would have attracted her built-up anger at her father too," said the sergeant, "since he exactly repeated her father's offense. So she decided, for the first time in her life, to strike back."

"Lydia put through her call to Daniel at Bergen Community College at about nine forty-five," continued Natalie. "My guess is she went down to her father's office to place the call, not wanting to risk being overheard by Sarah. I think Rose returned from aerobics just in time to listen in on the hall extension and hear her making an appointment for lunch with Daniel. Rose would have had no trouble identifying the potential for mischief in the conversation—signs which Daniel, on the other end of the phone, ignored. But that sort of thing was meat and gravy for Rose. Anyway, Lydia had to be in the office at some point to get the gun."

"The office was locked," ventured the sergeant.

Natalie smiled. "You speculated that there might be a spare key. Lydia certainly had one. In one of the letters she says she was in the office cleaning while her father was away. No need for speculation."

"I'm looking forward to reading those letters."

"At ten-thirty Sarah left for her appointment with Harry at the New Globe. At twelve-fifteen Lydia got into her car and drove off—Rose no doubt lurking somewhere at a safe distance. And somewhere along the way, Eric's private detective swung in behind Rose. The three of them headed for Bergenfield.

"We know about Daniel's meeting with Lydia. We know how—and why—Rose followed him home as he walked back to Cresskill." Natalie placed her hands on the table, palms down. "I knew that something traumatic had happened to Daniel the minute I heard from Rose about that long walk. Obsessive walking has always been his way of dealing with stress. He's claustrophobic, you see—and when he even *feels* trapped, the need kicks in.

"Anyway, we know what happened between Rose and Daniel. Then, at around three p.m. Rose left to do some quick shopping. We know that Eric's detective continued to follow her and that she certainly never met up with Lydia again. So she's out of it. From four o'clock on Daniel too is accounted for.

"We don't know where Lydia spent the afternoon, but now we know she was dead by six. After the murder, Harry raced back to the theater. In his horror over what he had done, he forgot to confirm the order for ice and the milk for the dinner show. That wasn't like him—he's a detail man. But he froze. He couldn't think...and no wonder. Everyone commented on how clear-headed Sarah was in the crisis—saving the show, driving down to Garden State Farms for the milk and cream.

"By the way, Sergeant." Natalie's tone grew delicate. "Sarah could not possibly have been hiding Lydia's body in the trunk of her car throughout that evening; she opened the trunk to put in the cases of milk."

Doubt, astonishment, embarrassment, and amusement trooped across the Sergeant's face in single file.

"Harry sat with Sarah during the show," continued Natalie. "It was a modest success. Then he went, still in Sarah's car, to the opening night party, which went on until two. Sarah dropped him off on the way home, and got a good night's sleep, never knowing that Lydia wasn't in the house.

"Harry had heard the weather report at the theater, and knew that a major storm was coming. He had to hurry. It was a short drive up Closter Dock Road to the parkway. He was lucky he wasn't seen—but then you have to be lucky to get rid of a body, I guess."

She took a deep breath. "Well, that's what I think happened, anyway. It all comes together when you get the history straight."

The sergeant stirred and rubbed his tired eyes. Then he contemplated her with a frown. "Miss Joday. I don't mean to be critical, but—why aren't you doing investigative journalism?"

Natalie was stymied by the contrast between words and tone, for once in her life slow to comprehend. When she at length fathomed their combined implication, she was touched beyond her capacity to understand. A sense of satisfaction welled up from deep within her, and a wide smile spread uncontrollably across her face. She closed her eyes, still smiling, feeling marvelous.

Eventually she opened eyes awash with feelings and looked at him. "I don't know why not. But I'll—find out."

"I'm sure you will, if you try." Sergeant Allan swallowed hard. "Good." He moistened his lips. "Well. I appreciate you sharing your thoughts with me." He stood up abruptly. "I'm overdue at Hackensack to take Suter's statement."

Natalie stood up more slowly, finding herself far from surefooted in this uncertain emotional territory.

At the door the sergeant stopped and turned. "By the way. I've been in touch with the DA's office about your brother. I'll do everything I can to make sure he's out in time to call his daughter." He looked down at his shoes. "If not I'll loan him my cell phone." He looked upward. "Hell, I'll dial the number for him and hand him the phone through the bars."

Natalie bowed her head. Satisfaction was joined by unbounded relief, overwhelming her whether she would or no. She put her hands to her face, covering both her smile and her tears.

"Natalie."

She thrilled to the sound of his voice invading her name.

He placed gentle hands upon her shoulders, and she moved forward, pressing herself against him. She rested her head upon the smooth fabric that covered his breast. She felt his arms encircling her, his hands sliding across her back, slipping past one another just above her waist.

Her head came up and she stepped back, reaching for his wrists and easing his hands away from her.

"Surely this is a violation of some polynomial regulation," she said in a practical voice.

"I'm going to rewrite the rule book," he said in a silken one.

Something caught Natalie's eye outside. "Do it fast." She nodded at the door.

He turned his head to see the tall officer coming up the walkway Natalie's keys in his hand.

The sergeant stepped back, and Natalie released his hands.

"What is it with the police?" she mused. "You always think you're the only ones who are allowed to bend the rules!"

He tipped his head back and studied her innocent face with a dubious eye. Then he gave it up, and smiled.

"I'll call," he said.

"Or die," she said.

He opened the door and held it with a courteous motion, but she hung back with equal courtesy, and gestured for him to go first. He acquiesced with his flickering smile, and went outside.

Natalie slipped a stealthy hand behind her back to make sure the revolver was still beneath her sweater. She rolled her eyes and let out a long breath as she stepped through the door. It was definitely time for a midnight trip to the Oradell Reservoir.

Epilogue

It was going to be another sunny, bountiful spring in Bergen County. Street after orderly street of vigorously landscaped and golf-course green yards were abloom with azalea, rhododendron, and dogwood, pink and white. Exotic, delicate, and old-fashioned flowers alike throve in the mild climate, perfuming the air with their mingled fragrances. Walking the streets of Bergen County in the springtime was like wandering through an impossibly vast botanical garden.

One morning, still early in April, Natalie and Sarah sat together on a rustic stone bench near the gates of the Westwood Cemetery. The funeral had been short and simple, the lack of numbers more than made up for by the benevolence of those who had come. Sarah was looking fit; a pink glow had been blown onto her cheeks by the gentle spring breeze, and there was an attractive absence of tension in her slender frame. Natalie was equally at ease, letting her thoughts wander where they would, inspired by the quiet beauty that surrounded them.

Sarah looked up at the drifting clouds. "What I really want to do is just—disappear! Give the whole estate to the New Globe—that would be appropriate—and bolt. Then I'd be out from under the whole mess. Funny how disappearing seems so attractive suddenly. Somehow I don't feel the same old anger against my mother. No, that's not right—I'm still angry. But—after what I almost did—I have an idea what she must have felt like; of how doing something terrible can seem perfectly reasonable when you're in so much pain. In comparison to some things, running away doesn't seem like such a bad option."

Sarah leaned down and picked up a fallen blossom of dogwood. "But, life goes on." She ran her fingers across the smooth white petals. "Even if I run away, Eric will still be here. How can I keep him from haunting me wherever I go? I've always been afraid of him. I don't want to live my life wondering when he's going to hurt me again. I want to be free of him! Still, isn't family—good or bad—all we've got in the world? Can I turn my back on him?" She looked at Natalie. "Would you?"

"Me?" Natalie came out of her reverie with a start. "I'm the last person you should ask." She raised her head thoughtfully, and a faraway look came into her eyes. "No, that's not true.

"I knew another father once. We loved him very much—my brother more than I, perhaps—or longer. But he was a man without judgment, without constancy, with another life beyond what we as children saw or understood. To the world he pretended to be more than he was; to his family he was always less than we needed. His life—and ours—was one epic downhill spiral. He used and destroyed everything and everyone, including our mother's health, her savings, and her trust. While she was alive there was some stability in our lives. But when she died, we were against the wind, my little brother and I.

"Our father was so unaccountable—talked big, never kept a job, hung out all hours with the kind of people who scare kids, never had money for things like schoolbooks or clothes. Jeez, I used to steal from him just so we'd be able to buy school lunches. But year after year he never ran out of excuses.

"And he used us, the same way he used everything. Did he need to make a late night pickup from one of his suppliers without arousing suspicion? The kids can do that! Did he think he could make a little extra cash selling dope to the local teenagers—the kids were in a perfect position for that! When I was fourteen, something happened—never mind what—and I wised up to it that what we were doing was not just a secret, it was illegal. I freaked, and then I made a stand. But I carried with me the fear that the police would catch up with me someday. Later I put myself through college and got the hell out of there.

"But Daniel—he so vulnerable. I realize now he was more dependent on our father from an earlier age. I think our mother died too soon for him. Anyway, he didn't see that what our father was doing was so wrong, although he didn't always like the way he did it. Or maybe he just didn't believe he had a choice. His teen years were a nightmare—he got busted for the first time at thirteen, and it was downhill from there.

"When he was twenty, things reached a very low point. He was desperate for money. He had just gotten married and had a baby to help take care of. He couldn't keep a job—nothing was good enough. He tried quick-money deals, buy cheap, sell fast, sometimes legal and sometimes not—but they never paid off. So once upon a time my father took my brother out for a heart-to-heart session that was supposed to result in a plan for Daniel's future. They both got high, and then they got higher, and together they set out to raid a liquor store in downtown Demarest. This was my father's top idea of how to help plan for his son's retirement. Daniel thought it was going to be a case of shoplifting, or whatever con game the situation called for. But my father had bigger plans. He pulled out a gun and told the guy at the counter to empty the till. Too bad he hadn't discussed it with Daniel first. My brother panicked, and bolted. My father grabbed him, and tried to calm him down, but he only made things worse. The boy in the store got a chance to hit the silent alarm. Daniel ran. My father—worried about his son, you see—chased him all the way down to Knickerbocker. They were easy to spot; they were picked up almost immediately.

Natalie looked up at the blue sky, her gray eyes searching. "I wasn't in the country at the time. I used to think…if only I had been there. I know better now.

"The courts were lenient with Daniel, I suppose—although I've always felt it was unfair of the DA to go for armed robbery. But they took a dim view of Rick. His sentence has a couple years still to run.

"So." She looked at Sarah. "Your question boils down to this: what will I do when he gets out? I don't honestly know, Sarah. I can't change the fact that he's my father, or that he's had an enormous influence on my life—even if his biggest legacy has been an aversion for legal institutions. But I know one thing—I'm not going to go to the party when he gets out. I'm not going to be responsible for him in any way. And, no matter what else happens, I'm not going to look to him for approval—ever.

"If my telling you the story helps you, Sarah, it'll be the first good thing that ever came of it."

Sarah's eyes were on the bobbing yellow tulips beneath the sandstone wall. "Thanks," she said, "it helps."

Up from the dell at the back of the cemetery, where Lydia's grave-marker rested in a circle of red roses, came Daniel, walking with a free-swinging stride. He smiled when he reached them, his clear gray eyes full of life.

"Ready," he said with a nod.

They went out the gate together and walked slowly to the parking lot. Preparing to cross Old Hook Road, Natalie noticed a woman standing next to Sarah's car. She was watching them. She was rather tall, and rather stout, and wore a fringed, pale green shawl over a flowing lavender dress. She was an unusual sight in affluent, conservative Bergen County.

With a start, Natalie remembered—the woman in the waiting room at the lawyer's office in Tenafly. Was this coincidence? Impossible! The odds were stacked against it.

Daniel stepped off the curb, but Natalie grabbed him by the arm in mid-stride and pulled him back. One foot in the air, he twirled unsteadily around, like a circus performer having a bad moment on the high wire. Regaining his balance, he looked at her in surprise.

"Let's take a walk over to Lakeview, Danny." She tugged at his arm. "We can feed the ducks."

"But—"

She flashed her eyes at him with a facetious smile. He looked at her suspiciously, but shut up. Natalie turned her back on him and faced Sarah, all innocence. “You go on home, Sarah. Call me later, okay?”

“Okay,” said Sarah. “Thanks for coming.” She hurried across Old Hook Road, her shining hair rippling in the sunlight.

Natalie and Daniel turned away, and walked arm in arm toward Kinderkamack, enjoying the glory of the day.

To receive a free catalog of Poisoned Pen Press titles, please contact us in one of the following ways:

Phone: 1-800-421-3976
Facsimile: 1-480-949-1707
Email: info@poisonedpenpress.com
Website: www.poisonedpenpress.com

Poisoned Pen Press
6962 E. First Ave. Ste 103
Scottsdale, AZ 85251